SEEDS

Little
DOZEN
press

SEEDS

Copyright 2018 by Rachel Starr Thomson
Visit the author at www.rachelstarrthomson.com

Published by Little Dozen Press
Crystal Beach, Ontario, Canada
www.littledozen.com

Cover design by Mercy Hope
Copyright 2018

ISBN: 978-1-927658-46-8

SEEDS

BOOK 1 OF THE CHRONICLES OF KEPOS GÉ

by Rachel Starr Thomson

Little Dozen Press

2018

PROLOGUE

Kepos Gé—The Garden World

In the year 1516, an alliance of nations called the Kaion Anthropon—born out of the remnants of an ancient empire 1500 years earlier—was torn apart by a series of wars. In the beginning, it was religious unity that created the Kaion—unity made in the worship of Father, Son, and Fire Within. Now, religious strife tore it apart. The conflict was called the Wars for Truth, as the Kaion split into factions, each claiming to hold exclusive truth and hope, not just for the Kaion, but for all mankind.

Of these factions, two became primary: the Sacramenti, keepers of the old ways, and the Puritani or Pure People, who claimed the old ways had become corrupt and that they were the new guardians of truth and freedom.

The Wars were bloody and seeming endless, raging for over a hundred years. As they split the Kaion into smaller and smaller entities, kings and nations sided with one faction or the other. In time, power shifted decisively to the Puritani, and the Sacramenti were largely driven underground. At last the Kepos Gé settled into an uneasy truce.

But even then, the splitting—and the attempts to find truth—did not end. From the Sacramenti was born an order called the Imitators, priests who sought to purify the Sacramenti from within and bring a renewal of their beliefs ... and of their influence. From the Puritani, a smaller group split away, objecting to the new Puritani alliances with political powers and seeking a more intimate and personal connection to Truth. These were called Luminari, but their strange practices soon had them nicknamed "Tremblers."

In the year 1629, King Aldous II of Angleland, an island nation belonging to the Puritani, granted to a troublemaking Trembler within his courts land in the New World across the sea. His name was Herman Melrose. Dreaming of a world in which peace might reign and tolerance lead every faction into unity and love through the influence of the Fire Within, Melrose crossed the ocean in a ship, meeting with the Colonies on the shores of the New World before beginning his river voyage inland—bound for the wooded mountains and valleys that now belonged to him.

Herman Melrose carried the challenge of forging a truly new order within the New World. With him was a small group of settlers. Ahead of him was an unknown world, inhabited by unknown tribes and deadly beasts.

And behind him, the Imitators trained up one of their own for a mission.

PART 1
ARRIVAL

CHAPTER

1

July 1642, The New World

Linette Cole rested her hands on the rail of the flat bottomed riverboat and gazed out at the green world unfurling before her. A long strand of strawberry-blonde hair, worked loose from her bun, blew across her face, and she tucked it behind her ear.

"Beautiful, isn't it?" asked a soldier behind her.

"That it is," she answered, keeping her eyes forward, fixed on the land before her. The crystal-clear river was wide and slow-moving here, and along its banks stretched a flat, sandy plain. Not a hundred feet beyond that, the land rose into hills and then mountains, covered with trees in a deep green darkness, a misty and mysterious world that called to her and frightened her both at once. She'd heard countless stories of the dangers of the wilderness—beasts, sheer cliffs, strange diseases, and terrible storms—only slightly more frightening than rumors of the tattooed and godless Outsiders. The stories had been told to her, offered to her like stones in a wall meant to keep her in the Colonies.

The frontier was no place for a woman, they said.

Not even a woman like her.

She glanced away from the scene beyond the river as the conversations and confrontations of her last days in New Cranwell flickered over her eyes like a film. Countless moments, woven into a painful cloak of shame and loss that she hoped never to wear again.

They'd told her there was another way—they, the authorities of the Puritani kirk and colony, not least among them her own father. They'd sworn that she would grow used to her new position in the Colonies, used to being an outcast and a byword, used to the constant reminders of her aching loss, and she would accept it and find peace.

But she did not believe them.

Her fingers tightened around the rail.

The soldier drew alongside her, standing a little too close for comfort. He was a young man, dressed in a fine red coat. A lieutenant, she thought—what was his name? Anderson.

"Those woods are as dangerous as they look," he said.

She knew where the conversation was going and thus tried to lead it astray. "Is it the Outsiders?"

"No, not here," the lieutenant said. "Make no mistake, they can be dangerous if they wish to be. But here they are mostly content to keep their distance. For now. Nay, it's the beasts. And the … other things."

She shivered, searching the dark green slopes with her gaze as they drifted slowly by. The sound of wood through water as the slaves poled their way along, propelling the boat by brown brawn and sinew rather than current, formed a rhythmic backdrop.

"You should reconsider settling here," the lieutenant said. Her heart sank a little, but her fingers holding tightly to the rail fortified her. So much for redirecting the conversation.

"I do not wish to reconsider," she said. "I have considered at great length, believe me."

He went on as though he hadn't heard her. "These wilds are no place for a woman, no matter what promises that self-styled governor makes. He may offer free land, but he can't offer protection. It's mostly Tremblers in these parts, and they will not even take up arms. They are fools to think they can live here without protection."

"They don't wish to mar the soil of a new world with blood," Linette said. She'd read the lengthy tracts of the Trembler, Herman Melrose, in the papers back east. The vision he propounded and others mocked inspired her more than she had dared admit—until the day she declared she was leaving for his frontier settlement herself. "Perhaps there is wisdom in that. They remember the Old World better than others—the way the Kaion tore itself apart. The Tremblers wish to put humanity back together."

"It cannot be done," Lieutenant Anderson said. He moved his hand as though he would touch her fingers, and she moved her hand away before he could reach her, resettling it on the rail just a few inches away. He did not pursue the touch. The woody vines that protruded from under his cuffs crossed the bank of his hands in an X-pattern.

As she gazed at the mountains, a flock of birds burst out from the trees near the river and flew white-winged against the deep green, the sun glancing off their wings as they rose. She caught her breath at the beauty of it—at their freedom.

"If I may offer a suggestion—"

Finally she turned and looked at him, directly into his stubbled young face. "I wish you wouldn't," she said. "As you may imagine, I did not make the decision to come here lightly."

Embarrassment flickered in his eyes, mixed with anger. "I only wish to suggest that you reconsider settling here and take another path—a middle road. Stay at Fort Collins. There is work for a woman to do around a military fort, and you would not have trouble finding a husband to protect you."

She flushed and felt the slender vines around her upper arms constrict. "Did I say I was looking for a husband?"

"What woman isn't?"

A smile, born of frustration, crossed her face, and she glanced at the deck beneath his feet. "Me. I am not looking for a husband, or for advice, Lieutenant. I've chosen my path; I'll thank you to leave me to it."

She pulled her hands away from the rail and stalked off, wishing—not for the first time—that on a vessel like this one it was possible to retreat further than forty feet from the soldiers. She did not fear them. They were men of honor, held to Puritani standards by their military training and punitive system if not by their hearts. A woman could not be safer with any other band of men.

But she felt their eyes on her and imagined their thoughts, of curiosity, of judgment. She hated it.

Fleetingly she considered throwing herself into the sparkling waters of the river and swimming to shore. She could walk the rest of the way to the settlement while the birds flew in freedom overhead.

Quietly, she chuckled at herself. *Sensible, Linette. Throw yourself to the beasts before you've even had your chance to start over, all because you can't take a little more judgment.*

That, in the end, was why she was going to join Herman Melrose's settlement in the deep forests of the frontier. She had read his words: his wonderful words not only describing a new life beyond the reach of the old violence and hatred, but also painting a dream of tolerance, freedom, and magnanimity. The Tremblers, talk said, were different from the Pure People in the Colonies and in the Old World. They accepted everyone just as they were, without questions, without measuring and assessing, without condemnation. They believed that Truth was something to be sought and found in direct contact with God, not simply dropped on someone from a pulpit like a fifty-pound weight.

In such a society, even she could find a place.

The breeze blowing up the river turned colder as she stalked the deck. She looked to the horizon ahead and saw dark clouds sinking down from the mountains as fog gathered and lowered itself into a storm. She paused to watch it, standing beside a silent slave who polled without offering a word of comment.

"Ma'am, best get inside," Captain Almon called out. "Lightning makes the water unsafe."

Reluctantly, Linette nodded and headed for the small shelter in the middle of the boat. She hoped the storm would blow over quickly and not delay them much longer. Three more days—that was how long it should take to reach the valley where Herman Melrose was governor. The valley where she would begin a whole new life as part of a new society.

Alone, but free.

Ezekiel, the old slave, watched her disappear inside. Without warning, a blow to his head pulled his attention back to the soldiers.

"Keep your eyes in your head," Captain Frederick Almon snapped.

"Sorry, sir," Ezekiel said. "Meant no harm."

"You know better than to look at a white woman. You do it again I'll have you dragged a half-mile."

Ezekiel gazed at the boards beneath his feet and poled in rhythm with the others. "Were an accident, sir," he said. "Won't do it again."

The captain moved on, satisfied. It was little more than a rote interaction, Ezekiel knew. The captain was one to say his lines.

So was Ezekiel. He had little choice about that. It was why he admired Linette. He hadn't tried to watch her, hadn't tried to listen, but there was little choice in a boat this small, and they'd all been together two weeks now. He'd heard and seen enough to know she was one who refused to say her lines any longer. She would go to the settlement and write a new script.

Rain began to spatter Ezekiel's exposed skin. It was cold. He felt the deep purple vines that grew from his waist over his back and down his legs and arms swell with pleasure at the rain. The wind picked up, growing brisk and threatening.

"Pole in!" the captain ordered. He drew alongside Ezekiel again and pointed toward a calm inlet just off the river, a sheltered pool surrounded by sandy bluffs. "We'll get off the water till it passes."

Without a word, Ezekiel changed his poling to head for the sheltered spot. The other six slaves on board did the same. They worked as one.

The rain continued to fall, growing stronger, droplets striking the ground like daggers. Thunder echoed through the mountains, and forked lightning spiked the sky over the river. Linette hiked up her skirts as she followed the soldiers inland in search of shelter. Behind her walked more soldiers, making twelve in all, and behind them the slaves, carrying the most important cargo from the boat on their shoulders.

The clouds overhead grew darker and more numerous until the whole sky was turned slate gray. Beneath them the river turned the same color, an ominous but beautiful transformation. Ahead of her the captain and his men turned worried glances upward. Linette could feel it too—the unmistakable threat in the air. But her blood rose to meet it, as did the sap in her vines. She could feel her own heartbeat and the earth's pulsing through her, alive, free.

Two soldiers had run ahead to scout out the landscape, and one of them ran back now, his coat a blood-red blot against the blue-green of the hills. He swept his arm through the air in a wide gesture and called out, "Here!"

Captain Almon led the way, through a cleft in the hills to a dug-out spot beneath the roots of overhanging trees and clumps of moss. They huddled together in the shelter. Water ran in rivulets down the limestone behind them, and the wind blew some rain into their faces and dampened their clothes, but the shelter was better by far than being in the open air.

The soldiers talked in low voices, and one drew fuel from his pack and started a fire in a dry spot deep under the overhang. As the wood began to smolder, Linette drew her woolen cloak closer and settled back on her heels, slightly away from the soldiers, closer to the slaves. Beyond the overhang the world grew almost black with the storm. Thunder crashed in her ears and shook the ground above them as the rain pelted down and formed a waterfall as it poured over the gap.

Linette reached beneath her cloak and fingered the wooden symbol that hung around her neck—a carved Book, sacred to the Puritani. It was meant to remind her of the Book, the word of the Father, their source of truth and security. Sometimes, in the Colonies, the talisman had comforted her with a sense of someone near her.

But now, it did not.

Wordlessly, she pulled the carving until the knot in its leather string loosened from around her neck and gave way. She held the wooden symbol up before her eyes. Light from the fire danced on it.

Slowly, she let her fingers relax until the talisman fell to the sandy soil beneath her.

A disconcerted sound from behind her startled her. She turned to see the big white eyes of a slave staring at her. He caught himself the moment she turned and looked away, with an expression that was both sincerely apologetic and afraid.

"It's all right," she said. "You can't help seeing what is right in front of you."

The slave hugged his knees and stared straight ahead, not looking at her. "Best you not talk to me, Mistress," he said.

Linette cocked her head and looked at the man a little more closely. She'd seen him before, of course—they'd been traveling on the same twenty-foot riverboat for a little over two weeks. But she hadn't really looked at him. What she saw now was a man who had been young long ago. His shoulders were strong but a little bent. His close-shorn, curly hair was gray at the temples, and she saw white in the stubble on his face. Like the other slaves he wore a loose-fitting cotton shirt over wool breeches, and his feet were shorn with ill-fitting leather.

"What's your name?" she asked.

"Best not talk," he repeated. Then, seeming caught between the risks of talking to a white woman and the risks of not talking to her when directly addressed, he added, "Ezekiel."

"A prophet's name," she said with a vague smile. "In the Book. Do you know the Book?"

"I don't read, ma'am." He still stared straight out at the falling rain, shoulders rigid, not daring to look at her.

"I may be done with the Book myself," she said, glancing down at the wooden talisman in the sand.

"Ain't right to say that," Ezekiel answered, sounding shocked. "Ain't safe."

Linette shivered as she stared at the symbol of her membership in the Pure People lying by her feet. She didn't know why she had dropped it. Didn't know why she would throw away such a sacred thing.

But she did not pick it back up.

CHAPTER 2

Jerusalem Valley Settlement—The New World

Herman Melrose looked over the letters laid before him and let out a deep sigh. In the corner of the room, Amos Thatcher rocked slightly on his heels.

"Everything all right, Governor?"

Herman leaned back in his birch-whittled chair and covered his brow with a hand. "Just a headache, Amos."

"Brought on by those letters, it would seem?"

Beneath his hand, Herman smiled. "Brought on by the duties of government."

The younger man, Herman's faithful clerk, let his frown creep into his tone of voice. "I don't understand why they worry you so, all the way out here. Can't they leave us be?"

Herman sat forward again and rested both hands on his desk. Ruefully, he noted how thick and gnarled the vines that grew up to his knuckles had become. Lately it seemed that every time he moved, he creaked and groaned with thickness and with age. He noticed, too, the scars that crept over his hands, backs and palms, like thin white tendrils. They reminded him of when he was a much younger man, and of how much he had to be thankful for now.

He turned and smiled at Amos. The young man wore gray cotton trousers stuffed into leather stocking boots traded from the Outsiders. The typical plain, collarless black coat of a Trembler covered the ensemble, completing the typical settler appearance: half-Colonial, half-frontier. Amos gave the look his own flair through his more-than-usually bookish expression and spectacles that always sat toward the end of his nose, as though he were an aging spinster and not a capable farmer of twenty-nine.

"Compared to life in the Colonies, my boy, they do leave us be. And that is nothing compared to the Old World, where they consider it right to harry a man into the ground for wishing to put an extra *e* on the end of a word or cross a *t* from left to right instead of right to left."

A shadow crossed Herman's face. The scars and vines alike seemed to ache more than the ordinary. His eyes drifted back to the letters, and again he sighed. Yes, they had much to be thankful for. Yet in moments like these he became acutely aware of how much further they had to go.

He stood, lifting his broad-shouldered, hefty form from the chair with some effort, and slapped a hand on Amos's shoulder. "I'm done with being indoors," he said. "The Creator never made man to sit in an office. We have done violence to his intentions most shamefully."

Amos moved toward the papers on the desk with a darting motion like a bird going in for a worm. Herman waved him off. "No, lad, not you either. Come, walk with me."

Amos froze in place for a moment before giving in. Together, he and Herman stepped out of the small room into the larger anteroom, decorated with a bearskin on the floor and a pair of antlers on the wall over a stone fireplace. The rough-hewn floorboards creaked under Herman's lumbering gait, and they stepped out onto the porch together.

Herman stopped there and took in a deep breath of humid evening air as he looked out upon the valley—the place where his lifelong labor had come closest to fruition.

The valley was a wide cleft in the mountains, widest in the east where it met the Mescahannec River. In twilight, the lowering sun lit the river on fire and turned the valley to a dusty gold at the base of the sloping mountains on the other three sides. The mountains themselves were a tumble of trees, tops rolling and rounded, their blue-green canopies shielding the world of shadow and moss beneath. Hidden paths, known by few but the Outsiders and the occasional trapper, crisscrossed that world.

These mountains were gentler, perhaps older, than the snowcapped peaks Herman had known in the Old World, yet with that age came a wilder and more foreboding aspect as well. It had always seemed to him that these were mountains that would embrace whom they chose, but equally, those who were not welcome risked being lost forever in their fog-drenched wilderness.

The valley floor had been largely wooded when they first came here five years earlier, except for the sandy banks of the Mescahannec. Herman had been strong with the strength and fire of a dream, and he had cleared trees and plowed new plots of land alongside the younger men and boys. Now as he looked across the valley, it was over golden heads of wheat and corn and backyard gardens, and the crowns of apple trees beginning to bear fruit. Thin columns of chimney smoke, each a few hundred feet from the next, rose in the evening, scenting the air with burning boughs and coal dug from the hills.

They had called their rough new home Jerusalem — the city of peace. They had come further in five years than Herman might have thought truly possible, even welcoming a wife or two and seeing the birth of several children. Yet in other ways they had not gone far. In some ways Herman feared they might even have gone backwards.

He took his walking stick in hand as he began to plod down the path from the rambling log house that served as the settlement's center of government, common meeting house, Sunday morning kirk (for the Puritani among the settlers), and occasional inn. Cornfields stretched down either side of the path, and he smiled at the gobbling of wild turkeys beyond them, tucked in to the base of the nearest mountain. Amos walked beside him with that nervous step of his, bathed in golden light.

It wasn't right to keep it from him, Herman decided.

"We have a letter from the Puritani synod in New Cranwell," he said. "They take issue with more of my teaching and ask me to curb it or to enter public debates with the parson, with the promise that I'll stop teaching if I lose. Evidently they've written to the parson already, but they write to inform me of their opinions as well. With much suspicion expressed that I may be leading their people spiritually astray."

"I … I see," Amos stammered. Apple boughs hung into the path from a wild tree, their fruit still small and hard. Herman stopped to finger an especially promising green apple within reach. "Of course I have no intention of debating the parson, or changing my teachings. I'll happily talk with any settler who wants to take issue with me. Our intention was to create a place where all are tolerated just as they are, synods and all."

"But you are troubled about it," Amos said.

"They also warn me to be on the lookout for Imitators," Herman said. "The elders think the Sacramenti may have sent an agent here."

Amos straightened his already straight posture as though physically impacted by the very thought. "But that ... that's impossible. We would have seen ..."

"Of course he is not yet here, if he is even coming," Herman said.

"Then we shall be on the watch indeed," Amos said.

Here Herman sighed again. "Shall we?" he asked. "And what do you suppose we should do if an Imitator arrives here?"

"Drive him out!" Amos said. His usually pale face flushed. "What else?"

"Can we drive anyone out of Jerusalem Valley, unless he provokes us to do it with violence?" Herman asked. "In all of Kepos Gé, we alone have declared our intention to welcome all with open arms and to view everyone as a child of the Creator. Can we exclude the Imitators and still hold our integrity?"

"But no one is guilty of greater violence than the Sacramenti," Amos said. "If we think the Puritani are bad ..."

Herman stopped and gazed at his clerk for a moment before patting the young man's cheek. "I'll think on it," he said. "Meanwhile I am more concerned about the potential of a visit from the synod. They had many words of advice for me. My fear is not that they will come and serve their parishioners well, but that they will stir up trouble and discontent in the valley."

They began again to meander through the golden air. "I do not think you need fear overmuch," Amos suggested. "Smith Foster is foremost of the Pure People here, and he is not one to be stirred up by anyone." His face fell a little. "Of course, there's also the preacher ..."

Herman chuckled and pointed his walking stick down the path as though identifying an enemy in the bend. "Toleration was easier to carry out when it was an ideal in a jail cell in the Old World," he said. "When all I had to do was forgive my enemies. Now that I have to govern them, I find my ideals strained."

"But not broken," Amos said. There was in his voice a hopeful note Herman did not miss. He turned and regarded his clerk once more. The young man's vines, strong and yellow in color, grew around both sides of his throat and nearly met at in the center like the golden torc of an ancient Celt. In the dusk, standing tall with the cornfields and the log governing house behind him, he looked like his father—a tree planted in new soil but still bearing the strength and dignity of the old.

Herman swallowed a lump. "Not broken," he agreed. "What your father and I started—I won't give up on it till I die."

Amos looked down. "May that day be far off," he said.

"I won't live forever, boy."

"It's not forever today," Amos answered.

Herman nodded. "Maybe the young preacher will prove to be right, and a purging of the kirk and the world will come with a great conflagration before I get a chance to die. We are all horribly misguided followers of the devil, and God will set us straight with an iron fist."

"You don't think so, do you?" Amos asked.

Herman chuckled, taking to the path again. His own crude house was not far, and though he'd not intended to go home quite yet, his feet were leading him there of their own volition. The turkeys sounded off again, and a flock of geese took off from the river and flew low over the valley, their hovering wings brushing the tops of the wheat.

It was a paradise, this place. His paradise.

"I ask the Fire Within," Herman said, "and it tells me nothing but to tend to my own cares, to my own fields—to the harvest I wish to reap. I think the young preacher is gripped of a fever from the Old World and wish he would be well. But that is just my opinion. If you are concerned, listen to him yourself, and ask the Fire Within, and be at peace."

Amos nodded. "Yes, sir."

"He was only a boy when we came here," Herman said. "A boy with a wild imagination. But then, many would have said the same of me."

"Your imagination created all this," Amos said. "This place. This peace. Those who called you a madman were wrong, Uncle."

"Maybe," Herman muttered as he looked over his valley once again. The sky overhead was darkening into night, hastened by the mountain shadows. A bird called out, long and lonely in the forest slopes. The plumes of chimney smoke were thicker now, and the air smelled of hickory and ash. This peace—did anyone else understand how truly fragile it was?

The peace here mattered more than anything Herman could imagine. But it was as fragile as the belief of a single woman or man.

"Maybe," he repeated. "We shall see."

CHAPTER
3

Port Tuscan, The Old World

The prison was dark and perpetually wet, its walls dripping with moisture and salt collected out of the air from the waterfront only meters away.

The prison was constructed, like a temple, in depths. Its outer court consisted of a holding pen for drunks and other rabble; its inner court was sectioned into fourteen cells, all of them holding prisoners in varying stages of more serious trouble—but likely to be tried, and out, to freedom or to death, within a span of weeks to a few years.

The prison's holy place, its innermost court, was nearest the sea and deepest underground. Its cells were little more than crypts hewn out of bedrock. Of its inhabitants, only one had been here fewer than thirty years.

That one huddled with her knees drawn up to her chest as the jangle-stamp of unexpected footsteps moved down the hall beyond her cell. The flare of a torch lit up the wall outside as the intruders came closer. The jangle indicated spurs—not prison guards, then, least of all the troll who lived here at all times, but someone who was still free to roam the outside world.

Hope flared high in her, followed closely by a fear that dragged her hopes down by the heels and hissed at her to bury them. This would not be help.

If anything, a visitor here meant a greater threat.

The torchlight grew brighter and brighter and then passed, followed by the shadows of three men. The troll, and the two men wearing spurs. Both wore the broad black hats of Puritani kirkmen—elders or deacons.

To her surprise, the footsteps stopped almost immediately after passing her cell. When they spoke, their voices carried.

"Do you remember me, cretin?" one of the kirkmen demanded. Serena's blood chilled at the sound of his voice. She remembered him, if the man in the cell next to her did not.

But he answered: "I do."

"The years have not been kind to you," Elder Crispin said. His voice dripped the condescension she knew so well. The utter and total disdain.

"Prison is not a good place to age." The prisoner's voice croaked. It sounded like he had not spoken in decades, which perhaps he had not. The troll was no conversationalist.

"You deserve this," Elder Crispin said. "Every moment of it, and more. When you come to the end of your years and the grave tips you into hell, you will go into the flames knowing you deserve every moment of eternity in torment."

The prisoner made a noise, and it took Serena a moment to realize it was laughter. When the spasm had ended he croaked out, "I'll see you there."

A crash made Serena jump—the elder or someone was shaking the bars. "Blaspheming dog, give glory to God!"

Serena closed her eyes. The words cut into her, deep into her soul, and burned there.

Burned strong.

The Fire Within, objecting fiercely to such a misrepresentation of the Creator.

She opened her eyes when the conversation resumed.

"Before you reach eternity, I have a proposal for you. A breath of freedom … perhaps a chance to repent."

"A chance to kill, you mean," the prisoner said.

The voices dipped too low to hear. Serena strained her ears and pulled against the chains that held her against the wall, unable to get closer to the door.

A few minutes later the torchlight brightened again, and the three men passed by her cell once more. This time they paused outside her door.

"Do you really believe we can trust him?" the third man, one she did not recognize, asked.

"Of course we can't trust him," Elder Crispin said. "But he'll do it. It's a job to his liking. What he does after that is none of our concern. He'll be too far from here to make trouble for us again."

He'll do what? she silently queried. *Where are they sending him?*

An image formed in her mind's eye.

She saw fields surrounded by mountains, golden fields ripe with wheat.

Then she saw a man's hand, holding a knife that dripped with blood.

"What can I do?" she whispered.

There was silence.

And then she knew.

"Am I going crazy, or was there a young woman in that cell?" Deacon Bure asked as he crossed the prison courtyard alongside the older kirkman.

"There was," Elder Crispin said. He did not slow his stride.

"A beauty, unless my eyes deceived me."

"Mmmm."

"Come on, man! Tell me who she is, and how she came to be in such a horrible place!"

Crispin stopped his stride abruptly and turned to face the captain. "Her name is Serena Vaquero. A Trembler. And a seditionist."

"The count's sister?"

"If I had my way we'd have burned her at the stake. The girl is a witch."

"And for once in your lifetime, you somehow were thwarted in getting your way?"

Crispin grimaced. "A necessary compromise. While she is alive we have leverage over her brother. If he leads a secession away from the Alliance it will give the Sacramenti the room they need to come rushing back in with their devil hordes. Our hold on the south is tentative as it is."

Crispin laid a gloved hand on the captain's shoulder. "Now tear your thoughts away from the count's troubled family and back to the matter at hand. Can I count on you for tonight?"

"Of course," the kirkman said. "Though I don't much like setting a creature like that loose in the world."

"Not our world," Crispin said. He allowed himself a smile. "Only the new one."

Serena sat awake that night as the torches and footsteps returned—quieter this time, lacking spurs. She watched the shadows flicker on the wall and heard the squeal of rusted hinges and the clanking of shackles, and the grunting of someone trying to remove manacles locked shut for decades. Then the shadows passed again, and this time there was another with them—a tall, menacing figure whose presence made her shiver.

But he was not her concern. Yet.

She passed the rest of the night in fitful sleep, and in the dim hours that marked daylight, she waited until the one she sought came again.

When he had drawn abreast of her cell without any hint of pausing, she called out, "I am sorry, Señor!"

She spotted the hitch in his step and took it as her opportunity. "I am sorry I ever called you a troll."

He stopped.

He stared at her.

For all the world, he did *look* like a troll.

"It … they … it's a nickname. They all use it. I should not have. It is wrong."

He turned away and continued his journey into the depths of the prison.

She leaned back against the damp wall, satisfied for now.

The next time he passed by, several hours later, she called out without moving, "You are a man like any other. You have your own story. I am truly sorry that I did not honor that."

Once again, he paused to stare before continuing on his way.

She drifted in and out of sleep for a while. In her half-awake state she whispered, "I am following you, Fire. You must lead me."

She wasn't sure when he came back, but she was startled out of sleep by his silhouette standing on the other side of her bars. Her eyes widened.

"What do you want?" he asked.

She inhaled with relief and wonder. She hadn't been sure he was capable of speech. In the months she'd been here, he had never once spoken to her or to anyone else in her hearing.

"I want to know your name," she said.

"The troll," he answered.

"Your real name."

"It is Banquo."

She smiled. "Thank you, Banquo. My name is Serena. Now neither of us is so alone as before."

The next morning when he passed, she called out, "Good morning, Banquo!"

Hours later, when he shoved her rations under the door and across the floor with a broomstick so she could reach them, she said, "I thank you."

He woke her again the next morning in the same startling way.

"I wish you wouldn't do that," she said, breathing hard.

"What do you want, Serena?" he said.

Her heart still beating double-time from the surprise of his sudden appearance, she felt the solemnity of a foreordained moment that had come. Though she knew there was no one nearby to hear, she lowered her voice.

"I want you to let me go," she said.

"I can't …"

"You will never have to lie about it; no one will ever ask you where I am. Nor will you suffer punishment for it. You are going to die, Banquo, tonight."

She saw the way her words startled him, and it moved her. That after all these years of existence here, of a subhuman life away from feeling or speech or light, he was still shocked by the prospect of death.

"Don't be afraid," she said, reaching out as though to comfort him. The chains dragged and clanked as she did. "You will die peacefully, in your sleep. It is just that your time has come. You have been here so long …"

"Sixty-five years," he said.

"Sixty-seven," she corrected him with a soft smile. "You've lost count."

"I …" he stopped, and a look of confusion crossed his face even in the shadows. "You're right. How can you know that?"

"The Fire knows you," she said. "And speaks to me. So please, Banquo, I hope you will let me go. I have work to do. I can't stay here."

He shook his head wordlessly. But she understood it did not mean no.

"And I hope you will take this chance to settle your soul," she said. "Your Creator would like to welcome you home."

He stiffened. "I am Puritani. I have given assent to all the confessions, and I—"

"You are lying," she said. "You are Sacramenti, hiding in secret because it is no longer safe to practice your faith as your fathers did. I know, Banquo. They were my fathers too. But that is not what I am asking. Don't think of confessions now. Are you at peace with the Creator? Is your trust in his Son—in his sacrifice for you? That is what matters. Your heart and his heart."

"What are you?" he asked.

"Right now I am only a child of God," she answered. "When you die tonight I want you to go home. Safe." She held up her hands wryly. "Whether or not you choose to remove these chains."

He looked away suddenly as though he heard someone coming, though the carved-out corridor was as silent as ever. "I will come back for you," he said in a hushed tone.

And vanished.

She leaned back again and closed her eyes in the dim darkness. The dripping of water lulled her back to sleep.

She did not know how much time had passed when she heard the sound of a key turning in a lock. She opened her eyes to total darkness. The air vents that let in faint sunlight during the day let nothing in now; it was night. Hinges squealed, and footsteps crossed the floor. She felt the presence of a human being nearby and heard him kneel before he took hold of the locks fastening her manacles in place and released them.

The chains fell off with a painful clank. She bit her lip as raw skin met damp air. A moment later the warmth of a cloak swept around her shoulders, and she felt something press into her hand.

The hilt of a knife.

She pushed it back. "I won't need this," she whispered.

The return was refused. "Keep it." It was Banquo's voice.

"I won't use it," she said. "Not against another human being."

"There are more uses for knives than stabbing people," Banquo said. "Keep it and get up."

Despite the shortness of his words, she felt kindness as he took her elbow and helped her to her feet, then tightened the cloak around her. "Keep silence," he said. "No one must hear you leave."

She nodded. He took her hand—the one not holding a knife—and began to lead her through the darkness. She bumped into the narrow walls of the corridor several times, unsteady on her bare feet. Her heart raced as they began to ascend the stone steps and then stepped out aboveground, into the inner cells, then rushed through them into the court outside.

Serena breathed salt air and thought her heart would break with the sensation of freedom. Banquo did not slow down, pulling her along with only a bare pause to unlock a gate and slip out into the night.

At last, on the cobbled street outside the prison walls, with the oil lights of the port city glimmering here and there in the darkness and the moon overhead casting its reflection off the waters of the port and onto the sides of ships that waited for morning, Banquo stopped and faced her.

"In sixty-seven years," he said, "no one has ever asked my name."

Tears ran down her face. "Thank you," she said. "About tonight … I'm so sorry …"

"Don't be," he said. "I am an old man, older even than you might think. I am glad you can't see me in the darkness, for I do not like to be seen."

"Have you made your peace?" she dared ask. "Are you ready to go home?"

"I think," he answered, "I can see my way to doing that. Thank you, dear girl."

Choking back tears, she nodded.

"You know your way?" he asked.

"I will find it," she said.

He turned to go. Above him, palm fronds waved gently in a warm breeze from the sea. He paused.

"Serena," he said.

"Yes?"

"Wash. You smell like the dungeon."

CHAPTER

4

Mescahannec River—The New World

Linette caught her first sight of the settlement just as dawn was slipping up over the mountains and dropping slanting rays of light into the valley west of the river. Thick fog hung close to the ground, cut by trees and the stalks of the valley's growing harvest. Hope bloomed in her chest, fresh and new, as the new day anointed the golden fields and orchards of the settlement. She balled her left hand up, feeling the throb of her pulse, as tears pricked at her eyes. Hope had brought her here. But she was not sure she had believed she would make it until now.

The boat began its slow angle toward the riverbank and the simple moorage awaiting it: a couple of wide wooden docks built on thick log posts sunk into the water. Shouts came from the fog-blanketed fields, and a small group of men emerged and ran for the docks, ready to greet them.

She swallowed a lump. If all was well, the governor would have received her letter and knew to expect her. She'd not waited in the Colonies long enough to receive a reply, so if he hadn't received her letter, or if for any reason she was not welcome here … well, she would have to handle that when she came to it.

A voice beside her, so quiet she almost missed it, said, "I wish you well, Miss. Hope it's all you're hoping it will be."

She glanced to the side and saw Ezekiel standing at his pole, relaxed for the moment—the intricacy of steering into port meant his pole needed to be out of the water for time being.

"Thank you," she said softly.

"I expect you're leaving somethin' behind you too. I pray what you find here makes it up."

"I hope so," she said, and swallowed again. His kindness was well meant, if misguided. Nothing could ever replace what she had left behind—but she had lost that before deciding to come.

It occurred to her suddenly that this man too might have dreams or hopes or things he was leaving behind. She opened her mouth to ask, but the shadow of a soldier fell across them both and interrupted.

"I wish you would reconsider my offer, ma'am," Lieutenant Anderson said. "You'd be safe in the fort. This is no place for one like you."

The boat jerked as it pulled up next to the dock, knocking Linette away from the rail for a moment. She regained her footing and gestured out at the awakening valley. "It looks like paradise to me."

"A deceptive façade," he answered. "The frontier is dangerous."

"You've made that clear, Lieutenant, but I'll take my chances here."

He nodded in a way that lingered at the end so he was unmistakably looking down his nose at her. "We'll be here a few days, dealing with king's business. If you decide to join us when we leave, no one will begrudge you the room aboard." He fixed his gaze so it held her eyes. "You would be *welcome* at the fort."

Suddenly deeply uncomfortable, Linette turned around so her back was to him. "I am welcome here," she said. "I have written the governor. Everything is prepared."

He clicked his heels in a salute and stalked away, leaving her alone with Ezekiel and the desperate hope that what she'd said was true.

Herman buttoned his simple coat without a collar and adjusted his black hat so it sat firmly atop his mostly white hair. Amos fidgeted by his door.

"They're waiting for you, sir," he said. "Scouts say the boat has arrived."

"Patience, Amos," Herman said. "We'll meet them in plenty of time to be polite."

They left the house together and greeted the other members of the welcoming contingent. John Hopewell, one of the original settlers, a man bigger even than Herman and a little younger. Smith Foster, the foremost of the settlement's Puritani, with his sixteen-year-old son Martin. Cleveland Moss, another of the original band. Together they made an imposing enough group, Herman hoped, to give the military officers a sense of their agency.

Whenever they had visitors from the fort, Herman got the strong sense that the king's army would gladly take control of the settlement, with or without the king's support. Their captain, Frederick Almon, was ambitious—and cruel, Herman thought, though he didn't show it.

Herman had been given this land by King Aldous himself, but that had not done much to legitimize him or the settlement in the eyes of the Colonies. He'd done his best to shift opinion through his tracts and editorials in the papers back east, but these small face-to-face encounters with the army seemed to him just as important. One never knew when the currents of political influence would change—and the king was a long way away, across the sea in the Old World. The more Herman could do to bend the currents in his favor, the better.

The Tremblers among the contingent wore their requisite collarless coats in black and gray along with their best trousers and heavy boots. Smith and his son had dressed up too, wearing green coats and felt hats instead of their usual furs. Together they plodded through the early morning fog down the path toward the river. The flat-bottomed boat came into sight, dotted with red coats and the white cotton shirts of slaves holding poles. On the dock, a small group had already disembarked and were talking with Silas Gromer and Clive Shilling, the men who minded the moorage.

Among them all was a quite unexpected sight: a dress, and a flash of light red hair.

"Bless my soul," Herman said. "I didn't think she would really come."

Cleveland Moss turned to him, his heavy grey eyebrows drawn into a frown. "You were expecting a woman?"

"She wrote to me. I didn't think ..."

"She must be a soldier's wife," Smith Foster said, peering at the group on the dock, which was beginning to fall into a formation as they saw the welcoming committee approach. "Don't see anyone else with her."

"She's no one's wife," Herman said, clearing his throat. "She's come alone."

John and Cleveland nearly stopped their march. "You authorized this?" John asked.

"We welcome all who wish to come," Herman said.

"How do you expect her to survive out here?" John asked. "We don't have the resources to run a charity camp, brother!"

Herman took John's arm. "We'll discuss this later," he said. "Here they come."

Tempers and words dropped as the military formation approached, with the young woman walking behind them. Herman and his contingent strode forward, and Herman stepped ahead with hand outstretched.

"Welcome," he said.

Captain Frederick Almon took his hand with a firm grip.

"Governor Melrose. Time is still being kind to you, I see."

Herman chuckled. "Is it polite to comment on an old man's age? Time has not had opportunity to be kind to you. Still, you are welcome even if your youth puts me to shame. Come, gentlemen, be at ease in our valley. We are ready for you."

He released Almon's hand and peered past him through the line of soldiers, who were breaking formation at a nod from their superior. "And Miss Cole," Herman said. He strode forward, through the soldiers, and took the young woman's hand. "You are most welcome too."

She who could only be Linette Cole, whose letter had impressed him but failed to convince him she would actually leave behind the comforts and protections of life in the Colonies, nodded as though she couldn't find words.

"Thank you," she finally stammered, "Governor Melrose, I ... it's an honor to meet you, sir."

"And you, I'm sure," he said. He waved to the group behind him. "Amos."

Amos hotfooted his way past the soldiers and joined them, bowing awkwardly.

"This is Amos Thatcher, my clerk. He'll see to your comfort until we can get you settled in properly."

Amos turned redder than a tomato, and Herman left him to manage without so much as a twinge of remorse.

Every young man should suffer this sort of embarrassment. There were far too few women in the valley, and not one unmarried Trembler woman.

From her style of dress, he knew that Linette was not a Trembler but Puritani, which made him a little unhappy. He had assumed from her letters she was one of them. At least this suggested an easy solution to housing her for the moment.

While John and Cleveland kept up obligatory small talk with the officers, Herman wove through the moving crowd to Smith.

"You'll take the girl in, won't you, Smith?" he said. "For a few weeks. Sarah won't mind?"

"She'll act put out for a moment, but I reckon she'll enjoy the company. What is this about, Herman?"

"She wrote to me months ago," Herman confessed. "She's been reading my tracts and avows that she's ablaze with our vision. She asked for permission to come and join us. I didn't think she would."

"Did you answer her?"

"I did, but she is here too soon. She can't have waited for my response."

He cast a glance behind him at the pretty young woman, whose conversation with Amos was turning his face even redder. Smith cast the same glance and laughed aloud. "You did that to Amos?"

"Amos needs more excitement in his life."

"If she's going to settle here he might just get it."

On the path ahead of them, a new contingent came to meet them, this one dressed in skirts and bonnets. Smith stepped forward to greet these first, kissing the foremost on the cheek.

"Hello, Sarah," he said.

Smith and Sarah's daughters, serious seventeen-year-old Letty and rosy fourteen-year-old Lila, held out arms full of fresh-baked bread and a basket of summer peaches to the soldiers.

"Welcome gifts for our visitors," Sarah declared. The soldiers took the gifts with surprised delight, and Sarah's sharp eyes quickly picked Linette out of the crowd. "And who is this?" she asked.

"A new settler, Sarah," Herman said. "Come to join us."

Sarah didn't bother to hide her surprise, but neither did she let it slow her down. She marched past the soldiers, whose arms were now too full of food for them to look overly imposing, and locked arms with Linette, dismissing Amos with a nod.

"Welcome," she said. "It's about time we had another woman in the valley."

"She's going to stay with us, Sarah," Smith said. "For a fortnight or so."

"It'll be tight," Sarah said, patting Linette's hand. "But it's a right sensible idea. Lord knows these lowborn farmers haven't prepared anywhere else for you."

A shadow crossed Linette's face. Herman saw it and intercepted. "We were expecting you, of course," he said. "Just not quite so soon, and I'm afraid events here have kept me unusually distracted of late. Don't let that trouble you, my dear."

One of the young officers, who had been listening intently, butted in. "If you're not prepared to receive her here, she could accompany us to the fort until you are better ready."

"Stuff and nonsense," Sarah Foster replied. "To do what, shine your boots? We've plenty of room here, and the sooner she settles in, the better."

Herman didn't miss the relief on Linette's face.

Government business took the better part of the day. That evening, with a fire flickering low in his office and gleaming off the eyes of the bearskin rug on the floor, Herman finally had a chance to meet with Linette.

"Please, have a seat," he said, gesturing to the chair fashioned from birch branches. "It's nothing much, but more comfortable than being on your feet all day."

Linette sank slowly into it. "I confess I'm still getting used to being back on land."

"Was your trip arduous?" Herman asked.

"No, not to complain of. It was slow. But peaceful, and the men were honorable. But I can't help feeling that I am intruding somehow. Please, if I—"

Herman sighed. He took off his reading glasses and laid his palms on the desk, facing her squarely. "Let me be painfully honest about that. I receive impassioned and idealistic letters like yours rather regularly these days, but not one in a hundred men comes here alone, and no woman ever has. There aren't many more than fifty of us all told, not counting a few trappers who come in and out. I wrote you back to tell you to come, but I also laid out the many difficulties of life here. I did not expect you to be willing to brave them, so I did not prepare for your arrival. That is my own fault. You made your intentions quite clear."

"I should have waited for your answer," she said, not meeting his eyes. He could see the way she was castigating herself inside.

"I am sure that whatever your reason for hurrying away instead of waiting, it was good."

Linette Cole was a pretty woman, in a fairly ordinary way. Her most striking feature was her strawberry-blonde hair, which curled and fell loose from her bun in an obstinate sort of way. Slender and green vines grew like ornaments over her ears and curled at her temples, as well as decorating her throat much like Amos's did.

Herman cleared his throat. "From your letter I assumed you were a Trembler," he said.

She stiffened. "Does that matter? I thought all were welcome here."

"All are," he said. "Puritani?"

He didn't miss her hesitation before she nodded.

"Smith and Sarah Foster are our most upstanding Pure People," Herman told her. "The kirk uses this very meeting house every Lord's Day. We even have our own preacher, a young fellow, very …" he frowned. "Passionate. So you will be well shepherded here."

"That is not really what I'm looking for," Linette said.

"If you don't mind my asking, Miss Cole, what *are* you looking for here?"

"A new life," she said.

"You are very young to be running away from a past," Herman said.

She startled.

"I know, it's not polite. But I take seriously my responsibility to every member of this settlement, Miss Cole—to care for their souls, no matter what sect they may belong to. I believe that every human being has some of God in them."

"I know," Linette said, eyes on the floor again. "You wrote about that in your tracts."

"I will not ask you what you are running from," Herman said. "But if you need to talk to someone about it, know that you do not have to be a stranger here. We all have pasts. Sometimes it is good to tell our stories."

He stood, ready to end the long day and unwilling to push her for more of her story. She looked up at him unexpectedly, and there were tears in her green eyes.

"I don't want to tell mine," she said. "I want to write a whole new one."

He smiled. "You do that," he said. "You do just that."

CHAPTER
5

Palacio del Quinte, Tempestano—The Old World

Martín Carlos Vaquero, the young count of the province of Tempestano, sat at wine in his winter palace and played with the edge of the letter.

"Sir?" Massimo Diego, captain of the guard, asked.

"Another threat is all," he said. "If I do not double my efforts to hunt down any remaining Sacramenti in my lands the southern synod will send troops to do it for me."

"It seems to me only the most foolish of Sacramenti would remain in a place like this."

"Or an Imitator. Which is perhaps the same thing."

Carlos sat back with a sigh. He dropped the letter and played with the stem of his bronze wineglass instead. "And then there is always the question: how much do I compromise with these buzzards before they see me as a puppet? How far is too far? How far makes me strong and wise, and how much loses me respect even from my own people?"

"That would be hard to lose, sir," Diego answered. "You have earned it at high price."

"But people are fickle." Carlos smiled sadly. "My father taught me that."

A commotion from out in the hall drew his attention away from the threatening letter and his wineglass alike. "What is that, Diego?"

"I'll have a look," his faithful soldier answered. But he didn't have time. The door swung open and a small whirlwind blew in, threw back her hood, and said, "Diego, leave us, please. I need to have a word with my brother."

Carlos leaped to his feet. "Serena!"

Serena threw herself into her brother's arms, not caring that Diego ignored her command and simply stepped back into the shadows rather than leaving.

Carlos sobbed once, overcome. "Serena, I … you … how can this be? Oh, thank God!"

"It's all right," she told him as his tears dampened her cloak. "It's all right, Carlos, I'm free."

She pushed back, letting him hang onto her arms but seeking out eye contact. "Brother, I need your help."

"Of course! Anything!" He tightened his grip on her elbows. "Serena, you must know I did everything I could. I didn't give up, please know that."

"I know, Carlos." She smiled. "It's all right. It wasn't your fault."

"But I couldn't protect you."

She laughed a little. "It is not your fault if your sister is always throwing herself in front of the firing squad."

He laughed, but the laugh faded as he slowly caught the meaning in her smile. "Serena, what?"

"Maybe you should sit down."

He did.

She gestured at the goblet. "Maybe you should drink a little more wine."

He groaned and covered his eyes. "Just tell me."

"I have to go to the New World."

He pulled his hand away and sat up straighter. "What? No!"

"You have to put me on a ship and give me passage to the New World. Brother Armando Melrose is in trouble."

"You don't have to go get him out of it."

"The Fire Within showed me."

Carlos groaned. "Why?" he asked the air. He knew perfectly well why. His sister got all the crazy assignments because she volunteered for them. At least, that was how he understood it.

Serena sat down across the table from him and leaned forward intently. "Elder Crispin came to the prison and set a prisoner free—a brutal man, a murderer from the wars. He is sending him to the New World to destroy Armando's colony by assassinating him. He has already been dispatched. I have to beat him to the Colonies or I won't reach Armando in time to warn him."

Her eyes drifted to the wine goblet and she took a quick drink before returning her attention fully to Carlos. "You must put me on your fastest ship and send me across the sea."

"Another would be able to warn him."

"No other can be spared."

"Serena, why do you think we can spare *you?*"

She smiled. "Moments ago I was good as dead in your mind. You have already learned to do without me."

Carlos stood and paced while Serena took another drink and began hunting around the table for something to eat.

"Diego, please call a servant and have them fetch something to eat," Carlos said.

Diego nodded and left the room. Serena stopped her hunting and sat with her hands in her lap. "You know I'm right, Carlos. And the Fire Within gave me a vision. He showed me what I am to do—that I must cross the sea and warn him. I can't simply give that to another."

"You're asking me to send you to your death. To give you up again."

"It isn't your choice."

"I'm your brother. I should be protecting you."

"You should be letting me be what I am. When you light a fire, does it burn fast or slow?"

"It … depends on the fuel."

"Show me."

Carlos picked up a scrap of paper and held it in the candle flame, knowing full well he was walking into some kind of trap but unable to resist Serena. "When I light a piece of paper, like this, it catches fast and flares up brightly," he said. "But it burns so fast that it soon burns out. If I light a good log of ash, dried out and seasoned, or a lump of coal, it burns long."

She caught his gaze. "I am like that flare. I caught fire fast and young, and I burn brightly. But I am not meant to burn long in this life. You know this to be true. Don't try to protect me from myself."

He looked at her for a long moment, then sighed. "There is a ship," Carlos said. "El *Ventarrón*."

"The Gale," Serena said with a smile.

"There is none faster, and it sets sail for the New World in two days' time."

"Can you send it faster?"

"No," Carlos said. He gazed at his sister with exasperation as much as with concern for her. "The captain has business to finish here; the ship cannot change its plans that fast. You will have to trust that it is fast and that the Fire Within can get you to Brother Armando on time."

Diego opened the door. "Pardon," he said. "Food."

Carlos nodded, and a servant carried in a tray and laid it on the table. Olives, dried figs, and apricots were arrayed around half a chicken and sliced bread, remnants from dinner.

"Thank you," he said. The servant left, but Carlos held out his hand to signal Diego to wait. "Diego will accompany you to port," he said. "I will send you with money and provisions and a letter to the captain of the ship. But I cannot do more. Our position here is tenuous, Serena. The synod does not much trust me. I can't be publicly known to be sending anyone to the Colonies, least of all you."

She nodded, apparently satisfied. "I could not ask for more," she said.

"You will be careful?"

Serena looked up at him with a spark in her dark brown eyes. "I will be brave. And sometimes careful."

Jonathan Applegate, young preacher and parson of the Puritani kirk in Jerusalem Valley, had fired the last of the lead shot from his flintlock pistol.

The creature stalking him through the pass knew it.

He was certain of that. Every instinct, every nerve cultivated by a sensitive and pessimistic nature coupled with five years on the frontier—the years in which he had transitioned from boy to man—told him he was prey.

His faithful mongrel, Rusty, trotted close to the heels of his mule, now and then finding himself an alternate path and passing them, only to circle back and go behind again. The mule made its surefooted way along the narrow path, which ran alongside steep rock to the right and terrifying drop to the left. Anoschi Pass was the only way through these mountains for many miles, but it was not a route for the faint of heart.

Creator, help me, he prayed in silence. He feared to speak the words, any words, aloud—as though if he kept silent, the creature would lose interest in him. His heart pounded, and he felt the weight of the small stone pendant he wore around his neck—a carving in the shape of the Book. His father had crafted it from the stones of the valley and given it to him the day he turned sixteen. It reminded him now that he wasn't alone.

He couldn't hear his pursuer anymore, though his heart knew it was not far behind. He'd seen it clearly yesterday, in a small meadow with thick woods behind it. He'd been with the Outsiders, and they had pulled him to cover and pointed to the beast as it stalked the grassy wild. It was a bear, in its primary form, the largest such bear he had ever seen, with a hump in its shoulders and long fur grizzled and matted.

Even from that distance, though, Jonathan could see the sun that glinted off scales under bare patches on its hindquarters, and he could imagine the curved claws that tore up the earth as it paced and the serpentine fangs that said this was no natural beast but one of the Malliku-Machkigen—what the Outsiders called the thorns.

He'd asked the Outsiders about their name for the creatures. They did not belong here, he'd been told, as thorns do not belong in a garden. They were born of *malliku,* witchcraft, planted here by an enemy.

What enemy? Jonathan had asked.

They could not—or would not—answer that.

Jonathan was not convinced the Outsiders did not hold the settlers themselves responsible for sowing the beasts in their garden, but they did not say so—not to him.

Rusty came from behind and hopped up on a crest of black rock jutting out above the path, jumping from rock to rock like a goat. He drew alongside Jonathan, looked back, and growled.

"Easy," Jonathan murmured. He fingered the sweaty steel of the pistol in his lap. He should not have tried to go home while the thorn-beast remained in the area. The Outsiders had told him as much. But when he'd insisted that he had to go, they'd let him leave.

Now, six pistol balls later and fairly certain the stony path with its dark green fir branches overhead was the last thing he would ever see, he regretted that decision.

Why had he been so foolish? All to get home and hold a service on the Sabbath. All to keep from missing a Lord's Day—a problem at all because he had been visiting the Outsiders.

"Forgive me, Creator," he muttered. And in his mind's eye, he saw the face of his earthly father and cried out, *Forgive me, Da.*

"Stay away from the Outsiders," his father had told him, seeing the fire in his eyes when he first saw the people of the forest. "I know they rouse your curiosity, but you're needed here. The settlers, not the Outsiders, are your calling, Jonathan. You stay here and make Jerusalem Valley a place the Puritani can be proud of."

"Yes, sir," Jonathan had said.

But he didn't know if he'd ever intended to obey. He cared deeply for the kirk. Young as he was, he took his position as their pastor seriously. Like his father, he admired Herman Melrose and his vision of a peaceful and just society that tolerated all who chose to live within it, and his sweat and muscle had helped build and plow the settlement, but he ultimately believed the Tremblers were dangerous. They had disavowed the Book, the revelation of the Creator, in favor of inner urgings, feelings, and thoughts of their own that they attributed to God. Like his father before him, Jonathan was deeply committed to nurturing a Puritani community in Jerusalem Valley so rooted and strong that eventually it would overshadow the Tremblers and earn the governance of the new settlement.

Also like his father, Jonathan believed the change needed to happen soon, before the Tremblers gained more influence. It was clear to him as he read the Book that within his own lifetime, possibly within the next few years, a great purging would come—a cleansing of the kirk and the governments of the world with terrible fire. In that day of judgment, Jonathan would answer for how he had won Jerusalem Valley for the Truth.

The son was like the father in nearly every way, except that where Jeconiah Applegate had been a hard man, the son was sensitive and even soft; and that where Jeconiah had been convinced the Outsiders were consigned eternally to the rule of darkness, Jonathan thought they could be reached.

That idea, that inkling that the strangers in the shadows were people who could also be won for the Book and the kirk, had seized Jonathan with a mighty grip and grown into a conviction that left him breathless and awake for hours in the night.

His father had opposed it unrelentingly, and Jonathan obeyed as long as Jeconiah lived. It was seven days after his father died, killed by a wild beast on a hunting excursion, that Jonathan made his first journey through the pass to find a rumored Outsider village. He'd gone with his heart bursting with sorrow, hope, joy, and shame.

That mix of emotions had never ceased attending him when he left the valley.

He could not leave the kirk without a shepherd, but neither could he leave the Outsiders without a witness.

A flock of crows burst out of the trees below the path, and Rusty barked. Jonathan's nerves, ragged and torn, screamed out in panic. His vines felt as though they would choke him, tightening around his neck and his hands and his upper arms. He twisted nearly all the way around in the saddle and searched the path behind him, but he could not see the creature.

When the bear attacked, he hoped his dog would run. If Rusty made his way to humanity in either direction, the Outsiders or the settlers would care for him.

Ahead, the path grew narrower and rounded a bulge in the rock face.

Jonathan found himself unable to see what was ahead any more than he could see the beast behind, and the moment of complete uncertainty—of hanging in figurative midair—made him catch his breath.

The mule kept on, faithfully plodding, nervous but not yet panicked. Rusty, out of landing places, jumped back down to the path and followed them as they rounded the corner. A foul scent on a sudden breeze let Jonathan know for certain the beast was not far.

On the other side of the bulge, Jonathan let out a breath. Water trickled down the rock here, joining other streams to become a small cataract through the leafy green below. It made a few steps of the path mossy and slippery, but the mule navigated them without trouble. A wider vista opened before them as the mountains fell away to the valley below. Jonathan knew the rest of the path: in a hundred feet more it would begin a steep and winding plunge downward, and he would be home in fewer than two hours.

For the first time, he realized what this meant. If the beast did not attack him—a contingency he had not seriously considered—he would be leading it straight to the settlers.

He weighed this. If he led the creature into the settlement, he would lead it toward other men with guns that were not out of ammunition, men who were not so foolish as to charge into the forest for five days with so few lead balls. Maybe, if he rode the mule hard and fast the moment he left the pass, he could reach them in time to give warning. Maybe they could gun the creature down before it could do any damage.

Maybe.

He closed his eyes and swallowed hard, feeling the muscles of the mule beneath him work as they neared the descent.

He thought of Letty Foster, who was nearly eighteen, not beautiful, and not witty, and whom Jonathan passionately loved.

What if she was out working the fields when he arrived, as was not only possible but likely? What if the bear charged her, or one of her little sisters or brothers, or their mother? The Fosters were the pride of his congregation. They were the kernel of his hopes for the future, and they were good people.

"Forgive me, Da," he said again. He reined in the mule hard, fighting it as it tossed its head and brayed, announcing its unhappiness with the plan. Reins in hand, he dismounted, careful of his footing on the treacherous path. Rusty ran to his heels and bowed as he dug a piece of paper and a pencil out of his saddlebag.

"Just stay put," he told his mule as he scrawled a note on the paper, trying to use his saddle as a writing surface. The mule shifted from foot to foot and made an atrocity of his handwriting, but he finished the missive and stuffed it back into the saddlebag.

He hesitated only a moment before tucking the reins away and slapping the mule as hard as he could on its hindquarters. The animal took off with a loud whinny, disappearing down the steep path in moments.

Jonathan watched it go, then drew his hunting knife and turned to face back the way he had come. Rusty hadn't followed the mule, but he didn't have the heart to send the dog away. He needed someone to strengthen him for what he was about to do.

From the west, the shadows were beginning to lengthen. With them, Jonathan heard it: the sound of footfalls on rock, of claws clicking at shale, of breath.

The scent, like rotting flesh, blew by him again. His fingers tightened around the knife. Carefully, he backtracked toward the sounds, over the slick spot where the water fell, then took hold of the nearest handhold in the rock face and hoisted himself up a foot—onto a small slab of rocky outcrop where Rusty had stood before. As though he climbed a treacherous staircase, he edged his way to the next such natural platform, raising himself a few inches higher.

Height was the merest advantage, but he needed every thread of help he could get.

The sun had nearly set on Jerusalem Valley when the mule came running like it would never stop. In the meeting house, they heard a shout and then hoofbeats. All stood to their feet simultaneously, but the young lieutenant, Anderson, was the first out the door.

"It's a horse!" he called, "Riderless!"

"Not a horse but a mule," Amos said, right behind him. Herman followed, slower and heavier, but he recognized the animal where Amos had not.

"It's Parson Applegate's," he said. "Catch the creature!"

Anderson was already in the path before Herman had finished speaking. The lieutenant was quick and even-handed, and he had the mule stopped and was calming it when Herman lumbered up to them.

"Thank you, young man," Herman said. Smith Foster, the source of the shout, ran up from the fields.

"That's Parson Applegate's mule," Smith said. "Came running out of the pass like a devil. What's going on?"

As though to answer his own question, Smith drew alongside the mule and rummaged in its saddlebag without hesitation. He pulled out a rolled-up piece of paper and unfurled it, holding it up to read in the half-light.

"What does it say, Smith?" Herman asked.

Smith rolled the paper back up and cast it aside. "Says he's in trouble— stalked by a bear in the pass. He's out of shot. He wasn't willing to lead it here but begs us to come to his aid immediately, before it's too late."

The young lieutenant turned to his captain. "Unusual behavior for a bear, isn't it?"

"The parson isn't a liar," Smith said.

Anderson stiffened. "Pardon, I wasn't implying that."

"Round up as many men as you can," Herman told Smith. "Can you find him in the darkness?"

Smith cast a worried eye toward the path. "There's only one path, but I'd worry for footing unless the moon is bright."

"It should be, tonight," Amos said.

Smith nodded. "We'll go." He stepped aside suddenly and drew close to Herman, taking him by the arm and leaning in. "Boy says it's a Machkigen. I'd keep the soldiers away."

Herman nodded and blew out a long breath of air. Smith was already advancing down the path into the growing shadows of the settlement, swinging a torch and calling for help from the nearest cabin.

"I'll send men with you," Captain Almon said.

"Better not," Herman answered. "Anoschi Pass is dangerous to anyone not familiar with these mountains. Our men will be safer alone. They can handle one bear."

He was glad the soldiers couldn't clearly see his face in the dim evening light—at least, he hoped they couldn't. He nodded at Amos. "Amos, fetch ammunition from the storehouse."

Amos nodded and jogged off into the darkness. With some effort, Herman lowered himself halfway to the ground to pick up the letter Smith had tossed aside. Ascertaining the captain wasn't close enough to read over his shoulder if he were so inclined, Herman unfurled the paper and read:

I am as good as dead. Don't come for me. I will do my best to slay the creature, so help me God, but I do not hold much hope that it can be done by one man so ill-armed as I find myself. Fortify yourselves, and give my love to Letty Foster.

CHAPTER 6

The commotion drew Linette from the loft room where she was unpacking her few things. Drawn by the noise, she descended the stairs into the heart of the Foster family home. She hung back awkwardly as the seven Foster children and Sarah clustered around Smith, who seemed to be fighting his way through them like a man cutting his way through waves to shore. He grabbed a flintlock rifle from the wall and tucked a large hunting knife at his waist.

"But Smith, in the dark?" Sarah said.

"The moon is nigh full. We'll be able to see the path some, and we'll take our steps carefully."

"If only you could wait till morning."

"If what the parson says is true, he won't last till morning." Smith gave a curt nod to his oldest daughter. "Sorry, Letty. I'll do all I can."

"But—"

Smith headed Sarah's protest off with a kiss on the cheek and then something said in low tones that made her turn pale as a sheet but step back and nod, argument won. Linette swallowed hard, unexpectedly gripped with fear. She didn't know what was happening, but she did know Sarah Foster was no coward. If anything about the woman was clear from first impressions, it was that. The gravity on her face now made it clear whatever was happening was serious.

Letty whisked open the curtains at the nearest window and stared into the darkness, cupping her eyes against the light in the house. "No moon," she said.

"What?" Smith asked, pausing with his hand on the latch of the door.

"There's no moon anymore. Clouds moved in."

Smith cursed, and Sarah reprimanded him. "Watch your mouth, Smith Foster. You know the Book says to let no foul speech proceed from your mouth." But both cast the door open together as though to prove their daughter's words wrong.

"When?" Smith asked. "It's been clear skies all day."

"Clouds been coming up the mountains since late afternoon," Letty said. Her face was almost expressionless, and her voice held little emotion. Yet Linette could see something in her eyes—something that said a fire burned inside this girl.

"Let me go with you," Linette said.

The words were out before she could take them back, but she didn't regret it, though her heart pounded at her own boldness. She had come here to make her home among dreamers and throw in her lot with them. What better way to do it than to offer the one small gift she could?

Smith and Sarah looked at her, uncomprehending. It was Letty who opened her mouth not to respond but to explain. "They're going into the high mountain pass to find the parson," she said. "He's trapped up there with a demon bear stalking him."

"A what?" Linette stammered.

"Outsiders call them Machkigen ... thorns. Beasts that are half serpent and half one thing else. They're not from earth and they're not like earthly beasts. Kill for the joy of killing and ain't easy to stop."

"Aren't," Sarah said.

Letty ignored her and fixed her intense eyes on Linette. "Why do you think *you* should go?"

"I ... I can light the way," Linette said. She saw the incomprehension in their expressions and decided it was easier to show than to tell what she meant. With a duck of her head, she passed Sarah and Smith and stood in the darkness outside the cabin. She shoved up both her sleeves, exposing the vines that coiled around her upper arms and elbows before trailing down to her wrists and hands. Lifting her hands a little, she closed her eyes and summoned the light.

She felt it coming like a warmth through her veins. It enveloped her arms and hands and throat, and when she opened her eyes it was shining.

"Phosphorescence," she explained. "It runs in my family."

The golden glow from the vines filled the air and lit the ground and trees around her in a wide swatch as effectively as any moon.

"I'll be," Smith said.

"But … you can't let her go," Sarah said. "Linette, you're a brave woman, but you'd be risking your life for a man you don't even know."

"I came here to be one of you," Linette said. "Believe me, I have nothing else. Please, let me help."

Smith and Sarah looked at one another. "It's not our choice to make," Smith said. He nodded, then trained his blue eyes on Linette. "You can come, depending on one thing. Can you keep a confidence?"

"Of course," Linette said.

"The soldiers are not to know we're facing anything but a bear out there."

"I understand," Linette said, though rightly speaking, she didn't. Why it was a secret that the settlement faced some kind of otherworldly threat, she did not know. Rumors of the frontier certainly suggested wilder things. She trusted someone would explain it later.

Smith hesitated, then reached into his coat and pulled out a flintlock pistol. "Can you shoot?" he asked.

"No."

"Take this anyway. If you find yourself looking a beast in the face, release the safety lock and pull the trigger."

He cracked half a smile. Linette nodded and gingerly took the pistol. It was heavy and cold. She didn't like the feel of it, but she tucked it away in her waistband and told herself she should be grateful for the protection.

After all, she had no real idea what they were about to face.

Smith turned to go. Linette began to follow. A hand on her arm stopped her. She turned to look into Letty's serious face.

"Alive or dead, bring the parson back," she said.

The way into the pass began in a patch of ground on the western side of the valley where a stand of firs had carpeted the valley floor in dry brown needles. In the light she gave off, Linette could see a rough path making its way through the stand and then steeply up the side of the mountain, through a groove worn by feet and hooves amidst exposed roots and stones.

Smith walked immediately behind her, closer than a shadow. She knew he would rather lead the way, but he needed the light she cast ahead to see where they were going. The path was narrow and mostly made of packed earth—easy ground to turn an ankle or slip. It also angled up so steeply she found herself quickly wishing for an easier way. Her heart pounded and the muscles in her legs were on fire. But she said nothing and kept going.

Above and ahead of them was nothing but impregnable darkness and a strange and oppressive silence. Behind them, eleven more men let out an occasional grunt at the steepness of the path. They carried lanterns that gave them a little more light in the hindmost of the party but did nothing to break the overall cloak of night.

They were strangers to her, every last one. Even Smith, close behind her, she'd known only for a day and not with any more than a few words exchanged.

Yet somehow, out here in the wilderness, in the foreign country that was night, with a band of armed strangers in her footsteps, she felt the deepest sense of belonging she had ever known.

If she died out here, tonight, she would not regret having come.

Step by step, flicker of light by flicker of light, they made their way up the mountain path. After what seemed an hour it leveled out and began to switchback. Linette charged forward, but Smith's hand and a low "Wait" stopped her. She turned to ask what he wanted, but he pressed a waterskin into her hand before she could ask.

Grateful, she took a drink, aware of her thirst even as she slaked it. The burn in her legs and the effort of breathing had kept her distracted even from that basic need.

She handed the skin back and saw a question in his eyes—was she all right, could she keep going? She nodded, and they continued on.

After a few more switchbacks the terrain changed, from dirt and roots to mossy rock. The path narrowed as it began to crawl along the edge of rock face. Looking up in the glow of her own light, Linette could see the high edge outlined against the sky far above.

"Watch your step," Smith whispered. "It's a sheer drop to your left."

Linette glanced to the side and shuddered. A mess of leaves and branches reflected the light, but she could tell they only curtained off a dangerous drop.

The smell hit her full in the face a moment later—a sharp rotting scent that turned her stomach. Her light flickered.

"That's the beast," Smith whispered. "It's close."

Linette stood frozen in place on the path, uncertain of what to do now. To light the way was one thing, to lead a charge quite another. The path was so narrow here there was barely space to let anyone move around her.

"I'll take the lead now," Smith said. He held out a hand to indicate she should stand against the rock face. She did, flattening herself as much as she could so he could pass easily. He gestured for others to follow. "Stay three behind me," he told her. "The light will still fall far enough ahead to help us, but you'll be protected."

She nodded, even though she knew as well as he did that it would not prove to be much protection. Somehow, without being told, she knew the beast they hunted was capable of taking every last one of them down. They were up here, out here, because they knew exactly what the creature could do to them, and they were unwilling to leave it free access to the valley or to surrender one of their own without a fight.

Two more men passed Linette, and she fell in behind them. They moved forward at a creep now, crouching, careful of every footstep. Just ahead was a bulge in the rock that would force them to go around it, walking a narrow ledge. Her heart pounded in her throat at the thought of what might be on the other side.

The smell had grown worse now, rank and demanding in the air. With it she recognized the copper smell of blood, and she found herself whispering a near-silent prayer for the parson she had never met.

Deep in her bones, an ache was settling in. She didn't know how much longer she could maintain the strength of the light.

Just long enough for the battle, she told herself, *and to get us all off this mountain. Then they'll all be glad to let you sleep.*

Smith stepped out toward the bulge, then hesitated and looked back. She realized it at the same time he did: once he rounded the corner, he would lose the light. Until she could follow him around, he'd be waiting in total darkness.

She opened her mouth to say she would go first after all, but before she could volunteer, he disappeared around the rock face. The others followed with hurried steps, and Linette went after them so quickly that she missed a loose piece of shale and slipped. She regained her footing quickly, but the clatter of the rock and the terrifying sensation of slipping impressed it so firmly on her rapidly beating heart that she thought it would leave a scar.

She saw it the moment she rounded the corner: about a hundred feet beyond the bulge was a dark, humped shape blocking the entire path.

Ahead of her, Smith called. "Linette. Come."

She inched forward, passing the two other men. Her light fell upon the shape, illuminating grizzled, matted fur, and something else—scales, shining through the fur on the creature's neck. She shuddered at the sight of an open mouth with long, curved fangs.

The beast was not moving.

Her light showed up dark patches of something on the path and the rock face as well: blood.

Smith took a cautious step forward, rifle in hand—then another, and another. The creature did not move. Linette followed, the light falling stronger and stronger upon the creature until they could all see plainly see the truth.

"It's dead," Smith said. He lowered his rifle and looked up and around helplessly. "But where is the parson?"

The men, all of them taciturn, burst into a collective relieved murmur. Linette edged closer to the beast, not because she wanted to but because she knew the men wanted a better look. She shivered at the sight of it. Its mouth hung open, a forked tongue displayed from between its teeth. The creature's shape was unmistakably a bear—although an enormous, nightmarish example of the species—yet the scales, the teeth, and the tongue were those of a serpent. She found herself grateful the eyes were closed.

The comments and relief gave way to search. "Parson!" Smith called. "Jonathan!"

No voice answered … but somewhere nearby, Linette heard a dog bark. The unexpected sound seemed to arrest the whole group in the darkness, knocking their calls silent and their search still. Then Smith said, "Rusty!"

The bark sounded again, more excited this time, followed by a mad rustle of leaves and a flurry of branches from the cliffside below. A small animal burst onto the path, jumping up the last few feet. Its eyes glowed in the light, set in a red-furred face with floppy ears and an earnest expression. Smith knelt down and reached for the dog.

"Here, Rusty! Good boy … good boy. Where's Jonathan?"

This time, a human voice answered—a low groan from somewhere below. He couldn't be far away.

Smith jumped up. "He's here!" He beckoned several of the men to his side and began giving orders. Some had already anticipated his commands and begun tying ropes around the nearest and sturdiest tree limbs or outcrops of rock so they could rappel down in search of their friend.

"Linette, come to the edge," Smith said, walking her forward like he would escort her to a safe place. Her head spun at the height she imagined below, but she drew as close as she dared to the drop-off and leaned forward slightly, holding her hands out so the light shone down and gave the men something to see by. Those who carried torches drew alongside her, and though their light did not add much to hers, she found herself grateful for their heat and for the men who stood grimly and silently beside her.

For the first time, she realized one of the men in the party was a boy, a teenager. She recognized him as having been part of the welcoming contingent when the ship first arrived at the port. He was Smith's son, Martin. He stood pale and wan beside her, hefting his torch high and peering over the edge with a strained expression. She wanted to comfort him, but something in her knew that would not be welcomed—that he was trying to become a man, and that for her to coddle him now would be an insult, even here where they faced the rot and prospect of death in the darkness.

Her mother-heart panged, and she swallowed a sudden hard lump in her throat.

"We found him!" came a shout from below where Smith and the others had rappelled down. More voices responded, and the ropes shifted and strained as they maneuvered in the trees below. In the movement of leaves and branches and shadows, Linette found herself growing dizzy. She closed her eyes, willing herself to stand firm and keep the light shining. In the force of concentration, she became aware of how much everything ached, her head not least of all, and of how hard she was finding it to concentrate or comprehend what was happening below.

"Easy," a voice beside her said. She opened her eyes just a slit, enough to see it was Smith's son who spoke to her. Comforting his would-be comforter. She smiled.

And then it was done. They were hauling the broken body of a young man up from the branches. She caught sight of his face in the glow of her light, saw the lines of pain pulling at his eyes and his mouth, and saw the wrongful bend of his limbs. His clothes were spattered with blood—in places drenched. Whether it was his or the beast's she didn't know. The smell was overpowering.

Smith's face near the young man's head gazed up into her light. The young man himself moaned.

That was the last thing she remembered.

CHAPTER 7

Torrentio Harbor, The Old World

Serena Vaquero waited impatiently while the scar-faced ship's captain counted out the money her brother had sent to pay her fare—coin by silver coin, clinking them one at a time into a small wooden chest that lay before him. At last he dropped the last coin and looked up, fixing her with a stare.

"Well?" she asked.

"It's enough," the captain said. Jones was his name. From all appearances he was as dishonest and disreputable a seaman as they came.

Serena bit her tongue. Of course it was enough. Never mind that her brother could have simply ordered the captain to take her and not bothered to pay at all. Carlos was a man of integrity, or this old sea dog wouldn't see a penny for his trouble. And here he was, not only *not* properly grateful for Carlos's kindness, but also daring to treat the count's sister like an inconvenience.

Forgive me, Fire, she prayed. *I am still too proud.*

The captain stood slowly, pushing back his chair. "We weigh anchor at dawn. Be aboard."

"I will," she said. "I am ready—more than ready."

Carlos wouldn't be happy with her for saying that.

And too impatient.

It occurred to her that she might ask the Fire Within to help her see this man with charity, the way she had unexpectedly seen Banquo, the prison guard—as a man, and not merely as an obstacle in her path.

But she didn't really want to.

Captain Jones turned his attention away from her and began to scratch out words on a long piece of parchment. She strained to make out the words from her upside-down vantage point and realized he was putting her name on a list of crew and passengers, to be submitted to the harbormasters for recordkeeping. Good enough. Satisfied, she turned to go.

The captain's "office" was an upstairs room above a pub a block from the harbor. Serena pulled the hood of her cloak over her head as she descended into the unseemly crowd, unwilling to draw undue attention to herself. The air was rank with smoke, alcohol, sailors too long away from anything like a bath, and the salt of the nearby sea.

She'd nearly made it through the front door when a voice said, "Excuse me, Miss?"

She put her head down and made to charge forward without responding, but the voice came out of the shadows accompanied by a man's tall and slender form, and before she could get away, he took her arm.

"Excuse my rudeness," he said. "You should not leave here alone."

Something inside told her not to react the way she wanted to—by casting the man's grip away, turning on him, and denouncing him as loudly as she could. Instead she kept her eyes forward and answered in a low voice, "Why?"

"You did not do a good job of concealing the money you carried when you entered. More than one man here will follow you out for it."

"I don't have it. I gave it to a captain for my fare on board his ship."

"They don't know that," the stranger pointed out.

She turned just enough to see his face: neither young nor old, with shoulder-length brown hair accented by a well-trimmed mustache and goatee along a sharply defined jaw. His green eyes were sharp and intelligent, and she noted that his face was not unpleasant to look at. He wore a green coat and matching gloves. He had neither the softness of a student nor the hardness of a sailor, and she wondered who and what he was.

"Allow me to escort you outside," he said. "If you are not alone I think your chances of escape are much better."

"And how do I know you are not going to rob me yourself?" she asked.

He smiled at that and pressed something into her hand. She recognized the feel of a pistol hilt and closed her fingers around it in shock.

"You will just have to trust me," he said. "And if you find that you can't, use that."

"You are inviting me to shoot you?"

"If you find it necessary I would rather you clobbered me in the head with it, but yes. I realize you have no protection but my word otherwise, and that doesn't seem fair."

She pushed the gun back into his hand. "I can't accept."

At this he seemed genuinely surprised, though they still stood side by side at an angle such that she couldn't clearly see his face. "May I ask why not?"

"I am a pacifist," she said.

"Then for certain, you *must* allow me to escort you out."

Serena looked around and realized their public position in the door meant far more eyes were on them than she liked. Hoping they looked like quarreling lovers, she allowed the stranger to propel her outside. With his gloved hand still on her arm, he began a brisk walk toward the harbor. She pumped her legs to keep up.

"Why so fast, Señor?" she asked. "Surely your next appointment can wait a few minutes longer for you to arrive."

He slowed his steps immediately. "I apologize. Of course, we can walk slower."

"Why are we walking at all?" she queried.

"Because I do not trust those fellows at the pub. I am not sure one of them will not still follow, and since you are a pacifist, I will have to fend them off alone."

Sometime in the course of the conversation, Serena had become convinced that the stranger's concern was genuine and his motives pure. She hastened her steps a little, allowing him to walk a bit faster—though not to equal his former speed.

"May I know your name, Señor?" she asked.

"It is Jacques," he said.

"Pardon me, *Monsieur,*" she said with a smile.

He waved a gloved hand, also with a smile, and angled his steps so he half-faced her as they walked. "No need for formality. Simply Jacques. And you, Miss?"

"Serena."

"It is a pleasure to meet you." He doffed his cap, and with his brown hair tousled, she thought he looked younger. His very intelligent eyes were large in a fine-boned face. "You must forgive my curiosity. You said you paid a fare with that rather large purse? You must be going quite some way."

"Indeed. I am going to the New World."

At this, both his eyebrows raised in genuine surprise. "So far! But this is a coincidence. I am also going to the New World, aboard the flying ship *Ventarrón.*"

"It flies?" Serena asked, laughing, in part to cover her own surprise. "This I did not know. I am afraid I am not dressed for traveling through the clouds."

He laughed as well. "Neither am I. I only mean the ship is said to sail so fast it must leave the water and soar on the wind. But I do not believe these rumors myself." But then his expression changed as he realized the meaning of her words. "But do you mean you are also sailing aboard the *Gale?*"

"The very same," Serena said. The young man, she thought, looked unaccountably pleased at this. And truth be told, she felt the same. What had promised to be a very long and lonely journey now held the prospect of a friend.

Jacques held out his arm. "In that case, allow me to be your escort for the remainder of the time you are abroad in the town. I cannot afford to lose a friend on the eve of such a voyage. I have so few as it is."

She took his arm, surprised at how comfortable it felt to walk alongside him. "I find that hard to believe, Monsieur."

Linette awoke to the sensation of a headache trying to cleave her skull in two.

"Shhh," said a voice, accompanied by the sensation of a cold cloth dabbing her forehead. "Lay back."

She didn't realize she'd been trying to sit up, but upon the voice's command she relaxed her muscles and let the feather pillow behind her head and shoulders receive her weight. She groaned. The headache made it hard to feel anything else, but she suspected every muscle and bone in her body was protesting the night before.

At least, she hoped it had only been one night.

"Did you know it would be like this?" the voice asked from somewhere further away—its owner had moved across the room. "The light? That it would affect you so badly?"

Linette considered nodding but didn't want to bear the consequences. She managed to grunt an answer that she hoped sounded like "yes."

"Well. We're all very grateful." This was a different voice, one she recognized as belonging to Sarah Foster. The earlier, inquisitive one must have been Letty.

Sarah continued. "When the men didn't come down the mountain last night, we feared the worst. Then Smith came down at first light with you and the parson both, and he told us what you did—how you kept their steps secure in the pass and helped them find Jonathan until your own strength gave out. Not many have that kind of grit. I'll admit I was glad to see another woman come to settle here, but a little trepidatious too. Now that you've shown what kind of woman you are, I'm nothing but glad."

Linette's eyes burned behind their lids. "Thank you," she managed to say through the thickness of her mouth.

"Letty, go and fetch a glass of water," Sarah said. Linette heard footsteps and the opening and closing of a door. When the girl was gone, Sarah said, "Smith tells me you've seen our secret too. I know he's already said it, but

I'll say it again—the thorns—what the Outsiders call Machkigen. Word of them doesn't leave this valley. Especially not with the soldiers."

Footsteps creaked across the floor, followed by the settling of skirts in a chair and the pressure of Sarah's hand on Linette's. "You're one of us now," she said. "I know you won't tell."

Voices from downstairs came up through the floorboards in a sudden burst of visitation—men's voices. "That'll be Governor Melrose," Sarah said. "He's been wantin' to see you. I know your eyes are still shut, but do you want visitors?"

Linette considered the question and managed to nod. The resulting peals of pain were less horrific than she'd expected. "And a … drink," she croaked out.

"Letty's gone to get you one. She'll be back any second."

As if to prove the point, the door opened and footsteps shuffled their way quickly across the floor. Linette opened her eyes a bare slit, just enough to make out a slightly stoop-shouldered figure in calico handing a glass toward her.

Linette tried to sit up, but Sarah's arm quickly circled her shoulders and gave her a resting place where she could drink. "No need to strain yourself," Sarah said. "Easy now."

The water, cold and clearer than any water Linette had ever tasted, washed down her throat with a soothing touch. She drained the whole glass, grateful for the instant relief it brought to her throat and her head as well. She opened her eyes again, this time attempting to focus on Sarah's face.

Sarah Foster, Linette noted, was a timeless woman. Likely she was only about eight years' Linette's senior, but her chestnut hair was streaked with grey. Her vines were dark brown, streaked with blue. She had an attractive, firm-jawed sort of face, one which didn't take guff from anyone and which managed to speak care and kindness to Linette without speaking fuss, judgment, or an overweening amount of concern.

Linette decided she liked her. Very much.

Sarah lowered Linette's head and shoulders back down and turned to Letty. "Letty, go tell the governor he may come up if he wishes, and bring another glass of water. I think Linette could drink down a whole well, and no wonder."

"Pa wants to come too."

Linette caught Sarah's eye and smiled her assent.

"He may," Sarah said. "But no more; we don't have room for a whole committee up here."

Letty withdrew to issue permissions, and in less than a minute, heavy footsteps creaked up the steps and paused at the door. Linette raised herself on her elbows and shifted back with Sarah's help until she could lean against the pillows and bed board comfortably.

"Come in," Sarah said when Linette was ready.

Governor Melrose doffed his broad-brimmed hat when he entered and stood presiding over Linette with an emotion she could not identify. There was a glow to his eyes that indicated concern and fondness, and there was something else. It might have been pride. She only knew her heart did a painful twist at the sight and that she would have given anything to see that look on her own father's face.

Behind the governor, three others piled into the small room: Smith Foster, with a similar expression on his face to Governor Melrose's; the governor's spindly secretary; and a hulking man the governor's age whose name Linette couldn't remember. The men fanned out and stood looking down at her with their hands clasped in front of them, all but Smith holding their black Trembler hats.

She cleared her throat to say something. Thankfully Sarah spared her the need.

"Well?" she said. "Say what you have to say and get on with you so Linette can rest. You needn't stand here like mourners at a funeral; she isn't dead."

Herman Melrose smiled. "Thankfully not. We only came to check on you, my dear, and to say our thanks. Because of you, a young man lives who otherwise might not have survived the night."

Linette smiled back. Her heart gave another painful beat at the way the governor looked at her. Like he was proud of her.

Like she belonged.

"It was my pleasure," she said.

The big man at the foot of her bed—John, that was his name; John Hopewell—barked a laugh. "Hardly that. You look like it nearly killed you."

To her relief, they all chuckled. She liked the way these people flowed together—the way they chided and corrected and argued with each other without any real tension at all, like family. And she didn't want them fussing over her.

"Nothing so severe," she said. "Just a headache. And a … well, everything aches. But it will pass."

For an instant the shadow of the past fell over her, but she shook it off. She wanted to remain here, in *this* moment. She hoped no one had seen the memory in her eyes.

"It must be a rare gift," Governor Melrose said. "I've never seen it before, and I flatter myself that I've seen nearly everything. What did you call it?"

"Phosphorescence," Linette said. She winced at the pain in her head. "It runs in my family. I think it … comes from the sun. We soak it up all day and release it at night when we want to."

The governor clucked his tongue. "Fascinating."

"It shone so brightly," Smith put in. "Turned the mountainside into daylight."

"Praise the Everlasting Arms for that," Sarah said.

Governor Melrose's face darkened suddenly. He leaned in. "So you saw … clearly, I mean …"

"The thorn?" Linette saw the surprise on all their faces—all but Smith's—and the quick exchange of glances. Sarah did not make any indication that she had spoken out of turn, though. "Smith and Sarah told me. You needn't fear. I'll keep it a secret."

The governor patted her hand. "Good."

His voice sounded thin with trouble. She glanced at the other men, but none met her eyes. "What are they?" she asked.

"I … I don't know," the governor said. "Something akin to the monsters in the sea, or the creatures that visit our dreams. Some embodiment of the Curse that plagues this world. They weren't here when we came—not that we ever saw them. They only began to appear a year ago."

"Are there many?"

"Too many," Governor Melrose answered. "We've lost livestock. They strike, destroy, and disappear. We've never killed one until now."

"Why don't you tell the army?" Linette asked. She hastened to placate the alarm on their faces. "I won't tell—you needn't fear that from me. But why do you keep it a secret? The army could send a detachment here if need be, help you defend against the beasts."

"Yes, they could. And that is precisely why we don't tell." The governor leaned in and smiled. "You've read my tracts. You tell me. What are the values this place is founded on?"

"Tolerance, goodness, and peace," Linette answered.

"And we have the ability to live by them only because the Colonial government holds no sway here. I am sovereign over this land by the king's command. But I hold that post by a thread. There are many who would like to cut it and take control for themselves. Fill this place with Colonial soldiers, and I fear we have little hope of maintaining anything like peace. If we accept their protection we also accept their authority, and we cannot do that."

Linette cast her eyes down and nodded. She realized she knew very little about how this place worked—the challenges these people faced in pursuit of their dream. She knew only that it was a dream she believed in.

Governor Melrose stood and laid a hand on her shoulder. "You're a woman of courage," he said. "I think you'll fit in well here."

Linette's heart warmed at that with greater heat than had throbbed through her vines the night before.

PART 2
CROSSING OVER

CHAPTER 8

September 1642—At Sea

"Eat this."

Jacques shoved the bowl of watery gruel in Serena's face, as was his custom. As was hers, she pushed it away.

"I don't want it."

His voice remained pleasant. "You must eat."

"Why? It all comes back up anyway."

"That is why you must eat. It does not *all* come back up, and what stays down keeps you alive."

She groaned and opened her eyes a touch, enough to see his hand holding the wooden bowl close enough for its contents to slosh around and speckle her face. It smelled awful.

"You're cruel."

"So you tell me."

"A tormentor. You're worse than the prison guards."

"I have heard."

Serena sighed and concentrated on the core of her body, checking to see whether she thought she could actually hold some of the gruel down. Jacques was absolutely right, of course; the trick for her was choosing her moments carefully.

She fought to sit up against the swimming in her head and waited with her hand against a post in the ship's stuffy hold for her vision to stop pitching the world back and forth more than it was actually doing. It calmed down after a moment, and she reached for the bowl. Jacques placed it in her hands.

"You know you are an angel."

"I am told that too."

Serena had been sick every day for the last fifty-two days—ever since an approximate thirty minutes after leaving the harbor in Torrentio. The ship's captain did not consider it his job to care, and without Jacques's patient tending, she was not sure she would have survived this far.

Truly, he was a gift from the Fire.

She peered at him as she tried to eat a bite. He sat patiently a foot away, on the floor with his back to a stack of barrels, ready to intervene if she needed something. While she had lost pounds and color and any shred of verve over the last month, he had hardly changed at all. His beard was a bit less kempt, given the difficulty of trimming accurately in a wooden tub that never stopped rising and tumbling over the changing peaks of the ocean. His face was a bit thinner (though his ability to keep food down in the worst of conditions was a gift she envied sorely). His eyes were as perceptive as the first time she'd met him … and he was every bit as enigmatic.

"I can't make you out," she said.

He shifted a little, out of the deeper shadows into a rainbow shaft of light that came through the spray and a window above. "Is that better?"

"That's not what I meant. You know that's not what I meant."

She swung her legs around the side of the bunk and held the bowl in her hands firmly, as though she thought it might try to escape while she was scrutinizing her companion.

"A whole month out here and I still don't know where you're going."

"I told you. I have business in the New World—prospects to explore. That is more than I know about what you are doing."

"I told you. I am going to stop a murderer."

Jacques's mouth twitched with a smile he didn't quite set free. "I do not think you are in the condition for that."

She held up her bowl. "I am eating."

"No thanks to yourself."

She smiled to herself and took another bite. For once it was settling her stomach rather than making it worse, so she followed that with another and another in quick succession. The gruel was awful, but it was food.

Jacques stood, his balance remarkable in the pitching hold.

"Where are you going?" she asked, alarmed. She wasn't ready for him to leave.

"I am going to find you some hardtack," he said. "You are eating better than I have seen you in weeks. I am not going to allow that opportunity to slip away from me. Maybe your stomach knows we are near land."

"How much longer?"

"The captain thinks we will see the shore of the New World any minute now. Then maybe two more days till we reach New Cranwell."

"Glory be," Serena said. "It can't come fast enough."

His expression sobered. "Eat your hardtack when I come back with it. Then I need to speak with you."

She raised an eyebrow. "Aren't we speaking now?"

"A different kind of speaking."

A knot formed in her stomach. She hadn't heard that tone from him since the day they met in the pub, when he'd been sharp and severe about her need to avoid robbers. For over a month, they had managed to live side by side on the ship, strangers among a crew that had a bond of its own, becoming in some way bound to one another—and yet she knew nothing about him. Not his destination, not his purpose, not his past. She was not even sure she knew his name. A growing conviction that he was hiding something—or everything—had taken root only a few days into the voyage, when she found him adept at talking about everything and revealing absolutely nothing. He did not lie. He simply did not tell the truth.

And yet she trusted him.

That was the deepest mystery of all.

Jacques reappeared with enough hardtack, wrapped in cloth, to keep her nibbling for an hour. She accepted it with her eyes glued to his face, which had lost none of its solemnity.

He knelt so they were at eye level. Her stomach fluttered. Was this it … was he going to tell her the truth about who he was?

"You are not safe," he said.

It wasn't what she'd expected to hear. "Excuse me?"

"I do not trust the captain of this ship," he said. "The Colonies, they are not friendly to Tremblers. I think the captain means to use you as some kind of example."

"What does Captain Jones care about religious squabbles?"

"I am only telling you what I believe to be true. I have overheard things … nothing that makes sense by itself. But I think when we land, they will try to arrest you. Your brother's position has protected you thus far, but the captain will make it look like he had nothing to do with this."

"My brother? How do you know about my brother?"

The smile came back to his lips. "You are not subtle, Mademoiselle Vaquero."

"Unlike you." She blew out a breath of frustrated air. "I don't want to believe you, but you, sir, are impossible to disbelieve."

He smiled this time softly … a smile that bespoke true concern and melted her heart. He confused her, this man. For the first several weeks she had tried to guard against his falling in love with her, but she'd given up trying when he simply gave no inclination that he was tempted to do so. And yet, at the very same time, it was clear that he *cared*. Now more than ever.

"Good," he said. "That settles it."

"Settles what?"

"It is not safe for you to land."

It was her time to smile. "And what do you suggest I do? Fly?"

"I suggest you *land* somewhere they are not expecting you. And early."

"Leave the ship somehow?"

"Steal a boat, I am afraid. But we will give it back. I think stealing is not in either of our codes of honor."

"You're right." She stared at the man looking back at her. "You said 'we.' You are coming with me?"

"I cannot let you go alone. You are my friend. And you have a murderer to stop."

She tried to read the expression in his eyes. She wanted to say something witty back—but the truth was, she had no idea what his purpose here was. Somehow he had simultaneously locked her out and invited her in.

"Thank you," she said.

"You are welcome."

"For being my friend."

"I knew that was what you meant."

"I am your friend also."

He smiled and reached out, touching her hand with his gloved one for a bare instant. "I know."

"So you think we should steal a skiff to leave the ship?"

"Once we have sighted land, yes. We should choose our timing carefully. If they come after us we may find out just how poor of a pilot I am."

He stood up and looked down at her for a moment later. "Eat your hardtack. It looks like your stomach is finally settling. Just in time to get back to shore where you will be sick all over again."

"Thank you for that reassurance."

He winked. "You're welcome."

"Jacques."

"Yes?"

"Are you a Trembler?"

The question hung in the air.

"No."

"Then what are you?"

Again, the question hung in the air. They faced each other, she searching his face intently.

"I am a man," he said at last.

"Can I bring my things?"

"The trunk you packed?"

"Yes."

"You had better not. I do not know how we will get it out of the hold and onto a skiff without being seen. Pack what is essential in a bag and carry it with you."

She nodded. No great loss. She had never been overly attached to things, and most of the contents of the trunk were only there in the first place to make her brother happy. He worried that she wouldn't have what she needed.

He always worried.

Serena woke in the middle of the night to a hand lightly touching her shoulder. She bit back a startled yell at the sound of Jacques's voice.

"Shhh. We must go now."

"Now?" she asked in a choked whisper. She sat up slowly in the pitch darkness of the hold, casting aside the scratchy woolen blankets she'd been sleeping under for the past fifty-some days. She'd grown so used to the sound of waves that she didn't notice them anymore, but now, in the strangeness of the night, they were all she could hear—rhythmic, beating, filling the hold.

She wrapped herself in her cloak and felt around for her small bag. She'd packed it right after yesterday's conversation ended and Jacques disappeared. He didn't often leave her alone, and she felt his absence. She wondered about him—wondered hard, wondered deeply. Wondered why she couldn't read him. She had always been a natural reader of people, and since the Fire Within had filled her, that skill was enhanced to a degree most people found frightening. But in this one very important case, the gift availed her nothing.

She found the bag and closed her fist around it. In the dark, Jacques took her other hand. She surrendered to his lead, heart racing as they crept through the darkness. Sailors slept all around them, and numerous obstacles littered the way, but Jacques led them expertly past it all. Up the ladder they climbed, and in a moment they were under the stars, breathing salt air.

Serena stared up at the wild sky and shook her head in wonder. Jacques didn't leave her much time to gaze. He pulled her hand insistently. "Come," he whispered.

"Why now?" she whispered back as she followed him across the deck, glad for the moonlight that showed up coils of rope and other obstacles clearly. The skiff—one of three—was lashed to the side of the ship, under a tarp. Jacques rolled the tarp back and began to undo the fastenings and prepare to lower the boat to the water. Serena followed his example, working alongside him. The tarp had kept things reasonably dry, and it wasn't too difficult to loosen the ropes.

"Because we are in sight of land now," he said.

"How do you know that? I can't see anything out here but the waves."

"I heard the sailors talking. We are closer than the captain said. When the sun comes up you will see it. Here, take this rope. We will lower it down together."

Obediently, she took the thick rope with both hands, bracing her feet against the ship's rail as they began the work of quietly lowering the skiff. Though it took some wrestling, it wasn't too heavy—or else Jacques was taking more than his fair share of the weight, though if that were the case she thought the whole thing would go askew and probably bang against the side of the ship and wake someone.

As they stood side by side and carefully lowered the skiff, a terrible thought struck her. What if Jacques was lying? What if there was no plot on the part of the captain? What if Jacques himself was the plotter, sent by Elder Crispin or some other enemy? Could it really be coincidence that he had shown up in the pub when he did, just in time to help her, and then turned out to be a fellow passenger on this ship? All of this time together, and all she knew about him was …

All she knew about him was that he had marvelously intelligent eyes and the ability to make her trust him without cause.

In other words, she knew nothing.

The whole scenario played itself out in her head, and she realized how much sense it made. This midnight escape was not an escape at all; it was a kidnapping. For a moment she considered letting go of the rope, losing the skiff, calling Jacques a liar, and maybe even calling for help.

But there was this one thing.

That she *did* trust him.

"Serena?"

She looked at him. He had a quizzical expression on his face … had probably been calling her while she was lost in thought.

"I'm sorry. What did you say?"

"I said it's time to go."

She nodded. "Lead the way."

"Not this time," he said, and though she could not quite make out his face in the dark, she could imagine he was smiling again. "After you. I will help you down. Here now."

She followed his voice to a long, thick rope full of knots, lowered over the side and dangling in the brisk wind toward the waves. She could just make out the dark shape of the skiff bobbing in the water, outlined by the white of water as it broke against the boat's sides. Jacques's gloved hands guided her as she took hold of the rope and began to lower herself over the side.

"No," she said, "wait a moment." She pulled herself back up and retied her bag of belongings around her waist. "That's better."

This time she began the climb down in earnest. Cold water splashed her, carried by the wind, as she worked her way down the knots toward the skiff. Her feet slipped off the rope, and she caught a scream in her throat until she'd managed to find the knots and steady herself again. Jacques called out no encouragement. Even if he'd seen the slip, they couldn't afford to be heard.

Just a little further, she told herself. *A little further. Fire Within, help me.*

She lowered herself past a covered porthole and resisted the temptation to nudge the cover aside and peer in at the sleeping sailors. She knew a lookout was probably awake somewhere on board the ship, missing their escape only because he wasn't watching for trouble on board. If Jacques was right about everything, leaving now was brilliant. The sailors would be so intent on reaching shore in the morning that they might not even notice their absence for some time.

If Jacques was wrong, or lying—well, she didn't want to think about that.

A wave swept through below and dashed the skiff against the ship. Serena swung wildly as the ship dipped and rolled with the wave. She stifled a yell as the rope swung her hard into the side of the ship, knocking the wind out of her. She fought to breathe as the rope swung back out and the aftermath of the wave separated skiff and ship again. She saw her moment and dropped.

She landed in the little boat, soaked with spray and spiked with pain from smacking the small of her back against the wooden seat in the boat, but she laughed with exhilaration at the sensation of having made it.

Of all the chances Serena Vaquero had taken in her life, skimming down a knotted rope and dropping into a skiff three feet below was among the least. Even before she had invited the Fire to kindle within and became a Trembler, she had seen little point in living life if it did not mean daring death at every corner.

Waves tossed the skiff, and she lay on her back and looked up at the shape of Jacques toiling down the rope on his way to her. No, this wasn't risk. Not compared to running with the bulls when she was only seven, or getting lost in the mountains when she was twelve, or standing trial before Elder Crispin for sedition and witchery.

Jacques landed in the boat with a satisfying thud and struggled to get his balance. Serena chuckled at him and rolled over with a groan, sitting up with some effort.

"Are you all right?" he asked.

"Fine, fine." She waved a hand at him. "Nothing a little land won't fix."

He cut the line to the ship with a knife. "You will not like the land."

She sank down in a seat as Jacques grabbed the oars, still waiting for the pain shooting through her back to pass. "I have always liked land."

"You will find it pitches and rocks while the sea stands still. For a few days. Then I think you will like the land again."

Serena took an experimental deep breath and found she could let it in and out without feeling as though she was going to crack a rib. She nodded and found another pair of oars under the seats. She picked one up and started to fit it to an oarlock.

"You do not need to do that," Jacques said. "Rest. Recover." He was already pulling the skiff away from the ship at a good clip, maneuvering the little boat expertly through the waves.

She raised an eyebrow. "You said you weren't a sailor."

"Maybe I am a natural."

She shook her head to rid herself of the thought: *Or maybe you are a liar.*

With a suddenness that took her breath away, the skiff seemed to catch a current and began to fly over the waves, into the stars and the dark sea—and there, far off where she could just make it out in the light of the moon and the stars, there on the horizon, lay the New World.

She gave up trying to wrestle the oar into the lock and just let it drop to the floor of the skiff again. Wind streamed through her hair and sprayed her face with salt, and this time she wanted to laugh but couldn't, because the wonder, the exhilaration, the sense of being alive was too much. It fell over her as a silence so deep it called to places in her own soul and spirit she didn't know existed.

Places where the Fire Within burned.

Her heart leaped as they skipped across the sea. Jacques, his own hair flying back in the wind, hardly seemed to the touch the oars. They were alone in the moment, alone with the universe and with the Spirit imbuing it all with meaning.

Serena trembled.

Jacques looked back at her. The moonlight caught in his green eyes, and he was part of the magic of this moment, this night, this flight.

I'm sorry I ever doubted you, she thought.

She wasn't sure if it was Jacques or the Fire Within she was apologizing to. Because it was the Fire, the Spirit, who had brought them together. Of course it was. It had to be. Even if Jacques claimed not to be a Trembler. He belonged with her and with people like her. He was one of them even if he didn't know it.

He looked away from her, back toward the shore. The dark, inviting shore: the one place within Kepos Gé where history had not yet been written.

In this moment, Serena was sure of one thing: they were going to write it.

CHAPTER

9

September 1642—Jerusalem Valley Settlement, The New World

The flat, whitewashed floorboards of the Trembler meeting house creaked, and in the creak Linette Cole heard the voice of God.

She stared at her hands and said nothing. The Tremblers were only supposed to hear God's voice in silence. This much Governor Melrose had patiently taught her as they took long, rambling walks together through the valley in the early days of her arrival, when she confessed to having thrown away her talisman of the Book—the mark of her membership in the kirk as one of the Puritani.

"That is a bold thing to do," Governor Melrose had told her when she confessed it. They were walking through a cornfield toward the small house he had ordered readied for her to dwell in. Some of the men were there at the time, hard at work. Linette carried a basket full of soiled clothing, to wash at the creek behind her house. It had quickly been identified as her role in the settlement: washerwoman for the many bachelors and widowers who made up the frontier community.

The task was far beneath the station to which she had been born in life, and she embraced it wholeheartedly.

As they walked together, more than two months after her arrival, her hands were raw and chapped from scrubbing wool and carefully working lye soap and cold water over buckskin, and her shoulders and back ached from carrying the baskets. She had never worked so hard, and she had never been so happy.

The one blight on her days was the kirk. She loved the Fosters and bore their morning devotions as a family tolerably well—Smith was not long-winded and managed to work none of the truisms she remembered from the Colonies into his comments on the Holy Scripture. Her first Lord's Day in the settlement, Smith filled the pulpit as well—uncomfortably. He struggled through the words on the page, and he preached on a single verse from the epistles, which read, "You shall reap what you sow." Linette stiffened when he announced the text, but he managed to make it about corn and potatoes, and she relaxed halfway through when she realized he wasn't going to apply it any more widely than that. The young parson, Jonathan Applegate, was as yet indisposed after his "unfortunate fall in the mountain pass," as the governor explained it to the redcoats before they left three days after arriving.

Sarah assured her after the sermon that Parson Applegate's messages were a good bit livelier and more, well, applicable. Smith overheard this and objected that his message had been plenty applicable. What was more relevant to the life of a settler than bringing in the corn crop? Linette felt secretly relieved that the parson hadn't been available, but she couldn't tell Sarah that.

When the young preacher did return to the pulpit, still walking on crutches and looking a bruised and pale fright for the beating he'd taken, his messages were indeed more full of fire than Smith's had been. Linette sat through the first message feeling as though someone was constricting her heart in a vice.

At the Smiths' over Sunday dinner that week, she was uncharacteristically quiet. She managed to compliment Letty on the young preacher's vivid way with words and to say something acceptable to Sarah about his handling of the Word, but all day she battled feelings of panic and the need to run away.

So it was two days later that she told Governor Melrose she'd thrown away her Book and that she wanted to know more about the Tremblers.

The Silence was the first thing he explained. Where the Puritani relied on the Book to hear from God, the Tremblers relied instead on the voice they felt inside, where the Fire Within dwelt. On the Lord's Day they would gather together, wait in silence, and hear the Creator speak from the depths of their souls.

It was a beautiful idea, and when Linette first visited the Trembler meeting house, she loved it. She soaked in the silence, listened as the others shared what they believed they heard, and wondered if she would ever begin to hear the Creator for herself.

So now there were the floorboards.

She was supposed to hear the Creator in the depth of her soul. She heard the Creator instead in the accidental, obtrusive, disruptive noise of the floorboards, alternately a groan, a creak, or a crack like a musket in the woods. She'd been hearing it for the past several weeks.

He always said the same thing.

I am here, Linette, underneath the floorboards. Remember.

She settled on the third backless pew in the women's section—the very back row—and eyed the whitewashed floor almost nervously, as though the Creator God, maker of Kepos Gé and all who dwelt within it, would come bursting up through it.

There was only one other Trembler woman in the settlement, the aging Agatha Moss, who took her seat on the front row but didn't obstruct Linette's view of the men as they filed in on the other side, creaking and cracking the floorboards as they came. They wore plain black coats without collars and and broad-brimmed hats for the Lord's Day, accompanied by good black leather shoes, made blacker with blacking polish. It was a marvel they didn't mark up the white floorboards something awful. For this solemn day, they had left behind their usual frontier accompaniments of buckskin leggings and moccasins.

Linette watched them enter with her eyes cast down. She wondered why black was the holy color and not white. She knew the Word as well as any good Puritani woman, so she knew it spoke of the saints clothed in white, and since they were not Sacramenti with their heretical ideas of an exclusive heavenly hierarchy, they knew themselves to be saints, counted among the number that would surround the throne of the Creator and make intercession for the world.

The last of the men filed in. They were the founders of Jerusalem Valley, these men who had accompanied Herman Melrose and gathered around his vision of a new society in the woods and mountains of the western frontier. There was a solemnity to them, to their history and their brotherhood, that Linette felt deeply.

Brother John Hopewell led them in a hymn and a prayer, and then as always, he sat down and they sank together into silence.

This was the way of the Tremblers. There was no preacher, no pulpit, no liturgy. They gathered on the firm conviction that the Creator speaks and his people can hear him, and so when they came together, they did not talk. They listened.

Someone shifted, and a floorboard popped like a firecracker and made everyone jump.

Someone on the men's side mumbled something. Linette didn't think it was a prayer—more likely a grumbling about the floorboards.

Things progressed as usual. Despite the lack of liturgy, the order of the Tremblers' meetings did not much change from Lord's Day to Lord's Day. Herman Melrose heard from the Creator first, and rose to speak a few words from the psalms; Sister Agatha Moss heard second and charged them all to labor faithfully at their labors, whatsoever they might be. Cleveland Moss gave a rousing exposition loosely drawn from the epistles of Paul. Despite the Puritani fear that Trembler silence would lead to them "hearing" wild heresies and imaginations, most of what was shared came straight from the Book, faithful enough to the Word to please even Sarah Foster.

Linette grew more and more nervous as she watched and listened. There was a roar growing in her ears, as when one is underwater or experiencing terrible fear. It made it difficult to take in what anyone was saying. Her eyes were nearly transfixed on the floorboards.

It had been weeks that she'd been hearing the Fire Within say the same thing, but today that thing was growing in power and growing in urgency and threatening to come out her mouth.

Linette had only officially been a Trembler for a month and a half, and she had never spoken up. She had hardly been one of their number long enough for anyone to recognize her right to hear from God.

The roar grew, and her nerves pulsed, until finally Cleveland sat down and she shot up onto her feet and blurted, "I hear the voice of the Creator under the floorboards. He says he is ... down there. Under the floor."

Every eye looked at her, no one bothering to hide that they were startled. And confused.

She faltered for words to explain herself more fully, but none came. She finished with a quiet, "That's all."

She sat down.

Everyone stared.

She shot back onto her feet again. "And one more thing. The voice says I'm to remember. Or we are. Someone is to remember."

She sat back down once more, and this time she wondered if she should have added "Thus saith the Fire," as Governor Melrose often did. She decided she'd done enough jumping up and down like a grasshopper on a hot rock, so that would be that for now.

Herman Melrose cornered her as soon as meeting let out and they were all dispersing in the street. He didn't immediately speak, just raised both of his white, bushy eyebrows.

Linette stuck out her chin. "It was the Fire Within. I'm sure it was."

He cleared his throat. He looked amused. "I didn't question you."

"But you don't believe me," Linette said.

"It seems strange of the Lord to hide under the floorboards. But his ways are beyond comprehending."

Linette eyed Herman suspiciously. Was he really accepting of her wild pronouncement, or was this the prelude to a lecture?

As though he could read her mind, he said, "It's not our way to correct the hearing of a sister among us. You must put those ways behind you—all the judgment."

"I'm only too glad to," Linette answered, "but I find it hard to rest in it. At home everything was about judgment. And even here ... Sarah ..."

The governor nodded and pointed down the dusty lane with his walking stick. "Shall I accompany you home?"

She nodded.

They left the meeting house together and meandered along the lane, under apple trees with leaves turned golden. The September day was warm, but the days were growing shorter, and Linette knew the cold was coming. She wondered what it would be like to face it, alone in her house—her first winter on the frontier.

They reached the split-rail fencing marking the front of Governor Melrose's property. Neat fields covered two acres, golden with wheat that would be ready to harvest before long. A garden grew closer to the house, and Linette recognized that it needed weeding. The house itself was rough and rudimentary, little more than a room with a stove and a pump.

When the governor first announced that Linette's home was ready for her, they had stopped here on their way. Governor Melrose sat on the buckboard of a wagon containing all Linette's earthly belongings: two suitcases, a chest of drawers, and a small oak table.

She'd assumed, when they pulled up to the house that was little more than a cabin, that it was hers. She remembered how her heart had sunk a little at its wildness, at the way it looked like a place a man should live, not a woman. Not a woman alone.

Maybe the governor saw the look on her face and understood, or maybe not, but he hastened to explain: "This is mine. It's on the way. I left something here I meant to give to you, so I thought we might just stop a moment if you don't mind."

"Of course not," she'd said, flooded with relief and then with worry. What could he have for her—this man to whom she already owed so much?

But when he came back out of the house, her eyes had filled with tears and her fears were forgotten for a moment. He came carrying a beautiful, hand-carved rocking chair. There was a quiet pride in his twinkling eyes.

"Made just for you," he said. "We didn't do a good job of welcoming you properly when you first arrived. I hope you'll accept this attempt at a second try. I thought you deserved something to make this valley feel like a home."

While Linette fumbled with words to try to explain her gratitude, he loaded the rocking chair into the wagon, clicked to his old horse, and off they went, to arrive just minutes later on the other side of a swatch of corn at a real house. A narrow, framed cabin with two stories, a cedar-shingled roof, and honeysuckle vines growing around a small front porch.

Quietly, with a voice subdued by emotions and memories, he'd said, "It's a good little place. I lived here once myself when we first came. Let it fall into ruin for reasons of my own. But we've patched it and fixed it up, and it's ready for living in."

"I know you say it isn't your way to judge another, but how do you *know* someone has heard the Fire Within?" Linette asked, pulling herself away from the memory as they drew near her cabin. "What if I am nothing more than a foolish woman trying to gain attention for myself, or a hysteric?"

"Are you either of those things?"

"No."

"And that is clear from your life. We do not judge, but we may occasionally look at fruit. When a hysteric or a fool speaks out and says they speak the words of the Creator, we doubt them. When you claim to speak the words of the Creator, we listen, even if you say he is living under our floorboards."

She flushed. "I don't think that's exactly what it means … what I said. I just couldn't stop those words from echoing in my head, over and over again until I had to say them."

"I know the feeling well."

"Is it always like that when the Fire speaks?"

"No."

"Then how do you …"

He held up a gnarled hand. "Sometimes, my dear, it is better to still your questions and simply be."

"You know that is the kind of thing Parson Applegate objects to so much."

"My advice?"

"Yes. Well, all of this reliance on feelings, and on being instead of thinking."

Governor Melrose sighed. A gust of wind blew fallen leaves by and rustled in the yellowed corn. "It is not one or the other, but I understand why he feels the way he does."

Linette frowned. "I wish you would say something to him about his sermons."

"He has a right to preach anything he desires to preach."

"Even if it encourages the settlers to question you?"

"I don't want them to obey me but to obey God, in whatever way they hear him."

Tears came to Linette's eyes. "But if you fall, the settlement will fall. When I came, you were so careful not to let the redcoats know anything. Yet Parson Applegate is sending regular reports to the Colonies, and he calls your governance into question as well as your beliefs. You must be aware of it."

"He reports to the synod. Yes. I know." Herman gathered Linette's hand and laid it to rest in the crook of his large arm. She soaked up his presence, the way he shielded her from the wind and the cold. This man had become everything to her. She'd dreamed he might become something to her, when she read his tracts. But to know him, to be truly with him in this wild place, was more than she could have dreamed. He had become more than a father to her.

They reached the beaten path to Linette's front door and stood together, neither in any hurry to leave.

"When I invited anyone and everyone to settle here, I knew the risks," Herman said. His brown eyes were sad, yet he smiled. "I didn't want a Trembler colony … one more place for one people and one people only, where we could put up walls and create enemies. I wanted a colony where anyone who loves peace and loves the Creator could choose to live together in harmony. I have never forgotten the sins of the Old World, Linette. I bear the scars of that violence and hatred on my body. We will never leave that awful history behind by doing the same things that led Sacramenti and Puritani to take up arms against each other. If we want a different future, we must change things in the present."

"But the Puritani aren't willing to accept you as a lover of the Creator.

I don't know how you can accept them. They say such awful things about you, even here."

Herman gave her a sharp look. "Don't allow yourself to be bitter against them, Linette. They are not our enemies. The Puritani here are committed to our cause."

"They are committed to their own," Linette said. "Not to yours."

"There we must disagree."

From the fields, a flock of swallows rose and dove as one, chasing one another through the sky and low over the wagon paths. Linette watched them, her own thoughts tumbling and diving like the birds. Dressed in his solemn black, Herman stood out against the white clouds of the sky and the dust of the road like an inkblot on parchment. Maybe, she mused, that was why the Tremblers wore black. So they might better write the Word with their lives for the world around to read.

"What do you think of the parson's talk of a purging? He thinks another war is coming, or something equally awful."

"I don't think of it."

"Do you know he hints that you may be a deceiver and a false prophet?"

"Linette."

Unwillingly, she turned and looked her elder in the eye. The rebuke in his gaze was clear. She flinched away from it.

"The parson may preach whatsoever he likes. I will not raise the law to stop him. That is not why I came into power."

"At least go and visit him," Linette said. "Speak to him about it. He makes himself into some kind of prophet. I don't think it's good for the Puritani here either."

"May I point out that it was you who spoke on the Creator's behalf today?"

"I'm not a prophet. I don't know even know what I meant."

"It doesn't matter what you meant, so much as what the Fire meant through you."

Linette sighed, exasperated. She really had no idea what the words she had spoken were supposed to mean. Unbidden, the question of what Sarah would think rose to her mind.

That didn't need asking. She knew what Sarah would think. Sarah had already told her.

And then hadn't spoken to her again, nor likely ever would.

She blinked tears away and saw Herman watching her closely. "What's wrong?" he asked.

"Nothing."

"It's a strange nothing that produces tears."

Linette wiped her eyes with the back of her hand, irritated with herself. "I'm glad to be one of the Tremblers. It's the right path. It's just ... it's just, I wish the Fosters would forgive me."

"They aren't speaking to you still?"

"Smith is civil. The children avoid me."

"And Sarah doesn't speak to you at all."

She nodded quickly. "That's right."

"I'm sorry," Herman said. He sounded deeply troubled. "Sarah Foster is a fiercely loyal and fiercely passionate woman. She loves the Book and believes wholeheartedly in the ways of the Pure People. It isn't *you*, Linette, it's just ..."

"I know. She thinks I'm a traitor and a heretic. She told me." Linette took a ragged breath and laid her hand on Herman's arm. "Thank you for your concern. You needn't worry about me."

He opened his mouth to say more, but she turned and fled into the house before he could.

Inside, she stood in the shadows with her back against the door and berated herself for being so emotional. When she'd told Smith and Sarah that she was leaving the kirk, she'd known they wouldn't be happy. Sarah, especially, wasn't happy—she acted as though she'd been personally betrayed. Linette tried to explain why she was doing it, but she wasn't sure herself.

"Truth matters, Linette," Sarah had said. "It matters more than anything. You can't just throw the Book away because you don't like what it says."

That wasn't it. It wasn't it at all. But Linette couldn't pull her words together well enough to make Sarah see that.

Their rejection was harder than she'd imagined it could be. For the first few horrible days after they fell out, Linette had lived in the torment of belief that the valley itself was rejecting her, that she would never belong here after all. But Herman and the other Tremblers had welcomed her, the others had remained cordial and even friendly, and in the end it was only Sarah whose friendship was lost to her.

Breathing hard, Linette pushed herself off the door, crossed the room, and pulled a small box from a crevice in the wall. She opened it to reveal writing paper, ink, and pens. Forcing herself to get her mind off the Fosters, she sat at the table and took out paper for a letter.

Brentwood Taylor, the trapper who ran the mail back and forth from Fort Collins, was due through the valley in a day or two. She would have a whole sheaf of letters for him this time.

There would be nothing for her in return, of course—for so many reasons, there couldn't be. It didn't matter. That wasn't why she wrote.

CHAPTER
10

The Coast—Eastern Shore of the New World

When the sun broke over the eastern horizon and lit the sea on fire, Serena and Jacques beheld the endless shore of the New World. It stretched without boundary to north and south, rising like an invitation. As the sun rose higher the shore shifted from uniform grey to blue and then to green and white; and from featureless to distinct, molded out of rocks and forests. Waves crashed off the inhospitable coastline, and rocks rose from the sea as they drew closer, treacherous islands more than capable of wrecking a vessel that drew too close.

The *Ventarrón*'s captain doubtless knew where to guide his ship safely into harbor. Serena and Jacques had no idea.

To her surprise, Jacques drew a looking glass from his coat and used it to sight the shoreline. "There," he said, pointing. "A wide river flows into the sea, there. I think we can row into the heart of the land if we use it."

"Where did you get that glass?" Serena asked.

"Stole it."

"Another reason to apologize."

"Lying and stealing are grave sins, but not as grave as allowing you to be betrayed into the hands of your enemies when I could prevent it."

Serena regarded her companion. As she did, a flash of vision passed before her eyes. She saw Jacques dressed in black robes and surrounded by redcoat soldiers who threatened him. The vision advanced, and she saw him standing trial before a magistrate.

"Who are you, really?" she asked.

He gazed back at her. "A stranger," he said.

"Is it only me you are protecting? Or would you have left the ship to protect yourself, even if I were not with you?"

He took a long time to answer. He seated himself at the oars, turned his back toward the shore, and began to row in the direction he had indicated. Finally he said, "What did you see?"

"You. Threatened with arrest. I do not think you are a friend of the Puritani."

"That is not inaccurate."

"But you are not a Trembler. You say."

"I am not."

"That leaves you only one affiliation that I know of."

A fleeting smile passed over Jacques's face. "If I say that out loud, you will be burdened with knowledge it is better for you not to have. I trust you will not be detained on your mission here. But if you are …"

Serena stared at her hands. "Let me help you row. It's harder now."

He nodded. She took the second pair of oars and fitted them to the locks. The rhythm of pulling the oars through the water strained every muscle in her back and shoulders. The effort felt good, bringing a sense of purpose and release to her tangled thoughts and feelings.

Jacques could only be one thing. It broke on her now like a wave on the shore. If her enemies needed one reason more to hang her, this would be more than enough: she was bringing one of the Sacramenti into the New World.

And not just an ordinary member of the faithful.

An Imitator.

And yet … the Fire Within had not warned her. Even in her vision, seeing him surrounded by his enemies, she had not felt a warning against him.

Why?

And why was he coming here?

They rowed in silence. He volunteered nothing, true to form, and she could not bring herself to ask. Any answer would change things. Any truth, spoken out loud, would make them mortal enemies. And she found she couldn't bear that.

Look deeper, Serena, said the Fire Within.

She objected, her heart bleeding with her prayer. *He is an Imitator. He is here to start a war. I have to oppose him.*

Look deeper.

She closed her eyes and pulled against the waves with all her strength. Her heart pounded as spray soaked her face. *The Imitators are the greatest threat to us. They would bring everything under the Hierarchy's control again.*

Look deeper.

She let out a sob and hoped that Jacques hadn't heard it, that the sound of waves drowned out the fight she couldn't help expressing. She opened her eyes and looked at him: the tall, strong man with compassionate green eyes and a spirit that had been faithful beside her for nearly two months at sea—gloved hands that had brought her porridge day after day and sometimes fed her when she couldn't lift her own head.

She was supposed to see an enemy when she looked at him, but she could only see a friend.

What if he is mine? asked the Fire.

But that is impossible.

What if it isn't?

Somehow she lost her grip on one of the oars, and caught by a wave, it slammed back and hit her in the shoulder. She yelled at the pain but shook her head fiercely at Jacques when he jumped to her aid.

"I'm fine. Keep rowing."

He looked at her strangely and went back to his own oars without a word as she grabbed onto the oar again and pulled.

I have put you together. You must stay together. You must go to Jerusalem Valley together. This is my will.

After an hour's hard rowing, Serena and Jacques found themselves in calmer, sandy waters where the river flowed into the sea. They rowed against this easier flow into a wide passage lined with pine trees and white boulders covered with lichen. Birds sang from the forest, and deer darted away from their approach. The new morning was rich and welcoming, its light sparkling off water and rock. Rather than pulling with regular strokes, they positioned themselves on either side of the skiff and began to paddle.

"There," Jacques said, pointing at a spot on the shore not far away. Rocks here gave way to a small, sandy cove. Serena nodded. Without another word, they directed the skiff to the spot. The bottom scuffed against sand as they approached, and the skiff lodged itself, unable to get any closer.

With a smile, Jacques lay down his oar and stepped out of the boat. The water reached to his knees. He held out a hand. "Brace yourself. It is cold."

She hesitated.

"You will have to choose to trust me," he said. "Like it or not, we are together, you and I."

"But what if I don't trust you?" she asked.

He looked around, taking in the tall pines and the depths of forest beyond them. To the other side lay the ocean, rough and blue under the new day's sun. Above stretched a sky that seemed bigger than it did in the Old World.

"Then we will find someplace where we can safely part ways," Jacques said. "But I do not think that place is here."

Serena nodded and took his hand.

He helped her out of the boat into water so cold it took her breath away. Her skirts became an instant heavy weight, wrapping around her legs as she tried to navigate the shallows with him. She gathered them and tried to lift them away from her legs with one hand while holding tightly to Jacques with the other. Only his steady strength kept her from tripping and falling in the water.

They reached the edge of the cove and left the water. The sensation of land—solid, unyielding land beneath her feet—greeted her violently. Water behind them, she tripped and fell after all.

Jacques caught her on the way down. The world spun mercilessly, and she heaved for breath.

"I told you that you would not like the land," he said.

She tried to nod. Instead, she fainted.

Serena awoke to the welcome sensation of heat on her skin. Her eyes fluttered open to the sight of flames licking at an expertly made tent of sticks and bark, balanced over ground that was a mix of white pebbles and dirt. Jacques's hand intruded on the vision, adding a thick branch wrapped in white bark to the fire. The flames dampened for a moment before surging higher at the new fuel.

The mesmerizing tongues of fire calmed her spirit for a moment—until their movement suddenly took in the rest of the world, and the ground tilted.

She groaned. "When will it stop?"

"It took you two months to become accustomed to the sea. Give yourself a day to come back to the earth."

"I don't have a day. I need to stop the killer."

Jacques settled himself across the fire from her, cross-legged on the ground. "I have been thinking about that. Tell me, how do you plan to stop this man?"

"By finding the governor. Warning him."

"I see. So you do not plan to go hand to hand with the murderer himself."

"That wasn't my intention, no."

"I confess I am relieved to hear that."

Serena managed a laugh. "Did you picture me challenging him to a duel?"

"I have not known you very long, but it seems to me something you might do. Even if you are a pacifist."

"If I thought it would work. But I have no idea how to find him, and I do know how to find the governor. At least, I did. From the harbor in New Cranwell. I don't know where we are now, and while I am grateful to be alive and free, I am a little unhappy about that."

"By my calculations we are not far from the harbor where you planned to land. On foot we can follow this river and make New Cranwell in two days. Or we can take the skiff upriver and make it in a day. You can find supplies and book passage inland from there."

That last *you* stuck in her ears. She raised her eyes to the grand, silent wilderness rising all around them and imagined pressing deeper into it—alone, or surrounded only by enemies.

It could not be done.

"And you?" she asked, finding the word stuck in her throat as well. "Where will you go?"

He looked intently at her. "That depends on where you want me to go. You know who I am; I saw that in your eyes. I will not defend or justify myself to you. But if you wish me to accompany you to Jerusalem Valley, I will."

She frowned. "I never told you I was going to Jerusalem Valley."

"I think you did."

She shook her head vehemently, thick black hair heavy on her shoulders. "I did not. I guarded that secret like you guard all of yours."

He seemed unperturbed. "Then perhaps I just assumed it. You are an escaped Trembler tracking a murderer to the New World to stop him from killing someone important to you and to your movement; who else but the legendary Governor Melrose?"

The thought came to her again that maybe he was lying. That their meeting in the pub had been no accident but a calculated encounter, that he had booked passage on the *Ventarrón* for the purpose of following her, that they had left the ship early because he had planned it so. How had he known where to pilot the skiff to find this quiet shore? Now it was clear he had known all along where she was going and to whom. And of all the enemies of Governor Melrose and his dream, the Hierarchy Jacques was sworn to serve were the most violent, the most voracious, the most opposed to everything Serena stood for.

It looked bad, all of it; it looked damning.

But the Fire had spoken so clearly. They were supposed to do this together.

And truly, she wanted him to come.

"I do wish you to accompany me," she said. "As selfish as that may be. I assume you have some purpose in being here other than helping me."

"Who says this does not serve my purposes as well as yours?"

She gazed at him over the pale flames, dancing in the daylight amidst the birch. "Those words should frighten me. By every history book your purposes and mine must be at odds."

"Must they be?" he asked. The usual veil over his thoughts lifted, and she saw a conflict in his green eyes something deep and torturous. Then it was gone, and his face was placid as usual. "I know our history, and I know what is said about the Tremblers. But if you will trust me to be me, and not just a member of an order opposed to yours, I promise you that I will not harm you or your friends. That is not why I came."

One final long pause, one final coming to terms with her fears, and Serena nodded.

"I will."

Jerusalem Valley Settlement—The New World

"The Book tells us that we must beware wolves among us, wolves dressed in sheep's clothing who would destroy the sheep. We cannot tolerate falsehoods even when they come from those who claim to speak for God. I tell you, my people, a purging is coming. A time of terrible trial and fire, brought about by God himself."

Jonathan Applegate clutched his rough-hewn pulpit and leaned forward, taking the weight off his leg. Though his wounds were healing, they were healing slowly—and poorly. The left leg was healing bent, and pain throbbed through it whenever he stood for any length of time. His small congregation, made up of the Foster family and six others, listened to him with a mix of rapt fascination and distaste. The latter came mostly from Smith Foster, which worried Jonathan but also spurred him on.

"The Book declares that everything that can be shaken will be shaken. The wheat will be sifted and separated from the chaff. A great purging comes, a day of fire and salt. I know in my heart it will come to pass soon."

Tears pricked at Jonathan's eyes, whether from the pain in his leg or the pain in trying to convey such strong feelings he was unsure.

"We must be faithful, more than we ever have been. We must press into our reading and our belief. We must be faithful to his Word. We must be merciless in purging the mixture from among ourselves. As he said himself, Will he find faith on the earth? Who will be found faithful? Who will be found *pure?*"

He tightened his fingers around the thick rim of oak. The kirk met in the anteroom of the governing house, which was transformed into a church only by hauling the heavy wooden pulpit out of its closet and setting up a couple of benches in front of the fireplace. A few embers smoldered there, remnants of a fire lit early to take off the autumn chill.

"As much as we all love this place," Jonathan went on, "even our loyalty to Jerusalem Valley must not be greater than our loyalty to king and kirk. The synod ..."

Smith stood. The bench groaned as he did, and every eye turned to him. The frontiersman cleared his throat. "Pardon me, Parson," he said. "The synod in New Cranwell has little to do with us."

Jonathan flushed. "The synod assures me that—"

"I don't care what they assure you. They should stay out of our business and let us attend to our own affairs."

Sarah was tugging at Smith's sleeve, but he ignored her. He swept his hat onto his head and nodded to Jonathan. "Good day, Parson," he said.

Jonathan watched Smith go with his mouth agape. He steeled his soul. It was the price to pay for faithfully preaching the Word—some would not tolerate it, preferring to placate their itchy ears with soft teaching and compromise. But his heart bled a little that it was Smith. His eyes sought out Letty, and he silently begged for her loyalty … her fealty to him even against her own father.

She looked back at him and nodded almost imperceptibly, and his heart eased.

Jonathan cleared his throat. "The synod is pleased with what we are building here, and they have promised to keep us supplied with books and teaching aids and to support us in their prayers as we hold our place against the darkness of these times. False teachers must not prevail. Jerusalem Valley will belong entirely to the Puritani faith, not because we use the strength of our arms, but because truth prevails."

Stifling a sigh, he closed the Book on the pulpit. Its pages closed over the letter he had tucked into his folds—a personal letter from the elder of New Cranwell. He didn't tell his congregation that the elder did not share all his convictions and had even rebuked him for some of them. The elders didn't know everything, after all. Why shouldn't the sharper insight belong to a young preacher on the frontier? God had chosen stranger prophets in the past.

Nor did he tell his congregation how much of his certainty came not from the Book, but from the dreams that had been plaguing him since he was carried home from Anoschi Pass that horrible night when he killed the thorn.

"Meanwhile, my friends, let us remember to perform all our labors as unto the Lord as we begin the harvest tomorrow," Jonathan said. "Let us pray."

He finished his prayer, and the few parishioners got up and milled about uncertainly. A heaviness hung in the air, left behind by Smith's exit. Some of the men began to put the benches away, and two maneuvered the heavy wood pulpit into the closet. Jonathan watched them with the sinking feeling that his authority and influence were being locked away with the pulpit, only to be brought out again a week from now. He feared when it reappeared, it would come out weak and sickly, like his slowly recovering body.

He brought his gaze back from the cupboard to find that Sarah Foster and her younger children were already gone, without the customary pleasantries toward him. His heart sank still further.

"Don't mind Pa."

He jumped. Letty had appeared out of nowhere, as she often did. He turned to her. She looked at him, expressionless. Strengthening.

"He doesn't like the Colonials. Wants them to stay out of here. But he still respects you."

"I'm not sure he does."

"He saved your life. Because it's worth something."

Jonathan looked away from her and wrung his hat in his hands. "I thought he did it because he's a good man."

"Maybe both."

None of the other parishioners seemed inclined to stay and speak with him. Outside, beyond the open door, Jonathan could see the black specks of Tremblers making their way home from their own meeting.

With no one else listening in, he allowed some of his heart to show. "I'm sorry to disappoint him, Letty. I truly am. But I must preach what I feel."

"Are you sure about it?" Letty asked. "The purging? This coming judgment?"

"The Book teaches it."

"But are you sure it teaches it *now?*"

"I am ..." He faltered. "I dream, Letty."

Concern crossed her face. The room had emptied out. With the furniture put away, they stood alone together in a bare space, overseen by bear rug and antlers and the few smoldering remnants of the fire.

"What kind of dreams?"

"Nightmares. I see the valley in flames, the Sacramenti ruling it with an iron fist. I see persecutions and war. I see the Tremblers opening the door to it all. I can't explain. It's terrible."

"How long?"

"Since the attack." Only half-aware of his own movements, he reached out for his crutch, leaning against the wall. Letty watched him silently as he positioned it under his arm and took the weight off his leg again. He knew he was not the handsome sight he'd been before the thorn tracked him through the pass. A gash in his cheek had scarred. He'd lost weight and muscle, and his skin was still pallid. The leg, he feared, would never be the same again.

He was grateful to her for remaining his friend, even as he was ashamed to be seen by her. Perhaps it was for the best if he lost favor with Smith. He'd hoped to be a good husband to Letty, but he feared there was little in his future but life as an invalid—at least until the day of purging arrived.

Letty reached for her bonnet. "I'll walk you home," she said.

"That should be my job."

"You're not up for walking that far."

He winced.

"I'm sorry, but it's true."

Letty reached up and fixed his hat, which was slightly askew. "There. Better."

They began to stroll together, he limping along on the crutch and wincing at the impact as they hobbled down the front steps and onto the lane through the valley. Trees and fields had turned brown and gold and red, ready for harvest. The sky overhead was bright blue but threatened by a low-lying bank of clouds moving in over the tops of the mountains.

"That will be rain," he remarked.

"If we're lucky it will move off before morning."

Shame filled Jonathan again. He would not be in the fields with the reapers come morning, nor would he be in the threshing floor or manning the cider vats. He would be sitting with the children, husking corn and doing other simple tasks. It was all he was fit for.

All because he'd been so stubborn in his desire to go to the Outsiders— to oppose his father's wishes.

A wind picked up, carrying the bank of clouds faster over the mountains. The sun disappeared behind a dark swath, and a deep chill fell over the valley. Letty took Jonathan's arm and squeezed it. "Storm's coming fast."

Jonathan stared at the gathering darkness, unable to look away. Fear fell over his heart, chilling him to the bone.

"Something's wrong," he muttered.

"It's just a storm."

He tightened his hand on hers. "No. It isn't."

"Jonathan?"

He looked over at her. Worry was clearly written across her face. "Something's wrong," he repeated.

Thunder crashed.

Jonathan's body went rigid, and he collapsed. The last thing he heard was Letty screaming for help.

CHAPTER 11

The Wilderness, south of New Cranwell—The New World

Rain pelted the river where Serena and Jacques trudged side by side, laboring over slick rocks and roots as they sought out a clear path in the forested ground. The sky grew darker as they stumbled along. Serena felt the charge of electricity in the air before the crash of thunder so loud it shook the ground. She threw her hands over her ears at the same moment that a fork of lightning surged over the river, breaking into a dozen branches over the water.

"Come on!" she saw, rather than heard, Jacques yelling. He grabbed her arm and pulled her away from the water, into the trees.

They'd lost the skiff in a tumble of rapids a quarter-mile back. Perhaps that was for the best—in this weather they were safer on foot.

The rain lashed at them so hard it half-blinded Serena as she tripped along behind Jacques, cursing the weight of her skirts and the way the ground even now did not want to remain still beneath her. Another crash of thunder deafened her. Unable to see the way, she concentrated on following Jacques.

Just ... stay ... with him.

He was yelling again, but she couldn't hear. He grabbed her arm and yanked. She half-fell after him, stumbling down a sudden and unexpected slope and then into his arms.

He lowered her to the half-dry floor of a den. She blinked. Over them, a thick tangle of tree roots formed a natural ceiling. They were crowded together in a hole in the ground, sheltered by the earth and the roots. It wasn't exactly dry, but the rain no longer pelted them, and the earthen walls of the hole created a hush.

"Thank you," she said, straightening her skirts out self-consciously.

"You're welcome." He looked up toward the storm, clearly worried. "We pray our tree doesn't get hit by lightning."

"Not a comforting thought."

"It feels safer here than out in the open."

"This is quite a welcome," Serena said with a laugh.

As the words left her mouth, thunder drowned out the world. The hole in the ground disappeared. Jacques disappeared. All that existed was the storm: wind, rain, thunder.

Lightning forked across her vision, and she saw a young man, doubled over a crutch on a country lane thrashed by rain, the ground around him swirling into mud and beginning to suck him down. She saw his eyes, wide and panicked, and his hand reaching for her as he called for help.

Lightning flashed again. She saw a pack of wolves, huge, fangs bared, a pack a thousand strong. They stood in the mountains and looked down on a valley.

Another flash. She saw a man wearing a cloak and holding a sword in his hand. The hand and the blade alike were covered in blood. The cloak fell back, and she cried out at the sight of his arm, now exposed—covered in scales like a snake. Something about the man looked familiar, but she could not see his face.

Lightning flashed. A droplet of rain, carrying grains of soil, fell on her face.

"Serena? Are you all right?"

She blinked and looked up at Jacques. "Something's wrong," she said.

"It's just a storm."

"No, no ... I saw something. I had a vision. Do you Sacramenti believe in visions?"

It was the first time she'd spoken the word out loud. She couldn't bring herself to say *Imitator*. He seemed to notice the weight of the word in the air, but to his credit he didn't react.

"Yes," he said simply. "We do.'

"I think I saw the valley. Jerusalem Valley. Something's wrong. I saw a … a man. With a sword."

"The murderer you're tracking."

"No, I don't think so." Her head was spinning, and for once it wasn't the effect of seasickness. She tried to remember the details—the horror of what she'd seen. "Or maybe. But it's not just a man. It's something else. They're under attack."

Jacques shifted position, squatting directly in front of her, and took her arms. His presence steadied her, calmed her. "What did you see?" he asked.

"I …" She forced herself to think, to remember. "A young man on crutches. Something was happening to him. He was caught in a storm—maybe this storm."

"That's impossible. Jerusalem Valley is three hundred miles from here."

A chill struck her at his words. How did he know the distance to Jerusalem Valley—an obscure settlement, after all, in the larger picture of things? It hit her again that he must have been planning all along to travel there. Their "accidental" meeting had to have been a sham.

The vision hadn't warned her against him.

Unless …

The man with the sword. She hadn't seen his face.

Her eyes widened as she stared back at Jacques. Muddy water ran down his face, dripping from above. His eyes were intense and focused on her.

"Serena. Tell me about your vision."

She squirmed away from Jacques's grip. "I told you. I saw a young man on crutches, in a storm, and something was wrong. And I saw wolves."

"Wolves."

"Thousands of them. In the mountains around the valley. I'm sure it was Jerusalem Valley. Where else could it be?"

He nodded and sat back. "I'm sorry for grabbing you like that. You looked afraid. I only meant to calm you."

"I … I know." Her emotions swirled now as much as her thoughts. If Jacques was an Imitator—and surely he was—here on a mission for the Hierarchy, then the vision spoke true by depicting him with a sword in his hand. Even the serpentine scales made sense: in some spiritual sense, perhaps he was a serpent prepared to strike.

But the Fire Within had made it so clear that they were supposed to be together. She held her head and moaned.

"You're not well," Jacques said, standing, as though there was something he could do. He ducked to avoid the roots, and clumps of wet dirt showered down from above.

"Sit," Serena said, waving him back down. "I am fine. I have to collect my thoughts, that is all."

Jacques sank back to his heels and watched her, clearly worried. "So," he said. "A young man in trouble. Wolves surrounding the valley. Was there anything else?"

Slowly, she shook her head. "No."

Her conscience panged her. But how could she tell him, when it might have been him in the vision? When he might be an enemy after all?

To her surprise, she saw hurt in his eyes. But he said nothing about it. "I do not know what your vision means," he said. "But I believe you must reach the valley urgently. It seems there are greater threats to them than simply this Reaper."

"The Reaper," Serena repeated. A trickle of cold water began to flow through the roots above and run down her neck and shoulder; she shifted to avoid it. The red vines that ran down her arms and the back of her neck, branching out into multiple vines that formed a symmetrical comb down her throat, swelled at the moisture. They were cold and clammy. She stared at her companion until he looked away.

"Jacques, how do you know his name?" Serena asked. "I never told you he is called the Reaper, just as I never told you I was going to the valley."

He didn't answer. She cleared her throat. "You have been a friend to me," she said. "I want to trust you. But right now, I am not sure how I can.

Jacques, whatever you are hiding from me, I need you to tell me before we take one more step together."

He folded his hands and nodded slowly. "Very well."

She didn't know if it was relief or fear that flooded her at this small recognition that she was right. Thankfully, he didn't leave her much time to sort it out.

"Our meeting in the pub was not an accident," he began.

She closed her eyes. Relief this time, at having something acknowledged that she was already convinced was true.

"I am an Imitator, as you know," he said. "I was sent here with a mission by my superiors. I cannot tell you all the details, but I have become convinced that a part of that mission is to watch over you. My order agreed with me that I should accompany you."

Her eyes snapped open, and she cocked her head. "What do the Imitators want with me?"

"My superiors believe you carry an important destiny," Jacques said. "You know as well as I do that many would like to stop you from carrying that out."

"What destiny?" Serena asked. There had been moments in her relatively young life when she felt that she had a glorious purpose, but here and now, sitting in a muddy hole in the ground in a vast wilderness land while she tried to unravel friend from foe, was not one of them.

"I am not one to answer that question … because I don't know, not because I am unwilling. But right now it would seem to have something to do with Governor Melrose and his … experiment."

"The Imitators cannot possibly be in favor of Armando Melrose's vision. He is no friend to the Sacramenti."

"Perhaps not," Jacques said, "but some among us have become convinced that his Jerusalem is necessary to the future of Kepos Gé. What he is doing … it may be what is needed to save us all. You asked me if we believe in visions, Serena. We do, and we have had some of our own. You may not believe that we can be friend to the Tremblers, but believe me when I say that we can be friend to the world. And that *I* can be a friend to you."

"How did you know anything about my journey?" she asked. "I escaped prison and booked passage on a ship. I told no one but my brother where I was going and why. How could you possibly have known where to find me, or where I was going?"

"We have spies," Jacques said, a little hesitantly, as though he knew he was confessing to something the whole world believed but the Imitators themselves had always vehemently denied. "Not in your brother's house … in the confidence of Elder Crispin. A name I think you know well. He learned of your escape and of your plans."

"How?" Serena burst out. "It is impossible!"

"Elder Crispin also has spies, and in his case, in your brother's house. Your brother has a servant, I think? One who hears nearly everything."

"Diego," Serena said. She scarcely remembered that he had been there when she burst in on her brother and insisted he send her overseas. Scarcely—but she did remember. He had been there, as he always was, so common she hadn't even bothered to check her words. "But if Diego is a traitor …"

"I do not think your brother has been harmed," Jacques said, reading her mind. "The elder finds it more useful to keep a mirror hanging on his wall than to bring the house down completely, if you understand my meaning."

"Nevertheless I must send word. Warn him."

"Perhaps," Jacques said. "In time. For now at least you know the watchers are being watched."

"Very few people in this world would find it comforting to know the Imitators are watching them."

"And yet I am an Imitator," Jacques said with a tiny smile. "Do you not find it comforting that I am watching you?"

She found the question surprisingly disconcerting, because the answer was yes—because he had been an angel on the voyage, and because even now, even wrestling with questions of trust, she did not want to take one more step into this foreign country without him. The knowledge that Elder Crispin knew of her mission made the thought of being alone even worse.

"Crispin paid the ship's captain double what your brother did to have you clapped in irons as soon as the boat reached shore in New Cranwell," Jacques said. "He would have charged you with sedition and made an example of you. I can only assume the captain sent a skiff ahead with word to the Puritani synod to expect you."

"So you saved my life with our little escape last night," Serena said. "And I haven't properly thanked you. Crispin would have had me put to death in the Old World, but I had friends. Here I have none."

"Incorrect," Jacques said with a smile. "You have one."

One I can't seem to help accusing of terrible things, Serena thought. Even now, she wrestled with the truth that he was an Imitator.

"Tell me again why the Imitators sent you to help me," Serena said.

"Because we believe something is happening that threatens all of Kepos Gé. You and I both have a role in stopping it."

"Threatens …"

Thunder rumbled again, but this time it was further away, and it lacked the soul-stopping violence of the earlier crashes. The rain too seemed to have ceased thrashing the forest and was instead falling in steady but calm waves.

"I do not know all my superiors have seen," Jacques said. "But I think perhaps you saw some of it … just now, in your own vision. The wolves, the boy."

"The wolves were threatening Jerusalem Valley," Serena said.

"And in some way, what threatens Jerusalem Valley threatens the world."

The water that trickled into the hole was collecting beneath her, turning the earth into fetid mud. She wrinkled her nose at the smell and pulled away, standing. Half out from the cover of the roots, the rain fell on her freshly, not carrying soil with it. She looked apologetically at Jacques and then grabbed a thick root to help her pull herself out of the hole, into the grey-blue blur of forest in the rain, into the cleansing water. He joined her without rebuke, and they walked side by side through the rain, back toward the river. Leaves and pine needles beneath her feet slipped and slid, but both she and Jacques managed to keep their balance.

They emerged from the woods onto a rocky outcrop overlooking the river. It soared along here, white caps crashing and tumbling down small slopes toward the ocean.

"I still don't understand," she said, raising her voice to be heard over the rain.

"You know what it means—Kepos Gé? In the Old Speech?"

"Of course. The Garden World. The place where the Creator planted all of his works as seed."

"There is a new seed in Jerusalem Valley," Jacques said. "And it must grow, for the sake of the whole world. What we have planted in the past, we have reaped in bloodshed and hatred. Those seeds go on being planted, and they will go on being reaped, no matter how hard some of us try to pull up the weeds. Monsieur Melrose, he is doing something different. He is planting a whole new seed, a whole new crop. It must be raised."

The rain slacked as she turned to him. "But he is a Trembler. You Imitators—you do not accept us."

He looked down at his waterlogged boots. "We believe all must return to the True Faith one day. But in the meantime, who can direct the hand of God? We only know the seed in Jerusalem Valley must not be stopped. That is why I am here. You are a woman of destiny, and Jerusalem Valley is a place with a destiny, and both are threatened."

"So your superiors sent you."

"Yes."

"Why you?"

His lips twitched. "That, perhaps you will have to find out for yourself. I think I have revealed enough secrets for one day. Do not make me boast about myself or I will tell enough tales to make us both sick."

She laughed.

Serena looked back out at the river, crashing its way down to the sea. She followed it inland until it was lost in the close horizon created by the rain—a dense, low-lying grey through which could only be seen the looming suggestions of tall trees and land rising to higher heights beyond.

He had not convinced her to trust him fully. But to accept him as her companion for now—that she could, and would, do.

CHAPTER

12

Palacio del Quinte, Tempestano, The Old World

Carlos Vaquero paced the length of the library of his summer palace, peering out the story-high windows at the rolling estate beyond. A steady rain blurred the vineyards and olive groves into a dull, subdued green.

The library door opened, and Carlos snapped to attention. "Diego. Good. I have been waiting."

The captain of the guard, a few years older than Carlos and his most trusted servant, bowed his head. His cloak and pants were rain-drenched. "Sir. I fear I have little to report."

Carlos waved his hand at his desk, covered with papers and open books. A fire burned beside it. "Draw up a chair. Warm yourself while we talk."

Carlos didn't wait for an answer, but sat in his own upholstered chair on the other side. He knew the answer he really wanted—to the question of Serena's welfare—would not and could not be forthcoming. Even if she had made landfall by now, the report of safe passage he had requested from the captain would not reach him for another two months at least. Even the fastest ship on earth could not make the journey across the great ocean faster than that.

Even so, enough had arisen in the time since Serena left to keep him, and Diego, up to their necks in reports and trials. Somehow Elder Crispin had discovered Serena's escape, and he had used it as an excuse to begin a new persecution against the Tremblers in Tempestano and other provinces of the South. Carlos himself was too wealthy and too well connected to be touched—yet—but he had his hands full trying to hide, protect, and defend the Tremblers in his territory without falling afoul of the neighboring princes, who were the real threat to him. If Crispin convinced one of them to launch an invasion of Tempestano, it could be disastrous. Carlos maintained his position of power only because Tempestano was too valuable and resource-rich for the Alliance to risk losing it. If he was simply invaded and overthrown, he would lose that leverage.

Carlos leaned back in his chair and rested his right foot on his knee. "Report."

"My men removed the Parrano family to safekeeping as you ordered," Diego said. "Messengers should have reached the further parts of the province by now to warn every Trembler meeting house of Crispin's aggression. If they take your advice they will have disbanded and scattered."

"You sound dubious."

Diego smiled thinly. "Tremblers are not known for taking advice. Or avoiding trouble."

"But you moved Phillipe and Elsa without trouble."

"They went. Not without trouble, but they went."

"The best we can hope for, I suppose."

Carlos balled a fist on the table and released it. "They should not have to move at all. Crispin has no jurisdiction here."

"Tell him that," Diego said.

"If only he would listen."

"You will have your chance to say your piece," Diego said, "though I would advise of course that you don't. That is the next piece of news to report. Elder Crispin is coming here."

"Here?" Carlos shot to his feet. "To the palace? When?"

"We received word just as I returned from this morning's relocation. I came straight here." The captain handed over a rolled-up letter.

Carlos unfurled it and scanned it quickly.

"Curse the man." Carlos caught himself and cursed again, under his breath. He was a man of God, or wanted to be. Curses should not come out his mouth. Armando Melrose himself had taught him that. *Only sweet water must come from the well of your soul, Carlos. Never bitter. Not even toward your enemies. Bitter water poisons us all.*

Carlos remembered the conversation well. He'd been complaining of his position. The young count of Tempestano wanted nothing to do with the privilege he'd been born into, with its inherited heartache and its burdens. Melrose, himself a man born into authority, had rebuked him. It was a gift to them all, he said. We do not choose our lot in life. We accept it, and we serve God in the station he has given.

Ironic, Carlos thought, for a man who had traversed the great ocean to found a colony where no one had any station except that which he earned through the respect of other men. Where everyone was equal and all people created their own lot in life after all.

Reports said Melrose's New World settlement was remote, cold, inhabited by savages, and dangerous. But right now, faced with a visit from one of the most influential and cruel men in the Old World, Carlos wished himself over the sea and beside Melrose on the most miserable day the New World could offer.

"He says he'll be here in only two days' time," Carlos said. "Diego, rally our troops. I want him to ride into a show of force ... a casual show, of course. Arm the men, swell their numbers with recruits from the countryside, give them money. Whatever you need to do to make it look like we are always powerful and happy."

Diego nodded with a smirk. "Did you want me to attempt to train the country bumpkins?"

"If you think you can teach them to make a good show of things."

Carlos bit his lip. "I need the south wing of the palace closed off. He mustn't see how depleted we are."

Diego hadn't left his seat. If anything, he looked more comfortable and relaxed as the warmth of the fire began to dry his clothes. "Sir, if I may, we wouldn't be so depleted if you were not so bent on feeding the refugees."

"We've talked about this before, Diego."

"Which is why I bring it up again. Señor Melrose's policies may be admirable, but they have not left you in a position of strength where your enemies are concerned."

Carlos closed his eyes and rested a hand on his forehead. "I know. I am laying up treasure for the next life."

"I am only afraid some of your good deeds will get you there faster. And those who depend on you at the same time. Like ..."

He held up a hand. "Don't say it."

Diego was a faithful soldier, even a good friend. But he was not a Trembler, and he did not understand or support Carlos's radical religious ways. Worst of all, he held the young count responsible for what had happened to Serena.

As did Carlos, himself.

It was because he held himself responsible that he could not bear to talk about it.

"Go, Diego. Make preparations. Leave me alone to wrestle out my guilt and my obligations."

Diego nodded and stood slowly, lingering by the fire a few minutes longer. Carlos turned away and stared out the windows at the dreary landscape.

The day of Serena's arrest had been the worst of his life.

He could only hope that what was about to come would not outdo it.

CHAPTER

13

Jerusalem Valley Settlement—The New World

Jonathan's body arced as he screamed out with pain. Letty followed close behind as her father and Cleveland Moss carried him into the governing house and laid him down on the bearskin rug.

"Letty, stoke up the fire," Smith ordered. "His skin is cold. He's shaking with chill."

She darted to obey, grabbing up the poker with tearful determination and attacking the embers as though she thought the fire responsible for Jonathan's condition. The door to the governor's office swung open. "What is this?" Amos Thatcher asked.

"Get help," Smith said. "Get Sarah, Agatha. Someone who can tend him."

Letty huddled near the fire, her legs drawn up under her skirt and her arms hugging her knees. She kept her eyes on Jonathan's face, pale and yet straining, as though something wanted to burst out of him.

Governor Melrose followed on Amos's heels. "Good God," he said.

Amos had already run out the door and into the lanes. Letty could hear him calling for help in a high, pitched voice.

Governor Melrose knelt laboriously beside Jonathan and laid a hand on his forehead. "Cold. I was sure he'd be burning with fever."

"Letty, the fire," Smith said again. The fire was already stoked up to a roar. Letty added two more logs to the flames and went after the coals again, raising the heat till it drew beads of sweat from her brow and caused the men to pull off their coats and hats.

Sarah arrived first, followed closely by Agatha Moss. Jonathan let out another scream as Sarah drew close to him, twisting and arcing.

"Hold him down," Sarah said. Smith and Cleveland struggled to obey. "Amos, help them."

Amos, newly returned, joined Smith in holding down Jonathan's shoulders while Cleveland held his feet. Letty watched helplessly in the soaring heat of the room and prayed her mother could help.

Sarah felt Jonathan's forehead and neck. She said nothing about the cold—the cold that turned him so white Letty thought he was even a little blue. Sarah paused as she ran her fingers over the vines that grew up Jonathan's spine and over his neck. "Smith, help me," she said. Quickly, she began to remove Jonathan's coat, her husband helping to turn him over and keep him still enough. Jonathan's eyes were wild and staring, and he got one arm free of Amos and backhanded Sarah in the jaw. Amos wrestled him back down.

"Stripping him?" Agatha asked as Sarah backed away, holding a hand to her mouth. "But the cold ..."

"I need to see the vines," Sarah said. She dropped her hand, revealing a split lip. "Something's wrong with them. They're where the cold is coming from. Maybe if the heat can get to them more directly ..."

She looked up from the flailing, struggling preacher and caught Letty's eyes as if she were seeing her for the first time.

"Letty, go," she said. "You don't need to be here."

"But ..."

"Go," Sarah ordered. There was no questioning her tone. Letty stood, her eyes still fixed to the young parson. The man she loved because he loved her—because he saw her, when no one else did.

"Letty," Smith cut in, "get Linette."

Letty froze. She anticipated her mother's objection before it even came out.

"No, don't," Sarah said. "We don't need her."

"We do," Smith said, fixing his steely gaze on his wife's. "We need to see more clearly. She can show us—"

"I won't work with her," Sarah said.

"Sarah. I know your falling-out was painful. Put it aside."

"She's a traitor to us," Sarah said. "To the Book, to the truth."

Agatha and Cleveland exchanged unmistakable glances and drew back a little.

"Can it really be truth, Sarah, if it doesn't include love?" Smith sighed with exasperation "Right now there is no 'us.' The parson needs help. Linette can give it. Letty, call her. She's likely at home. Go fetch her, and bring her back as soon as you can."

Letty nodded and tore out the door before she could hear any more of her mother's protests. A brisk walk turned to a run, and she raced through the cornfield lanes toward Linette's cabin as though the end of the world were chasing her down.

For her, it was.

She reached Linette's door, breathless and gasping for air. Pounded on it. Linette opened it so quickly she must have heard Letty stumping up her porch steps.

"Gracious, what is it?" she asked.

"It's the parson. We need your help."

Linette asked no questions, just reached for her cloak and followed Letty immediately. Overhead the storm was regathering clouds, and brown leaves blew past the women as they ran, side by side, toward the governing house.

They burst back in to find the parson stripped to the waist. He was still convulsing, still struggling, and five men and Agatha Moss were all employed in holding him down. Linette stood in the door, aghast.

Sarah, presiding over it all with a bleeding mouth, didn't look at her. "We need your light," was all she said.

Linette took a moment to regain her senses, then nodded and held out her hands. She closed her eyes. Softly, slowly, a glow filled the room.

As it did, it brought calm with it. Jonathan stopped convulsing and lay nearly still, shivering, whimpering. The light caused the vines on his body to stand out, and as they did, they began to turn color … from their usual yellow-green to black.

"What is it?" Amos asked, drawing back.

"Some kind of poison," Governor Melrose said.

Linette's hands trembled, but she held them steady. Jonathan's vines seemed to thicken to twice their usual size, and the black liquid inside them pulsed, visibly moving with a heartbeat of their own.

"When he faced the bear … the thorn … did it bite him?" Governor Melrose asked.

"No," Sarah said, "but there were scratches. Bad scratches, deep. Something could have gotten into him."

"What's it doing to him?" Amos asked.

"I don't know," Sarah said.

Thunder crashed outside. Letty jumped. With the sound, Jonathan let out another scream.

Governor Melrose's face had gone ashen. "There's nothing we can do," he said. "Pray."

"Is that all?" Letty burst out. "He's suffering."

She choked back a sob. Sarah was suddenly there beside her, her arms around her. "I told you to go," she said. "You shouldn't be in here." But she tucked Letty's head against her shoulder and stroked her hair.

"Pray," Governor Melrose repeated. With effort, he stood. "Tie him down so he can't hurt himself. Keep the fire hot. Linette, it's all right. We've seen enough."

Linette lowered her hands uncertainly, and the glow disappeared. Wind howled around the cabin, and a burst of rain battered its western wall like cannon shot.

Herman Melrose gazed down at the young man solemnly. The conflict on his face was evident to all.

"Pray," he repeated at long last. "And send word to the Outsiders."

"Sir?" Amos said, startling so badly his whole body jerked.

"We know nothing about this," Melrose said. "Perhaps they do."

"But those heathenish …"

"Send word," Melrose said. "We have no other choice."

"I'll go," Smith said.

"So will I," Linette followed.

"And … and I," Amos said.

The governor nodded. "You must hurry."

Less than an hour later, Linette found herself heading back up into the narrow mouth of Anoschi Pass. This time they pressed their way forward through wind and rain, but it was daylight, and she was not needed to lead the way. Smith went before her with Amos behind. Silently, she wondered why they'd even allowed her to come. Surely a washerwoman was not a necessary part of the expedition, and she would likely slow them down. In her heart she called down approbation on her skirts, which were already gathering mud and water like weights. She did at least have a decent pair of leather boots, made for her by Smith before she fell out with the Fosters over leaving the kirk.

The sight of Jonathan Applegate, his face twisted and white as a ghost, the vines that grew from his body thick and black, haunted her and made her sick in the pit of her stomach as she walked.

She'd not been able to stomach his sermons. His tone, his threats, it was all too familiar. Though she'd not admitted it to anyone, she'd been as much driven from the kirk by the young parson as drawn to the Tremblers by Herman Melrose. But whatever was happening to him—she would not wish it on anyone.

And she felt, in it, a threat to Jerusalem Valley. Something worse than Jonathan's ideology. Worse than the synod. Worse even than the thorns.

The driving rain battered them. Clouds overhead were thick and dark, but as they journeyed up into the pass they grew thicker and darker. Linette's steps slipped and slid in the leaves and mud. Smith stopped suddenly, turning so she nearly bumped into him.

"We can't go in this," he said, shouting to be heard over the rain. "We have to wait it out."

"But the parson—" she said.

"There's nothing we can do," Smith answered. He looked over her head at Amos, who nodded. "The pass is too dangerous. We'll slip and fall. That won't help the parson."

Surprised at her own reluctance to turn around, even frustration at being forced to, Linette nodded and turned. Amos led the way now—back toward the governing house. She waved at them both. "I'm going home!" she shouted through the pelting sheets of water. "Home! Unless you need me?"

Smith shook his head and waved. "Go!"

Putting her head down like a horse, Linette pushed through the rain. The cornfields whipped around her as though possessed by a thousand wild and boisterous spirits. The wind picked up even worse than before, and the rain seemed to turn to musket balls, pinging off Linette's head and shoulder with painful force.

It was with a sudden, sinking dread that she realized it was no longer rain.

The day before harvest was to begin, it was hail.

CHAPTER 14

Though his body felt as though it were turning to ice, in Jonathan Applegate's mind the world was burning to ash. He saw it over and over again in sweat-soaked, fevered visions: the purging, the mountains turning to monsters and rearing high above them, the sky peeling away like skin to reveal a skeletal creation beneath.

In the midst of it all, he saw his father.

His father, with his finger in Jonathan's face, pointing, accusing.

You disobeyed me.

This is your fault.

You are not my son.

As Jonathan's body arced and twisted against the ropes behind him, his eyes overflowed with tears. *Please. Please, I didn't mean to. I only thought to do what was right.*

Through the searing heat of his mind that made it impossible to think past the one terrible thought he was in, he could feel dread. Dread that the words would be spoken, the truth he'd buried deep inside him and refused to let out all these years.

The truth that he had killed his father. That if he had been there that night, instead of away up in the pass trying to trace a path through to the camps where he'd been forbidden to go, Jeconiah would be with them still.

So it was with relief that the shimmering apparition of his father visited him again in the midst of the apocalypse, and instead of accusing Jonathan, he accused another.

They killed me, the vision said as firebrands fell all around him. *I trusted them, and they put an end to my life.*

Through the torment of his dreaming he heard a voice saying his name.

"Jonathan. Jonathan."

He knew the voice and tried to go to it, to withdraw from the hell of his delusions and find shelter in the timber of his own name spoken by one in the land of the living. He managed to focus his eyes for a fleeting second on the cedar roof of the governing house and the antlers above the stone fireplace, and then closer to him, Letty's face leaning in toward his, grey eyes full of worry and fear and care, brow furrowed, calling to him.

Another sound accompanied her, an inconsistent pounding, beating behind her like drums or like musket fire.

The respite ended as the visions closed in once again. Jonathan heard himself crying out as he descended again into the poisoned world of his mind. He felt fingers wrapping around his and squeezed back, holding onto Letty's hand for his life.

A room away, Herman Melrose stood in his office looking out the window at the rapidly darkening world where hail such as he had never seen was falling. Jonathan's harrowing cries had fallen away. The hail pounded so loudly upon the roof and the porch outside the window that Herman wondered if he would hear him even if they had not.

Amos stood behind him, soaked to the bone with his hat in his hands.

"Do you think Linette made it home safely?" Herman asked. He could not bring himself to ask the question with any real feeling. It was a courtesy, the only thing he could think to say in the midst of such unmitigated disaster.

"I'm sure she did. Sir."

"That's ... that's good."

He turned away from the window and felt for his chair, sitting down heavily as though the breath had been knocked from his lungs. "What are we going to do, Amos?"

He didn't expect an answer. If he, the founder and governor of the fabled Jerusalem Valley settlement, was at a loss, his largely hapless secretary certainly would not have answers.

But Amos surprised him.

"We're going to have faith, sir," he said. "It's the only thing we can do."

"Yes," Herman said slowly. "Yes, you're right. Of course you're right. Faith … this will not be the end of us, Amos. This hail, if it destroys every stalk of food in the valley, will not destroy us. We *can't* fail here. We'll find a way to make it through the winter and begin again."

He looked up at the slender young man in a Trembler coat and buckskin leggings, spectacles perched on the end of his nose. "Do you understand, Amos, why it matters so much?"

"I … I'm not sure I do, sir."

Herman rose and patted the younger man on the cheek. "I'm grateful this is all the life you know. I'm grateful you and the young parson and the young Fosters have never seen the things I've seen. Nothing we may face here can be worse than what we left behind in the Old World. Here, the Fire Within will lead us to create a new beginning for everyone. A world where you and I and Smith Foster and even Jonathan Applegate can pursue our faith and conscience without the threat of someone trying to kill us for it in the name of the Creator. The rest of the world went terribly wrong somewhere, my young friend. We are trying to put it right."

Amos nodded, a jerky head bob. "I've read your pamphlets. If my father hadn't made the decision to come here with you, I think I would have come on my own. At least, I hope I would have. Sir."

"I don't doubt you, Amos," Herman said. "You're a good man. A courageous man with a good heart."

Amos smiled. Another cry from the next room drew them both away. Jonathan, tied down now, was thrashing again. Letty sat near his head, tears in her eyes. Sarah held a cup of something in her hands. It steamed. She looked up at Herman's entrance with an expression he'd never seen on her face—helplessness.

"I don't know whether to treat him for fever or hypothermia. He thrashes like a man possessed of fever, but his skin is cold as ice."

"Where's Smith?"

"Gone running home as fast as he can to see if … if he can protect anything. From the hail. And to check on the rest of the young'uns."

"I thank you, Sarah, for staying."

She set her jaw with a familiar obstinacy. "I'm not one to abandon our parson in his time of need."

Jonathan had settled down again, and he let out a whimper that tore at Herman's heart. It had been some years since he and the young man walked in close harmony with one another, but he had always believed deeply in Jonathan's call—both to the ministry and to this place, to the valley. The day the elder Applegate died was a day Herman would regret to his own dying hour, just as he regretted the wedge that had been there between valley Tremblers and Puritani ever since. Sarah maneuvered her way to Jonathan's side, and with Letty's help she attempted to give him a drink from the steaming cup.

Herman turned away. Outside, the crash and clamor of the hail grew louder. It filled his heart with dread.

He prayed the young preacher would survive the night. And that they all would survive whatever attack this was that had fallen upon them with such great fury.

The sun rose in Jerusalem Valley on a scene of utter desolation.

Linette walked through the ruins of the cornfield, trailing her fingers through the wreckage of the harvest, the sticky tendrils and filaments that remained of the yellowed husks and ripened ears of corn. Silent tears tracked down her face as she went. She'd left her house in shambles, the hail having driven holes through the roof and walls and pulverized her gardens. She could already see the broken and battered remnants of the Fosters' wheat fields ahead. Smoke rose from their chimney with a slow, curling, mournful climb.

Linette's path took her within sight of them. She stopped when she realized Smith and Sarah were standing together in the head of their field. Sarah's face was turned to his shoulder, and he held her with grim resolution.

Linette swallowed a lump in her throat. She had no regrets over leaving the Puritani kirk, except this one. Right now she would have tolerated many a damaging word from the pulpit if she could have gone to Sarah as a friend and offered comfort.

If, indeed, there was any comfort to give on a day like this.

A loud, garbled burst of sound cut through the morning: a bugle. Linette had seen it hanging in the governing house and knew it was calling the inhabitants of the valley to a rare council.

She wondered, as she changed her course in order to answer the call, if the parson had survived the night. Sarah's presence on her own property might mean he had turned a corner—or it might mean he had been lost in the darkness. She recalled the sight of his blackened, swollen vines, and shivered. How might have things have been different if the storm had not come? If she and Smith and Amos had been allowed to make their way up through the pass, to the Outsiders?

She glanced toward the mysterious mountains to the west of the valley. With the coming of autumn their covering had turned red and gold, and fog hung over them now like a tarnish. A wide swath of trees all around the valley now stood out broken against the sky, jagged branches and shards of trunks giving testament to the ferocity that had come against them all. This much was certain—had the hail not so suddenly changed their situation, they would be asking very different questions of this day.

It was awful to think that a storm could make one man's life seem so much less consequential, but it had. Whether Jonathan lived or not would make very little difference to the pressings needs of today.

"My friends, welcome," Herman said from the steps of the governing house when the last of the settlers had gathered in. His voice was heavy with emotion. Amos Thatcher, his coltish secretary, stood slightly to his side. Linette's eyes accidentally met Amos's, and to her surprise, she blushed as she looked away.

"None of us rejoices in the tidings of today," Herman said. "But as a wise man has reminded me, we must rally our faith. And of course, we must roll up our sleeves. Has the hail left anyone anything?"

There was a slight murmur as settler looked to settler, but no one volunteered good news.

Smith, leaning on a hoe he had carried with him from his farm, cleared his throat. "Our fields are in ruins, but with hard work, we can glean some usable wheat from the wreckage. Not enough. But … some."

"Aye," said another. "So can we."

Cleveland Moss raised a hand. "The corn is harder hit, but we can gather some of it too."

Herman nodded. "We must all work to gather whatever we can from our own fields and our neighbors. We will bring it all back here and store it up together. From the storehouse we can ration out portions for the winter."

"What about the fort?" Clive Shilling asked.

Herman's face darkened "What about it?"

"They may have extra provisions, or ability to get them. We can trade for them. Furs and maybe some of our handiwork."

"No," Herman said. "The fort mustn't know anything about this."

"But sir," Smith Foster said, "we are not talking about making ourselves comfortable. We are talking about survival. For us and our children."

"The fort may not be necessary," Herman said. "We've already laid aside some stores throughout the year …"

"Precious little," Cleveland answered. "The summer harvest was poor, you know that."

"We cannot alert the fort," Herman repeated. Linette had never seen him so stubborn, or veering so close to anger. "If New Cranwell learns of our predicament, we are through here. You all know this as well as I do."

"The soldiers are not demons," Sarah said, not looking Herman in the eyes. "They're good Puritani men. They can help us."

"They will not." Herman glared at Sarah and Smith. For the first time since she'd met him, Linette felt uncomfortable in the governor's presence. He seemed almost to attack the Fosters, and that unfairly. They were the only family with young children here, the ones with the most to lose.

And yet she of all people knew that Herman was not wrong to believe the Puritani of New Cranwell would overrun the valley if they could. The danger he saw in involving Fort Collins was real.

"The men of Fort Collins will not help us, they will conquer us," Herman said. "They have been watching for just such an opportunity for years."

Amos nodded, his usual fast, bobbing nod, and stammered out, "It's true. I see their letters; they are not friends to us."

"At a time like this I would say *friends* are those who will help me feed my children," Sarah said. She took a threatening step forward, and Smith grabbed her arm to stop her advancing any further.

"No one is starving yet," Herman said.

Sarah set her jaw. "And I will not watch a single one die because we would not act on common foresight! Will you? Which of our children would you sacrifice?"

"Sarah," Smith said.

"She's right!"

It was Linette. She looked around at the surprised faces that had turned to her and rushed to continue before she lost her courage.

"She's right. We can't risk her children or anyone else. And the governor is right too. We can't ask the fort for help. We might as well call on the government of New Cranwell directly. But can't we trade elsewhere?"

The settlers exchanged puzzled glances. "I mean the Outsiders," Linette said. "Can we not trade with them?"

The shocked buzz of response was at once defensive, outraged, and intrigued. "They'll have been as bad hit with the hail," John said.

"Maybe not," Smith answered. "You know the weather patterns in these mountains aren't constant. From the looks of the trees above us, it was only our valley that got hammered. And anyway, they have other trading partners and other sources of food further west."

"What do we have that they would want?" Cleveland asked. "We can't trade *them* furs. They have more than we do."

"We have blankets," Sarah said. "Clothing. Muskets."

"They like coffee," Amos volunteered.

Herman appeared troubled, but he nodded to Linette. "We'll send an envoy," he said. "See about trading with the Outsiders. Glean our fields as best we can and build up a storehouse here. John, when we've finished gleaning I'd advise fishing the river. We can preserve the fish like they did in the north in the old country."

Cleveland Moss barked out a laugh at that. "I'll eat my shoes before I'll eat that stinking mess. Fermented fish in a barrel. The Northmen are barbarians."

"Like Smith said," Herman answered, "this isn't about comfort; it's about survival. Now we'd best all get to work. The Smiths' fields to begin."

Linette turned to follow the Smiths toward their fields, but she paused as a sudden thought struck her. "Governor!" she asked, turned back. "Did the parson make it through the night?"

"Yes," Herman told her. "Praise the Creator, he did."

Linette nodded and turned again to follow the Smiths, but this time she hesitated with another thought. Drawing back from the crew trudging their way toward the bludgeoned fields, she nodded to Governor Melrose and made her way up the front steps of the meeting house. She twisted the handle of the door and poked her head inside.

Letty Foster looked up from her seat beside Jonathan. He was asleep on the bear rug, his chest rising and falling with labored breaths. A pallor still lay upon his skin, but the vines visible where his arms were uncovered by the wool blankets Sarah had brought had shrunk back to a more normal size and color.

Heavy dark circles dragged at Letty's eyes and made her look even plainer than she normally did. Yet beauty shone through her eyes as she sat there, standing her post with undying faith.

It's no wonder he loves her, Linette thought.

Letty's eyes clouded slightly at the sight of Linette. Fear gripped Linette, and she pushed it back.

"Do you need anything, Letty?" she asked. "Anything for him … or for yourself?"

Letty's expression softened. "No, but thank you for asking."

Linette managed a smile and a nod. She turned to go. Maybe it was the emotion of having lost so much in so little time, but she found herself flooded with emotions and words that wanted release. Between her and Letty things had been nearly as sore as they were between her and Sarah, compounded by Linette's obvious dislike of the young preacher and Letty's ardent devotion to him. Linette herself had reacted to their anger and rejection of her with a good deal of hurt, but she'd buried much of that beneath a strong sense of her own rightness in the matter and more than that, a strong sense of her right to be free.

The kirk had shadowed her every day of her life until she reached the valley. She refused to come under that shadow here too.

But now, with so much lost and so much still hanging in the balance—and the young preacher whom she'd so disdained lying tormented and barely escaped from death none of that seemed to matter as much as their need to be united. To be one family in a place that had become suddenly hostile to them all.

She felt all of that, but she could not find words to express it.

So instead she said, "If you need anything, just call for me. I don't imagine I'll be as much help out there as I'd like to be. They can spare me while I find what you need."

"Thank you," Letty said, her voice still subdued.

Linette nodded and hurried off to join the others.

Letty watched her go, the tall slender redhead who still carried herself with city airs even as she'd been appointed to position of washerwoman and largely ostracized by the Puritani in the valley—especially her own family. She couldn't help feeling a sense of remorse. It wasn't fair really. They'd cast Linette away without even hearing her side of things, Sarah especially.

It was all because of hurt, Letty mused. Sarah loved Linette like a sister, or wanted to. She'd been so alone here, in so many ways. When Linette told her she was leaving the kirk, she might as well have stabbed Sarah through the heart.

Still wasn't right. Hurt didn't justify causing more hurt.

"Letty."

Jonathan's voice was a bare croak, a dry murmur in the fire-warmed room. Letty heard it like a victory shot. She bent over him, low over his face, and grasped his searching hand.

"I'm here," she said. "I'm here."

"Letty," he said again. "I can't … I can't see."

He tightened his grasp on her hand. She winced at the strength of his grip.

"It's all right," she said. "You'll be all right."

CHAPTER

15

Port of New Cranwell—The New World

When the *Ventarrón* arrived in the port of New Cranwell, finding its place amidst a forest of ships' masts, a welcoming committee awaited it. The scar-faced captain sighed at the sight of them: six men, three of them churchmen dressed in black and three policemen awaiting their prisoner. They were all equally grim and all equally about to be angry.

He stumped along the creaking planks of the dock toward them. No use delaying it.

Elder Phinehas Cole stepped forward to greet him. "Captain Jones."

"Elder."

"We received your advance word. You have a prisoner to hand over?"

"I do not."

The elder and his compatriots exchanged troubled glances. The elder cleared his throat. "I had assurance that you were bringing a dangerous seditionist here and had been ordered to apprehend her."

"Dangerous my arse," Captain Jones grumbled. He squinted at the churchmen. "She was on board. I lost her."

"You ... sir, explain yourself!"

"She went overboard in the middle of the night. With a boat, so if yer smart, ye'll have your eyes open for her. Don't know where she was heading. Far as I knew she was coming here."

Jones made a long, slow show of rolling tobacco in his mouth before he leaned over and spat it into the harbor. The dock swayed beneath their feet.

"If you've good silver, I'll tell you somethin' else," he said.

The elder reddened. He was a tall, severe-looking man, with a close-cropped beard of silvered red, broad shoulders, and sharp eyes. Compared to the soft, rounded appearance of Elder Crispin back in the Old World, he looked like a giant and a warrior—a man worthy of his post.

And a man with some access to funds, or Jedidiah Jones was mistaken. And about money, he never was.

"You dare," the elder said. "You dare attempt to extort money from me mere seconds after admitting you failed to deliver on your last payment?"

"I won't fail to deliver on this one," Jones said, winking. "News I carry can't jump out of my ship in the middle of the night. Anyway, you keep your eyes open, you'll find your girl. Can't miss 'er. A real Southern beauty. She'll stick out around here like—"

"Never mind about that," Cole said. "Tell me your news."

"I will, sirrah, I will. After you pay up."

Jones watched out of his side vision as Cole considered his options. If he were Elder Crispin, he'd be threatening to clap the seafarer in irons already. But this man was a man of principle. Ruthless in his own way, yes, but not unjust and not one to abuse his power.

Not overmuch, anyhow.

Jones waited.

Finally Cole rustled in a bag at his waist and pulled out a silver coin.

"Two," Jones said.

"You're mad. Out with your news or I'll have your ship ejected from the port for bad conduct."

The captain reached out and closed his fingers around the edge of the coin, but Cole did not let go. He shook the forefinger of his other hand in Jones's face.

"If I decide your news isn't worth this coin, I'll be taking it back."

Jones scowled at him. "It's worth two. You be lucky I'm telling you at all."

Cole released the coin. "Well?"

"She had help," Jones said. "Tall fellow. Accent. Paid his way across the ocean with a purse no peasant can carry, yet had no name of nobility. Befriended her before they even got on the ship and then wouldn't leave her side. They went over the side together."

"So Serena Vaquero's taken a lover," Cole said. "I may be disgusted at Trembler moral character, but I'm hardly surprised—and I'll be wanting my silver back."

Jones tightened his own grip on the coin. "Not a lover. Not a Trembler. Something else ... something more interesting."

Suddenly, Cole looked truly interested. "What are you saying?"

"Of course a man trying to pass himself off as a commoner doesn't carry much across the sea, but what he did bring, I had myself a look at one day while he was seeing to your Trembler. Just a few clothes, a journal with nothing written in it—leastways nothin' I could make out, just some sketchin' and scribblin'—"

"Get to the point."

Jones chuckled. He reached into his coat and pulled out a carved symbol on a thin gold chain. He dangled it in front of the elder's face, triumphant. "And this."

Elder Cole's eyes widened. He took the carved symbol, a loaf of bread, and traced it almost reverently. "Sacramenti."

"Not just that. An Imitator, or I'm my own uncle. So unless they both drowned at sea, he's here somewhere with Serena Vaquero."

It was clear from the expression on Cole's face that he was thinking hard and fast. He turned to go, but he stopped and dug into his purse once more. To Jones's surprise, he tossed him a second coin.

"You were right," Cole said. "That was worth two. Now, if it's not too much trouble, you'll accompany these fine gentlemen to the jail and write out a full report. I want a full physical description and a report on everything he did or said while on the ship. Understood?"

"That's a lot of trouble," Jones said.

"And two silver coins. Not to mention you yourself will be allowed to sleep at an inn and not in the jail itself, notwithstanding your failure to do what you were hired to do."

Jones nodded. Barking a few orders at his men, he fell in step behind the police. He had little love for Elder Cole of the New Cranwell Puritani, but he was a fair man.

Wilderness, outside New Cranwell—The New World

Jacques had lit a fire on a hill overlooking the harbor city of New Cranwell. He and Serena sat together, tucked back into the trees, looking over the crest of the hill at the lights below. The city glow extended to the water and glimmered back as the sun sank over the world and night cast its first shadows over the forests, the city, the harbor docks with their clusters of ships, and the ocean beyond.

The city was small compared to anything in the Old World, a square laid out on a simple grid that made Serena think of prison bars. Horses and carriages moved along packed-earth streets past austere buildings, built in a tall, rectangular Colonial style that again made Serena think of prisons.

Maybe, she thought ruefully, that had less to do with New Cranwell itself and more to do with her life experience of late. She wondered if an inland journey to the wilderness frontier would cure her of thinking everything looked like a holding pen for troublesome human beings.

Once the rain stopped, reaching the city had been easier and faster than Serena and Jacques had feared. They'd followed the river as planned but soon come across outlying villages—with roads leading back to New Cranwell. They'd debated their course of action for a few minutes (some of them heated), but in the end aching feet and poor footwear won the day. Jacques paid a farmer to let them ride in his hay wagon, jumping out just before they entered the city itself.

They'd both decided they would rather climb this hill and get the lay of the city below before going blithely into it. As much as they needed supplies, a map, and likely a guide or escort of some kind, they both knew that

Captain Jones's arrival in the city would have put the local kirk and government on watch for Serena.

Whether she ought to enter the city at all had been a topic of argument for the last hour.

The little fire was threatening to go out. Jacques got up and went in search of more kindling to coax it back up. His voice drifted toward her from the trees. "I still say it isn't safe."

"And I still say this is my mission, and I want to talk to a guide myself. I'll be fine."

"I doubt that."

"I won't be conspicuous."

"Serena, how do I put this? You are always conspicuous."

She snapped a twig she was holding in her hands and considered throwing the pieces at him, but that felt childish even for her. "I don't want to be left out here alone. That doesn't feel safe to me."

"Nothing will eat you."

"I want to buy my own clothes. I need shoes. A good cloak. How are you going to find anything that fits me properly?"

Jacques walked back into Serena's field of vision. "I'll estimate," he said. "Serena, I know you don't like this. But think of it from another perspective. This is your mission, yes. So what happens if you go into the city and are seen and arrested? The kirk here throws you back into prison, or worse, and Jerusalem Valley never gets its warning."

Serena looked away petulantly and twisted a broken piece of twig. "You could warn them."

"You're being a child. Let me protect you. Stay here."

She nodded sharply but refused to look at him. For all the world this felt like having Carlos here. She wondered how her brother was doing. No doubt exerting all his energy in political games.

She felt ashamed as soon as she had the thought. Carlos's "games" were nothing he had chosen for himself, and scores of Trembler refugees owed their lives to his willingness to play them. She might be the public martyr of the Tempestano Tremblers, but Carlos was their savior, and she knew it. Perhaps he and Jacques were more alike than she'd realized.

"You will be careful?" she asked, finally turning to look at him. He looked ... relieved? Tired?

Very much, again, like Carlos.

"I am always careful."

"The captain may have told them to look out for you. He must know we escaped together."

"Even so they have much less reason to find me than you. And I am far less ..."

"Conspicuous."

His lips twitched. "Exactly so."

The night darkened, bringing out moon and stars over the city and the ocean that lay like a great black curtain beyond it. The fire cast a glow over their faces and warmed Serena's skin as she drew her cloak closer around her. The air here was colder and wetter than it ever felt at home. A wind blew, cutting right through the fine weaving of her cloak. If she'd ever entertained the idea of striking out for the frontier without buying new supplies, that wind would have ended the discussion.

Lights in the city winked out as night settled over everything like a heavy, brooding blanket. Sounds from the forest let Serena know they were not alone in this strange world. She shivered and felt grateful for Jacques's presence. He would not go until morning.

She was glad. It felt good to have him here. It felt ... safe.

Any illusion of safety shattered at the sound of a gunshot and the impact of a boot in her side, both so sudden that Serena awoke from a sound sleep. Jacques yelled something. She curled up instinctively against another kick but heard someone shout, "Stop, it's the woman!"

Hands grabbed at her arms, and as she was hauled to her feet, she felt the cold muzzle of a pistol against her neck. Any intention of fighting back left her. She raised her hands. Across the glowing embers of the fire, Jacques was similarly stymied. She could barely make out the figures of men dressed in black surrounding them both.

Jacques caught her eye and nodded slowly, a gesture meant to comfort and reassure. She took a deep breath and nodded back. One of their at-tackers grabbed her hands and pulled them behind her, shackling them. Someone did the same to Jacques.

"May we know whose acquaintance we are making?" Jacques asked.

"Shut up," a gruff voice answered.

Serena closed her eyes as hands steered her into the darkness. *Fire Within, help us. Speak to me.*

She saw a flash of vision: a tall man with red hair, dressed in black, his eyes boring into her. Elder Crispin stood behind him with a hand on his shoulder.

"Oh no," she said under her breath. Someone shoved her hard in the shoulder, sending her pitching forward and fighting to keep her feet.

"Quiet, wench."

"You might show a little respect to a lady," Jacques's voice came out of the darkness behind her. She heard the awful noise of something solid impacting flesh and bone, and Jacques cried out.

"Leave him alone!" she shouted, trying to twist to see behind her. Whoever was marching her through the darkness gripped her arm and stepped in front of her, grabbing her chin with his other hand. Through the shadows she could make out wide, weather-beaten features. She tried to get away from him, but he held her tight.

"I said quiet," the man said. "You give us any more trouble, I will kill your friend where he stands and say he abandoned you before we found you. Do you understand me?"

Reluctantly Serena nodded. The man let go of her chin. Behind them, she could hear Jacques moan with pain.

"Bring him quickly. I don't want to waste another minute out here in these God-forsaken shadows."

A quick though tortuous journey through the trees on the backside of the hill brought them to a road, where a wagon awaited. Serena was all but thrown into it, settling into a prickly and filthy mass of straw. Jacques was tossed in beside her. He groaned and caught his breath as he fell to the wagon floor.

"Are you all right?" she whispered.

He answered through clenched teeth. "That depends on how you define all right."

"So you define it for me."

"I think they dislocated my shoulder, but other than that, yes, I'm all right."

Serena cringed and shifted so that Jacques's head lay on her knee. "Here. Keep the pressure off your shoulder."

The first jolt of the wagon drew a cry of pain out of Jacques and disabused Serena of any notion that she was really helping. She twisted her hands in the cuffs as though she could slip them off, but they were small and too tightly fitted, and she could feel the skin of her wrists paying for her frustration. Three of the men had jumped up and rode in the back of the wagon, legs dangling off the end. The others—three more—sat up front. None of them said a word.

"Tell them nothing," Serena whispered to Jacques. She could only hope he understood what she meant. She could only imagine how much trouble she was in, but if he told them anything about himself, about his mission here and who had sent him, she feared for him. Maybe, if he would only stick with the story that he was nothing but a traveler who had befriended her on the ship, he could go free.

As the wagon edged forward, out of the forest darkness toward the city lights, she peered ahead at the narrow dirt streets and rising buildings on both sides. It was indeed much like a prison. Closing her eyes, she leaned her head back against the wagon. She had little hope these would turn out to be run-of-the-mill kidnappers. Jacques's suspicions had been right. Captain Jones must have alerted someone in the city to be on the lookout for her.

And just how much trouble she was actually in depended very much on who that someone was.

CHAPTER
16

New Cranwell—The New World

"Well," Phinehas Cole said, looking over his prisoners with grim satisfaction. "You were easier to find than I expected. When our questioning the locals yielded no sign that you had entered the city, we thought you must be nearby."

"A little much to send people to hunt us down in the middle of the night, still," Serena said. She glared at the tall, red-haired man—the man she'd seen in her vision. She'd known from the moment they were ushered into the upstairs room in the courthouse that he must be the elder of New Cranwell. Elder Crispin might not be physically standing behind him, but they clearly shared a common mission. "Taking risks with your men in the darkness. Couldn't wait for us to come into town in the morning?"

Phinehas Cole paced before them, looking at her almost curiously as she spoke—but she did not miss the dark edge of enmity in his bearing. He stopped in front of her.

"You, I did not wish to leave at large even minutes longer than necessary," he said. "We had a tip that you might be on that hill. We can dispense with your accusations, Miss Vaquero. I know who and what you are."

She looked to one side, refusing to meet his eyes. The room around them, tastefully outfitted with walnut furniture, a grandfather clock, and a deep red rug over polished floorboards, glowed with light from oil lamps.

Elder Cole moved across the room to a desk and picked up an unrolled piece of parchment. He held it up and shook it a bit as though she ought to recognize it.

"From the esteemed Elder Joseph Crispin, in the Old World," Phinehas said.

"A warning?" Serena asked.

"A conviction," the elder answered.

Despite herself, her body went rigid. "You'd jail me without a trial?"

"Look at me," the elder said.

Slowly, Serena looked up. The black-garbed churchman stood tall and imposing before her. His eyes, green and penetrating and cold and condemning as stone, held her gaze.

"This is not a jail sentence," he said. "It's a death order. Elder Crispin has found you guilty of witchcraft and sentenced you to be burned in the public square tomorrow."

"No," Serena said, her breath suddenly taken from her lungs. "That's impossible. He didn't find me guilty; he—"

"According to this letter, he was unable to execute you in the Old World due to the influence of powerful friends on your side. By good providence you escaped prison and came here, where you have no friends at all, and where you can be properly taken care of once and for all."

Serena couldn't breathe. She'd expected some difficulty in reaching the valley—but not this. Not the loss of her life so suddenly and so unjustly.

"I'm not guilty," she finally managed to whisper.

Elder Cole took a step closer. She was struck by how threatening his presence felt, in a way far more visceral and powerful than Elder Crispin's ever had. Her enemy in the Old World was cruel and calculating and politically powerful, but in person he'd always struck her as weak and almost flabby—a man whose power was ultimately a sham. This man was different. If Crispin was a sponge dripping poison, Cole was a rod of steel. He towered over her, and she knew in her heart he would show her no compassion, no kindness.

"Elder Crispin has written a damning report to the contrary. You see visions," he said.

"I do."

"And hear voices."

"I hear the Spirit of God. I see by the Spirit of God. The Fire Within gifts me, not some occult power."

"The Book condemns your kind."

"The Book *explains* my kind!" Serena's own gaze flared back at the unbending man before her. She pulled against the shackles again, instinctively wanting to talk with her hands. "You Puritani claim to be so allegiant to the Book, but you don't even know what it says!"

He stiffened, and she braced for a blow that didn't come. Instead he remained controlled, calm.

"You are not wise to attack me on my own ground," he said. "I have long suspected that Tremblers draw their power from the devil. I hope you will help me ascertain that for certain. Your response so far gives me nothing but assurance in that respect."

He folded his hands behind his back and began to pace again. "However, I will not simply send you to the stake on Crispin's orders without a hearing of my own. I wish to hear you condemn yourself with my own ears, and I do not wish to carry out any sentence that I have not myself confirmed. Much as I respect Elder Crispin, this is not his jurisdiction. It is mine. Do you wish me to find you an advocate?"

Serena could hardly believe her ears. But she stammered, "No. Sir. I thank you. I'll plead my own case."

"Serena …" Jacques said. She shot him a warning glare, but it was too late.

Cole turned to him next. "As for you," he said, "word of you has also preceded your arrival. I will give you to know, Imitator, that your presence with this woman is enough to convict her in its own right."

Desperately, Serena sharpened the glare she was sending Jacques. *Don't respond. Don't confirm or deny anything!*

To her relief, he said nothing. He simply straightened his stance. His skin under the lamplight was clammy and pale, and pain was evident in his face.

"He needs medical care," she said.

Cole waved her off. "We'll see to him. I intend to pack him off to the Old World in irons on the first ship available. Crispin can deal with him. Sacramenti are an Old World problem, thank the Creator."

He shifted his attention back to Serena. "Unlike you. As much as I am unwilling to burn you out of hand, I am grateful Crispin released you to me. It's about time the Tremblers had a good reason to fear."

"How dare you?" Serena said. "After all the Tremblers have done for you!"

"Done for us? Introduced confusion and darkness is all they have done. They seduce people away from the truth."

"They have brought peace!" Serena said. "Here, in Jerusalem Valley ..."

"Peace," Cole said. "Peace without truth is an evil. A sickness."

"That's what they said in the Old World during the wars," Jacques said.

Cole smiled. "And you are one to talk. Who spilled more blood in the wars than the Hierarchy? I know as well you do, my friend, that your presence here is not to bring peace. You invade the New World to spread your cancer. I know far more about your Hierarchy's plot than you imagine. Why do you think I refuse to make you a martyr here?"

Jacques looked at the floor. Serena felt an unwelcome tug at her heart. It was not lost on her that Jacques was denying nothing—and that he *was* here on some mission from the Hierarchy, an organization that, for all it had gone largely underground, had slaughtered tens of thousands and threatened the freedom of the whole Old World. If the kirk was evil, the Hierarchy was ten times worse.

He had told that part of his mission was protecting her. But even if that was true, it was only part. What else was he here to do?

"Peace without truth is an opiate," Cole went on. "We will have better. We will have the peace of purity. Beginning with the end of Jerusalem Valley."

"What?" Serena asked.

"Jerusalem Valley will not last another winter," Cole said. "The king was a fool to give Herman Melrose that land, and it will not survive without him."

Serena's soul shook. "Is he dead?"

"He soon will be. Melrose is a traitor. We have passed sentence of treason against him and given orders to our people in the valley to apprehend him. The valley will be left without a leader, and the New Cranwell synod is already poised to take that vacancy."

"And if the people of the valley don't wish to be under the synod?" Serena asked.

"The good men of Fort Collins will ensure the transition goes smoothly," Cole said.

"Do you know," Serena said, "when you said you were going to try me personally I thought, for a moment, you might be a good man. A man of honor. Now you tell us you're going to overthrow the rightful governor of Jerusalem Valley and take over the governance by hostile means. What little respect I felt stirring for you has flown."

"Do you think I care what you think of me, witch?" Cole asked. His voice lowered, growing darker, angrier. She had touched a nerve. "Herman Melrose is guilty of treason, a capital offense. He has declared himself monarch in Jerusalem Valley and intends to throw off the rule of the king. As a good citizen it is my duty to stop him."

Serena stuck out her chin. "And how do you know all this, from three hundred miles away? Are you somehow listening at his window at night?"

Stiffly, Cole answered, "I don't need to. I have an informant in the valley. Her letters tell me all I need to know."

Serena couldn't help glancing at Jacques. He looked as troubled as she felt. "An informant?" she asked, sick. "And you trust this liar?"

Cole smiled. "Indeed, I do. I could not trust her more. She's known to me. My own daughter, Linette."

Cole turned abruptly, leaving Serena to process what she'd heard. "Guards! Lock this man up. Captain, find me a ship that will take him back to the Old World where he belongs."

The captain of the guard nodded. "And the woman?"

"Put her in irons as well. I want her well-guarded and anything she says or does reported to me. As she does not desire an advocate, we will go to trial tomorrow. I will prosecute her myself."

The captain nodded and took Serena's arm while his compatriots man-handled Jacques, who cried out in pain.

"For God's sake, tend to his shoulder!" Serena burst out.

Jacques's warning glance as they roughly shoved him out the door was the last she saw of him that night.

Jerusalem Valley Settlement—The New World

Gleaning the fields took every ounce of time and energy every inhabitant of the valley had to give, but after a day and a half it was clear there would not be nearly enough. The hail had done worse damage even than they'd realized at first.

The settlers gathered at the governing house to see off their envoy to the Outsiders. Herman had appointed them: Cleveland Moss and Smith Foster. Cleveland's age and founding stature would invite respect from the Outsiders; he would function as Herman's emissary. Smith was better with a gun and better in the woods than any man in the settlement.

When Herman announced Smith's name, Sarah simply tightened her mouth and nodded. It wasn't a good time to send a father and husband away, but someone capable needed to go. This was their best hope to make it through the winter.

The settlers stood in a little crowd around the governing house, fifty-some people: all the Fosters but Letty in a little circle, the older men standing around Herman, Linette hanging toward the back. She stared at the broken ground unhappily as Herman said a few words of encouragement. She found she couldn't hang onto his words. They entered the air and vanished like warm breath on a cold morning. This man had inspired her more than any living being, but even his words felt meaningless in the face of their task.

Herman finished his speech and clapped Cleveland and Smith on their shoulders. "May it go well with you and your mission," he said. "Hurry back to us. We need every good man we have." Herman glanced through the crowd, and his eyes found Linette. He smiled. "And every good woman."

Sarah stepped forward as if on cue and unraveled a long, red scarf. She held it up to Smith. "Take this," she said. "Trade it."

Smith looked conflicted. "But this is …"

"I know what it is. Trade it to save our children."

He looked at her for a long moment, then bent to kiss his wife good-bye.

As he did, the door to the governing house opened. Letty stood in the doorframe—with Jonathan Applegate leaning on her.

"Wait," Jonathan said. He let go of Letty's shoulder and limped forward. He was pale and looked as though he'd been stretched on a rack the last two days, but he'd left his crutch behind. "I'm going with you."

"Don't be a fool, lad," Cleveland said. "Go back to bed."

"I'm no fool." Jonathan exchanged a glance with Letty before squaring his shoulders and hobbling down off the porch and into the crowd. "I am going. You need me."

Linette watched Smith for his reaction. If anyone would decide this, it was him. To her surprise, he simply folded his hands and said, "Speak on."

"I am not proud of my disobedience to my father," Jonathan said. His voice trembled. "But because I disobeyed, and went to the Outsiders as he instructed me not to, I alone among us know the way well. I have been to the camp of the Outsiders many times. They know me, and I know them. Without me, your chances of making a successful bargain are poor. With me they go up significantly."

Smith pursed his lips. "Can you make it over the pass?"

Jonathan tried to stand taller. "I'll make it."

Despite herself, Linette's heart went out to him. He'd nearly met an awful death in the pass, and in some way, what had happened there was still affecting him—it had nearly killed him again over the last few days. She'd seen it boiling and bubbling in his vines even as it turned his body to ice.

And yet, as Herman slowly nodded and Smith sent one of his sons for more supplies for Jonathan, Linette rebelled against the thought of these men going into the pass together—back toward the death that had nearly claimed the preacher.

"I'm going too."

The words were out of her mouth before she even understood why she'd said them.

The crowd turned. She felt all eyes on her, staring. She couldn't meet their eyes. For a horrible moment she was back there, in the past, when all eyes had condemned. She forced herself back to the present—this place, these people, and this need.

"You might need my light."

"Unnecessary," Jonathan Applegate said. "We can handle this without her."

"Says a man who has twice been saved in great part by my light," Linette said. Her face flushed, and she raised her eyes to meet his. She saw barely concealed enmity there and wanted to recoil from it, but instead she pressed forward. She felt like a schoolgirl arguing her way against an older boy in class, and she knew the justice of her cause and refused to back down.

"Smith, let me come," she said. "I can help."

She didn't voice the deeper drive inside her—that she needed to go, for her own sake, because she needed to go through that pass and look the Outsiders in the face, and she didn't even know why. And the lesser but still present need to be there if Jonathan was there. To not let him go with Smith and Cleveland alone.

Did she want to protect them? Was that what she was feeling?

How did that even make any sense?

Linette shook her head slightly as though she could dislodge her confused thoughts. It was enough that she wanted to go, needed to go.

"We don't know what will happen," Smith said. "Might want to travel at night. Get back here faster. She'd be a boon then. Light might help scare off ... things. Too. If they're out there."

He didn't say *thorns,* nor the word that gave Linette shivers up and down her spine—*Machkigen.*

"If he gets sick again," Sarah said to Linette's surprise, nodding at Jonathan, "she can help. Light showed up what was happening in his vines. It helped us know what to do."

Linette looked Sarah's way, hoping to make some connection. Sarah didn't return the look, keeping her eyes fixed ahead. Herman was shaking his heavy head.

"Governor, please," Linette said. She drew his full attention and held his gaze. "Please, let me do my part. I want to go."

"Very well," Herman said. "If you want to go and they will have you, I'll not make it my job to stop you. Cleveland?"

Cleveland Moss huffed. "Don't really see the use of her coming, but I'm not one to say no to an offer of help. Who knows? Maybe we'll need a woman's viewpoint in the talks. Creator knows Agatha can think her way through a bushel of problems before I even see 'em coming."

Linette nodded gratefully to him. He didn't come out and say he wanted her along so he wouldn't be outnumbered by Puritani, but she suspected that was true too. Smith was such an ecumenical soul she was tempted to forget sometimes that he belonged to the kirk, but Jonathan carried enough partisan heat for three men.

"How long do you need to prepare for the journey?" Herman asked Linette and Jonathan both.

"Less than an hour," Linette said.

"I can go now," Jonathan replied.

Herman nodded to Linette first. "Go get what you need. And boy, you dress yourself warm and get yourself armed. No need to be foolhardy."

Jonathan flushed and nodded. Linette turned her back and headed home. She didn't need much—just boots suitable for trekking in, a warm cloak, and her hunting knife. She didn't own a gun and couldn't aim one anyway. She ran the last few feet to the house, jumped up the porch, and made herself ready as quickly as possible, stuffing a few extras in a saddlebag she would hang from her belt. She paused over her writing implements— paper and pen.

Her hand hovered over them for a moment. No, she decided, she didn't need them. There would be no time for writing letters.

But she couldn't bring herself to leave them behind. Annoyed with herself, she grabbed them and placed them inside the bag beside a scarf, leather gloves, a roll of bandages, and a few hard apples. Cleveland and Smith had already packed the real supplies. This was just to make herself feel prepared.

Prepared for what, she wasn't really sure.

CHAPTER 17

Province of Tempestano—The Old World

Elder Crispin arrived in style three hours after Carlos was expecting him. The man was fabled to possess many virtues. Punctuality was not one of them.

Carlos could not find it in himself to complain about this. He would have preferred it if Crispin had never arrived at all. In fact, he fantasized about it. He couldn't bring himself to wish the man ambushed and murdered by bandits in the road, so instead he imagined the famed leader of the Old World Puritani lost in the border country between Tempestano and its nearest neighbor, wandering eternally in circles in the terraced hills.

The elder swept into Carlos's expansive front hall flanked by armed men dressed in black. He raised his hands while an aide swept his cloak away. Carlos noted that his fingers, festooned with rings, were thicker than he remembered. In fact, the man in his entirety had grown larger and softer. Apparently power agreed with him.

Carlos wasn't prepared for the wave of hatred that hit him at the sight of the Puritani elder. When they'd last seen one another face-to-face, it had been at Serena's trial. Carlos could never forget what this man had tried to do to his sister in the name of God. If he'd held any hope that the Puritani were not evil, only misguided, he'd given it up then.

But they were powerful. The greatest power, in fact, in the Old World, with kings and magistrates equally in their pockets and very few independent lords still free of their control. So playing chess with this stuffed snake was Carlos's cross to bear.

"Welcome," Carlos said stiffly.

"Thank you, Conde Vaquero," Elder Crispin said. "I trust you know why I've come?"

"What, no pleasantries?"

"I'm not a man with an abundance of time on my hands," Crispin said.

Although apparently a man with an abundance of everything else, Carlos thought, observing the quality of the elder's cloak, his fur-trimmed cuffs, and the heavy jewelry on his hands. There was a time when the Puritani made their stand on austerity of lifestyle and of soul, in contrast to the opulence and self-indulgence of the Hierarchy at the apex of their power. Evidently that claim to superiority had gone by the wayside.

"We have word that you are harboring Trembler congregations in Tempestano," Elder Crispin said. He held out a hand, and an aide placed a scroll in it. He unfurled it and handed it to Carlos. Carlos scanned it. It was an order, signed by three key leaders of the Southern Alliance, to round up and imprison anyone found gathering in Trembler fashion. Nothing new, but also nothing that had been enforced in Tempestano.

Carlos handed it back. "I think you are mistaken. There are no Trembler gatherings left in Tempestano, thanks to your thorough work."

"Not one?" Elder Crispin asked, raising an eyebrow as he looked over the notice himself. "I am to believe you are especially zealous at rooting them out, then. I have found them notoriously hard to be rid of even in lands where I have direct governance. Frankly, your reputation and ... family connections ... do not suggest the kind of zealotry necessary to empty a province of these vermin."

Carlos held his tongue and his temper with some effort. "I did not interfere when you arrested my sister. Records will show I have been a loyal and faithful subject. I do not lack family feeling, Señor, but I know enough not to put everything I have at risk."

"Then there are no Sacramenti hiding out in your lands, either? No secret base of Imitator operations?"

The question caught Carlos completely off guard. He tried not to let it show. "I don't know what you're talking about."

Elder Crispin rolled up the scroll and smacked his palm with it before handing it back off to his aide. "We shall see. We've had reports, Conde Vaquero, that rather contradict your protests. Accordingly, I am here to set up an inquisition."

Carlos flushed. "You have no right. This is my land. Magisterial authority here is mine."

"Not anymore. I have orders from the Alliance. They have given the synod direct control over inquiries here in Tempestano, and any judicial procedures arising from them, with me as their representative of course."

Crispin smiled, an impossibly smug smile that capitalized on Carlos's speechlessness. "I'll need an office, a courthouse, and troops answering to me. I've brought the captains to oversee them. Oh, and I'll need a room and due provision for the remainder of my stay."

Carlos found his tongue at last. He said none of the things that burned in his heart to say. Instead, he simply said, "Of course. I'll make arrangements."

Carlos turned on his heel, but before he could go, Elder Crispin halted him with a question. "Have you had any word from your sister?"

"What are you talking about?" Carlos said, turning back. "My sister is in the belly of a prison, where you put her."

"We both know that's not true," Crispin said. "She escaped. Came here, unless I miss my guess. By this time she should be in the New World."

Carlos's blood ran cold. If Crispin knew this much about Serena's whereabouts ...

"I only asked because I thought, if you'd had word from her, it might add to the case against her in the New World. Not that they need further proof to carry out the sentence I recommended. But anything we can use here, to let people know the truth ... it would help in the cause against the Tremblers."

Elder Crispin caught Carlos's eyes in an unmistakable threat. "Of course, it might also implicate you. So I suppose it is best for us all that you haven't heard from her."

He turned away, into conference with his aides. Carlos stalked away, heart pounding. He tore away his coat as he entered his library and threw it aside. Diego entered on his heels.

"Calmly, sir," he said.

Carlos round on him. "You heard him! He knows where Serena's gone! Find out more, Diego. Find out what he's done!"

"Respectfully, sir, your bigger problems are here. If he finds Tremblers in Tempestano …"

"You've warned them all."

"But they haven't all gone."

"They're not gathering. If they don't gather, they aren't afoul of the law."

"You hope they aren't gathering. I can't promise that."

"And what did he mean about Sacramenti? Diego? Are there Sacramenti here?"

Diego didn't meet his eyes. "I don't know."

"You've just finished sweeping the whole countryside for religious dissidents. You saw nothing to indicate the presence of Sacramenti enclaves?"

"I wasn't looking for them, I was looking for Tremblers. Frankly, sir, if Sacramenti are hiding in numbers anywhere in this part of the world, it's likely they're here. Your Trembler tolerance is not a secret."

Carlos cursed and quickly sent another inward apology for his language heavenward. "But Crispin can't prove anything against me."

"If he finds Sacramenti here, he might be able to convict you on that basis alone. Especially if he's right and there are Imitators operating in Tempestano … or if he can make it look like there are."

Carlos stood in his library in his shirtsleeves, feeling the helplessness of his position crash over him. He couldn't throw Elder Crispin out. He couldn't control the Tremblers in his province—make them play by the rules. He couldn't even help Serena.

He closed his eyes and sent up a prayer for her, and for them all. When the Puritani first went to war with the Hierarchy a hundred years before, it had been with the promise of making a better world. Now that they had won, the Sacramenti had gone underground and the kirk with its synods reigned supreme, that better world didn't look much different from the old one.

If he admitted it to himself, Carlos had hoped Serena's crazy determination to sail west and save the settlement of Armando Melrose would result in a true new world. In saving the dream of a new beginning—a place where Carlos himself might go one day.

If she was lost, so was the Jerusalem Valley settlement.

So was everything.

And with the wolf breathing down his neck, there was nothing Carlos could do about it.

Anoschi Pass, West of Jerusalem Valley—The New World

An early snow began to fall as the envoy made their way up the pass—light, swirling snowflakes, looping across their path against a backdrop of brown trees and grey rock, with smatterings of red and orange still painting the remaining leaves. It wasn't a good omen, Linette knew. Snow meant winter, and winter without the harvest meant a struggle to survive unlike anything she'd ever known.

Smith led the way with Cleveland just behind him. Linette followed in Cleveland's tracks, unable to keep up with their confident, long-legged pace as well as she wanted to. Jonathan lagged even further behind, which was some small consolation to her pride—though considering how sick he'd been just twenty-four hours ago, she knew she wasn't setting the bar high by comparison.

Their march through the pass felt grim. The air grew colder, knifing Linette's face when the wind blew. They passed over the place where her last journey here had ended—the bulge in the rock, rounding it to a narrow path. Falling leaves had cleared much of the foliage that had obscured the mountainside before, and now broken branches, crumbled rock, and dark stains that might have been blood could be clearly seen where the men had sent the carcass of the thorn tumbling off the path after drawing Jonathan up from where his broken body was cradled in the branches of the trees.

Linette shivered as they passed by, but she couldn't help looking for the humped body of the creature she remembered. It was nowhere to be seen.

She cast a glance over her shoulder and saw that Jonathan's face was drawn and his hands balled into fists. She'd been there to hear his story when he first told it in the Fosters' home, from his bed where Letty tended to him night and day. Certain that he was good as dead, he had determined to do whatever damage to the creature he could before it reached the valley and the unsuspecting settlement. He'd climbed the rocks above the path, then waited for the beast to appear. When it did, he had swallowed his fear and leaped upon it from above, his one thought to hang onto a handful of fur with one hand and stab with the other, inflicting wounds with all the strength he could muster.

It had been a fight, and that he had killed the creature was a shock to Jonathan. In fact, when he first told the story, everything about it seemed a shock to him—the beast, his own courage, and his survival most of all. Linette's heart had gone out to him, and she'd admired his pluck and self-sacrificing actions.

All of that had faded. With time, the shock in his story gave way to bravado and then what Linette considered arrogance—a smug belief that his survival made him right about all things, especially about the Word of the Creator, the path the settlement ought to take, and the dangers of Trembling.

But being back here, she felt her heart soften a little again. No one had forced Jonathan to return to this place, nor to put himself at risk by attempting to make this journey in the condition he was in.

Smith pushed ahead without stopping, or even pausing, and Linette scampered to catch up. She realized she couldn't hear footsteps behind her, and she stopped and turned. Jonathan stood in the narrow path just where the bear had gone over the side, staring at the broken trees and bloodstains with rapt fascination.

"Jonathan," Cleveland called out, gruffly. "No time to stop."

Jonathan blushed and pulled himself away. He caught Linette looking at him and scowled. She dipped her head apologetically. He'd meant that moment to be private. She shouldn't have intruded.

As they pushed on, Linette found her eyes again and again drawn away from the path before them and over the sweeping mountainside above and below. She felt a sense of something ominous—the approach of winter, perhaps, or something else. In the wind's biting cold was a presence, watching them malevolently.

She tried to shake off the feeling as she stumbled over a broken piece of rock in the path. Chips of shale crumbled away and slid noisily down the mountainside. Smith turned and raised his musket as though to signal them.

"Are you all right?" he called.

"Fine," she called back, blushing. Leave it to Smith to notice her one misstep. She refused to look back at Jonathan.

But as she took another step forward, the path beneath her feet seemed to shift.

For an instant, she was not standing on a narrow trail high on a mountainside. Instead, she stood at the edge of a cliff, looking down on a broad plain she had never seen before. It was littered with corpses—the bodies of soldiers, dressed in all colors, all the regiments of the world in a single bloodied heap.

Over them, staring up at her with greedy yellow eyes, were enormous wolves.

She gasped, drawing cold air into her lungs that filled her whole body with ice and struck her voiceless.

"Linette?" It was Smith. He'd come back a few feet, concern on his weathered face. "Are you all right?"

She nodded and trailed a hand across her brow in what she hoped was a nonchalant gesture. "I'm fine. Just a little ... a little winded."

"We should take a break," Smith said.

"Is that wise?" Cleveland asked.

Smith looked Linette over, and beyond her to Jonathan, who even despite the pause was still lagging a good fifteen feet behind.

"Yes," he said. "We can all use a rest. The Outsiders will be there for us when we're back on our feet. We hope."

"We hope?" Linette asked, trying to put the grisly vision out of her mind but genuinely surprised by Smith's words. "What do you mean? Don't we know where they live?"

"They move," Smith said. "Got a village on the other side of this pass, but they're not always there."

"They should be at this time of year," Jonathan said, panting, as he drew near and limped to a stop. "They've never left this early."

"But it's cold," Smith said. "Cold early. Think that will make a difference?"

"It might." Jonathan sat down on a rocky outcrop and pulled a chaw of tobacco from his bag. He bit off a chunk and handed the rest to Smith and then Cleveland. Both men partook; no one offered Linette anything. Self-consciously, she pulled a green apple from her own bag and took a bite. Sour.

"I don't think so, though," Jonathan said. "Can't read the weather and the signs like they can, but my gut tells me they'll still be there. Anyway, five minutes' rest here shouldn't make a difference."

Smith regarded Jonathan curiously. "You're moving faster than I thought you would. Weren't you still on crutches a few days ago?"

Jonathan shrugged, but Linette noticed he didn't meet Smith's eyes. "I feel stronger than I did before I was sick. Maybe I sweat something out of me."

"You didn't sweat," Linette said. Everyone looked at her. She cleared her throat, self-conscious again. "You were cold as ice. You never sweat."

"Even so," Jonathan said around the tobacco in his mouth, sounding annoyed, "seems it did me some good in the end. I'm feeling stronger, and good thing too. You're going to need me in the village."

He didn't seem to want a reply, so Linette didn't offer one. Instead, she cast a surreptitious glance at the ends of his vines, showing at the cuffs of his sleeves. They were dark grey and almost stony, as though the black ichor she'd seen pulsing there had stained them.

She pulled her gaze away, disturbed. Though every muscle in her legs ached from the upward climb and her body protested at the thought of moving again, she stood. She wanted to move away from this place.

"I'm rested," she announced.

Smith raised his eyebrows. "Well, then," he said, looking around at the others. No one protested. "Let's go."

The day wore on, and as it did, the clouds seemed to sink, gathering lower and heavier around the mountains until at last they wrapped the path in fog. Linette walked with one hand trailing the rock face, able to see only a few steps ahead of her before the world was lost in white haze. Smith slowed their pace to a crawl, and they huddled close together, unwilling to lose anyone in the fog. They did not speak.

Despite the limits of their sight, Linette could tell when the path began to slope downward—gently at first, and then sharply, until every step had to be measured to keep from slipping on unsteady footing below. The fog was so thick Linette felt as though she was stepping down into another realm, another reality, one in which ground was only an unconvincing possibility until one's foot was firmly on it.

This, she thought, was what faith felt like.

Her foot slipped, and Jonathan above reached down and steadied her with a hand on her shoulder. Cleveland waited attentively just below. She grew embarrassed, aware that they were all fussing over her far more than over each other—and with good reason. She was the only one whose steps continually threatened to fly out from beneath her. She'd come to be a help, not a hindrance, and she silently breathed an imprecation upon her city upbringing and her unreliable strength.

The steep drop abruptly came to an end, and Linette sighed with relief and fell into a more surefooted gait, slow though the going still was thanks to the blanket of fog. The cold, almost icy water clung to her cloak and skirts and managed to soak through at her collar and cuffs. Drops gathered and fell from the brim of her hat. What had been bright white in the mountains turned dark grey here, a fog that was suffocating and seemed, to Linette, to harbor threatening shapes—things that darted away just beyond the edge of sight.

And then, all of a sudden, they were there.

She could smell wood fires and animal hides, and there it was, looming out of the mist: a tall, domed structure covered in sheets of bark and brown animal skins. Smoke curled from an opening in the top of its roof. Now that they were here, the fog seemed to clear a little, and Linette could make out other shelters—wigwams—around them, arranged roughly in a circle. A taller, longer structure formed the heart of the village. Smith took her arm and pointed toward it.

"The longhouse," he said. "We'll meet with them there."

"Ho!" Jonathan called out. "Greetings, brothers!"

With a shiver, Linette became aware of eyes on them—and then that they weren't alone, that figures were standing behind them and around them. They had melted through the fog so silently she hadn't known they were there. She turned, slowly, to face them.

The man who stood before them was tall. He wore buckskin leggings and a rich blue mantle that draped over his shoulder and hung to the waist. A leather pouch hung from his neck. Long white hair, gathered with a strap, hung over his shoulder as well, and his forehead and cheeks were lined with strange markings—tattoos, she thought.

The men around him, mostly younger, were shaved except for a scalp lock. One or two of them wore a bright red headdress at the base of the lock, standing straight up, and their faces were painted with brilliant red. A few of them wore cotton shirts like the settlers, belted with leather over buckskin leggings and breechclouts.

"Chief Capenokanickon," Jonathan said, stepping forward. "We have come to speak with you."

The chief regarded Jonathan sternly, hardly changing his expression or moving. Linette found herself strangely awed by his presence. Awed, overwhelmed, and deeply uncomfortable even as she felt suddenly and deeply at home.

"You are a long time gone, little brother," Capenokanickon said.

"It's a long story," Jonathan said. "I was tracked by a Machkigen and killed it."

The warriors looked at one another with evident surprise. "You killed a Machkigen?" one of them burst out.

Capenokanickon didn't react. He continued to stare at Jonathan with a piercing look that Linette couldn't read. "Eat first," he said. "Talk after. Come, friends. We will feed you."

An hour later, Linette sat in the midst of the crowded longhouse among tribesmen and women, with Smith on one side of her and Cleveland on the other. Her belly was full of venison, shellfish, maize, and squash, and the dense, warm, smoky air of the wigwam threatened to lull her to sleep.

Her body, aching from the journey through the pass but finally trading the chill for warmth, was relaxing despite herself, her limbs growing heavier the longer she sat. If she wasn't so keenly aware of being a stranger in a strange place, she might have given into the sensation. As it was, she kept herself awake and tried to pay close attention to everything around her.

It was a losing battle. She found these people, this place, overwhelming. The frontier settlement had been a new experience, yes, the dangers and triumphs of life both standing out in sharper relief here where life was so much more closely dependent on the whims of land, river, and sky. But this—

This was a new world indeed. All the powers of her imagination had never really come close to believing it existed.

But perhaps what struck her most strongly, as she sat here amidst a people so unlike anyone she had ever known, in a place so unlike any place she had ever been, was that it was not a new world to them.

Jonathan was telling his story of encountering the bear—the thorn, the Machkigen—in the pass. The chief had wanted to hear it. Jonathan described how it stalked him through the forest beyond the Outsider village and then up into the pass. He told how he'd hoped to lose it, prayed with every step that it would turn back, but had realized with growing dread that it would not.

He described an otherworldly terror that gripped him as he fled. As he spoke of it, Linette remembered back to the fog and her sense of things tracking them in it—of something watching.

She had shed her damp cloak in favor of an animal hide robe when they first sat down together. She drew it around her now, strangely comforted by its weight and its unfamiliar smell. It belonged here, in a way she didn't, and it knew, perhaps, more than she did about what hid in the woods and the mists.

Finally Jonathan told the story again, of how he had leaped down on the bear from above and stabbed it over and over again, even as it thrashed and buffeted him against the rock face, and how at last he was flung off and thought he would die—but the trees caught him, bore him up as if in their arms. And the bear remained above, on the pass, a hulking, dark shape in the night, dripping blood and poison down the side of the mountain.

Linette listened as though she'd never heard the story before. And she hadn't—not like this. Jonathan told it in a subdued, almost childlike voice. In the chief's presence he lost his bravado and his shock alike and simply related what had happened ... humbly.

She'd never liked him as much as she did here and now.

"And you lived," Capenokanickon said. "Tell us that tale, little brother."

Jonathan was quiet for a minute. He seemed to be collecting his thoughts. He didn't look up. "I remember only little," he said. "I was only half-awake. I remember pain. The moon high up, but then swallowed up by clouds. And then there was a light."

To Linette's surprise, he looked up and met her eyes. "The valley people got my note and sent men after me. This man—" he pointed at Smith. "And others. They came to my rescue."

"In the middle of the night?" Capenokanickon asked.

"They had a light," Jonathan repeated. Halfheartedly, he gestured to Linette. "She had a light."

The Outsider chief smiled. It was the last thing Linette expected. She realized suddenly that everyone was looking at her, and she shifted uncomfortably, wishing she could shake off the urge to sleep that even now kept her drowsy and slow. Was there something she should say? Something she should do?

"The vine light is a rare gift," Capenokanickon said. "Rare and honored. I saw it in her when you first arrived." The chief turned to Linette. "Your light will discover what is in darkness," he said. "It will show what hides in shadows."

Linette shifted again. "I ... I'm not sure what you mean."

The chief didn't seem inclined to explain. "You must all stay here to-night," he said. "You cannot journey further in the fog, and I wish to know more about all these things."

"We have not even begun to tell you why we have come," Smith said. "We are not here simply to talk. We want to trade with you."

Capenokanickon waved him away as though banishing a fly. "In time. First I want to know more." He pointed a pipe, carved out of a thin, shiny material Linette couldn't identify, at Jonathan. "You have been well?"

"I ... no." The young preacher seemed caught off guard by the question. "I have been ill, Chief."

Linette sensed a sudden change in the atmosphere of the longhouse, though so subtle it was hardly perceptible. The chief looked sharply at Jonathan. "Ill with white man's disease?"

"I had a fever. I'm better now ... better than before, even." He looked at Smith as though seeking some kind of help. Apparently he sensed the change too, and didn't know what to make of it—a fact Linette hardly found comforting.

Capenokanickon stood. The move was so unexpected that the warriors around him seemed to fall back, and Linette felt herself shrinking into her animal-hide robe as though she could find a way to leave the longhouse through it. Not that she was desirous to go out into the night. The world around them felt more wild and strange than anything she'd known at home or in Jerusalem Valley.

The chief gestured to his guests. "You will stay tonight," he said. "We talk in the morning of trade." He looked to Smith and Cleveland. "Is the woman yours?"

"No," Cleveland said, so hurriedly Linette thought he might hurt himself. "No, she's ... she's her own."

"She can stay with my daughters," Capenokanickon said.

So it was that Linette found herself bundled up in animal skins on the floor of a round wigwam, watching sparks from the fire drift up toward the hole in the roof and the brilliant stars beyond it—visible now that the fog had cleared. She lay on a pile of skins that in turn covered mats woven from grass. There were four other women in the wigwam, at least two of whom were Capenokanickon's daughters—who the other two were, she wasn't sure. They didn't seem to speak English. They were all young. Two of them snored.

Linette stared up at the stars and the smoke. Now that she was out of the longhouse, relatively alone, and able to sleep, she was wide awake.

She felt … not safe. That wasn't the right word. "Safe" could not begin to describe the electrifying currents flowing through her. Though she did not feel in danger either.

She knew she was meant to be here. Every fiber of her soul told that she was here for a reason. That her steps had brought her to this night and this place for some reason she could not yet fathom, but which would surely become clear.

And she knew that they were wrong to call these people "Outsiders."

They weren't the Outsiders at all.

In her short time in the valley, she'd become aware that Herman strongly opposed the idea of forming any relationship with the tribes who lived in the wilderness. In five years, contact between settlers and these people had been rare. Jonathan was the only exception. Much as she respected and loved Herman, she felt strongly that he'd been wrong.

She thought back to the chief's words. *Your light will discover what is in darkness. It will show what hides in shadows.* She'd always understood her light, the phosphorescence that ran in her bloodline, as little more than a useful trick. A way to see where you were going and save on lantern oil. Yet the chief seemed to indicate it was more than that. She remembered using the light to see what was happening in Jonathan's vines. She hadn't known she could do that. Smith had called for her—and Sarah had told her to shine the light. Sarah had known, somehow, that the light would do more than just brighten the room. How had she known?

Beyond the mats of bark and grass and skin that covered the wigwam, the sounds of the forest in November sharpened Linette's sense of being alone in a wild place. A bird called—a looping, three-syllable, strangely haunting call they sometimes heard in the valley. A whippoorwill, she remembered. Some of the settlers claimed the whippoorwill's call was an omen of death.

Another sound.

Outside the wigwam, something moving.

Linette's heart beat faster. She heard the sound again. Someone was there—just outside the door.

And then her name, whispered. "Linette."

Heart still beating double-time, she gathered her wits together and slowly pushed away the animal skins covering her. She gathered up her cloak and pulled it around her shoulders. The air in the wigwam was close and warm, and she stepped out the door into a biting chill. She pulled her cloak tighter.

Smith stood outside the door, accompanied by two warriors. They stood in deep shadows. Without thinking about it, Linette summoned the glow in her vines until it revealed the expression on Smith's face. He looked deeply perturbed, but not afraid.

One of the warriors beckoned for her to come with them. Smith nodded to her. It was all right.

She let the light die back to a dim glow and followed them away from the wigwam. They passed through the village and beyond the longhouse, into the woods. The light from her vines allowed her to see just clearly enough to know where to put her feet. The Outsiders seemed to know the path by memory.

The quick journey through the trees brought them to a sheer rock face that rose from the forest floor. The light of a fire danced off the rock, highlighting ancient carvings in the stone—figures of animals and men, mostly. Capenokanickon sat at the base of the rock beyond the fire, cross-legged. He indicated that they should sit down.

A full moon rode high above in a sky that had finally cleared. Linette let her light die completely as she sat down, close to the warmth of the fire. The whippoorwill sounded again, loud and clear—closer here.

"We must be sitting right on top of him," Smith said, remarking on the call.

Capenokanickon raised his pipe. "He is a mile away. His call carries. But if we were sitting on top of him, we would not see him. He hides himself among the leaves."

"Such a conspicuous call," Linette said. "It's hard to believe he could hide."

"Many powerful things wear plain clothes," Capenokanickon said. "But he is late. Late at night, and late in the year. He should be gone now, flown away before the winter. Perhaps he has stayed to tell us something."

Linette glanced at Smith. He did not look any more comfortable here than he had in the longhouse. She wondered if he knew the superstition about the bird.

She wondered if it was more than superstition.

Smith cleared his throat. "You didn't call us out here to talk about a bird. Why this midnight conversation? What do you have to say that you couldn't say in the longhouse?"

Capenokanickon seemed unperturbed by Smith's interrogation … and yet Linette could see in his expression that something was wrong. "I did not wish to speak in front of the little brother," he said.

"Jonathan?" Smith asked. "Why ever not? He's your friend, isn't he?"

"Not anymore. He has become something else."

Linette found that she was holding her breath. Under the full moon's light, she felt as though the world was about to shift irreparably beneath her. As though to confirm her intuition, Capenokanickon gestured toward her. "She has seen it," he said. "Her light has shown what he has become."

Smith looked questioningly at her. "When he was sick," she said, "I saw something in his vines … something black. Some kind of poison."

"It is malliku," Capenokanickon said. "Witchcraft. It entered him when he fought with the bear. Jonathan has become a Machkigen."

Smith sat back as though he'd been hit with a musket ball. "What kind of nonsense are you talking? Jonathan is Jonathan."

"Jonathan is lost," the chief said. "I see it in his eyes. He is not the same little brother who came to us bearing words from the Creator. He comes bearing poison now. He is becoming poison. You must kill him."

"What? No!" Smith burst out, jumping to his feet. Linette thought he might throttle the chief, who remained undisturbed—though the young warriors tensed, ready to interfere.

Smith stood his ground, more agitated than Linette had ever seen him. "We are God-fearing men. We don't kill our own."

Capenokanickon's eyes burned. "He is no longer your own."

"You said he is *becoming* poison," Linette said. "Is there hope for him? Any other way that you can see?"

Unlike Smith, she didn't try to argue that Jonathan was all right. She'd seen the poison for herself. Something deep inside told her the chief was right.

"We do not know any other way," the chief said. "There is a war inside of him. Maybe he can win it. Animals do not. But he is a man. So maybe there is hope. But you risk everything if you leave that to chance. He will kill."

"How is it that you don't know more?" Smith said, sinking back down. "This is your world; haven't any of your people ever become infected?"

The chief's eyes blazed again. "This is not our malliku. We never saw it before you white men came. You brought it with you."

"That's impossible!" Smith burst out. "We are the Creator's people; we don't bring witchcraft with us."

"We never saw it before you came," the chief insisted. "The black-coated fathers came to the valley, and we welcomed them, but they were not friends to us. Only the little brother took our hands. But even before he grew to be our friend, the Malliku-Machkigen appeared. First it was a wolf. We killed it when it attacked our village and found the scales and the black blood that hisses and burns. We called them thorns, because they do not belong here. Someone else planted these serpent creatures. We did not."

"We won't kill the boy," Smith insisted. "He is one of us."

One of the warriors behind Smith stepped forward. "I will do it for them," he said.

"No," Capenokanickon said quickly. "To kill will bring consequences. I do want not blood on our hands."

"But you want us to get it on ours," Smith said. Linette wanted to reach out and touch him, to calm him—but she didn't feel that she had the right, and in any case, this whole conversation made her dizzy with questions.

"The malliku came with you," Capenokanickon repeated. "It is the fault of the settlers, so the settlers must bear the guilt of his death. It is the only way to stop the poison. I find no gladness in this, settler-man. I will grieve for him."

Smith had not stopped shaking his head. "There has to be another way. I'll not take the boy's life."

"Then you must bear the guilt of his life," Capenokanickon said. "What he does with the poison inside will be on your head."

The chief stood and held out his hand. One of his warriors placed a tomahawk in it. Linette tensed, every nerve suddenly on alert. But the chief made no threat. Instead, he held the weapon out … to Linette.

She took it hesitantly, mouth open as she searched for words.

"You have no weapon," the chief said. "If you travel with the little brother, you may need it."

"I … thank you."

The chief bowed his head in evident pain. Fire bounced off his skin, the deep blue of his mantle, and the tattooed markings on his face. "We will hold a mourning ceremony for our brother. He is gone, even if you will not kill him. Then we must leave. Our winter country has not seen the Machkigen. I will make my people safe there."

As though she were waking from a spell, Linette remembered in a flash why they had come. She reached out. "Smith. The hail."

Smith hung his own head, clearly searching for words. He found them with some great effort. "Chief," he said, "we came to ask you to trade with us. Our harvest—our crops were destroyed by the hail."

The chief listened without speaking. If he knew of the hail—despite the lack of destruction on this side of the pass—he did not say.

Smith cleared his throat and continued. "We have lost more than we can live without. We thought … we have blankets, some tools and muskets. We thought we could trade for maize and venison."

His words fell away. In the light of the fire, Capenokanickon still did not speak. Linette shifted from one foot to the other uncomfortably. When she was with her own people, she could read their faces while they thought.

The expression on Capenokanickon's face was unreadable, at least to her.

At last he answered. "We will give you what we can before we go, but we have only a little here."

"We hoped you might send traders back, with more from your winter country."

He shook his head. "We will not come back while the Machkigen remains in your midst. I will not risk my people's safety."

Smith's voice sounded half-strangled. "One boy," he said.

"I have sought the Creator," Capenokanickon said. "And he answered me with a vision. I saw hungry wolves surrounding your valley. They were not the wolves of the forest, but the wolves of malliku. They wanted to devour everything in their sight. You settlers could not stand against them. We cannot come back here, white man. This is not our fight."

Without another word, he turned and headed back toward the village. The warriors began to put out the fire, and one by one, the carvings in the rock winked out of sight.

CHAPTER
18

Outsider Village, west of Anoschi Pass—The New World

Morning was solemn and unhappy. Smith told Jonathan and Cleveland that he had met privately with Capenokanickon in the night and that he had promised to send traders to the valley with a little food, but that there would not be more.

Linette laced up her leather boots while the men talked. Cleveland sounded bewildered and a little angry. Jonathan sounded hurt.

"You're sure you didn't dream it?" he asked. "Why would Capenokanickon talk to you without me?"

"How should I know the mind of an Outsider?" Smith shot back. "He didn't tell me why. Maybe because he took me for the leader."

"He should have called Cleveland, then," Jonathan said. "They honor age. That's why we brought him."

Cleveland snorted. "I'm not that old, boy."

Jonathan ignored him. When it was clear that Smith could tell him nothing more, he looked around rapidly until he caught sight of a warrior he knew. He dashed across the clearing through the village.

"Anasan!" he called.

Linette watched with a sinking heart as Jonathan ran up to the red-painted warrior, a young man not much older than he. The warrior stared at him for a moment before turning his back.

Jonathan stood facing the back of a man he must have counted a friend, looking lost and frightened.

For the first time, Linette's heart went out to him fully. Whatever was happening inside of him, he didn't deserve to be rejected by people he'd cared about, even risked greatly for. She knew the story of how Jonathan had first gone to the people beyond the pass, against his father's wishes, against Herman's warnings, and with no guarantee that they would be friendly to him. Letty had told her. She rose, not sure what she intended to do but wishing to comfort him somehow.

He stood staring at Anasan's back for a few seconds later before suddenly turning and walking toward his companions. He brushed past Linette without a word.

"Jonathan—" she said.

"Not now, woman," he growled.

Linette looked to the ground. Cleveland stirred himself as though to come to her defense, but she raised a hand to forestall him. She understood.

Smith looked back and forth between them. "Well," he said. "We should go."

If their journey to the village had been mostly wordless, the beginning of their journey back was frigid. The air had grown colder, and Linette's breath formed clouds as she started up the steep path back into the mountains. This time Jonathan went ahead of them all. She noticed with some surprise that he'd become even stronger than before. His recovery from the illness was remarkable.

The word *malliku* rose into her mind, accompanied by the flickering of flames on the carved rock wall and the tattoos on Capenokanickon's face. She pushed the word and its accompanying memory back into the recesses of her mind, but with every striding step that Jonathan led up into the pass, her sense of foreboding grew stronger.

As it did out of Jerusalem Valley, the pass here began in a steep, almost vertical climb. It took them up the side of the mountain and looked down on the village. The group paused, and with each hand on a rock to help her up, Linette looked backward and down. She could just make out the domed shapes of the wigwams. Smoke rose from them in thin spirals.

Higher up, Jonathan seemed to have the better view. She realized he had stopped them—stopped for the purpose of looking back.

"Someone has died," he said. "They're beginning a mourning ceremony. Someone has died, and ..."

He didn't finish the sentence. Didn't say, *And they didn't tell me. I thought they trusted me. I thought they were my brothers.*

And once again, Linette understood. She wanted to try to explain. To tell him they were grieving for him, that they had not rejected him in their hearts.

She wanted to say all the things to him that she'd wished, during so many long and lonely days in New Cranwell, that someone would say to her.

In her case, she knew it wouldn't have been true. But that made it even harder to say nothing now ... to this man who wouldn't want to hear it from her anyway, and wouldn't likely believe her.

And of course, they couldn't tell him what the chief had said about him. That he was poisoned and had to die.

She blinked away tears that froze in the corners of her eyes and stung. When she looked up, the rocks and the steep, narrow path through the mountains beckoned like a fate that would take all of her effort to meet and then punish her for reaching it.

Even knowing they had no good news to bring the settlement, the end of this journey through the pass couldn't come fast enough for her.

Jailhouse, New Cranwell—The New World

The New Cranwell jailhouse was much like any other. It was damp. It had rats. There was one other prisoner, brought in drunk and unconscious and not awake yet. The accents of the jailers were different, but other than that, it was as unpleasant and unremarkable as any prison Serena had known in the Old World.

The worst of it all, Serena decided, was having lost Jacques. Their tête-à-tête with Elder Cole had ended with their separation—Jacques dragged off to who knew where, in order to be packed in irons and sent back over the ocean without her. Cole had suggested a good flogging beforehand as well. Serena was sent here, to wait for her public examination and its certain conclusion. Cole's commitment to examine her himself showed some integrity—or at the very least, a desire to operate independently of the cabal in the Old World under Crispin. She couldn't blame him for that. Crispin made a show of piety, but from the time she had spent as his favorite scapegoat, she knew perfectly well that his ambitions stretched across the Old World and even into the New, and there was nothing holy about them. His forebears might have fought the Wars for Truth in order to attain freedom, but Crispin would see the world under bondage again, with only the masters having changed.

That, all of it, was why it mattered so deeply that she reach Jerusalem Valley. Herman Melrose had seen what was happening in the upper levels of the Puritani kirk and taken a stand against it. He'd helped pioneer a whole new way of relating to God, hearing directly from him, reading the Book with different ears. He had articulated a vision of self-governance, tolerance, and peace. He'd been beaten, hounded from province to province, jailed, and targeted for assassination. Yet against all odds, he had lived, and he had become free. The small religious movement of which he was a part, the Tremblers, had grown in size and influence among the common people.

Thanks in great part to his father, the foremost of Angleland's generals, he had been given protection and favor by the king of Angleland—and then gifted with land in the New World.

What he was trying to do there, in the settlement he called Jerusalem, was the only hope for something better to rise out of the ashes of the Old World. He was planting seeds of tolerance, of new ways of thinking, learning, and being, that alone could draw the poison of hatred and violence that had done so much damage in the country of Serena's youth.

She well remembered the day when Melrose had visited Tempestano. She was only four years old, but it had engraved itself in her memory forever. It was the first day she felt the stirring of the Fire Within and heard the voice of the Creator speaking to her—telling her she was known, beloved, and chosen.

If Melrose could succeed in his daring project, if he could teach all the peoples of the world to hear that voice—everything would change.

But if he died, with his project still in fragile infancy; if the seeds he'd planted were uprooted before they'd even begun to grow; she could not see any hope beyond that. Assassination would cause the kirk to declare Jerusalem Valley a failure and petition the king for control of Melrose's lands. According to Cole, the kirk was trying to wrest control away from the Tremblers even while Melrose lived. How much worse would things get if the Reaper carried out his mission?

Not for the first time, Serena pondered the vulnerability of human beings and the movements that rode on them. How was it right that something so important should rest in vessels that were so easily broken?

Who says it rests on you? asked the voice she knew as belonging to the Creator.

You do, she answered in her heart. *You are the one who has called and chosen us for this task.*

Then I bear the ultimate responsibility, not you.

It made her feel better.

A little.

"Serena."

It took her a moment to realize the voice, rasping at the corner of her consciousness, wasn't in her thoughts or spirit. Rather, it was sounding into the room, beneath the snores of her drunken cellmate. For that matter, she realized suddenly, that all the while she'd been lost in thought, there had been another noise—a scratching sound.

"Serena!" the voice hissed again.

She turned, scanning the grimy cell for the source of the voice. "Jacques?" she whispered back. There, in the far corner—a tiny shaft of light. Ignoring the filth on the floor, she got down on her knees next to a small hole in the brick wall. "Is that you?"

"Serena, take hold."

It *was* Jacques. And something was needling its way through the hole … a piece of string. Serena grasped the end with her finger and thumb and pulled it through to her side, gently.

"Pull it all the way through," Jacques's voice said. More muffled, as though someone was standing behind or beside him, she heard another voice say something. Who …?

Figuring it was easier to obey than to question, she pulled the string. A weight now made pulling it harder, and something clanked and stuck. "Hold on," Jacques's voice said. She heard the scraping sound of something moving, and the string twisted. "Now, pull again."

She did, this time giving the string a solid yank. Her eyes widened as it came all the way through—and tied to its end, a key.

"Now wait," Jacques said. "You'll know when."

Stuffing all of her questions back with some effort, Serena slipped the key into a skirt pocket and stood slowly, looking around. Lost in thought before, now her mind and body alike stood alert, watching and listening for danger or a signal. The door to the anteroom, where guards sat watching and occasionally talking, remained closed. In the Old World, the guards would be playing cards or dice. She doubted very much that kind of behavior would be tolerated here. Crispin might be wolfish in his appetites, but Cole seemed more an iron fist, determined to force righteousness upon the populace whether they liked it or not.

For what felt like a horribly long time, nothing happened. Then she heard a sound, with the familiar scent of burning accompanying it … and then smoke was curling under the door, then billowing, and the stirring in the anteroom had turned to shouts and banging doors.

Smoke filled the room until Serena could barely see. She pulled up her skirt to cover her mouth and nose and sank to her hands and knees, trying to get under the noxious fumes. Heat was growing in the room, pressing and urgent. She crawled forward, feeling her way across the floor until she found the cell door. Careful not to touch the metal bars for fear they had already grown hot, she passed her small hand through the bars and tried the key in the lock. It turned. Coughing, she turned her back against the door and pushed. It swung open on protesting hinges.

The anteroom door flew open, filling the room with more smoke. A figure in the door beckoned wildly. "Serena! Come on!"

Coughing instead of answering, she pushed herself to her feet and sprinted for the door. Jacques sprang backward, out of her path. "Here! This way!"

Holding her skirt over her nose and mouth, she followed him. The smoke made it impossible to see precisely where they were going, but in a minute they tumbled out into the street—through a back door. Smoke was pouring out the windows of the jailhouse, galvanizing passersby and jailers alike. Shouts filled the air. No one was paying attention to the back door.

"Were you trying to burn me alive before the kirk could do it?" Serena asked when she caught her breath. Her throat scratched.

"What, you don't trust me?"

"I'm starting to wonder."

"Wonder later."

Jacques grabbed Serena's hand. She let go of her skirt and breathed in the salty-fresh air as he pulled her down the narrow, cobbled street behind the jailhouse, which backed on a row of tall, formal-looking two-story buildings. Behind them, footsteps pounded the cobblestones. Serena pulled against Jacques's hand, trying to twist around to see their pursuers. "Jacques! Behind us!"

He cast a quick glance back. "They're friends," he said.

Serena had little time to ponder that as he continued to run down the street, away from the jail. They had run perhaps a block when Jacques abruptly stopped, said "Here," and all but shoved Serena through a door.

She found herself in a dimly lit room with a clapboard floor and brick walls. Dusty furniture looked as though it had been cobbled together from the cast-offs of others and then abandoned. The coals in the fireplace surely had not been kindled in months.

Their followers burst through the door directly after them and shut it, barring it quickly. Serena got a good look at them for the first time, and her eyes widened with surprise. The "friends" Jacques had somehow found were a black man and a child of the same persuasion, most likely the man's son.

"How did …"

"Serena, meet Eben Axel," Jacques said. "And his son, Josiah. They are going to Jerusalem Valley and they wish to accompany us there."

"But how …"

"They agreed to help me get you out of the jail, using their ingenious bag of … tricks, I think they called it? In return for our patronage getting to the frontier. I thought it was a good exchange."

Serena realized she was staring and tore her eyes away. The man, a tall, limber fellow wearing cast-off clothing that was too big for him and a wide-brimmed hat over close-cropped hair, had already loped across the room and thrown open a dusty chest. He pulled out clothing and threw it at Serena. "Here. Put this on."

She caught the bundle of cloth and unfolded it to find a stained frock and petticoat. Without warning, a heavy black bodice, white collar, and hooded cloak followed them. Serena caught them out of the air and looked around helplessly for a place to change.

"About-face, if you please, gentlemen," Jacques said. All three turned around, facing the door and the street protectively. Serena hurriedly changed, mourning the loss of the quality clothing her brother had supplied her with. It was too thin for the climate, but what she was wearing now smelled like it hadn't been washed in a decade, and it scratched.

"It's all right," Serena said when she had managed to transform herself into a Puritani woman of the New World—a poor one with no access to a laundry.

All three turned back. The boy turned last of all. Serena regarded him curiously: he was young, perhaps fifteen, and thinner than his father. His hair was longer, curly and falling half into his face. Enormous brown eyes fixed on her.

"Good," Jacques said. "And now we wait. I have already found us a room in an inn."

"Wait?" Serena said. "Don't you mean now we flee? We must get to Jerusalem Valley before any more time passes!"

He shook his head resolutely. "That is the worst thing we could do. We need an escort, and the authorities will be looking for a woman and a man fleeing New Cranwell and trying to reach the frontier. They will find us if we approach anyone to help us or if we run on our own. If we stay here, under their noses, we will remain undetected."

"That is a big chance, Jacques," Serena said.

"No bigger than tryin' to run now," Eben said. "Man's right."

Serena bit back a retort to the effect that it was none of Eben's business. In some way or other he had been instrumental in getting her out of the jail, most likely at some risk to himself. She owed him a debt of gratitude and as much courtesy as she could muster.

"Well, but we can't just stay here forever. How do you suggest we get to the frontier if we cannot set out for it now?"

Jacques looked to Eben. The tall man said, "Been listenin' for a chance to go west some time now. Learned there a small bunch o' soldiers leavin' for Fort Collins six days from now. They escortin' some high muckety-muck out there."

"You're suggesting we join a detachment of soldiers? How will they not recognize us at once?"

"We don't join them at once," Jacques said. "We follow them for a while and join them once they're several days into the wilderness. Eben assures me he can help us."

"And then we come out of the forest pretending to be what, lost pioneers in need of help?"

"Something like that."

"They'll see through us."

"Mebbe they do, mebbe they don't," Eben said. "What's sure is, they won't send you back. Too few men an' it's too late in the year; they delay, they run into snow enough to stop them gettin' where they need to go. They arrest you, they'll take you to Fort Collins. You find a way to break out from there."

Serena laughed, unbelieving. "You're truly suggesting we volunteer to be placed under arrest? Surrounded by redcoat soldiers in some well-guarded wilderness fort?"

Eben shrugged. "It's the frontier. That's where you wanna go, ain't it?"

"He's right, Serena," Jacques said. "I fear we cannot lose our enemies at this point. Let us harness them instead."

Serena laughed again. Though she hated to admit it, it was exactly the kind of plan she herself would have come up with if she'd been given the time and information. The only real reason she was resisting it was that it wasn't her idea.

Carlos would have a fit.

Carlos always had a fit.

"It's a good idea," she finally confessed.

This time it was Jacques's turn to laugh. "I don't know if I would go quite that far," he said. "But it is an idea, and the only one we really have. I assume you do not wish to wait out the winter here."

"A truer word was never spoken." Serena looked down at herself and tried to hide her dismay at the sorry condition of her appearance. "Take me to this inn you found. If we have to hide for a few days, we might as well get it underway."

Anoschi Pass, west of Jerusalem Valley—The New World

The snow began falling when Linette and the men were three hours into the pass. It came out of seemingly nowhere, turning a blue sky into a steel-grey one. At first the snow was dry and light, nothing that threatened their passage. But it turned quickly into something heavier, wetter, and more ominous. Within thirty minutes it had ceased to be passable. Snow clinging to the path made it slippery and treacherous, and it swirled around them in a howling wind that made it nearly impossible to see. "We have to get off the path!" Smith finally yelled. "We need to take shelter!"

The pass here was not as narrow and steep as elsewhere, and Smith led the way down the slope, fighting through the blizzard into a stand of tall, majestic pines. The snow fell more slowly here, and the trees dampened the sound and force of the wind, even though they swayed in its blasts. Smith gestured them all toward a low spot in the ground beneath two trees that grew close together, providing a natural shelter.

He hunkered down first and waved for Linette to follow him. She slipped down the needled slope and settled in close to Smith's warmth. Cleveland lumbered after them ... and stopped as the sound of a musket fired through the stand.

Cleveland's eyes widened, and he pitched forward with an agonized sound.

Linette couldn't breathe as Cleveland's body fell at her feet. The hole in his back was clearly visible.

Both she and Smith looked up into the face of Jonathan Applegate, who held a musket in his hands and stared at them with eyes that had lost their whites and turned the same black, noxious color that Linette had seen in his vines.

Slowly, she summoned her light. As it fell on Jonathan, the vines around his neck and wrists were clearly seen to be black and full of poison.

Machkigen.

"Jonathan," Smith said, his voice tight and trembling, "what have you done?"

"Have to kill you all," Jonathan said. "Rid the earth of the Tremblers."

"Why?" Smith asked. Slowly, he began to rise so that he stood halfway between Jonathan and Linette, holding his arm out protectively in front of her. "Who says you have to do that?"

"My father," Jonathan said.

"Jonathan, your father is dead," Smith said. "He's been dead for years. We are your family now. We are, the Puritani and the Tremblers of the valley."

"No," Jonathan said, shaking his head slowly. He still held the smoking musket, unloaded now. Linette couldn't tear her eyes away from him. Behind Smith, she also stood slowly. The howling wind and blowing snow ripped at the image before her eyes, of a dead man and his killer. "My father told me. It's all coming to an end, all of the wars and the world itself. It will all be purged away in the fires, when the defilers are gone and only the pure remain."

"It's a lie, Jonathan," Smith said. "Your father is dead, and we are not your enemies."

Jonathan looked down at the musket in his hands. His movements were sluggish, as though he moved through a film. He cast the gun aside, into a slowly growing snowbank, and drew his hunting knife from his belt.

"Move, Smith," he said. "I don't have to kill you."

"I won't let you near Linette," Smith answered. "This isn't you. Fight it, boy!"

In answer, Jonathan snarled—an inhuman, animalian snarl that made Linette's blood run cold. Knife in hand, he lunged at Smith. Linette screamed as both men went down, tumbling on the ground. To her horror, Jonathan jumped back. His knife dripped with blood. Smith rolled onto his back with a groan. His hand, covered in blood, clutched his side along his ribcage.

Linette's eyes fixed on Jonathan, but he was still focused on Smith. He snarled again, raised the knife, and went for the kill.

Linette darted forward and grabbed Jonathan's wrist before he could finish the blow. It took every ounce of her strength, all of her weight, to knock the blow aside and hang onto him.

And her vines blazed with light.

Her hand, pressing around the poisoned vines on his wrist, seared with heat as though their flesh was fusing together.

"No!" she shouted. "I won't let you kill him! He's a father ... a husband. Jonathan, think of Letty! Think of Sarah!"

It seemed to her that Jonathan faltered a moment. His eyes seemed to clear, just a little, and he took a step backward.

"Drop the knife!" she commanded. The dazzling light that radiated from her in pulsing waves pushed away the shadows, the snow, even the wind. Jonathan whined and dropped to his knees. The knife fell from his hand. Behind them, Smith groaned. "Linette ..."

She twisted her head to look back at him. "It's going to be all ..."

She couldn't get the words out before her world went suddenly dark. She felt herself falling. That was all.

CHAPTER
19

Province of Tempestano—The Old World

Carlos awoke on the first morning of Elder Crispin's occupation to a pounding on his door. He answered it hurriedly, half-dressed and afraid of what it might portend.

A young servant nervously stood before him when he yanked open his bedroom door.

"The elder summons you, my lord," the boy said.

"Summons me? In my own house? Through my own servant?"

The boy ducked his head as though he expected a cuffing. "I'm sorry, sir, he didn't give me a choice."

Carlos breathed in deeply, trying to calm himself. "No, that's all right. Of course not. I'm not angry with you. Do you know what it's about?"

"Something about the Tremblers, sir."

Carlos began to shut his door, already lost in thought. "I'll be there shortly."

Fifteen minutes later, he strode down the hall with Diego on his heels. He'd awakened his captain himself, banging on his door just as unceremoniously as the servant boy had done on his and with less patience as to a response. If he had to jump to Elder Crispin's every call, he wouldn't be the only one.

Elder Crispin stood in the front hall, fully dressed and pulling on riding gloves. "We are going to conduct an inquisition," he declared when he saw Carlos. He didn't bother with a greeting. "Your presence is requested."

"Requested or required?"

"I have no jurisdiction to *require* you do anything, Conde. I only suggest you should be happy to join us on official kirk business."

He didn't miss the underlying threat, the clear tone that said he did *not* have a choice, no matter what the elder actually said about it. He cast a quick glance at Diego. The captain seemed a little ashen. The early morning, maybe, or the shared understanding that the elder had a plan and it wasn't good.

"What do you intend to do?" Carlos asked.

"I will ride out on an inspection of the town business this fine morning," Elder Crispin said. "But you look disturbed. From what you told me yesterday, surely you have nothing to fear."

"It isn't fear you read on my face, it's annoyance," Carlos said. "I object to you pretending greater authority than you have in my territory. But never fear, I will play your game. I know the consequences if I don't."

"Good then," Elder Crispin said. His eyes still clearly veiled something, and he smiled thinly. "I'm glad we all understand the rules."

Carlos grew grimmer as he entered the palace courtyard and saw a full detachment of soldiers on horseback, arrayed in formation and ready to ride out. This didn't look like an inspection. It looked like a raid … and it looked like they expected to find something.

He leaned toward Diego and whispered, "You did warn every Trembler congregation to clear out?"

Before Diego could answer, Elder Crispin invaded the few square feet around them. "Mount up, Conde," he said. "We wouldn't want to ride out without you."

Troubled by his growing sense that something was wrong, Carlos called for his horse. He mounted the proud chestnut stallion and reined it in behind Crispin. There was no point in pretending he was leading this expedition. In any case, whatever was about to happen, he didn't want it to look to his people like he was at the helm. For once, it was better that they see his true position and know he was doing all he could for them. He might look weak, but at least he could retain their trust in his intentions.

The gates opened at Crispin's command, and the detachment rode out. Their hoofbeats were sharp and measured, a drumbeat down the main street of the town arrayed at the base of the palace. In the early morning, peasants and merchants gathered and gaped. Carlos did not meet their eyes.

Suddenly, they stopped outside a small tavern. Crispin flicked his hand, and his captain gave a command for his men to dismount. A dozen of them did so, drew weapons, and advanced on the tavern door.

Behind him, Carlos heard Diego say, "I'm sorry."

Jerusalem Valley Settlement—The New World

A day passed from the time the envoy was expected back. Then two.

Sarah Foster advanced on the governing house and pounded Herman's desk. "We have to send someone after my husband. Something's wrong."

"Perhaps they are still negotiating," Amos offered from the corner. "It would speak distrust to the Outsiders if we sent others after them too soon."

"What can there be to negotiate that would take so long? Either the Outsiders are willing to trade or they are not. Something has happened. The longer we wait to find out what, the greater trouble Smith could be in."

"No one values Smith more than I do," Herman began.

Sarah flared up at that. "I do. His children do."

"Of course." Herman sighed. "I'm sorry, Sarah. For a moment, the politician in me came out. But you must believe me. I value Smith highly, and Cleveland, and Linette. I'm worried too, but I think we are still within the bounds of a reasonable time frame for negotiating, and I hesitate to threaten the results of negotiation by doing something rash. If we send the Outsiders another signal that we don't trust them or view them as enemies, it could put their mission in jeopardy. It's bad enough that we haven't formed a relationship with them before now. I don't need to remind you how badly we need our men to succeed."

"One more day," Sarah said. "One more day, and we send men after them."

Herman nodded but said, "Two more."

"I *don't* trust them," Sarah said. It came out like an after-shot, a belated volley in a pitched battle. "What if the Outsiders turned on them?"

"You trust Jonathan, don't you?" Herman said. "He has always assured us the Outsiders can be trusted, that they are people of honor."

"Yet you've never seen fit to believe him until now."

Regret passed over Herman's face. "I decided when we arrived that our business was our own—that we had no room in Jerusalem Valley for the heathen. I am not sure now that I was right. Alliance would help us dearly right now."

Sarah nodded. She drifted helplessly toward the door. "Herman? Don't wait. As soon as two more days pass, if they aren't back, send someone without delay. I'm worried. About all of them."

Amos watched Sarah leave with concern written across his face. "Governor, will you excuse me for the day?" he asked.

"Of course," Herman said wearily. "We're done with our letters and paper for now. Go and be of help wherever you can."

At those words, a small smile formed on Amos's face—as though he'd just been given a greater permission than Herman realized. He hurried out the door after Sarah.

Anoschi Pass, west of Jerusalem Valley—The New World

Linette crouched beneath a spray of slender branches covered in snow. She hovered over Smith, protecting him, glancing back every minute to make sure he was still breathing. He had not spoken or moved in hours. His face was nearly as white as the snow that had fallen on them and around them.

Somewhere beyond the trees, Jonathan was stalking them. Every now and again she got a glimpse of him through the stark bare tree trunks and low branches. He paced like a beast, with a strong, frightening swagger. She knew he was not in his right mind.

Why he had not killed her while she lay unconscious, victim to the powerful unleashing of her own light, she did not know. Perhaps she'd been protected by some supernatural power. Or maybe he was still afraid of her. Maybe, unconscious, she'd continued to glow.

She didn't know. She thanked the Fire Within for keeping her safe, and for Smith's life, still tenuously present. And she kept her eyes forward with her heart in her throat, searching the trees for the threat.

Heavy, dark grey clouds overhead threatened more snow. She prayed the Outsiders would be able to get through to the valley with the promised food and that she herself would get through, would make it home … to save Smith and to save Jonathan.

Smith's pistol in her right hand shook while she waited. She would shoot him if she had to, but not unless she absolutely had to. Better to use the light, to push him back … to push the dark magic in him back until she could find a way to help him. Or rather, until *they* could find a way to help him.

The snow, ironically, had brought greater warmth. She made a small burrow in it, beneath the trees, and it stilled the air and made it a little warmer. She shivered. Her heavy coat, brought from the valley, covered Smith now. A small fire she'd managed to build without going too far to gather more kindling helped against the chill as well.

But they couldn't stay here. Smith had lost too much blood. She had used the red scarf Sarah had sent with him to staunch the bleeding as best she could; and she'd made a winter's poultice from chewed bark and pine needles, as Agatha had showed her how to do, to guard him against infection. But it was poor tending for a bad wound, and she knew it. He needed to get home, where it was truly warm and where the wound could be cleaned properly, stitched up, and watched over. He needed his wife and his children.

And as for Jonathan—Linette had seen something when the full force of her light shined upon him. Something that gave her hope that he could be saved. Capenokanickon had suggested that maybe, just maybe, they could find a way to reach the human being in Jonathan, and Linette was now convinced he'd been right.

But seeing was one thing. Knowing how to act on what she saw was another, and for that, she'd become convinced, she needed Sarah.

Sarah, somehow, had known that Linette's light would reveal what was happening inside Jonathan. Sarah, somehow, had understood more than anyone. Something in Linette's gut told her that Sarah would understand how to deal with what she'd seen too.

If Linette could only reach Jerusalem Valley, everything could be all right.

But Jonathan stood between her and home, and he was armed and murderous.

She worked through the problems one by one in her mind. She couldn't move Smith by herself—he was too heavy for her, and if she tried to drag him somehow, she feared making his injuries worse. So she would have to reach the valley on her own and get the men to return for Smith. The trouble there, of course, was that she risked Smith's life if she left him unguarded. What if Jonathan came back to finish what he'd started?

The more she thought about it, the more convinced she became that she'd have to draw Jonathan off after her. It was her he'd wanted to kill anyway; Smith had just gotten between them.

But that presented problems too. Drawing Jonathan away necessarily meant getting close enough to him for him to follow her, and it meant *not* using the light to drive him away. If he caught her and killed her, it was over for all of them. If he didn't catch her—if he just stayed on her trail all the way to the settlement—she'd be bringing a murderer into the valley with no ability to warn the settlers first.

Tears pricked her eyes at the irony. She well remembered when Jonathan's mule had come running into the valley, bearing a letter that commanded the settlers to stay away. He'd faced much the same choice she did now: lead the Machkigen into the settlement or stay in the pass and give his own life to stop it.

But she had Smith to complicate matters, and Jonathan too. Even if she were willing to give her own life, she couldn't sacrifice either of them.

The sloping forest on both sides of the pass remained silent beneath the snow. There was no sign of Jonathan for the moment, but no signs of other life either—no birds, no beasts moving in the trees. The only movement was the slight curl of smoke from her sorry fire.

Unbidden, thoughts of her father came to mind.

Her father would have told her to have no mercy. Evil must be purged. The best thing to do would be to turn the force of her light on Jonathan until he was incapacitated, then use the pistol. Shoot him dead and eradicate the witchery from their midst.

And yet, before Jonathan had suddenly turned into a monster, her father would have supported his vendetta. Maybe even now he would support it. The real enemies were the Tremblers. Herman. Cleveland. Amos.

Herself.

Shame smote her. She remembered the token she'd thrown away when she came: the carved image of a Book she'd worn around her neck. Sarah had one just like it. Smith probably did too. They were people of the Book like her father—Puritani, Pure People, faithful to the end to the written word of the Creator. Living it and enforcing it.

And she had thrown it away as though it were worthless and embraced a new faith. A new religion. One that cut ties with her family and everything that mattered in the past.

She was fiercely proud of herself for it, fiercely certain that this was who she was. And yet she was ashamed.

How could that be?

She shook off the feelings of pain and confusion and refocused on the present moment. On the pass, the snow, the life-threatening journey she had to make.

Fire Within, she prayed. *Spirit of the Creator. Help me. Help Smith, help Jonathan.*

That was it, her whole prayer—the only thing she knew to ask for. Help.

Her father would know better how to pray. He would pray whole passages of the Book, the very words of the Creator. He would discern what was happening here and how it fit the big plans of God.

She was much smaller than he was, and yet she felt closer to the heart of the Creator here, trapped in a pass in the wilderness, calling for help, than she ever had sitting beneath his pulpit in New Cranwell.

That was why she'd become a Trembler. She wasn't sure why she'd thrown away the token of the Book—as an act of rebellion? As a sign of independence from her father? But she'd become a Trembler because Herman Melrose made her believe she could feel close to God.

And by some miracle, she did.

Movement in the woods caused her to tense. She saw a flash of dull color, something in the trees—Jonathan's coat, or a flash of light off the muzzle of his gun.

She twisted her neck to look at Smith behind her. He remained deathly still except for the barely perceptible rise and fall of his chest.

She knew what she had to do.

Closing her eyes, she sent up one more prayer for help. She tucked the tomahawk given to her by Capenokanickon close to Smith's hand. And then she broke cover and ran toward the movement in the trees.

"Here!" she shouted. "I'm here! Come and get me!" She kept running, full-tilt over the broken ground, leather boots leaving impressions in soft patches of earth and sailing over rock and roots. Without her coat, the cold air bit through her bodice and white sleeves. She stopped abruptly at the tree line, looking wildly around for the one she should be running from but instead ran toward.

She saw him an instant before he fired. She screamed and ducked, but the musket shot went wild. Before she could think, she brought her hands up in front of her and blasted him with the light. Not twenty paces away, he staggered backward, still clutching the musket. Heart in her throat, Linette took two steps forward, advancing on him even as he stumbled back, ducking his head away from the light like a frightened animal. His vines throbbed black.

But she had to drop the light.

If she kept it up it would render her unconscious again, and there would be nothing and no one to protect Smith.

She let her hands fall. The light dimmed. There were tears of desperation in her eyes. "Come after me," she said.

Then she turned and ran through the trees, downhill—away from Smith, away from the pass, and into the wild.

CHAPTER
20

Province of Tempestano—The Old World

The first face Carlos saw when the tavern door was kicked open by Crispin's soldiers was that of Philippe Parrano, and behind him, his wife.

Behind her, their children.

It was then that he knew all was lost. Diego had assured him the Parranos were gone—that they had left the province. If they were not gone, if they had stubbornly remained despite his warnings and continued to gather the Tremblers around them, then this moment had become a tragedy. Philippe and Elsa were the closest thing Tempestano's Tremblers had to successors of Armando Melrose. Serena had been the movement's heroine, their martyr and symbol of the struggle, but the Parranos were the mother and father raising spiritual children to maturity. Their influence was such that any public meeting they convened would attract most of the region's Tremblers to it.

From the looks of things, there were easily a hundred in the tavern.

Philippe stepped forward. His hands were empty. Unarmed—as he would always be, on principle. The Tremblers refused to take up arms to spread their ideology as the Hierarchy and Puritani before them had done. They refused to spill blood in the name of God. Better that their own blood be spilled, they said.

Carlos saw it all as if it happened in a dream, as if time moved too slowly and all that he beheld was covered by a veneer of unreality. He saw the soldiers charge into the tavern, bayonets forward. He saw Philippe stabbed through the heart and heard the musket fire that filled the tavern and the square with smoke, the screams and desperate dashing for escape that could not be found. A window shattered from within, shards of glass blasting into the square. He saw townsfolk all around running toward the tavern and stopping in horror as smoke began to billow out from the open window and the soldiers retreated.

They brought no one out with them.

He had to do something. There must be something he could do. But he couldn't … couldn't move. Couldn't think. Could hardly breathe.

He didn't know if seconds passed or minutes. The soldiers barred the doors and threw a torch in through the open window, adding to the fire that had already begun. His people were in there. Children were in there.

Pushing against the freeze that held him, he tried to pull his foot from a stirrup and dismount, tried to run for the doors and unbar them. But hands were on him, soldiers were pulling him down from his horse.

Everything snapped back into living color as soldiers forced Carlos onto his knees, the muzzle of a pistol pressed into the back of his neck. His arms were wrenched behind him and hands tied. He felt the heat of the fire on his face as screams rent the air.

"Don't worry," a cold voice said beside him. Crispin. "Most of them are already dead. The fire is only meant to finish cleaning up the infestation."

Crispin nodded over Carlos's head. "Take him back to the palace. Keep him in irons. We will deal with his treason later."

The Wilderness—The New World

Linette led Jonathan on a hunt across the wilderness, relentlessly downhill and then up the slopes again, through pines and stands of barren deciduous trees, through ravines and half-frozen streams. She kept him close enough that when she turned and looked behind her, she could always see him there—following, hunting her. She could not risk losing him. If she did, he might return to Smith.

But that was the other threat, of course—that she would lose her own way. That she would not be able to return to Smith when she needed to get him home. She watched the landmarks and did her best to map them out in her mind, but the unceasing adrenaline of the hunt made her thoughts hard to process through. She could only hope she was doing it right.

Linette's long red-blonde hair had come loose from its pins and now hung in a ragged braid down her back, wisps floating around her face. She was cold, but she kept a dim glow alight in her vines, and it kept her fingers and toes from going numb. She scrambled up the far side of a ravine and turned to scan the trees behind it for Jonathan. It was becoming a familiar rhythm. Run, turn, look. See the threat, keep going.

She couldn't do this forever. The energy needed to keep her vines alight even slightly drained her, and she knew she would need another burst before this was over. Jonathan did not seem to have tired at all. Though he kept himself at a wary distance, he did not fall behind in the way of a man growing weary.

She knew what he was doing. Running her to ground. Waiting for her to grow tired before he moved in for the kill. She didn't want to admit to herself that it might work.

Somewhere in the distance, she heard a dog bark.

With a frown, she looked away from the trees she was searching toward the sound. In the same instant the sound of a shot peeled through the ravine, and a musket ball tore through her arm just above her elbow.

Linette cried out and crumpled to her knees as pain ripped at her senses. Instinctively she covered the wound with her hand, but blood soaked her sleeve and seeped through her fingers. Her hand was shaking—her whole body was shaking.

She fought for control of herself. *Look at the wound.* She pulled her hand away and fought down bile at the sight of blood and torn, open flesh. But it was good news, what she saw. The musket ball had torn through skin and muscle but not shattered bone, and it had gone through her, slicing a gash through the outside of her arm rather than lodging itself within. She could wrap it up, stop the bleeding—

But he was coming now.

The sound of snapping branches and crunching snow alerted her. She looked up to see Jonathan crossing the distance between them at a rapid pace, faster than a walk, a little slower than a run. He wore the musket across his back in a sheath, but his hunting knife was in his hand. The sun glinted off it as he ran. She had no time.

Ignoring the pain as best she could, Linette turned, scrambled the rest of the way out of the ravine, and broke into a dead run.

Branches tore at her. Her light died—she didn't have the energy to keep it alive while she ran. Her arm ached and grew heavy, threatening to slow her down, to pull her down. Her sleeve was soaked, and her fingers grew sticky and dripped. She reached up to steady herself against a tree trunk, and when she pulled away again its grey bark was smeared red. She tried to keep running, but her footsteps grew more sluggish, and then she fell.

She didn't even know how she'd fallen—only that she lay sprawled on the earth, one hand grimy with dirt, splayed across a patch of moss, the other almost black with spilled blood. Her stomach heaved, and she rolled over and looked up at a patch of blue sky through the trees.

A shadow fell over her. Jonathan stepped into sight.

A dog was barking. Closer now.

She raised her good hand as though she could ward him off. "N … o," she got out. "Jonathan. No."

He raised the knife. She closed her eyes and summoned the light. This was the confrontation she'd been leading him toward, but it wasn't supposed to happen like this—with her already half-dead, already bleeding her life away in the snow. She didn't know if she could survive the blast of light.

But she called it up anyway. She felt the growing heat as light coursed through the veins in her arms, her hands, her legs, up her back and around her throat. She closed her eyes, loosed the light, and screamed.

Flooded with light as though a well had burst from beneath the ground, Jonathan staggered backward and dropped the knife. The poison in his vines surged, filling his body with pain and with heat. He dropped to his knees and opened his mouth in an incoherent cry of agony. His hand searched the ground for the knife he'd dropped.

Stop her. Kill her. Stop the light, drummed the voice inside.

Somehow, through the pain and confusion another voice seeped up. Why did he want to do this—to kill a helpless, injured woman in the woods, one who had trusted him and tried to help him when he was ill?

When had she become his enemy?

He stuffed the voice away. His hand closed around the knife hilt.

The light was dimming.

As the light shrank back, he could see again. He saw the woman lying unconscious before him, still glowing, but with a glow that died away as fast as the blood drained from the ugly wound in her arm. He could see the twisted arms of trees angled overhead and the clouds and rocks marring the landscape above and around them.

He knew she'd meant the light to incapacitate him completely, but she did not have the strength.

He snarled. What had been pain shooting through his vines congealed into a familiar heaviness, a throbbing presence that drove him and gave him strength. He pulled the knife back to plunge it into her heart. His thoughts narrowed to a single point.

Be rid of her, rid of the confusion she brought, rid of the light.

But before he could, a red-brown streak shot through the woods and positioned itself between him and Linette, barking.

Jonathan shook his head, confused. Rusty?

Rusty growled and showed his teeth. His ears flattened against his head, and he crouched, tail held high, like he was ready to attack.

Jonathan took a step back. He didn't understand.

The mongrel lowered its head even further ...

And then Linette's hand drifted up and took hold of Rusty's fur, clutching it like she would hold him back. Jonathan's eyes returned to her face. She was pale and unmoving, but her green eyes met Jonathan's and held him.

Held him fast.

"Jonathan," she said. "Come back."

His hand swam. His vision blurred and blanked in and out as though black swatches of cloth were being ripped apart inside his eyes. The little red dog still crouched between them, head lowered, teeth bared. At him.

The dog ... the dog was his friend.

"Come back," Linette said again.

The mountainside tilted, and Jonathan was a boy. He made his way up the pass, heart bursting with excitement, Rusty jogging along at his heels. It was summer. The pass invited him deep into the heart of the wilderness, toward the Outsider village ...

Away from his father.

Pain tore at his heart.

"Jonathan," a woman's voice said.

Linette.

He snapped back to the present and sank to his knees. A heavy hunting knife dropped from his hand. Suddenly he felt tired ... exhausted.

The hand clutching Rusty's fur let go and reached for him instead. Slender fingers grazed his cheek.

"Jonathan," Linette whispered, her voice little more than a rasp, "help me."

CHAPTER
21

Anoschi Pass—The New World

Amos Thatcher stumbled and slipped through the cold, snowy pass for a mile before he spotted a thin wisp of smoke coming from the trees below. His heart leaped. He'd found them.

Nearly tripping over his own feet in his haste to reach the little band they'd sent from the settlement, Amos found his thoughts crowded with possibilities. They were here, so they hadn't been killed or abducted by the Outsiders. Maybe there had been an accident? Maybe a storm? Maybe …

His thoughts halted along with his feet when he came upon the smoldering embers and the dead body of Smith Foster lying next to them.

Smith was alone. Blood soaked his clothing on the left side. Linette's heavy coat partially covered him.

Foreboding filled Amos, and with his feet rooted to the ground, he looked slowly around. Through the trees nearby he could make out another form—humped shoulders, a body lying face-down on the ground. From the size and black coat he recognized it as Cleveland.

They had been attacked after all. The Outsiders must have ambushed them after they left the village. Linette and Jonathan must have been abducted. He would go back and get a posse of men together, and …

Smith groaned.

The sound startled Amos so badly he dropped the rifle in his hands. He fell to his knees next to Smith.

"Smith! Smith, can you hear me? What happened?"

"Amos." Smith's eyes were barely open, but he reached up and clapped a surprisingly strong hand on Amos's arm. "Help me ... sit up."

Amos nodded. He slid an arm behind Smith's shoulders and lifted, and together they shifted Smith enough to lean him against the flat side of the boulder that sheltered the little spot beneath the trees. Smith groaned again and kept his eyes closed, but his mind seemed to be clearing. He waved Amos off when he tried to get a closer look at the wound.

"Linette ... wrapped it. Gotta ... find her."

"The Outsiders ..."

Smith shook his head with surprising vehemence. "Wasn't the Outsiders. Was Jonathan."

Amos didn't think he could have heard right. "What?"

"Jonathan, he's ... sick. Violent. He shot Cleveland and tried to kill Linette. I ... got in the way."

Panic rushed Amos, filling every one of his senses. He leaped to his feet, only vaguely aware of Smith grabbing at his pant leg like he would hold him back. "Where is she?" He looked wildly around, vainly searching the trees and sloping ground. "Where did she go?"

"Don't know. She ... ran. He's after her. Have to ... find her."

Fear pulsed in Amos's chest, but Smith grabbed a tighter hold of his pant leg. The farmer forced his eyes open wider and looked fiercely into Amos's. "Careful," he said. "He's dangerous."

"Jonathan, yes," Amos said.

"Shoot him ... on sight."

"What?"

"Shoot him!" Smith repeated. Spittle edged his bottom lip. He swallowed hard. "He's ... poisoned. Out of his mind. You have to kill him."

Amos's mouth opened with an objection, but he could not find words. He was a Trembler. A pacifist. His kind did not kill.

But if he found Jonathan threatening Linette …

A dog barked.

The sound took a moment to register. Then it did—for both of them. Amos and Smith turned their heads simultaneously, and both at once saw the little red mongrel running up the slope toward them, wagging its tail and barking.

Jonathan's dog.

What … ?

And then, behind the dog, a figure came through the trees.

No, two.

It was Jonathan. And he was carrying Linette in his arms. Her head lolled on his shoulder as though she were unconscious.

Or maybe dead.

Amos took off, straight toward them, not even able to gather his thoughts enough to know whether he should be drawing a weapon or preparing to help. He heard Smith shout his name behind him. But Jonathan began to run too, jogging across the uneven ground as soon as he saw them. There was no threat in the way he moved, no sign of aggression or enmity— only, rather, an exhaustion so deep it seemed like Jonathan was trying to outrun it.

Without speaking a word, Jonathan transferred Linette into Amos's arms before collapsing on the ground. He curled his legs up toward his waist with a groan.

Amos looked down into Linette's pale face. Her clothing was blood-soaked. One arm was layered in it, congealed and dark but with fresh blood still flowing bright red over it. Her eyes were open but seemed to want to roll back into her head. She fixed them on Amos.

Trying to tell him something.

"What is it?" he asked softly. He wanted to weep. And to hold her closer. To save her, somehow.

And he didn't know if he could.

"Help … him," she said.

Amos blinked. He transferred his gaze to Jonathan, who had curled up in a ball on the ground. His shoulders shook. He was crying.

Jonathan looked up into Amos's face unexpectedly. Tear tracks lined the dirt on his face. "Kill me," he said. "Please, kill me, before it comes back."

A hand tightened on Amos's arm—Linette's good hand. "No," she said.

Slowly, Amos lowered Linette to the ground. He crouched between them—the killer on one side, rolled into a ball with tears streaming down his face; and his victim on the other. Amos looked up, needing help. Needing someone besides himself to make the decisions here.

Smith, still sitting against the boulder, shook his head at him. "Amos," he croaked out, his voice carrying through the still winter air. "Amos, kill him!"

Oblivious to the question at hand, Rusty trotted around Jonathan's rocking form and began to lick the tears from his master's face.

Amos's rifle still lay back by the embers at Smith's feet where he had dropped it. He reached a shaking hand into his boot to withdraw a hunting knife. Jonathan had killed Cleveland—the faithful old Trembler's body lay nearby, a hulking backdrop to the scene. He had incapacitated Smith and from the looks of things, nearly killed Linette. Perhaps he *had* killed her. She was still bleeding. How much longer could she last?

If he was truly responsible for this, he was a monster. He needed to die. He *wanted* to die.

Amos's hand trembled. He and Jonathan were nearly the same age— Amos was just a year older. They had both come to the valley as boys, had grown up side by side. They had helped cut the first trees and plow the first fields. They had raised the meeting house together, both sitting perched high in the rafters on the frame, young men with daring and energy. They had never been good friends. Jonathan's father, Jeconiah, made no bones about his anti-Trembler sentiments. He believed in the political vision of Jerusalem Valley but did not want his boy growing close to a Trembler.

Yet, there had always been something in the son that Amos admired. His conviction—his spirit. As much as he had followed in his father's foot-steps, becoming a preacher at the kirk and continuing to uphold the doctrines of the Puritani, he had carved his own path too. He had been the only one in the valley with the courage to cross the pass to the Outsiders. He had preached things Amos didn't agree with, but he preached them with sincerity—with all his heart.

Amos still remembered the night Jonathan's father had died. He'd watched the young man, the only one in the valley who could have been his brother, go out alone into the night to mourn, and he'd wished things were different and that he could offer comfort.

Now the proud young man lay in the frosted mud and cried, and Amos was supposed to put a knife in him.

He couldn't do it.

"Amos."

He turned his gaze away from the young preacher. Linette's green eyes held his. "Amos, help him."

What did she mean? Did she—could she—mean that she wanted him to kill too—that Jonathan could only be helped by death? Bile rose in his throat at the thought.

But no. That wasn't what she meant. An expression crossed her face as she looked at him—almost a smile, despite the pain and the terrible weakness she displayed.

She closed her eyes.

And golden light began to emanate from her.

It rose from where she lay and spread across the ground in a circle, taking both Amos and Jonathan within its rays. He looked at Jonathan, and his eyes grew wide as the young preacher's skin grew translucent and he saw, running all through his body, black veins of poison—spidering from his heart through his vines and to every part of his body.

But no ... not from his heart.

From ... something else.

And then Amos saw himself going to Jonathan and rolling him over, sitting him up. He saw himself tying Jonathan's hands behind his back and securing his ankles to each other and then to a tree. He saw himself carrying Linette away with Rusty staying behind to guard his master.

He blinked. The light died away, plunging the forest back into its normal winter interplay of shadows and brightness. The vision was gone.

"Just … until you can come … back for him," Linette got out.

Then her eyes closed, and it seemed to Amos like another light went out.

Desperately afraid, he knelt over her and laid his hand on her cheek, then her throat, checking for a pulse. He found one—but it was faint. He clutched her good arm, wanting to do something—anything. His tears fell on her face, and he cursed himself for being so weak.

Amos didn't know when he'd begun to feel so much for Linette. Or even what these feelings were. He just knew he couldn't let her die out here.

That resolution galvanized him. He looked around, eyes suddenly sharp. His mother, God rest her soul, had taught him what she knew about healing. He could find something to help stop the bleeding. Something to patch her up. To give her a chance.

And then he was going to carry her home.

Jerusalem Valley Settlement—The New World

Sarah was in the fields gleaning the last of the corn from the Mosses' ruined harvest when she heard a ragged voice shouting her name.

"Sarah! John! Anybody! Help me! Sarah!"

She gathered her skirt and ran toward the voice, heart in her throat. Was it Smith?

Through the early dusk she could make out a tall, spindly figure staggering through the fields from the pass. It wasn't Smith, it was Amos. When had he gone out there? And who was he carrying? She let her feet carry her forward toward the answers and fairly burst upon Amos. In the shadows it took a moment to recognize the blood soaking both him and Linette.

"Dear God," she said.

Sarah swallowed back revulsion and fear as she reached for Linette, moving the edges of Amos's coat back enough to see the recently bound wound above her elbow. Strips of cloth torn from someone's clothing had been tied tightly around her arm, holding some type of poultice in place, but blood had saturated the bindings.

"Musket ball, I think," Amos said. "Hit something it shouldn't have hit."

Sarah looked over her shoulder and yelled for her sons, simultaneously gathering Linette out of Amos's arms. He let go only reluctantly. He was shaking from the exertion of carrying her all this way, and breathing like a winded stag. He must have run a mile.

"Where's Smith?" Sarah asked as she shifted Linette's weight into her arms and nodded to her boys as they arrived. Martin took Linette's legs, helping Sarah carry her.

"He's alive," Amos said. "He's going to be all right. We need to go get him."

Sarah closed her eyes for a half-second. She wanted to know everything, and she wanted to know it now. But she knew, from the state Linette was in and from the mix of grit and fear in Amos's eyes, that there was no time for that.

"Samuel, get John Hopewell," Sarah told her other son. "Tell him to call all the men to the meeting house. Amos, go find the governor and tell him everything. He's in his office."

"What about …"

"I'm taking her home. I'll do everything I can for her. From the looks of it, you've already done a good job patching her." Sarah looked down at Linette's wound again and felt the blood drain from her own face. She took a deep breath. *Steady.* "Go, Amos. Send the men to get Smith and do whatever else you need to do, and then send Samuel back to me to tell me everything. Understand?"

Amos nodded. Without another word, he turned and ran through the dusk toward the meeting house.

Sarah watched him go with a heart that was suddenly bleak. She could imagine too many possibilities for what had happened out there in the pass or beyond it, and none of them bode well for the valley. *Smith.* She shook her head. Amos had said he was all right.

She could do nothing for now but try to save Linette.

CHAPTER

22

Province of Tempestano—The Old World

Carlos sat in a chair in his library. His arms were tied tightly to the arms of the chair, his legs to its legs. Heat from a roaring fire in the hearth crackled on his swollen face. Blood dripped from his lip, but he could not wipe it away.

Elder Crispin barely cast him a glance as he entered the room and poured himself a glass of wine.

Finished, he raised the glass in Carlos's direction and smiled. "Cheers," he said, and drank the wine down.

Carlos watched him. Silently.

Crispin put the goblet down and smacked his lips loudly. "Delicious. Only the best, no, Conde? Only the best for traitors and treasonous princes."

"You should talk," Carlos forced past his swollen lip.

"You should know I didn't actually order them to break your face. You must have provoked them."

Carlos glared at him but said nothing.

He could hardly remember what he'd said or done when Crispin's men brought him here. He'd raged. He'd grieved. His heart had been torn in pieces, and he knew with certainty that all was lost. Not only were a hundred or more Tremblers dead, the rest had only hours to flee before Crispin would unleash his full wrath upon them.

And the presence of Tremblers openly, blatantly gathering in the province, clearly sanctioned by Carlos's own authorities, had given Crispin the proof he needed to remove Carlos from power. The neighboring princes, and the synod that controlled them, would take over.

Carlos had lost. He didn't understand how, but he had lost. And people who had trusted him, who had put their lives and futures in his hands, were dead.

He clenched his fingers into tight fists. He almost welcomed the pain in his face. He deserved it.

What would Serena think, if she could see him now?

Crispin leaned back against the small table, regarding Carlos smugly. "I don't have to explain to you what all this means, do I?" Crispin asked.

"Are you waiting for me to lash out at you?" Carlos answered. "I don't see any reason to give you the satisfaction. I know what you've done. You'll answer to God for it, not to me."

"Is that so?" Crispin moved so he stood directly in front of Carlos. He still held the wine goblet in his hand, loosely, carelessly. "So you know I've clearly implicated you in the hiding and abetting of religious factions? Not that it took much effort. Unlike your sister, you are actually guilty."

Carlos knew—he *knew*—the words were meant to get a reaction.

And though he hated himself for it, they did.

"What about Serena?"

"You were allowing them—hundreds of them!—to meet here in plain sight. Did you really think your neighbors would not jump at the chance to invade?"

Carlos pulled against his restraints as though he could tear himself free and attack the man in front of him. "What about Serena?"

"Temper," Crispin said.

"Tell me what you're talking about!"

"Very well." Crispin set the goblet down and crouched so he was eye-to-eye with Carlos. "Do *you* know where your sister is?"

Carlos opened his mouth, momentarily stopped. It seemed clear that

Crispin knew. If Carlos played along, he would learn more. But what if he was wrong? What if Crispin didn't know what Serena was doing, and this conversation was meant to get it out of him?

Crispin rolled his eyes slightly. "Let me help you begin. Serena is in the New World, on her way to Jerusalem Valley. At least, that is the plan. No?"

Carlos decided his desire to know overran any need for discretion. Even if he did give away something he shouldn't—unlikely, considering how little he actually knew—it would be months before Crispin could send anyone or anything across the ocean to interfere with Serena's mission.

"Yes," Carlos said.

"Why?" Crispin asked.

He knew—he had to know. Carlos would play along.

"She went to stop a man you sent from murdering Melrose. Someone called the Reaper."

Crispin chuckled. He straightened his legs and stood to his full height. "Serena will not stop the Reaper."

"So sure?" Carlos asked. "You have a history of underestimating her."

"Serena will never stop the Reaper," Crispin went on, "because I already did. I killed him myself, two days after I let him out of prison."

Confusion filled Carlos's heart. He knew it was reflected on his face. "What?"

"The man was a murderer, a beast of a human being. I sent him to a well-deserved meeting with his Maker."

"But Serena …"

"Serena thinks she's chasing the Reaper across the ocean, yes, I know," Crispin said. "She's wrong. Actually, she's going to murder Melrose her-self—to help murder him anyway, anyway. So plainly and so horrifically that Jerusalem Valley will not possibly be able to continue its independence any longer. A military takeover will be clearly necessary."

"I don't understand," Carlos said. He almost wanted to laugh. "Serena is no killer. She would never help you, not even unknowingly."

"She is already helping me," Crispin said, "more than you can imagine.

No, you're right, Serena wouldn't do the deed herself. Instead, she's ushering a murderer right to the valley, right into the bosom of Herman Melrose … because Melrose trusts her, more fool he. And soon the news will spread across the New World, and then reach us here in the Old: that Serena Vaquero, the infamous Trembler from Tempestano, colluded with the Hierarchy to destroy the last best hope of mankind. So much for tolerance."

Carlos's head was swimming. "The Hierarchy? What are you talking about?"

"Do you think the Sacramenti are just sitting idly by while we fight over the future of the world?" Crispin snapped. "They have been biding their time behind the scenes, moving players into place and preparing to rise again."

"It's impossible," Carlos said. "They've been defeated."

"You've heard of the Imitators?"

"Their order of fanatics and spies? Of course."

"One of those fanatics and spies has been ordered to murder Herman Melrose and set up a Sacramenti takeover in Jerusalem Valley. As it happens, he was on the same ship you put your sister on."

"How can you possibly know that?" Carlos asked. "The secret dealings of the Hierarchy … how can you know them?"

"I have spies of my own." There was a weight to his tone—like Carlos was meant to understand more by these words than he did.

He shook his head, dazed. "I still don't understand what you're saying."

"That's because," Crispin said, shaking a finger at Carlos like he was lecturing a poor student, "you fail to understand the significance of that settlement. You think we, Puritani and Sacramenti, are content to fight over the scraps of the Old World when there is an entirely new horizon, an entirely new beginning to be shaped? The New World is the future. I understand that. The Hierarchy understand it. Melrose understands it."

"What does the New World have to do with you? It's already under governance."

"Poor governance."

"Phinehas Cole is one of you. Puritani of the finest order."

Crispin looked disgusted. "Puritani of the worst kind … the fanatical kind. I thought Cole could be trusted, but he's got too much of an independent streak. He's been angling for some time for a new model of kirk governance, with the congregations breaking away from synod control. He would take the unity of our movement and break it into a thousand kirk-sized fractions. And then there's his penchant for embracing 'causes' … abolition of the black slaves, educating the Outsiders. No, Cole has served his purpose and will not serve it much longer. I told him Serena was coming, of course—ordered him to execute her. But he will not be able to hold her. I've seen to that too. And when he fails, I will charge him with secretly helping her to escape. And then there's Melrose, governor of Jerusalem Valley by the gift of Angleland's king. The greatest mistake of all, and the greatest opportunity. When the dream of Jerusalem Valley falls, when it comes to a decisive end, control of the New World will fall with it—from Angleland, and from New Cranwell, to me."

Carlos shook his head. "And Serena? I still don't understand what she has to do with all of this."

"Serena will do exactly what I want her to do," Crispin smirked. "She will fascinate the Imitator, befriend him, and trust him. She'll take him straight to Melrose, and when he carries out his task and murders Brother Herman, the whole world will know that the Tremblers and Sacramenti have joined in an unholy union. All the Trembler speech about peace and tolerance and a new era of living by side by side—it will all be seen to be a lie, nothing but a cloak to cover up the activities of the Hierarchy. We Puritani will have no choice but to move against the settlement and take over—and to launch a full-scale inquisition to eradicate both Tremblers and Sacramenti from both worlds. People think the Wars for Truth were a blight. The blight is only that we didn't finish them. We should have wiped out every last one of our enemies while we had the chance. I intend to give us a second opportunity."

"But you can't control all of that!" Carlos said. The enormity of what was happening was beginning to dawn on him, along with the sinking feeling that Serena truly was into something much more deeply than even she knew. But Crispin's plan … how could it possibly be relied upon to work? He needed Serena to befriend the Imitator and take him to the valley. He needed Serena to escape from Cole, he needed them both to reach the valley against all obstacles, and he needed the Imitator to act successfully on a supposed plan to assassinate Melrose.

"Your plan ... there are too many factors, too many pieces outside of your control."

Crispin smiled. "You misunderstand me. I do not control anyone, Conde. I find tools and I manipulate them. And your sister is an excellent tool."

Carlos closed his eyes. Something Crispin had earlier said was drumming through his head, making his beaten face throb. *I have spies of my own.*

The last missing piece clicked in Carlos's mind. He remembered Diego turning to him just before the soldiers began to massacre the Tremblers gathered at the tavern. *I'm sorry,* he had said.

A tear ran down Carlos's face. It stung all the way down.

"Yes," Crispin said. "You've lost. You, your Tremblers, your sister. Your movement. I am about to wipe the Tremblers from Kepos Gé forever—to purify the world for good. I have just one more execution to order for today. Would you like to say anything more before you die? To me ... or perhaps to your faithful captain?"

In the corner of his vision, Carlos saw Diego step out of the shadows. He could not read the look on his friend's face. His friend, the man who had lied to him, who had not warned the Tremblers to leave at all, who had led Crispin right to them.

He did want to say one thing more. To ask a question. To ask why.

But he could not bring himself to say the word, for he did not think he could bear the answer.

Instead he simply hung his head. Other soldiers came out of the shadows, and rough hands grabbed his shoulders.

Fire Within, he prayed, *receive my soul.*

And please ... help Serena.

The Wilderness, west of New Cranwell—The New World

Two feet of snow fell overnight while Serena, Jacques, Eben, and Josiah slept in an abandoned trapper's cabin on the edge of a lake in the wilderness. Serena woke early, crept to the window, and looked out at a breathtaking world blanketed in white. She caught her breath and whispered a word of worship at the beauty of it. A pair of birds, electric blue in color, dove from a tree branch and chased one another through the air and back to the branches. She laughed.

"That will not be easy to cross."

She jumped. Jacques's voice behind her was grim—a far contrast to her own mood.

"It's beautiful," she said.

"It's thick. It will slow us down—too much. We will not be able to keep up with the soldiers."

"So maybe today is the day?"

She turned to look at him in the gloom of the cabin. He was as tall and handsome as ever, but his face looked gaunt. The anxiety of all that had happened since they reached New Cranwell weighed heavy on him. His hair had grown longer and more untrimmed over the last several weeks, so that but for his fine leather gloves, he almost looked the part of a frontiersman.

She finished her thought. "Maybe today we get ourselves captured and ride the rest of the way to the valley."

He shook his head. "It's too soon. They might send a detachment to take us back to the city instead of going on to Fort Collins. We can't risk that."

She nodded. He was right, of course—not that she minded. She was not yet travel-weary enough to make the thought of being bundled into a small prison beneath the deck of a riverboat and made to ride in darkness the rest of the way to Jerusalem Valley sound attractive. They would find some other solution to the problem and keep going on foot.

"Well, then, we'll just have to find a way."

Jacques grimaced. "You don't seem to appreciate that we have a real problem here. The snow will slow us far too much."

She looked askance at him. When had his mood soured so much? "I appreciate it," she said. "I just choose not to worry. I have faith."

She stressed the last word and didn't miss the annoyance in his expression. Good. She'd meant that to dig at him. She didn't know what exactly Imitators believed, but she knew they claimed some kind of faith in the Creator just like everybody else. About time he activated his.

Belatedly, she realized he didn't deserve her accusations. Jacques had acted with more faith, and faithfulness too, throughout this journey than most men showed in their lifetimes.

She opened her mouth to apologize, but Eben interrupted. He pulled the door open from outside, letting in a blast of cold air and ice crystals that blew in and danced in the cabin's interior. The cold burned Serena's lungs and made her throat constrict. Eben dusted snow off his legs and coat as he shut the door behind him. She hadn't realized he was outside.

"What you two on about?"

Jacques swept his hand to indicate the pristine panorama on the other side of the door and window. "The snow. It's going to slow us down too much."

"A little," Eben said. "Till we finish these." He nodded to a handful of something Serena hadn't noticed. Strips of leather?

"What is that?" Jacques asked.

"Rawhide," Eben said. "Lucky for us, trapper left it here, gettin' nice and seasoned. Just gotta cut us some good strong ash and soak it and dry it for a while. Lace it up with rawhide and we got us shoes that will walk right over the snow. Learned it from some Outsiders on my way up from the south."

"How long will it take to finish them?" Jacques asked.

"Few days."

"Days?" Jacques straightened like someone had shot lightning through him. "We don't have days. If we don't keep up with those soldiers, we'll end up stranded out here for the winter. We can't survive that."

Eben regarded him sideways. "Speak for yourself, white man."

"Jacques," Serena said, trying to relieve some of the tension, "maybe the snow will melt."

"Just gonna fall again," Eben said. He'd turned his back on them and was searching the walls for something. After a moment he found it: he took a hatchet down from its place over the doorway and hefted it in his hand. "We take a few days and make shoes, we can move fast. Don't have to stop every time the weather say so. We don' take these few days, we end up bogged down in the snow and never catch up with the soldiers. That what you want?"

"There has to be another way," Jacques said.

Eben lifted the hatchet in a half-salute. "Goin' out to cut wood with my boy. You figure out another way; we get the shoes ready."

He walked out without another word. Looking around the cabin, Serena realized Josiah was gone too. Both had gotten up and left the cabin before she or Jacques were even awake.

"He might be right," she said. "If we lose a few days only to gain more later, we'll come out ahead."

Jacques shook his head. "We'll fall too far behind. We might even lose them. It's bad enough that they're on a boat and we're on foot. This whole plan is too full of holes."

"We didn't have a better one," Serena offered. He looked up at her, and she smiled—trying to make peace. "We knew it might not work when we decided to do it. But then, you and I … we are doing a lot of things that might not work. Trusting that the Fire … that the Creator is guiding us. So far we have crossed an ocean, you have escaped a prison and gotten me out of one, and we are on the road to the valley. I am not going to allow a snowfall or a few days' delay make me believe we're not going to make it."

He stared at her for a moment before nodding, and the ghost of a smile reached his lips. "You are right," he said.

"I didn't thank you," she said.

He looked up. "For what?"

"For saving my life in New Cranwell. For risking your own life to come back for me."

He smiled fully then. "Did you think I would abandon you?"

"I wouldn't have blamed you if you had."

"Yes, you would have."

She laughed. "Maybe. I'm not known for being reasonable. You didn't have to come back for me. You could have gone on alone."

"You were never meant to do this alone," Jacques said. "Like you, I have a mission in Jerusalem Valley. But part of it is accompanying you. Helping you."

And why is that? Serena wanted to ask. *Your superiors sent you to the valley. Why?*

But those were questions she knew she couldn't ask … or at least, that she couldn't expect him to answer. Instead she said, "I didn't ask you how you escaped from Cole."

"It was Eben," Jacques said. "He was working on the docks where they delivered me to be put in irons on board a ship. I tried to bribe the soldiers to let me go—with an appeal to conscience, and then with money. They did not listen. Eben did. He and his son snuck aboard the ship and released me. Don't ask me how they managed all the details of that."

"Did they take the money?" Serena asked, curious.

"Didn't want it." It was Eben—returned, and lurking in the doorway again. He leaned against the doorframe with his arms folded. Josiah stood behind him with his hands full of something that looked to Serena like the outline of a large and unwieldy basket.

Eben smiled. "All I wanted was a new life. Get outta New Cranwell and go somewhere better. For me and my boy. Didn't think I could do it alone. You folks gave me a way out."

"You mentioned Jerusalem Valley when you appealed to the soldiers?" Serena asked Jacques.

He shrugged. "Appealing to conscience. I told them I needed to reach the valley with an important message for Governor Melrose. Many in this city believe in Melrose's vision."

"Do you have a message for Governor Melrose?"

Something flickered in his eyes at that. She couldn't read it.

"You do," was all he said.

"Melrose may be crazy," Eben said, "but I'm hopin' he'll let us be crazy with him. World needs a new start." He broke into a wide smile. "And we got one. Show 'em, boy."

Josiah held up his armful of wood. He held what appeared to be teardrop-shaped frames of polished wood.

"Shoe frames. Don't have to wait days after all," Eben said triumphantly. "Trapper must have been plannin' to sell 'em, 'cause they's enough for all of us. Just gimme an hour to lace 'em up and we be on our way."

"Are we stealing the trapper's work?" Serena asked, frowning.

A shadow passed over Eben's face. "Won't make no difference to him."

"But these must be valuable. They …"

"I said, it won't make no difference." Eben exchanged a troubled glance with his son. "We found 'im. Out by the lake. Man's dead."

Serena swallowed. "Oh."

"What killed him?" Jacques asked. "Something we should worry about?"

"Nothin' we can catch. Musket ball in his gut. Got in a fight, that's all."

"Could it have been Outsiders?" Serena asked, fear pricking at her skin. They hadn't talked about the presence of the others in the wilderness—others who were neither Trembler nor Puritani nor Sacramenti, but foreign and possibly hostile. Hadn't talked about it because it wasn't a kind of trouble they were equipped to deal with. There was no sense in dwelling on the possibilities.

"No," Eben said sharply.

"How can you be sure?" Jacques asked.

"I'm sure. Told you, I've known Outsiders. Learned from 'em. This wasn't their work."

Jacques gave Serena a knowing look. She read it well. He didn't trust Eben's assessment in this regard.

Once they strapped on the shoes and began their journey through the snowy world, they would be on their guard even more than before.

CHAPTER
23

Jerusalem Valley Settlement—The New World

Laying Linette down on the rough-hewn dining room table Smith had built for his family, Sarah moved the bandages and poultice Amos had applied, exposing the wide-open gash through Linette's arm, just above the elbow. She caught a glimpse of exposed veins and bone before the bleeding started again. Her stomach threatened to revolt, and she threw a hand up to cover her mouth.

"Letty," she called out to her daughter in the doorway, "boil water and bring me a needle and thread. Quickly."

Letty nodded and turned on her heel, running to the kitchen to obey. Linette convulsed with pain, and Sarah moved to her head and brushed Linette's hair back from her pale forehead.

"It's all right," she said. "It's going to be all right."

She wished it wasn't such a lie.

"Sarah," Linette got out, "don't let them … hurt him."

"Hurt who?" Sarah asked.

"Jonathan," Linette said.

Confusion covered Sarah's features. "What are you talking about? Linette, who did this to you?"

"Jonathan … did it."

"No. No, it couldn't have been. It was the Outsiders, it …"

Somehow, Linette found the energy to shake her head vehemently. "Tell them not to hurt him. We can save him. I … saw it. In the light. Tell them."

"Listen, Linette," Sarah said. "I don't know what happened to you out there, but I can't leave you to go tell them anything. If we don't close this wound up properly you're going to bleed to death."

Linette smiled. "You always tell the truth," she said.

Something about Linette's sudden clarity, sudden cohesion, scared Sarah. She had the sense that this was the moment of calm before death.

Linette reached up her good hand and clutched Sarah's elbow.

"You can't close the wound," she said. "He hit an artery. I'm going to bleed to death."

"Not if I can stop it," Sarah said.

"You can't."

"I'm going to try!" Sarah pulled away angrily. Linette was a traitor to the Puritani cause and a constant source of pain to her heart, but that didn't mean she was just going to let her bleed out on the table.

"Not like this," Linette said. "You can't sew it up. Have to … sear it shut."

"You're not in your right mind," Sarah said. "We can't possibly …"

"I can do it. With the light."

Sarah stopped and stared. Deep in her heart, she knew Linette was right. "Do it then," she said. "Use the light."

Linette shook her head weakly. "Don't have enough strength. I need your help."

"Mine?" Sarah asked.

She didn't understand.

And yet, somehow … she did.

Linette closed her eyes. Her grasp on Sarah's elbow tightened.

And Sarah closed her eyes in return, surrendered to the grasp, and closed her hand over Linette's elbow as well.

Deep inside, Sarah felt something awaken. Something alive—something seeking. An energy inside of her pulsed. She could feel her vines expanding and contracting, the life in them moving toward Linette.

The vines at her wrists began to grow. They crept further out of her skin and found the thick vine at Linette's elbow, twisted themselves together with it, and began to root themselves in the mass of muscle, tendon, and vine that surrounded Linette's bones. After them, the vines at Sarah's elbow stretched out and connected with the vines at Linette's wrist.

They bowed their heads, life connected to life.

Sarah gritted her teeth as her vines began to send strength and vitality out of her toward the great need in Linette. Linette's grasp grew stronger, her breathing deeper and more regular. It was working.

"Now," Sarah whispered.

In answer, Linette let the light inside of her blaze out.

Sarah cried out as fire and light rushed up through her vines, filling her body, filling her heart. Her nails dug into Linette's skin as she fought to maintain the hold. Behind her eyelids, she felt as though she were staring into the sun.

Linette let go. Sarah's vines retracted, and she slumped forward onto the table.

"Mother!" Letty rushed into the room and grabbed Sarah's shoulders. Sarah reached up and covered her hand.

"It's all right."

She opened her eyes and lifted her head. Linette's eyes were still closed, but she was breathing regularly, strongly—and there was a smile on her face.

Sarah looked breathlessly to Linette's arm. The wound was closed. A bright red and white line like a burn scar ran the length of it.

The bleeding had stopped.

"It worked," Sarah said.

"What just happened?" Letty asked.

"I'm not sure," Sarah said. "But it worked." A smile of wonder crept over her face—wonder and gratitude. Somehow they had just beaten death back from the threshold.

Maybe they could do it again.

Maybe they would *have to* do it again.

She tightened her hand over Letty's fingers. "Letty, run for the meeting house. Tell the men that whatever they do, they can't hurt Jonathan."

"What?" Letty asked. Her voice broke with fear and confusion.

"I'll follow you," Sarah said. "I have to make sure Linette's all right. But get there. Don't let them send a posse without promising they won't hurt Jonathan."

Letty nodded. "O-okay."

"Good girl." Sarah smiled at her oldest daughter, willing her to take courage. "Now go."

Letty nodded again, then turned and ran from the cabin.

Sarah watched her go, the smile on her face giving way to a heavy seriousness.

She turned back to regard Linette. She appeared to be sleeping.

"Dear Creator," Sarah prayed aloud. "I don't know what's happening. But we need your help."

She took a step toward the kitchen, but her foot didn't quite find the floor. She was only vaguely aware that she was falling before everything went black.

Letty ran across the fields as fast as her legs would carry her and burst in on a gathering of every man in the valley—as many, at least, as Amos Thatcher had been able to find. There were a dozen or so of them, mostly armed or carrying pitchforks or hoes, in from working the fields as late as possible. They stood around the meeting house and Governor Melrose. John Hopewell held the reins of a mule. Though Letty was not versed in the procedures of posse-forming, it looked to her like they were about to leave.

"Wait!" she shouted. "Wait, please wait!"

She stopped and nearly doubled over as she tried to catch her breath. Governor Melrose held up a concerned hand, stopping whatever proceedings from carrying on. "What is it, Letty?"

"You can't … you can't hurt Jonathan," she panted.

She didn't miss the looks that passed between the governor, John, and Amos Thatcher. In a rush, it seemed to her that she was surrounded by the enemy. These men were all Tremblers. They had all opposed Jonathan in the past. He'd warned her against their ways. They had all the power now—but she wouldn't let them abuse it.

"I won't let you!" she yelled, straightening. A hand pressed down on her shoulder. Governor Melrose.

"Peace, little one," he said. "We're not going to hurt him."

"You're not?" she asked.

"Amos has told us what happened and that Linette believes Jonathan can be helped. We'll do our best for him."

Letty blinked back tears and sucked in gasps of air. The turnaround confused her, and she realized how in the dark she herself was. She *didn't* know what had happened—what they were talking about. Why her mother had sent her. She felt like a child and wished someone would explain it all to her.

Jonathan would, if he were here.

As though the discussion were closed, Governor Melrose nodded to the handful of men around the mule. Amos and John were among them. "Get going," he said. "The sooner you reach Smith, the better."

Smith? "What about Father?" Letty asked.

The governor's hand pressed even more heavily on her shoulder. He meant it to comfort her, but she felt trapped.

"I'll explain everything," Herman said. "First we need to let these men go."

Letty nodded tearfully. "As long as you promise."

Amos stopped and faced her. He bent so he was at eye level with her. His gaze behind his spectacles was utterly earnest. He was a lot more handsome, Letty thought, than she'd ever realized. She'd always thought of Amos as the scarecrow Trembler who lived across the valley and who seemed more comfortable in the governor's office than he did in the fields. But the look on his face in this moment changed something in her opinion of him, and she knew it would never go back.

"I promise," he said. "We're going to bring back your father and Jonathan. We'll do everything we can for them. I will."

She nodded. "Thank you."

Amos glanced up at Herman Melrose before dropping his voice and asking, "Is Linette …"

"She's …" Letty searched for words. "She's all right. Mother stopped the bleeding. She's sleeping, I think."

How to explain what she'd seen and heard in the cabin before Sarah sent her away? The blast of bright, hot light? The vines growing between Sarah and Linette, pulsing with energy before they retracted again? The fear and wonder on her mother's face—her mother, who was never startled or awed by anything?

She couldn't.

So she didn't try. The men said a few good-byes and headed off toward the pass in the gathering gloom.

"It's dark," she said.

"Yes," Herman answered.

"I thought it wasn't safe to travel through the pass in the dark. Last time Linette went with them to light the way."

"Yes," Herman said again. "But your father's been hurt, Letty. And Jonathan's … not well. We don't want to risk leaving them up there alone. The men will find them, tend to them, and stay with them until daylight when they can bring them back. It will be slow getting to them with only torchlight, but if they go carefully it's better than leaving them overnight."

Letty shivered and wrapped her arms around herself. "I wish Linette could go with them again."

"So do I," Herman said. "But she's already given all she has this time, I think."

He smiled at Letty. His hand, still on her shoulder, had stopped feeling like a weight and felt more like the comfort it was meant to be. "Come into the office, Letty," he said. "I'll tell you all I know."

Letty shook her head. "I think you'd better walk back to the cabin with me. Mother might need me, and … and there's something else you should know."

Herman sat holding Linette's hand. Sarah had moved her onto a pile of skins and blankets in the corner of the dining room and now leaned against the wall opposite them, arms folded at her waist—listening as Linette recounted the story of what had happened in the pass. Linette was still pale and her voice weak, but she was visibly growing stronger by the hour.

"The Outsiders agreed to help us," Linette said, "but only once. They don't want to chance coming into contact with the poison."

The fire flickered across Herman's features, accenting the troubled expression there. "And they believe we brought this poison with us—that the beasts had not begun to appear before we settled here?"

"That's what they said."

"I don't understand how that's possible. We came here to plant a work of God, not to bring witchcraft. Could some of the settlers ..." He shook his shaggy head as though to beat back his own suspicions. "No. We would know. I would know."

Sarah shifted against the wall. "Governor, respectfully, there is much going on here that we don't know anything about. I don't believe any of the settlers are practicing witchcraft. But Linette saw something in Jonathan. Something I don't understand but that we need to pay attention to."

"Linette?" Melrose asked.

"I saw a seed," she said. "Planted in his heart. Not the vine-seed, but one that was sending out tendrils of poison that fed into his vines. The poison in him didn't come from something on the outside ... the bear. It's coming from inside him."

"And you could see this?"

"When I let the light shine, to protect myself ... it showed me what was happening inside him."

"Didn't you already do that here? When he was sick?"

"I used the light to reveal the poison in his vines, but I didn't go deeper than that. When he attacked me, the light just ... burst out. So strong it revealed more. I didn't mean to look, but I couldn't help seeing what I saw. I showed it to Amos as well. At least, I think he could see it."

Herman held his head in his hands. "So we've sent our men to bring back someone with a poisonous seed in his heart that turns him into a murderous monster without warning."

Linette struggled to sit up higher. Herman helped her, and she leaned up against the wall. "I think we can help him," she said. "Uproot the seed somehow. Even Capenokanickon thought it might be possible to reach him. We have to try."

"We're not meant to go digging around in the souls of other people," Herman said.

"We're not meant to see into them either," Sarah said, pushing herself off the wall, "but we did. Governor, I think we must view this as a gift of the Creator. Linette's light has shown us what we could not have otherwise seen. Can it be a coincidence that she came to us when she did—just in time to help us see what is in Jonathan's heart?"

The governor shook his head slowly. "But what do you want us to do, Sarah? Try to dig the seed out with a surgeon's knife? He wouldn't survive. I promised your daughter we wouldn't hurt him. I can't allow some kind of butchery even if it seems to be our only hope."

"Maybe we can heal him by joining vines," Sarah said. "We told you what happened with Linette ... I was able to share enough life energy to power her light. Maybe if we connect into Jonathan's vine network in the same way we can send him some kind of healing."

"Or maybe his poison will come flooding into you," Herman said sharply. "No. I'm grateful for whatever you and Linette were able to do to save a life, but I won't allow either of you to risk yours. Or anyone else either. The last thing we need is this spreading."

He patted Linette's hand, then stood. "When the men come back we'll put Jonathan into quarantine."

"You'll have to keep him restrained," Linette said. "And guarded."

"Of course."

"And then what?" Sarah asked.

"I don't know," Governor Melrose said.

The governor left, and Sarah went to the window to watch him go. She turned and wiped her hands on her apron.

"Thank you," she said brusquely.

"For what?" Linette asked.

"For protecting Jonathan's life. You don't owe us that, you know."

"I didn't do it out of debt," Linette said. "I did it because he needs help."

"Well," Sarah said. "I suppose I'm just surprised you feel that way."

"You aren't my enemies," Linette said. "And I'm not yours."

Sarah stood without moving for a moment as though she couldn't decide what to do or say next. Then she turned and headed for the kitchen. Linette said nothing more ... for a few minutes.

Then she drew herself up on the makeshift bed and called out quietly, "Sarah."

Sarah reappeared in the doorway from the kitchen. "What is it? What do you need?"

"Nothing. I'm fine. I just wanted to know who will preach at the kirk now that Jonathan is ill?"

Sarah's lips tightened. "I don't know. No one. The synod will have to send us someone."

Linette shook her head. Something was bothering her, deep inside. A strong sense that the kirk could not be left bereft at a time like this.

"You do it," she said.

Sarah straightened her already straight posture, clearly startled. "What are you talking about? Women don't do that."

"You know the Book better than any of them," Linette said. "I know you do. You can't leave the kirk without the Word. Not right now."

"They have the Book," Sarah said. "They can read it for themselves."

"If they will," Linette said. "Are you sure they will? You can't let them go without seeds. They need to be strengthened. They need to be given life."

Sarah shook her head. "Linette, what are you talking about? You're delirious."

"I'm not. I know I sound it. I don't completely understand what I'm feeling. But the seed ... the seed inside Jonathan. Someone planted it there.

Someone … spoke it into him. Words are seeds. They contain life. They take root, and when they do, they grow. You can't let the kirk be without the Creator's Word right now. You have to keep planting the seeds, or we won't survive the famine."

The words out, Linette fell back, exhausted. Sarah stared at her as though she had two heads.

"Don't preach then," Linette whispered. "Just read. Women can do that. You can do it. You need to do it. They need you."

Sarah shook her head. "I can't."

But Linette just smiled to herself. She hadn't known Sarah long before they parted ways. But she knew her well enough to be sure of this—Sarah would see the necessity of what she'd said, and she would shore herself up and do it.

The men returned the following day with Smith and Jonathan carried on the backs of the mules. Smith was in a bad way, but he declared loudly as he was taken down off the mule's back and into his wife's arms that he would be fine. There was no real reason not to believe him. As for Jonathan, his hands and feet were bound, and he did not say a word. There was a small room in the back of the governing house, and there Jonathan was conveyed. Some of the men nailed heavy wooden bars across the window. He was given a cot and a rough-hewn chair and desk in an attempt to make it homey. Men were posted at the door in shifts, heavily armed.

Agatha Moss appointed herself to bringing him meals, such as they were—with famine looming, no one could eat better than he did, but neither did he eat worse than anyone else. Cleveland's death hung over the exchange. She did not say a word about it, to Jonathan or anyone else. Jonathan accepted the beneficence in sullen quiet.

The valley settled into a tense and unhappy waiting. They put their efforts into gleaning the last of the fields.

Winter threatened.

PART 3
WINTER

CHAPTER
24

November 15, 1642—The Wilderness, west of New Cranwell—The New World

The silence was what struck Serena most about the wilderness under winter—under the snow. They walked over the white drifts in the flat, wide shoes the shape of beaver tails, made of rawhide and treated wood. She marveled at the way the shoes only sank far enough to leave shallow impressions in the snow, despite their weight. The width of the shoes forced them to walk further apart than they had before—a distance particularly enforced after Serena stepped on the back of Jacques's shoes one too many times and finally sent him sprawling in the snow. She caught sight of Josiah Axel hiding a smile as Jacques struggled back to his feet, his hair and beard dusted with crystals of white. The smile was infectious. She laughed.

And trailed further behind, after that.

Eben led the way. They all seemed to understand that he knew this wilderness better than anyone else, even though they were following the sound of the river. Jacques followed him, then Serena, then Josiah. The effort of trekking in the snowshoes and the distance between them kept them all silent.

And so it seemed to Serena that they walked through another world. A world where the only sounds were muffled breathing and the constancy of the river. Mercifully, it was such a strange and delightful landscape that it kept her from becoming lost in thought. Whenever her thoughts had a moment to collect themselves, they focused too much on the odds against them—that and the threat of the Outsiders.

Maybe, the Fire Within said, *you are worrying about the wrong things.*

Well, she snipped back, what are the right things to worry about then?

There are no right things to worry about.

From there her thoughts drifted to Eben. From his brief account, he'd spent time with the Outsiders—learned from them. He didn't seem afraid of their potential presence in these woods. He'd also mentioned coming up from the south. She wondered about that. She knew that along the southern coast of the New World, slavery was a common practice, with the most commonly enslaved being those with skin like Eben's ... like his son's.

The Trembler community in the Old World had taken an unequivocal stance against the practice, but theirs was only a theoretical battle. Tremblers here had to face the real thing and try to make a difference.

She wondered if Melrose had been outspoken about the issue and if that was why Eben would undertake an arduous journey like this one. She wondered if he had run away from the south and if anyone pursued him.

If so, they might have one more thing to worry about.

She considered trying to speed her steps over the snow and talk with Jacques about it, but decided against it. They couldn't very well have a private conversation out in the open like this, and besides, if anyone was jeopardizing their chances of reaching Jerusalem Valley by virtue of having enemies, it was she and Jacques. She could hardly begrudge Eben a bid for freedom.

Eben stopped abruptly and waited. The others drew abreast of him one by one, Serena carefully watching how far her shoes extended to keep from tangling up with Jacques again. He watched her come with good humor sparkling in his eyes. She was grateful for him.

When they formed a line, Eben pointed ahead through the trees. "The ford is there, less than half a mile. It's the best place to get ourselves caught, once they on the other side."

"You're sure we will have beat them here?" Jacques asked.

"Not sure, but hopin'. Snow will have slowed them some too. Not as much as us, but some."

Serena nodded. "All right then. I'm ready."

"As am I," Jacques said.

Serena looked expectantly at their guide, instinctively waiting for him to add his declaration of readiness. Instead, for the first time she noticed a look of uncertainty on Eben's face, but he quickly hid it behind a hardened expression that she realized was practiced.

"Boy," he said gruffly, "you don't come with us yet."

"What?" Serena burst out. "What do you expect him to do?"

Eben glared at her. Jacques gave her a look that let her know she was speaking out of turn—something which, belatedly, she realized on her own.

"We go get ourselves caught like we talked about," Eben said. "You stay out in the woods till we see how things go. They good, I signal you. You join us then. If I don't signal you, you turn around and go back to New Cranwell. Understand me?"

Josiah nodded. "Yes, sir."

Eben glanced back at her. The anger was gone from his expression, but she saw clearly that he owed her no explanation.

He gave one anyway, graciously. "Things go bad for us, they go real bad. I didn't come all the way out here to see my boy sold back into the bondage I got away from."

She nodded. "I'm sorry. I spoke out of turn. You've been nothing but a good father." He nodded and seemed to accept the apology. She still had misgivings—what if Josiah *did* have to turn back? Was he really capable of finding his way to New Cranwell alone? What would he do when he got there? Or did Eben have some other kind of plan up his sleeve? Maybe he thought the Outsiders would find his son, or he would find them, and they would help him.

It was an oddly new thought. In the Old World, tales of the Outsiders always centered around fearsome stories of warmongering and savagery. The righteous conquest of the New World by the people of God always meant conquering the people who lived in it, and although the Puritani talk of battle and conquest didn't sit well with the Tremblers generally, they didn't really question the idea that the two peoples could not coexist. Civilization and savagery were so different as to make the people who embodied them entirely different in kind. The Outsiders were hardly human.

Then again, she reflected, in the south not far from here, the general belief was that people like Eben and Josiah were hardly human either—at worst animals; at best hapless children. And here they were, risking their lives to see Serena and Jacques safely on their journey, and accomplishing the impossible through Eben's considerable knowledge, courage, and skill.

Maybe there was more to this world and its people than she had realized.

"So we go quiet now," Eben said. "Voices carry in this kinda place. Stay quiet till we reach the ford. All goes well, we get there before them. Then we follow the plan when they cross. If we don' beat them there, all we gotta do is catch up. They can't be far. Stick to the plan as much as possible."

Jacques nodded and gave Serena a slightly concerned look. "Are you ready?" he asked.

"Of course. When am I ever not ready?"

He smiled. She felt suddenly overwhelmed by the awareness of how much they had been through together. Despite her doubts, despite her fears, and despite the gulf between their faiths, she had never had a truer friend.

For a moment she wondered if that gulf could really be as great as she thought it was.

But how could it not? The Sacramenti had ruled the Old World with an iron fist, controlling the minds and hearts of all. When the Puritani rose to oppose them, they were fierce and violent in persecuting them, and the Puritani were saved only because enough princes took their side to give them military might to fight back. Together the two groups had plunged the world into war for more than a hundred years. The Puritani had been just as ruthless in opposing the Tremblers in recent years, but in the minds of nearly everyone, a resurgence of the Sacramenti would be even worse.

The Imitators were a secret order of spies and fanatics, rumored to be attempting to undermine and overthrow Puritani strongholds all over the world. Given the opportunity, they would take over again and plunge the world back into darkness.

And yet … if Jacques were truly an Imitator—and by his own account, he was—how could the accounts she knew be true? Jacques was kind, brave, and faithful. In all his dealings with her, he had been pure and selfless. She had never known another man quite like him.

She pushed her thoughts aside and focused her attention on Eben again. Satisfied with their responses, he had begun the forward move once more.

Step by wide, awkward step, they traversed across the snow toward the sound of the water, still free of ice—though not for much longer, if Eben was to be believed. He had told them that the soldiers would be delayed at the ford, because the water was shallow here and would have iced over. They would have to break up the ice to let their boat through, and once they'd made it across, they would be little inclined to turn back for the sake of delivering prisoners. It was the perfect place to prompt their own arrest.

Serena still held some faint hope that they would not be recognized. Maybe these soldiers would have left town before word of her escape was spread, and they would not be taken prisoner at all—instead they would be taken in as lost travelers and ushered to Fort Collins under the army's protection. Puritani were known to care for their own with conscientious honor, especially when women were involved. Of course, that assumed the soldiers would believe the likes of Serena, Jacques, and Eben belonged to their own ... but she could hope.

She looked behind her at Josiah, who was struggling along without complaint in his oversized snowshoes. For all their sakes, she hoped the faint possibility would come to pass.

She knew it wasn't likely.

As they drew closer to the river, they heard a heartening sound—the thudding and cracking of ice being battered and broken through. Soon the shouts of men joined the sound. The soldiers were at the ford. They'd made it in time.

Jacques looked back and nodded to her, a silent signal of reassurance and commitment. Eben waved them forward, and they pressed into a thick stand of barren trees mingled with dark green firs. In the tangle of roots and branches it was hard to find a clear place to step. Serena was relieved when Eben stopped and signaled for them to do the same, then bent down and began to unlace his snowshoes. They had agreed to leave them behind, much as the loss was unfortunate. Their story of being lost in the wilderness would not be helped if they looked like experienced frontiersmen— even if the truth was they had stumbled across the shoes by accident. Almost certainly they would have to be arrested, but if there was any chance at all that they could pass themselves off as lost homesteaders instead, they would take it.

Serena followed Eben's lead, grateful to be leaving the unwieldy objects behind. Her gratitude changed focus a moment later, though, as she sank knee-deep into the snow and felt the cold closing around her legs, falling into her boots, and soaking her leggings and skirts. Her first attempt to take a step forward nearly threw her onto her face. She spotted Jacques silently laughing at her and barely restrained herself from sticking out her tongue.

Arms swinging to give themselves more momentum, they struggled through the snow. After two or three steps, she had forgotten about the cold as heat surged through her from the effort. No wonder Eben had insisted they not leave the cabin without snowshoes. They wouldn't have made it a mile in this.

As they crested a low ridge above the river, Eben paused and laid a finger on his lips, gesturing to them all to make sure they would keep silent. He needn't have warned them. They were all breathing so hard from the effort of getting through the snow that talking was hardly an option.

The ridge was lined with small, twisted firs. The river was visible below, as were the red coats of soldiers working to break up the ice with picks. The boat, a large, flat-bottomed barge designed to be poled up the river, waited on the other side of the ice. On the shore was a small cluster of officers with six horses.

The firs provided cover as Eben led his little band off to the left and down toward the river. Below them, the soldiers broke through the last of the ice and shouted for their companions to pole the boat through. It moved with a creak and a groan, and the small band of officers led their horses along the bank to the other side. This was the moment they'd been waiting for.

With Eben in the lead, they half-tumbled down the gentle slope toward the river bed, still keeping out of sight. Serena's heart began to beat faster, and not only because of the effort. It was time.

A thousand wild suggestions presented themselves even as her feet carried her toward fate. Maybe this wouldn't work at all. Maybe the soldiers would be ordered to shoot on sight rather than arresting her. Maybe they would be mistaken for Outsiders and likewise shot on sight. Maybe ...

It didn't matter. She had to do it.

Finding her feet in the snow, which was not so deep here, sheltered by the riverbanks, she grabbed her skirts with one hand and broke into a stumbling, faltering run. She waved and shouted.

"Help!" she called out. "Please, help me!"

The soldiers nearest her turned in obvious surprise, several of them drawing knives or hefting muskets. They relaxed the weapons the moment they recognized her as a woman, and her faint hope gathered strength. Would they buy it?

Then the shout: "Arrest her! That's Serena Vaquero!"

No. Her steps faltered, and she waited while the soldiers looked behind them in confusion. One of the officers was striding forward none too gracefully through the snow drifts, pointing at her and waving his hand. A dark coat billowed around him.

"I tell you, that's Serena Vaquero. Place her under arrest at once!"

Faintly aware that Jacques and Eben were edging their way toward her, hands held high to show they meant no threat, Serena squinted at the man who seemed so certain of her identity. He seemed … familiar.

Out of breath, the officer drew alongside the soldiers, who had just enough presence of mind to lift their muskets in her direction again—as well as pointing them at Jacques and Eben. He *was* familiar. She knew this man from the Old World. His name was Principio Premislav, and he was both a decorated military commander and a close associate of Elder Crispin.

Nevertheless, she relaxed. "Hello, Premislav," she called out.

He blustered in response. "You're under arrest." He gestured at the soldiers to hurry it up, and they finally snapped out of their hesitation and blundered forward toward her. She gave herself up without a struggle, allowing two of the soldiers to flank her with their weapons at the ready.

"We surrender!" she said, gesturing to the men by her side. "These are my companions. We are unarmed, and we surrender to your superior force."

Premislav trudged forward and glowered into Serena's face. "What are you up to?" he asked.

"We are lost," Serena said. "We were trying to reach Fort Collins. Alas, in the snow we lost our way, and you found us. We surrender, as I said."

More soldiers had reached Eben and Jacques, and they pulled their hands down and cuffed them behind their backs. Neither man put up a struggle.

Premislav wiggled his large grey eyebrows. "You were trying to reach Fort Collins, unarmed. Not even a carabine to protect yourselves from, say, the wolves."

"We might have had weapons before," Serena said. "We didn't think it was prudent to be carrying them when we met you, as seemed inevitable."

He waved a giant hand at the soldiers. "Search the woods along the ridge. I think you'll find a cache of weapons. Valuable, out here."

"There's a boy," Serena said in a rush. "Take him prisoner as well; he's with us. He's harmless."

Premislav drew a breath and shouted after the soldiers who were already lumbering up the hill toward the top of the ridge, "There's a boy also! Arrest him!"

Serena cast an anxious glance at Eben, who looked hard at her before pursing his lips and whistling. The whistle rose high and clear: his signal.

Serena relaxed as she turned back to their unexpected captor. "I heard the soldiers were escorting someone west. I didn't expect it to be you."

"No more than I expected, when I crossed the entire ocean to come here, that I would ever run into you again. But here we are."

"Why are you going west?" Serena asked. "What is your purpose?"

"As though I would tell you that."

"I'm no threat to you. You know that."

Premislav grimaced. "And yet you are here, and you are heading to Fort Collins, which at the moment happens to be at the center of Crispin's plans."

"I'm almost surprised you're still carrying out Crispin's plans."

Another grimace. "As I have told you at least a hundred times, I am a man of this world with my interests fully placed in my pocketbook and in the power I can garner from serving powerful men. You keep trying to convince me that I'm a better man than I am, but it is not going to work."

Serena smiled even as the soldiers on either side responded to a nod from Premislav and took her arms, propelling her toward the boat. "Maybe," she called back.

When the boat was firmly settled on the western side of the ford, it let out a plank of wood to allow for reboarding. Serena, Jacques, and Eben were huddled together, with Josiah trailing after under the control of a soldier whose friends followed with armloads of muskets and other scattered weaponry and tools. One of them even carried the snowshoes. The red-coated captain, reaching the plank at the same time they did, drew near with a stormy expression.

"What is the meaning of this?"

"These are the escaped prisoners we were told to watch for, sir," said a young private. "They just came out of the woods ahead of us. Commander Premislav ordered us to arrest them, sir."

"Of all the … what are we supposed to do with them?"

"Stable them in with the horses, put them under guard, and deliver them to Fort Collins," said Commander Premislav, lumbering up behind them. "We'll send word to Elder Cole from there."

The captain chewed his lip. "I'd much rather be rid of them now. Send a detachment back with them."

"And lose your men for the rest of the season? They'll not get back through the ford once the ice settles in. I shouldn't need to remind you, Captain, that you are in a race against time."

As though in agreement, a flock of crows burst out of the trees over the river bed and flew west, cawing as they went, winging their way toward the icy horizon. The captain watched them go with evident displeasure before he snapped, "Fine. Do as the commander says and secure them in the stable."

"All of them?" the young private asked.

"Yes, all of them. Don't take pity on this woman, boy. She's an infamous heretic and a seditionist."

None of the four put up a fight as they were propelled onto the boat and across the deck to an enclosure in the center, stacked with bales of hay and smelling of manure. They were piled into a corner, and Serena's and Josiah's hands were tied to match the others. From there, the soldiers secured ropes around each of them that attached them to the boards making up the slatted stable wall. They were left enough freedom to shift position, but not enough to twist around and untie the ropes. Likewise, each was positioned just too far from the next to be of any help to one another.

Serena leaned her head against a slat and shivered in the cold. She was glad for her heavy winter garments, courtesy of Eben, and that the horses would soon be secured in here as well. Their body heat would go a long way toward keeping them from freezing on the journey ahead. If only the soldiers knew they needn't have bothered so carefully about keeping them secured. They wouldn't make any effort to escape—at least, not until they reached Fort Collins.

For now, it was back to a life Serena had much experience with: that of being a prisoner. She wondered how much the others had known the same, and remembered with a shiver that Eben's experience was likely far more extensive than hers. As for Jacques, how could she know? That part of his life, like nearly everything else, was a mystery.

Commander Principio Premislav passed by the enclosure and stopped for a moment with his hand resting atop the slats. She couldn't see his face to know if he was looking down at them. He went on his way before she could say anything.

"You know him?" Jacques asked.

"He's an old enemy. Or an old friend. Sometimes I forget the difference." She opened her eyes and saw all three of the others were waiting expectantly for her to go on. "He's a military commander, a very good one. Works for Elder Crispin in the Old World. He says all he cares about is money, but I don't believe him. He's a fair man, even a kind one. We couldn't really ask for a better enemy on a trip like this."

Eben snorted. "That's comforting."

She smiled. "This whole thing was *your* idea."

"Keep your voice down," Jacques said mildly. In obedience to his own injunction, he dropped his till the words were hardly audible. "This is all supposed to look like an accident."

CHAPTER
25

Jerusalem Valley Settlement—The New World

Capenokanickon and his people appeared without warning from the pass two days after the settlers had finished gleaning every last scrap from their fields. They carried baskets of food balanced on their hips and strapped to their backs. Along with maize, and root vegetables the settlers could bury to keep cold, they brought a generous amount of dried meat and fish, and even a heap of furs, as though they felt the long and hard winter ahead would need extra warmth.

Generosity, in fact, seemed the best word to describe their coming. They stood in the barren field just beneath the pass, the dyed-red feathers in their hair a blaze of color against a greying mountain backdrop. Martin and Samuel Foster spotted them first, dropped what they were doing, and ran helter-skelter for their parents.

The Outsiders waited until a small contingent came to meet them, made up of a limping Smith Foster, Amos, John Hopewell, and Herman Melrose. Linette spotted them filing through the fields, caught a glimpse of red near the base of the mountains, and hurried out after them.

Capenokanickon waited until they drew near before raising a hand in greeting. He motioned for his warriors to set their bounty on the ground, and they did—basket after basket, the furs, skins sewn around strips of dried meat.

"We thank you," Governor Melrose said. Linette had never seen him looking so discomfited, face-to-face with people whose existence he had refused to ever really acknowledge or deal with. People who were now treating him with great grace.

Melrose had found his place on the map of a world drawn along exactly three lines: Puritani, Sacramenti, and Trembler. The Outsiders meant there were other pieces to the map, other lines, other pictures. He did not know where he fit on that map, and so he had never tried.

Capenokanickon nodded. His eyes scanned the little group, seeing everything—Smith Foster's wan cheeks and limp, the absence of Jonathan. He even saw the change in Linette. How he could see that, she didn't know—but he did. To her surprise, her heart constricted at the idea that he and his people were leaving. That for the rest of this season, this man would not be on the other side of the pass. She felt bereft.

Governor Melrose was breathing heavily from the fast jaunt across the fields. "We have payment," he said. "Please, come back with us to the governing house, and we ..."

"No," Capenokanickon said. "We will take nothing. This is not a trade; it is a mourning feast."

Linette understood. She touched Governor Melrose's elbow. "For Jonathan," she whispered. "They think he's gone and they're honoring him." She knew she shouldn't, but she stepped forward and said, "Thank you for your kindness and for honoring our brother. Please, come and eat with us."

She heard the spat of whispers from the others, especially protest from John Hopewell—they didn't have food to share. The whole point of this exchange was to receive stores for the winter. But Smith stepped forward alongside her and said, "Yes. Come. Mourn with us."

She watched Melrose carefully, looking for some sign of which way he would turn. To her relief, he nodded.

"Please," he added. "You are welcome."

Less than an hour later, the governing house was filled with tattooed warriors, and the porch and mucky yard were spread with blankets to sit and eat together. Silas Cromer, standing sentry at the door of Jonathan's room, let his musket hang loosely in his arms and watched the goings-on with evident discomfort.

Linette passed the door, and Silas beckoned to her. In a whisper he said, "Do they know he's alive?"

She nodded. "I think so. They are not mourning because he's dead, but because he's gone."

"Is he?" Silas asked.

"I don't know," she finally answered. "I hope not."

A young warrior she recognized as Anasan drew out of the crowd milling through the house and nodded to her. "The daughters of Capenokanickon send greetings to you," he said.

Linette smiled. "And I send mine in return. Thank you." Her heart felt unusually full. Outside, Sarah was cooking a pot of stew in a hanging iron kettle over a fire, and the steam blew off in clouds and wisped away to the west. Warriors lit pipes and solemnly passed them to the settlers.

Locked behind the door, Jonathan remained cut away from it all. They couldn't risk letting him out. But Linette hoped something of the honor being paid him seeped through the door. And with it, some kind of hope.

She could still see the seed near his heart. The black, poisoned seed. All they had to do to save him was root it out somehow.

She was determined to find a way.

The mourning feast was still underway when Sarah Foster withdrew and let herself into the guarded room where Jonathan sat. Silas protested, but Sarah won.

Jonathan eyed her miserably as she seated herself by the barred window. He sat on the floor in the corner, his arms folded over his midsection, hunched forward as though he were in pain.

As perhaps he was.

She looked back at him with her heart aching. Her daughter loved this boy. And despite his youth, Sarah herself had looked up to him, deferred to him—respected him as the representative of the synod, who were the guardians and representatives of the truth, the words of the Father contained in the Book.

"You should go out and join them," Jonathan said after a few minutes passed without words. "No need to keep my bad company."

"You're not bad company, Jonathan."

"I'm a threat."

"You're sick."

Jonathan leaned back and looked to the ceiling with a groan. "Maybe I'm being judged. Purged."

"By who?" Sarah asked. "For what?"

"For my rebellion. Seeking out the Outsiders even though my father told me not to."

She stared at him for a minute. She'd been aware of some conflict between father and son over Jonathan's desire to reach the heathen. But she hadn't known it still plagued him, all this time after his father's death.

"You honored your father his whole life, Jonathan. You never went to the Outsiders until after he died."

"I was looking for a way through the pass that night. When he … fell. If I'd been there …"

"'What ifs' will only make you sicker," Sarah said. "Maybe you did wrong. Don't you think there's grace for that?"

"God is a harsh judge."

"You were trying to serve God by going to them."

"Was I?"

Sarah bit her lip. She didn't know what to make of this boy. She'd known him much of his life, but right now he felt like a stranger—and not because of the things he'd done or the poison in his veins. Because of the things coming out his mouth.

"You know the gospel," she said. "God sent his Son into the world to save sinners, of whom we are all chief. He loved us before we loved him.

If the Son can die for you, don't you think he can forgive a wrongful step made out of a good heart?"

"No sacrifice remains for those who trample underfoot the blood of the Son of God," Jonathan said.

"Do you really think that's what you've done? By trying to share the gospel with others? By doing something your father would surely have eventually agreed was a good thing?"

He fixed his eyes back on her. They were empty and haunted—and hard. "None of us are good, Sarah. None of us are worthy. We're all worms in his sight. You know that."

She stood. Smoothed out her skirt. "I know something like that. But I'm starting to think you and I don't read quite the same Book."

It was the most heretical thing she'd ever said.

Her heart pounded hard as she left the room and returned to the feast.

Mescahannec River—The New World

Serena thought her hands might turn to ice.

Prisons were familiar to her. This was different. There were no rats. No mildew. Just unrelenting, icy cold, mitigated but not erased by the warm breath and bodies of the horses and the heat and smell of manure. The others, like her, sat huddled with their hands tucked under their arms, trying in vain to keep warm. They didn't talk. Their faces and lips were numb with cold. They just stared at each other, or through the slats at the slate-grey water of the river, reflecting the clouds above. And waited.

A day had passed, then a night. They didn't sleep much. Morning dawned, but its scant sun wasn't much relief.

Three soldiers appeared and opened the stable door. Two began to undo the ropes that tied them to the stable slats, while the third gestured with his pistol. "On your feet," he said. "Premislav's orders. We're to walk you around."

Every muscle screamed as Serena tried to stand. Surely the blood had frozen in her veins.

"I did not think tormenting prisoners was your style," Jacques said.

Premislav's voice boomed from the other side. "I won't have you losing limbs to the cold on my watch just because no one got you up and walked you around."

Serena chuckled. "You make us sound like horses."

Premislav ran a hand over his beard. "You smell like them."

Josiah stumbled and nearly fell as one of the soldiers helped him up, catching himself on the slats and pushing himself back up. The boy hadn't complained once, but his lips were blue, and misery was writ large in his face. Jacques watched with evident concern. As all four prisoners shuffled out onto the main deck, he turned to Premislav.

"Thank you for your kindness, Monsieur," he said. "May I be so bold as to suggest a benefit to you? Our servants are no threat to you or your men. Put them to work poling the ship, or tending your horses—doing some useful task. They can spell your men off and keep them fresher. To keep them confined does you no good and threatens the boy. He is young; he cannot withstand this cold."

The commander appeared to consider the suggestion. Serena waited with bated breath. At last he nodded, and at the same time motioned for Jacques and Serena to walk. They staggered forward, painful steps made harder by the motion of the river beneath them, threatening to throw off their balance with each step.

"I'm not too proud to take suggestions from a prisoner," Premislav said from behind them, "when the suggestion is a smart one."

"But, Commander," one of the soldiers began to protest, but Premislav waved him silent. "None of that," he said. "These people are no threat to us."

Serena smiled to herself as she fought to stay balanced. Her feet burned and stabbed with every step, but she knew walking was the best thing she could do. Jacques drew close to her, so close that if his gloved hands hadn't been bound, he might have taken hers. She looked up to see if he wanted to say something, but he just smiled down at her. Care and kindness filled his green eyes.

He was the best man she had ever known, she decided. Imitator or no.

To her surprise, footsteps stumped along behind her and Premislav began to walk on her other side. His hands *were* free, and he put out an arm to steady her as they walked. He nodded to Jacques in a friendly way that indicated he needn't fall back. The commander was happy to walk with both prisoners.

"I won't be putting you back in that stable," Premislav said abruptly. "No sense in letting any of you suffer lasting damage. Summer is one thing; winter is another, especially in this cursed wilderness." He looked over Serena's head at Jacques. "Can you pole?"

"I can learn."

"Good. I'd just as soon sit you down with a cup of tea and demand you give me some good conversation; you seem an intelligent fellow. But my men will revolt if I don't work you at least as hard as I work them."

"Understood," Jacques said, seeming amused and a little befuddled. "I thank you for the compliment."

Premislav looked down at Serena. "There's a captain's cabin; that's the only place fit for you to sleep. I can't put you down with the men. You'll have to trust me to share it with you, but I'm a man of honor."

"I know," Serena said. "Why are you doing this? Simpler for you just to let us fight out the cold."

"Simpler, but a constant drag on my conscience. I prefer to avoid that."

"And you say you're not a good man," Serena said.

He cleared his throat. "Not a *good* man. A self-interested one."

A cold wind swept up, howling over the mountains and down to the river from somewhere in the north. Serena could feel the blood circulating through her limbs again, but the wind blasted against her and sent her hair flying in a dark tangle. She shivered violently. Jacques moved between her and the wind, but his tall frame didn't do much to shield her from it.

An hour later Serena found herself bundled away in the captain's cabin, seated behind a curtain on a small, built-in bed with a thin mattress, under a pile of blankets. It was cold in here too, but a few coals smoldered in a brazier on the other side of the curtain, and warmth filtered up from beneath it. She had left Jacques, Eben, and Josiah poling the boat—kept warm both by the activity and also by the extra coats, gloves, and scarves Premislav had issued them from the soldiers' stores. If the crew was prone to grumble about it, the imposing commander had glared them quickly into silence.

Sitting alone now in the darkness of the cabin, she found herself relaxing to a degree that surprised her. It was over, for now, all of it—the tension, the threats, the need to find their own way. She could simply wait and let the river take them, sheltered in the presence of enemies who were more like friends.

The unexpected appearance of Principio Premislav had been a true surprise. It felt to her like a gift from heaven—a sign that she had been right all along in her confidence that God was sending her on this mission. In the Old World, Premislav had served Crispin with unmatched military skill—but he had also been willing to look the other way where the Tremblers were concerned, and during the long period of Serena's arrest and trial, he had made conditions tolerable for her by interceding on her behalf more than once. He was brilliant at covering his tracks and somehow kept himself lily white in Crispin's sight, but she knew him better than his allies did. True to his name, he was a man of principle.

Released at last from any need to be on her guard, figure out a plan, or counter unexpected circumstances, Serena gradually grew warm and fell asleep.

She awoke to the sound of a voice on the other side of the curtain. At first she thought she was eavesdropping on a conversation. Then she realized the voice was talking to her.

"I am not sure why you predicated your own arrest out there, but I'm not foolish enough to believe you were truly lost, or that your ultimate goal is Fort Collins. Given the nature of this wilderness I can only believe you're trying to reach the Tremblers in Jerusalem Valley."

Serena fought to pull her mind far enough out of the dark, warm fog of sleep to understand what was being said and why. Premislav rambled on, apparently uncaring whether she was listening or not—or just assuming she would wake up and pay attention eventually.

"I think you should know that the Puritani synod has Jerusalem Valley in its sights. In fact, that's why I'm going west right now. I'm to take charge of the troops in Fort Collins and await the signal to stage a takeover of the government there."

"What signal?" Serena asked, her voice like her thoughts still fuzzy and dragging more slowly than she wanted it to.

"Word that Herman Melrose is dead."

"An assassination," Serena said. "I know. That's why I'm going west … to stop the Reaper."

"The Reaper?" This time Premislav sounded surprised. "You don't have to stop him. He's already dead."

"What?" Serena sat up straight, suddenly fully awake, and shuffled off some of the blankets that had been swathing her in warmth.

"Crispin ordered his assassination in Torrentio after he escaped prison."

Her mind swam. "But Crispin let him out!" Serena exclaimed. "I was there; I heard him. He released the Reaper and commanded him to go to Jerusalem Valley and kill Armando. That's why I'm here."

Premislav was silent long enough to let Serena know this was new information to him. "Strange," he finally said. "What is that weasel trying for?"

"He's not a weasel, he's a snake," Serena said. Her vision from earlier on the journey, of a man's scaled arm holding a bloody knife, came back to her memory. At the time she'd been convinced, against logic, that the man in the vision was not the Reaper. Now she knew that was true. She'd suspected Jacques—but that was no longer a thought she could even countenance. So who … ?

"Rumor has it there's an Imitator abroad," Premislav said. "Charged to carry out one more piece of the Hierarchy's plot to regain control of the world."

"Nothing but a story," Serena said, peering hard at the curtain. "It's not even possible. I've encountered Sacramenti; they're a scattered, persecuted few—weaker than the Tremblers. They cannot rise."

"You underestimate them," Premislav said. "They've appointed a new leader, a father, as they say. They have spies. They plan to infiltrate and destabilize their old strongholds. If they can do it, it will not be hard for them to reassert themselves. There are far more of the old believers left than the Puritani want to admit."

Like you? It was a new thought, and Serena wondered if it had come from her own thoughts, born out of the uncertainties of the moment and the strangeness of this conversation, or if the Fire had given it to her. Maybe Premislav had more secrets than just his Trembler sympathies. She tried to remember if she'd ever noticed him wearing a Book, the talisman of the Puritani. But she couldn't recall.

"If there *is* an Imitator on the loose," Premislav went on, "and if he is heading for Jerusalem Valley, Crispin may be trying to implicate the Sacramenti in what happens there. It would be bad for everyone if he succeeds."

"How could they know if an Imitator was headed there?" Serena asked. "They aren't working together. Are they?"

"More likely they're working from the reports of their own spies. And Crispin, true to form, is trying to pull as many strings as he can to gain control."

"Elder Cole said he had an informant in the valley," Serena said. It was the first time she had really thought about the conversation with Phinehas Cole since escaping the prison in New Cranwell. "He said his own daughter is there and keeps him informed. And he also said Melrose would be overthrown by the valley Puritani. Did he know about you?"

"He knows I am here and taking command of Fort Collins, but he does not know my full mission, and he knows nothing about the assassination as far as I know. Crispin is no friend to him either. After the valley falls, taking control of New Cranwell will be next. That is unlikely to be a job given to me, thank God. But it will happen."

"Crispin is a madman. He wants to rule the whole world."

"He may manage it, if no one arises to oppose him. The new Kaion Anthropon, made in the image of one power-crazy elder."

"So why are you telling me all this?" Serena asked.

"Because I think you can oppose him. And because I think you may be bringing the Imitator to the valley yourself."

Serena stiffened. She knew exactly what he meant—and she didn't want to. She didn't respond, so he filled in the blanks for her. "Your friend. The tall one."

"Jacques is not a threat."

"Mmm. But to whom? A friend to one is an enemy to another. In our world full of lines and sides, that is how it must be."

"No," she said, shaking her head. "He wouldn't harm anyone, least of all a good man like Armando. I trust him."

"But you don't deny he's an Imitator."

She was silent again. She wanted to lie. But the Fire Within would give her no rest if she did. Confusion assailed her. The Fire Within had set her on this journey—to stop the Reaper. Except that the Reaper wasn't here, wasn't even alive. And along the way, the Fire had given her a companion who was, officially, an enemy of everything she stood for, everything the Puritani stood for, and everything Jerusalem Valley stood for.

All appearances indicated that rather than saving the valley and its precious dream, she would be complicit in destroying it.

She was supposed to save the valley.

Wasn't she?

Fire, she implored. *What am I supposed to do?*

There was no answer.

From that she gathered one thing: her commission hadn't changed.

She was supposed to go on. Go to the valley. Take Jacques with her.

And do something, somehow, to save it from the enemies who threatened to overrun it.

There was a scraping sound as Premislav pushed himself up. He must have been sitting on the floor. "Think on what I've told you, and make your decisions from there. I hate to see you playing the pawn again."

She flushed. She'd been a pawn in the past, yes. A tool for Crispin to use to shore up his own power by exposing the "spiritual threat" people like her posed. But she'd always been doing her best to follow the Fire, the spirit of the Creator. That was all she could do. Consequences had to be left up to God.

A question struck her, and she blurted it out before Premislav could leave. "But if the Reaper isn't heading to the valley, who is supposed to kill Armando? You said you're waiting for the signal that he's dead."

"That shouldn't be too difficult to figure out," Premislav said. "You said yourself Cole has an informant in the valley. His own people will do it. The Puritani settlers."

"But … no," Serena said, and her eyes filled with unexpected tears. "Armando has created a place where Puritani and Trembler live at peace with one another. Where the dream of harmony is realized."

"That was the dream, yes," Premislav said. "But it has already failed. The lines are drawn; the two peoples cannot live together. The synod has ordered his death, and the Puritani will carry it out. Cole may only plan for them to take over governance, but Crispin must have sent his own orders to someone."

"But you know!" Serena burst out. She rocked forward, cursing the small space where she was trapped. Why must so much of her life be spent trapped in small spaces? "You know it's coming; you can stop it. March your men to the valley and arrest the dissidents. Keep the peace, like you were commissioned to do!"

Premislav let out a rough sigh. "I have told you so many times, Serena, I am not a good man. I was hired to serve the interests of the kirk and the governments in league with it, and that is what I will do."

She slumped back against the wall, feeling the vibration of the boat moving through water. "And yet," she said, "you're telling me this."

"I will do what I was sent to do. You must do the same."

She put out a hand against the wall to her right, steadying herself. "How much time do we have?"

"I am being positioned to take control of the valley almost immediately after arrival. Listen to me carefully, Serena: Fort Collins is only ten miles from Jerusalem Valley, down a south fork of the river. We will pass the junction three days from now. I can't help you get off this boat. But you may find the cabin is left open. And it may happen that we will drift by the junction at night, when it is not easy to see."

"But what about the others?" Serena said. "Jacques, Eben … the boy."

"If you all escape it will look too much like you had help. I can't have that kind of word getting back to Crispin, or even to Cole. The freedmen can plead they were only servants and knew nothing of your mission."

"And Jacques?"

A pause. "He may be needed on deck three days from now."

Again the suspicion—even a growing conviction—that Premislav had his own secret.

"Why would you help him?" she asked. She shouldn't pry. But Serena often did things she shouldn't.

"If I bring him to the fort and he is discovered, he'll be executed," Premislav said.

He said nothing more. She finished it herself. Premislav couldn't allow that to happen on his watch.

For reasons of his own.

"Don't tarry," he said. "Once you leave the boat, you'll have only days to stop whatever is to happen from happening. If that."

Banquo. Jacques. Now Premislav. As she sank back into the darkness and listened to Premislav leave the cabin, she marveled at having found so many allies among those considered by the whole world to be enemies.

CHAPTER
26

Jerusalem Valley Settlement—The New World

Two days after the visit of Capenokanickon and his people, the last mail run of the year came to the valley by way of Brentwood Taylor, fresh from Fort Collins. Linette saw him coming and met with him quickly and privately to give him her letters. He tipped his raccoon-skin cap and winked. "Secret as always, ma'am," he said as he tucked them away. "I'll be back to the fort in a week's time and deliver them then. Don't know when they'll get them out east. Not much travel happening the rest of this season, once the new commander arrives."

Linette frowned. "New commander?"

Brentwood didn't answer, instead looking up at the approach of Smith and Sarah, coming down the well-beaten path from the governing house. The former leaned a little on his wife's shoulder. He was healing well, but the knife wound still seemed to sap a good bit of strength out of him.

Linette's heart panged to see them coming. There would be one conspicuous absence in the letters going east: any missive confessing the famine and asking either Fort Collins or New Cranwell for help. The Fosters had chosen to take their chances in solidarity with the Tremblers. Linette knew how much they risked in order to do it.

As usual, hiding her letters caused her some distress. But it was better this way. She'd told Herman when she first arrived that she did not wish to tell her story. She wished to write a new one. That was still true.

Brentwood held up a handful of letters, tied with string. "Mail!" he announced.

Smith nodded to him with a grimace. "You're welcome, as usual. Will you take supper with us?"

"No," Brentwood said, and Linette noticed the relief in Smith's expression. They couldn't afford to give away the little they had, but neither could they afford to let anyone outside the valley know of their predicament. "I'd best be getting further into the hills before sundown," the trapper explained. "Looks to be snow on the way."

He ruffled through the letters. "Let's see. Got three for the governor."

Smith reached out. "I'll take them."

"And one, marked highly private, for the parson of the Puritani kirk."

Smith and Sarah exchanged a glance. To Linette's surprise, Sarah held out her hand. "I'll take that," she said.

Brentwood held it out of reach. "I don't know. Says it's for the preacher and only the preacher."

Sarah looked annoyed. "It doesn't say anything of the kind, and you can hardly read more than the bare names you've memorized. Give it to me. I'll see the preacher gets it."

The trapper eyed her curiously, though Linette doubted he would push her much further. Sarah could be formidable when she wanted to be.

"Where's the preacher now? He's usually first out to meet me, except when I happen upon Miss Cole here."

Sarah ignored his question and snatched the letter from his hand while he was off guard. She glared at him. "The parson's indisposed."

"Sorry to hear it. Bad time of year to fall ill." Brentwood Taylor cast a glance at the clouds gathering like a heavy cloak across the sky. "I'd best be moving on myself, though I'll take a little whiskey to refill my stores. As payment for the mail."

"You know we don't drink it here," Smith said. "Not much use for demon liquor in God's colony."

"Come on, brother," Brentwood said. "I know better than that. Saints are only saints till the weather gets cold enough."

Smith grimaced and gestured with his head toward the governing house. "You'll find a bottle in the shed. We keep it for medicine. Fill up your flask if you must."

Brentwood tipped his hat again, a comical gesture for a garment made of fur. With its brim sitting closer to his eyes, he hoofed it off to the shed. Smith watched him go.

"He won't go into the governing house, will he?" Sarah asked, worried.

"Doubt that," Smith said. "He's not the kind to be much governed." He looked at Linette suddenly with a sharp expression she didn't expect and couldn't read. It took her aback. "You meet him alone often when he comes here?" Smith asked.

It took a moment for the question and its implications to sink in. "No," Linette stammered. "Never. I mean ... only to get the mail."

"Funny, because I think I've seen you two standing in the road talking like this before."

"Only to get the mail, I swear," Linette said. "And ... and to give him something to send back east, once in a while."

Sarah laid a comforting hand on Linette's shoulder. "Don't mind Smith; he's not accusing you. Just feeling protective. Brentwood's the lawless kind frontiers usually attract. We've had a little trouble with him before, especially if he's been drinking. For a few months Martin was a mite taken by him. We worried he might lead him down a bad path. He showed some interest in Letty for a time too. He and the parson had words."

Linette looked after the trapper, who was digging around in the shed. He emerged triumphant, hefting a half-filled bottle of whiskey high. From the looks of things, he planned to take the whole bottle—never mind filling his flask.

Smith huffed. "Good thing I didn't tell him where to find the whole cache."

Linette managed a pale smile at Smith. "I promise, there's nothing between me and Brentwood Taylor but this length of laneway here."

She tried not to show how shaken she felt. The guilt of her letters must be weighing on her more than she thought. Smith had risked his life for her more than once. For her to now think of him as a threat of some kind, just because he'd asked an innocent question …

For the first time, she wanted to tell them. Things between her and Sarah had changed after the healing. They were allies again. Maybe they could all be close.

If she didn't continue to keep secrets.

But could she really risk baring her soul—letting those things be seen that had ended her life in New Cranwell forever?

Smith nodded to Sarah and Linette. "I'll take the mail to the governor," he said.

Sarah held up the one she'd snatched. "What about this one?"

Smith glanced at it. "What's it say?"

Sarah read the front of it. "It's for Jonathan. Marked private. The seal is the New Cranwell synod."

Linette paled. She tried to shake it off. Of course the synod was in touch with the kirk here. That was their business: shepherding the Puritani all over the New World. They must have been in touch with Jonathan all along, and she hadn't been any the worse for it.

She tried to shake off the feeling that her two worlds were about to collide in a way she was entirely unprepared for.

"Take it home," Smith said. "You should read it."

Sarah shook her head, eyes widening. "It's for the parson."

"The parson is a crazed lunatic who killed one good man and nearly took the lives of two more."

"Then the governor should have it."

Smith smiled at that. "The governor doesn't much qualify as leader of the Puritani kirk. I'm afraid that's you and me, Sarah. And I'm not much of a reader. Synod wants to write to the local kirk, you'll have to be the one to read it."

Sarah nodded and stuffed the letter in her pocket. She didn't look pleased about it. Linette wondered if she'd given any more thought to her suggestion that she take over reading the Book in the kirk meetings. Given that she didn't attend, she didn't know what the kirk had been doing in the week and a half since Jonathan traded his honored position for that of a madman locked in a closet.

"Walk with me?" Sarah asked.

Linette nodded. The invitation was a surprise. She tried not to feel afraid. She and Sarah were allies again—but they had not come all the way back to being friends.

Sarah headed toward her home, across the fields from the governing house. Linette fell in beside her. Four of Sarah's children, scraping the light snow from the ground and packing it into balls to throw at one another, nearly burst into them when they were sixty feet from the house.

Sarah pushed the oldest girl away. "Lila, Samuel, off with you! I'm too old for that."

The children laughed more but obeyed. Linette watched them go with a mist in her eyes. Sarah seemed to notice it.

"I wanted to say I'm sorry for Smith," she said. "He didn't mean to attack you like that. If you were … that is, if you did have some interest in Brentwood Taylor, we wouldn't think worse of you."

Linette flushed. "It's all right, Sarah, really."

"Well, you couldn't know what he is. We should have warned you earlier. Of course you should be interested in—"

Linette didn't want her to finish. "I didn't come to the frontier looking for a man. I came for a new life. I've found one, and I'm glad for it. If loneliness is some of the price to be paid for it, it is worth it to me."

Sarah fell silent, and they walked side by side a little further while the children's laughter rang in the cold air. Then Sarah stopped. "I know I don't know everything about your past. Or really, anything at all. But leaving a place doesn't mean you have to leave every dream God ever placed inside you. When we came here, Smith and me, I thought I was facing a death. And maybe in some ways I was. But in most ways I just rediscovered everything that really mattered to me—out here, where the air is clearer."

Tears stung at Linette's eyes. She laughed as Lila smashed a handful of snow in Samuel's face, and he hollered and chased across the furrows of the field. She prayed they would make it through this winter, all of them—that the laughter would not die to give way to something more visceral and lasting.

Sarah didn't miss the wistful look on Linette's face. "It's not too late for you, Linette. That's what I'm trying to say. You may yet be a mother of children."

And with that, Linette couldn't hold it in anymore. She had to tell. She *wanted* to tell. She wanted to be known, fully known. For what she was and not only for what she wanted to be.

"I am already the mother of one," she choked out. "And seeing as I left her in the east, alone, I am not fit to bear more."

Sarah gazed steadily at her. Her eyes filled with sudden understanding, sudden *seeing*. Linette cringed, ready for the judgment that would surely come.

But instead, Sarah said, "It was not your choice to leave her, was it?"

Linette bit her lip, holding back a swell of emotion she couldn't even name. "I chose to come here."

"But not to be without your daughter. Do not take on yourself the sins of others, Linette. Who forced you away from your child?"

Linette stared at the ground. Sarah's hand closed around her arm and squeezed slightly, a gesture of embrace. Of encouragement.

"My father did," Linette finally said. "I was not married. My family was not willing to bear the shame."

After what felt like a very long time, she dared look up at Sarah. Her hazel eyes showed nothing but compassion and a level of understanding Linette had not expected to see there—or in the eyes of anyone, ever again.

"The Book says the Son bore our shame," Sarah said. "I don't hold much truck with those who want to put it on people."

The words unlocked something inside Linette that she hadn't known was shut. She swallowed a sob. "The Book says that?"

"Of course it does. It says he was proud to bear our shame and our cross so he could call us all family. We're all sinners, Linette." A smile flitted across her face. "Guess that's what really unites us, since it seems governments and kirks don't."

Sarah stuck out her hand. It took Linette a moment to realize she was being asked to shake it.

"I'm sorry too," Sarah said. "It wasn't right of me to treat you like an enemy. I knew you weren't one. Just thought I was supposed to draw that line and not compromise on it. Smith, he told me truth couldn't really be truth if it didn't include love. I didn't want to hear what he meant, because it meant me putting down my pride. But I hear him now. And you've always deserved better."

With a lump in her throat, Linette shook Sarah's hand. And then tossed caution to the wind, threw her arms around her, and hugged her as hard as she could.

Sarah patted her back. "It's all right," she said as Linette cried. "You're home with us."

Smith stumped inside the governing house. The moment he entered, the hair on the back of his arms stood straight up. A long wailing sound filled the air—from behind the door where Jonathan was sequestered.

It was Martin's turn to stand guard. He was pale and clearly shaken.

"Pa," Martin said. "He's been goin' on like that for an hour."

The door to the governor's office swung open. Herman Melrose gazed across the anteroom at the locked door. He nodded gravely to Smith.

"Uncanny, isn't it?" he said.

"Unearthly," Smith said. "I don't like it."

The wail was a half-cry, like a child; half-howl—like a wolf. One thing was certain: whatever was on the other side of that door didn't sound human.

By circuitous thought, it reminded him of why he'd come. He reached into his coat and pulled out the handful of letters. "Taylor came through," he said. "These are for you. There was another—for him, from the kirk."

He nodded at the door. "I told Sarah she and I might as well open letters for the parson now."

"Those affairs are your own, of course," Herman said, "but to me that seems a sound decision."

Smith cleared his throat. The wailing made it hard to concentrate. He tilted his head to the door. "Step outside a moment? I'd like a word, but I can't even hear my own thoughts with that racket."

"Of course," Herman said. He reached for his coat and scarf, and Smith nodded to his son. "Stiff neck, Martin. You'll be done in an hour and let someone else beat their eardrums for a while."

On the colder but quieter porch, Smith stuffed his hands in his coat pockets. "I wanted to ask you, Governor, what you might think of a woman reading the Book in the kirk meetings. Sarah, to be specific."

Herman smiled. "You know we have always allowed women to speak among the Tremblers. We don't believe the Spirit of God discriminates between the sexes."

"But the kirk doesn't much cotton to it," Smith said. "Thing is, with the parson gone, our meetings don't have much to go on. I'm a poor preacher, and I don't read so well. My boys take after me, I'm afraid. But Sarah, now ..."

"I think even the New Cranwell kirk couldn't object to the Book being read by a woman, given the absence of other options." Herman cast a worried glance behind him. "But all things being equal, you should perhaps begin to think about requesting a new parson. I want to believe he'll pull through this somehow, but ..."

"You believe what the Outsiders said about witchcraft?" Smith asked abruptly. "Think that could be the cause of this?"

"Call it whatever you like, the cause is that seed Linette saw planted inside him. Unless we can find some way to kill it, I don't know how much hope we can hold out for him."

Smith shook his head slowly. "It's a terrible shame. I keep thinking of his father—how he would have felt."

"His father had no love for you," Herman said, peering sidelong at Smith.

"True enough. He thought we were too soft on the Tremblers." Smith barked a small laugh. "But I just can't imagine if that was one of my own boys in there. I don't know what I'd do."

Across the valley, Sarah sank into a rough-hewn chair at her table. She'd lit a single candle to battle the growing gloom of evening. Linette was gone—they'd parted ways after a long hard cry in the field. Sarah had invited her back to the house, but Linette said she wanted to sit in her own rooms and pray.

Tired now, Sarah drew the letter from the synod out of her pocket and gazed at it. The envelope paper was yellowed from the journey. She turned it over. The wax seal on the back sat fat and dark like a spider.

Feeling a bit like a thief, she broke the seal.

Smith was right. They were still the kirk of Jerusalem Valley, with or without their parson, and the synod bore responsibility for their souls. They couldn't just let correspondence lie until Jonathan was fit to read it again.

As he would be, she told herself. As he had to be. They *would* find a way to bring him back to himself, for Letty's sake if for no one else.

Slowly, she withdrew the letter and unfolded it. Her eyes read the first few lines of greeting. And beyond.

She sat up, ramrod straight, heart suddenly beating like a drum.

She had to tell the governor.

She left the candle burning as she ran into the night.

Inside the governing house, Martin Foster watched the growing light beneath the door with concern.

The wailing hadn't stopped, except that it tended now less toward crying and more toward an animalian howl. The governor and his father still stood outside on the porch, talking. As evening dropped over the valley, it had grown darker everywhere, especially inside the cabin.

Except, apparently, in the room he was guarding.

A howl in the room turned high and short—a shriek.

Martin laid his hand on the door. It was hot.

Fire.

Another shriek.

His heart raced with fear and indecision, but he couldn't let Jonathan burn to death.

He threw open the door.

CHAPTER 27

Jerusalem Valley Settlement—The New World

Sarah Foster ran across the fields toward the governing house with all her strength, tiredness completely forgotten. She held the letter clutched in her hand—the damnable letter that exposed as lies far too many things she had taken for granted as truth.

"Smith!" she yelled as she approached, spotting someone on the path in the gloom.

But it wasn't Smith.

She pulled herself up short, stumbling to a halt, and took a step backward. "Jonathan?" she asked carefully.

A growl answered.

Sarah's blood ran cold. He'd come from the governing house. Smith had been there. Martin too.

"Where is my husband?" she demanded. "Where is my son? Jonathan, speak to me!"

Another low, menacing growl answered. She could hardly see in the gloom, but as he drew closer, she could make out a weird, hunched shape to Jonathan's back and shoulders. His eyes glowed like a beast's, except there was no light in the sky for them to reflect.

That Sarah herself was in danger only occurred to her now. She drew back another step and reached for the small knife she kept tucked into her bodice.

Something told her it would not be much help.

"Jonathan," she said slowly, "listen to me. You are not an animal."

She could smell blood as the wind shifted, and she shivered. But continued. "You are not an animal. You are a man, a brave man. My daughter, Letty, loves you. Smith cares for you as his own son."

Jonathan whined. It was the sound a wolf might make, not a sound that should come from a human form. She closed her eyes against the reality of what faced her in the darkness.

A story came to her, from the Book.

A rich man went out and planted wheat in his field. But when it grew, tares grew up with it. When his reapers went to harvest, they asked, "Who planted these tares?" And he said, "An enemy has done this."

The story tugged at her heart. It seemed to her that her whole world was full of tares. The letter in her hand. The young man facing her in the pathway. The seed in his heart.

We're all sinners, she had told Linette not an hour before. *Maybe that's what really unites us.*

The field is the world, the story went on. *The wheat are the children of the kingdom, and the tares are the children of the evil one. The reapers are the angels. "Do not pull up the tares until the end of the age," the rich man said, "lest you pull up the wheat with it. But let both grow up together until the end."*

"The end is not yet," she whispered. "Jonathan. What have you done?"

With another blood-curdling whine, his shape in the darkness changed—it seemed to shrink, to become less than it had been a moment ago. He bowed, head to the dirt, like a dog.

Her hands shook as she pulled out the knife and kept it close to her side where she hoped he couldn't see it. She reached her other hand out, a peace offering. He had come out of these fits before, become human again. Perhaps she could coax him back.

"Jonathan," she whispered, "I know. I know what they told you to do. I know you resisted them. I read their letter. It's all there. You refused to do what they told you. You stood up for what was right. Now resist this. Resist whatever is trying to poison your heart."

She inched forward as she spoke until she could crouch down just in front of him, hand held out. The other hand still held a knife, tucked back and away, where she hoped not to use it. But she knew that she would be a fool not to arm herself.

Slowly, she lowered her hand until it brushed the top of his thick hair. He reacted as though he'd been burned—leaping back and growling so swiftly it left her heart pounding in her throat. With a cry, he ran.

Away toward the mountains.

In the darkness, she lost sight of him almost immediately.

On her knees in the path, she slumped forward and let her hands hold her up.

And then she remembered.

Smith. Martin.

Sarah leaped to her feet and ran for the governing house once more, screaming her husband's name.

She fairly burst upon them—both of them. Smith and Martin, both alive, bloodied, and kneeling over a still figure on the porch.

Smith looked up at her. In the light escaping the windows of the governing house, she could see the haunted expression in his eyes.

"He's dead," he said.

He moved back so she could see. Her stomach turned with revulsion, but there was no mistaking the result of the carnage.

Jonathan had killed Herman Melrose.

Linette was seated alone in the darkness of her cabin when she was startled out of her thoughts by a pounding on the door. She'd come here after pouring out her heart to Sarah in the field. She'd needed time to wonder at it, to be amazed that she had been embraced and not rejected. And to mull over what Sarah had said.

The Book says the Son bore our shame. It says he was proud to bear our shame and our cross so he could call us all family.

She'd heard her father read the Book all her life, but she'd never heard that before. At least, she'd never heard it in a way that really took.

Just before the pounding interrupted her, Linette did something she'd never done before.

She called up her light, let her own skin grow translucent, and looked inside.

She saw what she'd half-expected, somehow, to see, and her eyes and smile grew wide with wonder. A seed, tiny but pulsing with a life of its own, newly lodged in the side of the vine near her right hand. It was already sending out thin tendrils of life, of energy.

Words are seeds, she remembered saying.

She hadn't realized how true that was before now.

"Linette!" The voice that accompanied the pounding was Smith's. "Open the door!"

Wonder forgotten, Linette jumped up and ran to the door. She pulled back the latch and hauled it open. Smith, Sarah, and Martin stood on her porch, all three of them flushed and breathing heavily. Martin and Smith held muskets out and in their arms.

"The governor's dead," Sarah said without preamble. "Jonathan killed him. He's on the loose. You're not safe here, and we need you."

Growing numb as she tried to take in what Sarah had just said, Linette simply nodded. She reached for her coat, scarf, and gloves and hurriedly pulled them on. "Where are we ..."

"Back to the governing house," Smith said. "It's the only place big enough for all of us. We can keep watch over each other and keep the valley safe."

Still bewildered, Linette nodded and followed the others out onto the porch. Then she stopped, dogged by a strange feeling that she might be leaving her house for the last time. "Wait," she said. "I need one thing."

"We don't have time," Smith said.

"Sarah, please. It's for ... you know who it's for."

Sarah nodded. "Quickly." She put a hand on Smith's arm. "We can wait just a minute."

Linette ran back inside, pulled a loose board away from the cabin wall, and removed the small box she kept there. She tucked it inside her coat and ran back.

"All right."

They told her the story in rushed tones as they ran back together. "Martin thought he saw flames under the door and felt the heat of a fire. Jonathan started screaming, and he threw the door open to rescue him. But there was no fire, just Jonathan, and Jonathan—changed."

Smith's grim expression could be heard in his words if not seen in his face. "I was on the porch with the governor. We didn't see him coming. He threw Martin out of the way, opened the door, and … he killed Herman."

They were in sight of the house. Smith stopped, scanning the few trees around it before indicating they should cross the yard. Linette trembled at the thought of approaching the place where Herman had died.

Herman. Her own Governor Melrose. The man who had built her a house, made her a rocking chair. Given her a home and a new start. The man whose tracts had set her heart on fire and assured there could be such a thing as a place without judgment or shame, a place where anyone could belong no matter their past or their party.

He had made it true. One man had gathered this handful of settlers within his expansive heart and made the dream real.

It was a dream that was supposed to thrive under his governance, grow as more and more settlers came, and spread—by example, by force of conviction—to other provinces and other settlements. It was supposed to change the New World into a place entirely unlike the old.

But it needed Herman. And now he was dead.

Linette hardly had the time or the space to process her personal grief. Right now this all felt bigger than that. The valley was bigger. The dream was bigger.

Torches bobbed in the darkness … other settlers, answering the summons that Smith and Sarah had sent out via Martin and Samuel and others, despite the risk of them running into Jonathan.

"Why … why are we gathering?" Linette asked. "To keep us safe?"

"In part," Smith said. "And to talk. There's more news. It can't wait till morning."

"What do you mean?"

They hurried across the flattened brown grass with its patches of white snow shining under the scant moonlight.

"We're under attack," Sarah told her. "The synod is trying to destroy us. They've sent men. They could be here any minute. We can't let them catch us without a plan in place. We need a new governor, and we need a way to hide what has happened to Jonathan."

Linette's thoughts churned. She didn't miss the tone in Sarah's voice, resignation and shock overlaying grief. Sarah was Puritani of the truest kind: absolutely loyal, convinced of the truth of the Pure People's ways and teachings. And now not only had her preacher turned into a murderer, but the synod she trusted to shepherd them had turned against her home and everything she had tried to build alongside her husband. This had to be killing her.

But Linette was relieved to find, now that the worst had happened, that Sarah was as committed to standing with the valley as she was.

They made it inside the governing house, and Smith immediately began to clear aside the wreckage that Jonathan had left behind. Sarah pulled a letter from her coat and held it up.

"It's a letter removing Jonathan from authority over the valley kirk," she said. "From the New Cranwell synod. The letter is clear about why. They've been corresponding with him for some time, and several months ago they ordered Jonathan to rally the Puritani and take control of the settlement, even if it meant killing the governor. He refused, and apparently accused them of collaborating with the devil. All this time we thought he was opposing Herman, he was trying to protect him. He was trying to protect all of us."

"But I don't understand," Linette said. "You said there was a new threat."

"This letter declares that Jonathan is to step down immediately upon pain of arrest and prosecution and says the military has been commanded to take control without delay."

"On what grounds?" Linette asked. "This settlement is authorized and protected by the king!"

"As long as Herman is alive and in good standing with the king, yes," Sarah said. "But according to the letter, the Tremblers of the valley, Herman included, have been accused of colluding with the Hierarchy. You all stand charged with sedition. Herman's governance is forfeit and the synod will take control until the charges have been investigated."

"The Hierarchy," Linette said, more bewildered by the second. "What nonsense. How could he … I mean, they …" She shook her head and closed her eyes before holding out her hand. "May I see the letter?"

She felt the weight of it in her hand and opened her eyes. Unfurling it, she scanned quickly down to the bottom, looking for the familiar signature.

It was there.

Phinehas Cole, Elder of the Kirk of New Cranwell.

Her father.

Boots stamped on the porch. The door swung open and the settlers piled in, grizzled and fretted. For the next half-hour they poured in. Linette wasn't sure she'd ever seen them all in one place before, and certainly not all crammed indoors. They filled every nook of the house. Agatha Moss arrived last, escorted by Amos and Martin Foster.

Every man had a weapon in his hand, even Martin. Their faces were grim. With the summons to the house, the news of Herman's death had also been spread.

Silas Cromer was one of the first to speak. "We gotta kill the preacher," he said. "I been as sorry for him as anyone, but we can't risk him killing again."

An uproar answered. Sarah shouted over it. "We're not going to kill the preacher. We're going to rescue him."

"How?" Silas demanded. "By lockin' him in a back room again so another of your boys can let him out?"

"That's enough," Smith said, quelling the clamor of voices by raising his own. His voice boomed out with clear and unquestionable authority.

In the wake of it, Agatha Moss tremored, "We Tremblers don't kill. I believe the boy can be saved."

"He killed your husband," Silas pointed out.

"He wasn't in his right mind. And if I can forgive him, so can you."

Silas grumbled but didn't reply to that. Everyone knew Agatha had been caring for Jonathan since the men brought him down from the pass. That kind of moral weight, nobody could argue with.

"Jonathan is only one of our concerns right now, and he's not why we called you here," Smith said. That quieted everyone even more than Agatha's response had.

"We have a bigger threat on our hands," he said. "The synod in New Cranwell has charged us with sedition and ordered the military to take control of the valley. They may be here any day—even at first light. We cannot present them with a dead governor and no defense and expect them to leave us control of the settlement."

The chorus of "whats" and "whys?" that greeted Smith's announcement took some time to calm. The few who knew the facts did their best to explain them.

"Let me see that letter," Silas said, stepped forward.

To Linette's surprise and confusion, a shadow passed across Sarah's face—and rather than hand the letter over, she tucked it beneath her arm and said, "No. We've told you what it says; we don't have time to let you labor through it. We need to discuss the plan."

"And we're supposed to trust you?" Silas bit out. "For all we know you're in cahoots with the synod! We surely all know where your loyalty's been all these years."

"I read it too," Linette shouted over the noise. It was only partly true— she'd read little more than the signature. But she trusted Sarah's instincts. "All they say is true. And Sarah's right; we don't have time to distrust each other. If we don't stick together now, we're going to lose the valley."

Big John Hopewell cleared his throat with a harrumphing sound that drew all attention to him. "They're right," he said. "Smith, Sarah, you've known about this longer than any of us. Has a plan suggested itself to you?"

"We need to elect a new governor," Smith said. "Right now, before the military arrives. The best thing we can do is present them with a unified, organized front, including a government capable of denying the charge of sedition and applying for more time to defend ourselves against it."

"I elect John Hopewell," Silas said.

"I second," Amos said.

"And I decline," John answered. The tight crowd parted for him, and he walked up to stand beside Smith. "It's the Tremblers who stand accused of sedition, you said?"

"Yes," Sarah answered.

"Then for the sake of countering their expectations, we should elect a Puritani governor. Smith Foster, I elect you."

A buzz arose in response. Linette looked down at the floor. Of the fifty or so settlers, the majority were and always had been Tremblers. She was no stranger to the tension that had existed between the two groups, despite their commitment to work alongside one another. The ideals that had created the settlement all came out of Trembler ideas, Trembler ways. She couldn't blame any Trembler settler for being uncomfortable with the idea of turning over control to the Puritani.

But right now it didn't matter so much that Smith was Puritani. It mattered that Smith was Smith.

She held her breath, waiting for a seconder.

"I second," Amos said again.

"Let's make this quick," John said. "Any opposed?"

He glared around the room, gaze landing on Smith just as much as anyone else. No one voiced opposition. Linette let out her breath.

"Very good," John said. "Now then, Governor. You best lead the rest of this meeting."

The big man stepped aside, letting Smith take center stage once again.

He doffed his hat and held it in his hand. "We're charged with collusion with the Hierarchy," he said. "If anyone knows anything about that, best you speak up now. Everyone in this room will be lenient and even protect you. The same isn't true of the army."

A small murmur of voices rose again, but no one confessed anything—or appeared to have anything to confess.

"Good," Smith said. "Amos, I'm promoting you. I don't much need a secretary. You'll serve as my deputy. John, you're sheriff."

John nodded.

"I'm afraid we need to dig Herman's grave tonight. It isn't decorous and it doesn't do him honor like we should, but we don't have time, and I don't want the army to see what happened to him. It isn't pretty. When they arrive, we tell them he died in an accident and we buried him. It's not a lie. Will you all agree to that?"

Nods and assents filled the room. "We deny all charges of sedition and make our appeal to the king. With the governance of the valley having changed, I don't believe their charges can hold as they are now. If they choose to act unjustly we don't have much recourse, but we can hope they are righteous men and that they are merely carrying out orders. If we appeal to a higher authority they may consider their orders changed.

"Jonathan is our second problem. They're not to know anything about him."

"But where is he?" someone asked. "How can we hide him if we don't even know where he is?"

"I believe he's left the valley," Sarah said. "I met him—on the path heading toward the pass. He seemed tormented, and he did not threaten me. We can hope he's gone for a while."

"That's a mighty big hope," Silas said. "With all due respect, he hasn't shown much desire to kill you Puritani. Just us Tremblers in his sights. Even Smith there only got knifed 'cause he got in the way, or so the story goes."

"We'll find a way to help Jonathan," Smith said. "But in the meantime, we'll help him and help ourselves by keeping him a secret. If anyone sees him, report to me immediately."

Silas nodded. So did the others. It wasn't a plan. But at least it was agreement.

"We'll have to tell the soldiers something about him," Sarah said. "The letter removes him from authority in the kirk. There's a good chance he'll be wanted for questioning, if not arrest."

"We'll tell them he went through the pass," Smith said. "If they ask why, we tell them he's built a friendship with the Outsiders. That's all."

"And the famine?" Agatha asked.

Everyone turned to face her. Her voice trembled as it always had done since Cleveland's death. "If they come here we need to feed them," she said. "If we don't we'll look like enemies, and if they ask questions and find out how bad off we are, we'll risk losing control again."

It was true. The silence that fell throughout the cabin testified to the intractability of the problem.

"We'll just have to give them as little reason to stay as we can," Smith said. "They'll feed their own men; it's only the officers we'll need to dine. We have decent food from the Outsiders and the last of our own stores. If it's a little thinner than usual they'll forgive us with winter coming on."

He didn't address the larger problem—that famine more than likely still faced them all, that they still had to find a way to feed themselves through the winter, even without giving away their best to unwelcome guests.

One problem at a time, Linette thought. God knew they had more than they could handle just in the next few days, never mind the rest of the winter.

"Above all," Smith said, "it's important we stick together. That we renew our reason for being here in the first place. We all came here because we were tired of reaping the fruit of old feuds and old hatred. We wanted to plant something new. Herman led us. I'm not ready to give up on his dream. If we truly believe that God is Father to us all, Trembler and Puritani alike, and that every man has the right to believe as his heart leads him to believe and to be free from fear because of it, we can't let this go without a fight."

Linette's heart warmed. She still couldn't believe Herman was gone. Even as several of the men filed out to dig a grave in the cold but not yet frozen earth, her heart refused to come to terms with it.

Smith laid a hand on her shoulder. "Linette, Agatha, you shouldn't go home tonight. Stay here in the governing house. In case Jonathan is still in the valley."

Linette nodded. She didn't like it, but Smith was right.

Her gaze drifted across the room to the porch, where Herman's body was wrapped in blankets.

She wanted to go and say good-bye, but her feet seemed rooted to the floor.

A sudden lump in her throat and heat in her eyes threatened to overwhelm her. She shuffled across the room and took Agatha Moss's arm, covering the older woman's hand in comfort.

She needed to comfort another, because in this moment she could not face the rawness of her own grief.

Agatha tightened her arm so Linette was drawn close. Thankfully, she seemed to understand.

Later that night, Linette burrowed into a makeshift bed on the floor of the governor's office. On the other side of the door, oil light still flickered as Smith, John, and a few others talked in hushed tones. Across the room from Linette, heavy breathing let her know that the Foster girls were asleep.

They must be exhausted, poor things, Linette thought. She could only imagine how Letty felt.

The door opened, and footsteps padding across the floor accompanied a dark silhouette that settled down next to Linette without a word.

"Sarah," Linette asked after a few minutes in which Sarah stayed sitting up, silently, beside her.

"Yes?"

"Why wouldn't you show them the letter?"

In the darkness, she couldn't see anything. Sarah was silent. Lost in thought … or constructing an answer.

"Because we don't need any more reasons not to trust each other," Sarah said finally.

"Wouldn't reading the letter help with that?"

Sarah was blunt. "The letter names you, Linette. Linette Cole. I don't know why I never saw it before. I guess I just couldn't have imagined a child of Phinehas Cole choosing to come here. A daughter especially."

Linette felt suddenly very small. There was no judgment in Sarah's voice. She sounded hurt—yet Linette understood that the hurt wasn't directed at her. That it was about the betrayal of the synod, and the revelation of more about Phinehas Cole's true character than Sarah had ever wanted to know. She knew things now that she wished she could unlearn.

Linette wasn't the only one whose world was unraveling.

"What do you mean it names me?"

"The letter says his daughter has been sending him information. He names you as Herman's accuser, the one who gave word of the Tremblers' sedition."

Linette sat straight up at that, nearly bumping her head on the desk. "It's not true! I've never written him a word since coming here!"

"I know," Sarah said. "That's why I wouldn't let them read the letter. Some of the others might not believe you."

"But you do."

"Yes."

"Why?"

Sarah sighed. "I told you, Linette … I was wrong to treat you the way I did. From the moment you arrived here, you've done nothing but prove yourself. We have no reason not to trust you, especially when the accusation comes from …"

She fell silent again.

"I'm sorry he's not what you thought," Linette said. "He's not as bad as … as you may be imagining. If he's willing to lie, it's because he truly believes it's for the greater good."

"We don't believe in doing evil that good may come," Sarah said bitterly.

"That's a quote, isn't it? From the Book?"

Sarah shifted, maybe half-turning toward Linette. In the shadows she couldn't tell. "Yes."

Linette shook her head. "I think you know more of the Book than my father does. And he knows enough to quote it for an hour."

"I can speak it out," Sarah said. "But do I really know it? Not as well as I thought I did."

"The little bit you know is enough to change people. Change lives. You know," Linette said, "I don't think your faith is in the Puritani as much as you think it is. I think it's in the Book itself. And beyond that, in the Creator who spoke the Book. And if we Tremblers put our faith in the Creator too, and listen for his voice, then there's not much difference between us at all."

This time, she could hear the smile in Sarah's voice. "Maybe that's true," she said.

CHAPTER
28

Morning, Jerusalem Valley—The New World

Linette woke up to a floorboard ache in all of her bones, a chill from sleeping in a room without a fire burning, and a low headache that reminded her of everything that was about to break upon them.

And to a memory. *I am here, Linette,* she had heard the voice say. *Under the floorboards. Remember.*

She opened her eyes slowly and peered around her. The light filtering through the windows indicated it was very early. Agatha Moss slept in a chair on the other side of the room, her head slumped onto her black-clothed chest. The Foster girls were arrayed around the floor. Sarah was gone.

Linette tried to sit up, and grief spiked through her like an ice pick in her heart. So full of people, the office felt empty.

She spread her hands out before her and looked at the slender vines curling around her wrists and spidering across the backs of her hands and between her fingers. *What are we?* she wondered. *Puritani, Trembler, Sacramenti, Outsider. We all grow here, together. We all receive seeds and bring forth life or death, light or darkness. And we all die.*

Herman Melrose had died prematurely, like the harvest destroyed by hail. In her heavy heart, it seemed to Linette that the same enemy had felled them both, and had twisted Jonathan, and had even, long before, planted in her father's heart the seeds of judgment and pride that had now grown into persecution and injustice.

She swallowed hard at the thought that her father had lied about her in his letter. Had implicated her in what was about to happen. Why? She was content to go away and consider herself as dead to her family. Why couldn't he do the same?

That he was intent on destroying her was a hard thing to swallow.

Something deep inside her twisted, and she imagined it was her vines, knotting up near her heart in a painful lump that would grow hard and petrify over time.

And suddenly, she knew.

She knew why Jonathan had become the Machkigen.

It was so simple.

And so terrible, too.

Capenokanickon had been right. The settlers themselves had brought the witchcraft here—they and the soldiers in Fort Collins. It had come in their hearts, carried from the Old World, and planted in the soil of the New it had taken a new and terrible form. It had come in the form of old hatred, bitterness, and unforgiveness. It had come in the form of judgments and lies and shame. Herman had tried to overcome it, but he hadn't. His new society welcomed Puritani, but kept them out of positions of leadership. He proclaimed tolerance but refused to deal in any way with the Outsiders—or even to recognize that they were not "outside" at all in the Creator's eyes, but only in the eyes of settlers who saw them as less than human.

Most strange and even wondrous of all, it had somehow come alongside the truth of the Creator's voice, of his Book, of his message that he did not condemn or shame mankind but instead wished to dwell among them, to speak to them, to sanctify them all.

Jonathan's father had drilled the seed into him. He had condemned the Tremblers even as he worked alongside them. He had assured Jonathan that their friends and neighbors would burn in hell and that it was their duty to one day wrest control from them. He had told him that the voice of God was the voice of the devil. He had weighted the words of the Book with condemnation. He had opposed Jonathan's desire to know the Outsiders and filled his heart with shame because of it.

And then he had died. And Jonathan blamed the Tremblers for his death … them, and himself.

And somehow, that weight of fear and shame and grief and blame had compressed into the black seed Linette had seen in Jonathan's heart, and he was becoming lost in its poison.

The same thing, she realized, could happen to her.

It could happen to any of them. In fact, perhaps it already had. It had just happened to manifest itself in Jonathan in a most terrible and terrifying way.

The knowledge of this, all of this, was terrifying.

But she knew something else too.

She knew how to save him.

And it, too, was simple.

She had to tell Smith and Sarah. Gingerly, her heart pounding with revelation but unwilling to wake up the girls, she untangled herself from the blankets on the floor and stood stiffly. Sleeping on the floor made her feel just as much like an old woman as sleeping outdoors.

Before she could reach the office door, she heard a shout from outside and realized it was a lookout.

Someone was coming from the river.

They were out of time.

On the path to the mooring, Linette joined a quickly gathering band of settlers led by John Hopewell and Amos Thatcher. They didn't pause to discuss their approach, instead striding as one toward the river and the newcomers.

But the figures that appeared on the horizon, walking toward them from the river, were nothing like what Linette had expected.

Flashes of red, yes—but not redcoats. Instead, the red was the dyed feathers of six of Capenokanickon's warriors. And escorted by them were not soldiers, but a tall man in a green coat and gloves and a small, dark-haired woman who strode toward them like a storm cloud.

As they drew nearer, the woman broke into a run. "Where is the governor?" she called out in thickly accented English. "We must see Armando Melrose!"

The groups met, standing at some twelve feet apart except for the small woman, who crossed the gap and all but grabbed John Hopewell to shake him. "Where is Governor Melrose?" she asked again. "I must see him at once."

"I'm afraid you can't," John said, clearing his throat.

"But I must, sir. His life is in danger. We have come to warn him."

She looked from John's face to those of others in the group. They must have told her what she needed to know, for her own face fell. "Oh, no," she said. "No, no. Please tell me we are not too late."

"I'm afraid you are, Miss …"

"Vaquero. My name is Serena Vaquero."

John Hopewell's bushy white eyebrows shot up. It was clear to Linette that the name meant something to him. To her, it sounded vaguely familiar … but she couldn't place why.

"Miss Vaquero, it's an honor," John said. "But I'm afraid our dear governor is gone. He left us last night … victim to a tragic accident."

"An accident?" Serena's sharp eyes went from person to person in the group, and she closed her eyes. Linette had the strong and strange sensation that she was listening. When she opened her eyes again, her long lashes were dusted with tears.

"I see," she said. "So they were wrong—the serpents who thought they could entrap you were wrong. And yet you are still trapped. So what is to be done?"

The tall man in a green coat stepped forward. He was very handsome, Linette thought, though tall and rough-shaven. He didn't look like their journey had been kind to him.

"Pardon my interruption," he said. His English was also heavily accented—though with a different accent, Linette noted. "My name is Jacques. We have traveled far to find you. I am sorry to hear of your loss. Might we meet together somewhere more private, where we can share with you information that may be of use? We have just come from keeping company with a band of soldiers headed for Fort Collins. You should know they also plan to come here."

"We do," John said. "In fact we expected them when we heard a boat had come. It's you we didn't expect."

The big Trembler was eyeing the newcomers with unmistakable suspicion, though Linette detected genuine respect for Serena in his bearing. *Serena Vaquero.* Where had she heard that name?

It broke upon her suddenly. In his tracts, the pamphlets and newspaper articles she'd read in New Cranwell that first lit the fire of Jerusalem Valley in her heart, Herman Melrose had talked of his past in the Old World and the plight of the Tremblers there. He had argued that a new form of government was needed, one in which princes and kings were not knit to kirks and hierarchies, so that truth could be allowed to take root and grow as it would, without anyone being condemned or killed if their search for it took them down a different path. He had argued that truth needed freedom in order to be known and to grow.

Among the stories he told were those of a young nobleman from the South and his sister, Serena Vaquero. He told of their heroism and courage in defending the Tremblers through their province, and he told of the unjust arrest and trial of Serena, who had nearly escaped burning as a witch. She had become a martyr and heroine of the cause, known to Tremblers across the world.

And now here she stood, in Jerusalem Valley. Linette could hardly comprehend it.

She lifted her eyes to the warriors standing behind Serena and her tall companion. She recognized Anasan, Jonathan's friend, among them.

The Outsiders were supposed to have gone west. Capenokanickon had made it clear they would not help them again. And yet, here they were.

"John," she said, moving alongside John Hopewell. She nodded toward the Outsiders and hoped he would understand what she meant.

To her relief, he did. He lifted his voice to address them. "And welcome to you, my friends. Please, come and join us. Our new governor will want to know how you came to be here, together." He looked over at Linette and gave her a wan smile. "I suspect we all have stories to tell."

John cleared his throat in his loud, commanding way. "My name is John Hopewell," he said. "I'm the sheriff here. Please, all of you come with me. We'll feed you a hot meal and sit you down with our governor. I'm afraid things are in some disarray. But we'll do our best by you all."

Serena scanned the motley crew of settlers who had come to meet them as she, Jacques, and the Outsiders followed them toward a large, ungainly cabin with a front porch and smoke curling from its chimney. Her eyes rested on the young red-haired woman who walked next to the sheriff. The family resemblance was unmistakable—this had to be Phinehas Cole's daughter. The informant. Serena would have to reveal her at the nearest possible opportunity, but she would do it discreetly—as soon as she had met the new governor and had time to take a measure of him.

In all her worst fears, this was not what she had expected to find. Armando, gone—but not killed by a conspiracy, but by …

She didn't know. The Spirit had shown her something when she asked, out in the lane, but she didn't understand what she'd seen, and it shook her. She did know that in some profound and important way, Elder Crispin's efforts had failed. Armando had not been betrayed by the Puritani settlers. Indeed, from this brief appearance, the settlers seemed more united than ever.

Jacques, walking beside her, comforted her with his presence. That these settlers had somehow managed to avoid the fate Crispin had laid out for them comforted her too. They might all be pawns in his game, but at least one significant group of pawns had liberated themselves. She and Jacques could surely do the same.

At least she knew now, beyond any shadow of doubt, that Jacques was not the one responsible to kill Melrose.

She hated the fact that the possibility had dwelt in her mind at all, not to mention clung so tenaciously, all this time. But now that it was gone for good, she felt as though a weight had been removed.

The warriors walking behind them still unnerved her. From the moment they'd appeared, as though called out of the night, to usher her and Jacques away from the army boat, she'd been awed by them. She didn't know why they were here. Why they had come. Why they had helped them. How they had known anything about what was happening.

Just trust me, the Fire reminded her.

They had passed by the fork in the river at the time Premislav had indicated, and as he had promised, when Serena tried the door of the cabin she found it unlocked. She also found herself unguarded and the deck suspiciously empty of people. A few soldiers manned the poles, of course, and a handful huddled at the far end, but overall it was surprisingly quiet.

At the same time, Jacques was just standing on the deck. Not poling, not occupied with anything. Just waiting for her, as though he thought he was invisible. In the darkness he nearly was.

She hadn't yet had the chance to ask him how that had come about.

He took her arm nearly as soon as she stepped free of the cabin and steered her toward the far end of the ship, and there stood Eben and Josiah, each handling a pole. They nodded to Jacques without a word and tipped their heads toward the water. Serena thought she and Jacques were going to plunge into the icy cold and swim for shore.

But instead, when she looked down, a dugout canoe waited alongside the boat, with three extraordinary tattooed and feathered men in it. Another waited just beyond.

And so Serena Vaquero, stubbornly suspicious and afraid of the people called Outsiders, left the army boat and dropped into their canoe, to be paddled away under the light of the moon.

Just before she went over the side, she heard Jacques tell Eben, "We'll come for you. Both of you."

"You just get yourselves to that valley," Eben had answered.

So they had. Or more accurately, the warriors had. They'd said few words to either she or Jacques; she wondered if they could speak English. Shortly before they arrived at the moorings of the legendary settlement at dawn, they turned and said, "We are here. The governor's house is straight up that path."

Apparently they could.

A nearby howling sound brought her back to the present. Behind her, the warriors grabbed at their weapons—drawing tomahawks and knives. The crowd of settlers in front of her likewise whirled around, eyes full of fear.

Full of fear, but full of knowing.

Serena and Jacques were the only ones here who didn't know what creature had made that sound.

Except …

Jacques put out a hand in front of Serena, as much to signal her to stand her ground as to protect her. Then he reached into his coat and drew out a long, thin, silver blade, about the length and width of an arrow. It was like nothing Serena had ever seen before.

How long had he been carrying that?

What even *was* it?

His eyes were scanning the valley intently. Everything in his stance was expectant—and prepared.

Maybe, after all, she was the *only* one here who didn't know what had made the sound.

"Jacques?" she asked.

"Shhh," he said.

The howl rose from the snow-patched fields again. It sounded like a wolf—but this time it choked off in a crying sound like a child.

Serena's skin crawled. Although the sound seemed to be coming from somewhere close by, she lifted her eyes to the mountains that surrounded the valley on three sides. As she did, her vision shifted, deepening and sharpening—and she saw, on every ridge and rock and even in the clouds, the wolves. Great, grey, slack-jawed wolves, eyes narrowed as they gazed down at the valley. Their legs and shoulders were patchy with serpent scales. Long, forked tongues lolled from their mouths.

She blinked. It was gone. But she knew from Jacques's steadfast stare at the mountains and the long, thin blade still in his hand that he had seen it too.

They were both so intent on the vision in the mountains that neither noticed John Hopewell stepping up behind Jacques until the big man laid a hand on Jacques's shoulder, frightening them both.

"I suggest you put that blade away," he said. He nodded to the Outsider warriors. "You too, if you would. We don't want violence."

"The Machkigen …" one of the young warriors began.

"It's all right." The new voice pulled Serena's eyes away from Jacques and rested them on Linette Cole. "It's all right, Anasan. We can heal him. I know how." The slender young woman gazed out at the fields. "We just need to find him."

The howl rose again.

Serena put it together piece by piece. The childlike sound hadn't been her imagination. It was a human being howling in that field—howling like a wolf. She knew that his hands and arms were scaled like a serpent's and that they were still bloodstained, just as she'd seen in her vision. He had killed the governor, and for some reason the settlers were protecting him— most certainly because he was one of them.

John turned to Serena and Jacques with trouble in his eyes. "How long until the soldiers come?"

"You should have a few days at least. Premislav is waiting for a signal … one they haven't yet had time to receive, though I think he will likely send emissaries himself looking for it."

"Who?" John asked, then checked himself. "No, never mind that now. It's good that we have time."

"You do not." It was Anasan. He pointed out toward the river at a thin column of smoke rising from the other side. "We have been watching. The soldiers are here now."

"Now?" Serena burst out. "But how can they possibly …"

"Maybe they are pursuing us," Jacques said.

Serena lowered her voice. "But Premislav let us go. Why would he order his men to chase us down?"

Jacques frowned toward the water. "Maybe it isn't Premislav." He turned and, to Serena's surprise, addressed Linette. "You must take me to the monster."

She stiffened. "He's not a monster. He's our friend."

"I know what is happening to him," Jacques said. "That is why I have come. To put an end to it."

A tall, gangly young man with spectacles and a broad-brimmed Trembler hat stepped up next to Linette. "With all due respect, sir, we won't allow that."

Jacques shook his head in frustration. "I don't want to hurt him. I want to free him."

"What?" Serena grabbed Jacques's arm. "What are you talking about?"

"Forgive me, Serena," Jacques said. "I could not explain everything to you before. I will, I promise. If I see you again."

"If ... what are you ..."

Jacques turned to Linette and the young man next to her. "Please, I know you have no reason to trust me. But I have come a very long way to be of use to you now. Your friend is tormented by a creature in his dreams that drives him to madness. I can set him free."

"It's not true," Linette said. "Jonathan is sick because of a seed in his heart. We saw it. And I know how to heal him."

"But it is true." This time a young girl stepped forward. She was plain but beautiful in the earnestness of her expression. Tears filled her eyes. Serena looked between them all with astonishment—Jacques most of all.

"He does dream terrible things," the girl said. "He told me. I didn't tell anyone because I didn't want anyone to think badly of him. But ..."

"The soldiers are at the mooring," the warrior, Anasan, interrupted. "They are here. You have no more time."

The howl rose again.

Linette nodded to John. "I'm going after him. Keep the soldiers away."

"I'm going with you," Jacques said. "You do not have a choice. You cannot do this without me."

Serena looked aghast at her friend. He smiled softly at her. "Trust me," he said.

Two of the settlers had run ahead and were now holding a rushed conference with others on the porch of the rambling cabin. They ran back to the newcomers, and a woman took Serena's arm. "Come with me," she said. "We'll hide you."

Serena turned toward Jacques with her mouth open to protest, but the look on his face told her everything the Fire Within was trying to tell her as well—only she wasn't listening.

Now was not the time for her to act. Now was the time for her to trust, to let others take the lead, and to see for herself what kind of world-changing magic was afoot in Jerusalem Valley.

CHAPTER
29

Outside Jerusalem Valley—The New World

Jonathan had descended into hell.

The valley was on fire even as the ground beneath his feet was frozen. He ran for the pass, desperate to escape the flames, but the shape of his father, huge and dark, loomed in the entrance. He pointed his finger at Jonathan as the trees around him grew and bent forward, grasping for his soul.

"You dare go back to the Outsiders?" His father's voice shattered boulders in the mountains. You dare defy me? And you have not done what we have commanded you! The Tremblers still live!"

Jonathan fell to his knees and hugged his own head, curling away from the shape of his father. "I killed the governor," he moaned. "Please let me go."

"It's not enough!" his father shouted. The trees glowered down, and within their shadows Jonathan saw eyes and teeth—wolves. "Others still live! The traitor Linette Cole still lives! And even now others are arriving. They are overrunning the valley because *you* have failed! Because you run back to your rebellion and your disobedience every chance you get!"

"No, please," Jonathan whined. He panted with the heat and shook with the cold. "Please, I didn't mean to disobey you. I didn't mean to let them kill you."

"You might as well have killed me yourself," his father said. Before Jonathan's terrified eyes, he drew a pistol from his belt and cocked it, pointing it at his son.

"Now get up," his father said. "Get up and finish the job I gave you to do. Kill that woman before she can spread her treachery. Kill all of them and purify the valley. Begin the purging!"

Jonathan squeezed his eyes shut. Tears dripped from beneath his lids and ran down his face. He felt them splash off the backs of his hands, and when he looked down, he saw they were black.

He wanted to fight. He wanted to tell his father no. He couldn't run back into the fires filling the valley, and he couldn't kill one more person, guilty or no.

He just wanted to die.

He panted for air. He couldn't fight back. He was too weak.

His skin prickled.

Someone was approaching.

Slowly, Jonathan turned. The fires in the valley seared his vision, but he saw through the burning the faded image of Linette Cole, walking toward him through the dead fields.

And beside her, a man.

Unlike Linette and the rest of the valley, all of which seemed to be filtered through ash and smoke, the man was vivid. He was tall, and his green eyes blazed with light. His clothing and his entire figure seemed to be wreathed in electric blue. In his hand he held a thin silver blade—a dagger or an arrow, Jonathan could not tell.

His eyes were not on Jonathan, but on his father.

Somehow Jonathan knew this was strange. That no one else should be able to see his father, or the fires, or the wolves hiding in the trees. No one but himself should be able to see that the world was ending.

"Jonathan," the man said, although he didn't know how he could know his name, "come here."

Jonathan's eyes fixed on the blade in the man's hand. Slender as it was, there was something deadly about it. It made him afraid.

"Don't hurt my father," he tremored.

"That is not your father," the tall man said. His eyes were still fixed on the giant figure in the entrance to the pass. "Please, Jonathan. You have to trust me. Your father would not speak to you the way this creature speaks to you. Your father loved you. He would not tell you to kill."

All the time he spoke, the man's eyes did not leave the figure in the pass. Dead stalks rustled beside Jonathan as someone settled in close beside him and whispered his name, surrounding his shoulders with her arms.

Linette.

And his father shrieked.

"Do it now, my son! Kill her now!"

"Jonathan, don't be afraid," Linette said.

Her voice was low and soothing. He didn't think she could hear the command echoing through every chamber of his mind.

"Jonathan," she said again, "it's all right. You can be well."

A hellish wind began to blow from the mountains, sere and blazing, and before Jonathan's eyes, his father grew and grew, becoming a giant as tall as the mountains themselves.

"Kill her!" he commanded.

Linette's arms tightened around him. Her silky hair brushed his cheek.

And Jonathan whispered, "No."

His eyes widened as the giant changed form. From the familiar hunched shoulders and gnarled, weathered hands of Jeconiah Applegate, he became a great, broad-shouldered man with steel-grey eyes and red hair. Phinehas Cole, the Elder of New Cranwell.

"I ordered you to take over control of the valley," Cole said. Displeasure and disapproval dripped from his voice. "You were to lead the Puritani and make Jerusalem Valley a bastion of the Pure People, and you refused. I've sent my men to do what you wouldn't. You have one last chance to redeem yourself, boy. Kill that girl."

"Your own daughter?" Jonathan's voice cracked, and he raised his eyes to Cole's, high in the sky.

"Who are you talking to?" Linette asked. Her voice sounded like it came from far away, but he could feel her arms, her warmth—she was crouching over him protectively, like the mother he couldn't remember might have tried to protect her son.

"That isn't who you think," the tall man wreathed in blue light said. "Resist him, Jonathan. You're doing it. Keep doing it. Resist him."

The giant's form changed once more. This time it was someone Jonathan didn't recognize, a corpulent man dressed like a Puritani elder. His dark, hateful eyes glared at them all.

"So it's you," the tall man said.

He stepped forward, into the searing wind. The blue light surrounding him deepened and spread. His coat fell away. Around his neck, a leather string held the talisman of a loaf of bread. The gloves he wore melted from his hands, and Jonathan's eyes widened.

Both the man's hands were pierced.

"Go," he said. "Linette, get him out of here. Get him healed. I'll deal with this creature."

Linette couldn't understand what was happening. They'd found Jonathan on his knees in the cold mud amidst brown, broken stalks of grass and wheat. A wind howled toward them from the mountains. Her every instinct told her they were surrounded by an enemy. Jonathan held his head and talked to himself. His hands were streaked with black, the remnants of tears that also stained his face like streaks of coal. She couldn't follow the things he said. It was about her, some of it.

All she really knew was that he was fighting.

And Jacques, the stranger who had come to the valley with Serena, stood facing the pass and talking to Jonathan about something she couldn't see. His long brown hair blew wildly in the wind, and he held the thin blade in his hand.

It wasn't a blade, she realized suddenly.

It was a stake.

A nail.

"Go, Linette!" Jacques shouted into the growing wind. "Get him healed. I'll deal with this creature!"

When the words left his mouth, she saw it.

A giant, standing in the pass.

It was her father.

She nearly vomited at the sight. It felt like someone had kicked her in the gut. The figure locked eyes on her, lifted a finger to point it at her as though he was ordering her execution. She gasped for words to defend herself before him.

But it wasn't him.

"Linette! Go!"

Jacques's voice broke through. She scrambled to her feet and pulled at Jonathan. She knew with every fiber in her being that this—thing—would pursue them if it could, but Jacques would hold it off.

At least for a while.

However long that "while" was, that was how long she had to set Jonathan free.

Somehow, she got Jonathan to his feet. Locking her arm with his, she half-ran, half-pulled him through the valley toward the Trembler meeting house.

She could still remember the words. The words she'd thought might just be her imagination—but that had never left her.

I am here, Linette. Underneath the floorboards.

Remember.

Jacques de la Croix, Imitator of the Son, bearer of the Sacraments, and Hunter of the darkness faced the demon with the silver nail in his hand.

"You know what this is," he said.

"You don't frighten me," the giant answered.

RACHEL STARR THOMSON 293

Jacques smiled grimly. "Only because you are a fool."

"Get out of my way," the creature snarled. "I have my rights."

"Not much longer."

"She'll never free him. She isn't strong enough."

"She doesn't have to be. She only has to know where to put her faith. And that battle is already won." Jacques's face grew grim. "Now stand down, gargoyle. I will not let you by."

"You know that if you cast me out before the boy is healed, it will be worse for him the end. He'll call me back, and I'll grow stronger and bring more."

"I know. But he will be healed. For now all I have to do is keep you clear of him long enough for that to happen."

The creature breathed in, and Jacques saw the fire burning in its throat. It lost all semblance of humanity and became instead a thing out of a nightmare: wolf and dragon and man and bone, with a fire burning in its gut and glowing through its skin.

It let out a belch of fire large enough to consume Jacques where he stood.

In a single fluid motion, Jacques knelt, laid his hand on the ground, and stabbed the nail through it.

The door of the Trembler meeting house creaked open with a loud protest as Linette shoved it with her shoulder. She half-tumbled inside, hauling Jonathan after her. He was crying, and he could hardly walk on his own. They had barely made it past the column of soldiers in the lane without being seen.

Jonathan crumbled to his knees, shoulders shaking.

"Leave me be, Linette," he said. "Get the men and tell them to kill me. I killed the governor. I killed Herman. You can't trust me. I might kill you. It keeps telling me to kill you."

"It's not telling you to do anything right now. Jacques's holding it back—he's battling it to give you a chance."

Linette spoke with her eyes on the floorboards. She set her hands on her hips. The floorboards lay flat and white and chipping—an unimpressive barrier. She needed some way to break through. She could run home for an axe, but she would risk being seen by the army.

And besides, they didn't have time.

Then she remembered.

Capenokanickon's tomahawk.

It had come back with Smith from the mountain pass. She'd been uncomfortable with it in her house—too many awful memories—so she left it here, in the meeting house—over the door.

Almost laughing with relief, she ran for the door and stood on her tiptoes, reaching for the tomahawk. It was there. She pulled it down and jammed the stone edge under a promising floorboard, trying to wrench it upward. The board strained but didn't give. Wiping a strand of hair out of her eyes, she hefted the hatchet and swung it down at the board instead. The first blow splintered it lengthwise. She hit it again and got another long, narrow splinter. She wasn't strong enough. This was going to take too long.

She looked up. "Jonathan. Help me."

He stared back at her, uncomprehending. She held the tomahawk out.

He jumped back as though he'd shocked her. "What are you thinking?" he said. "I told you, that … thing … wants me to kill you! You can't give me that!"

"It's not talking to you right now, is it?" she demanded. She locked eyes on him, old frustrations bubbling up. Why did she care so much about the fool preacher anyway?

Her chest heaved with frustration and anger and fear. "I've already risked everything for the chance to heal you, and so has Jacques, and so have a lot of others. Now get over here and help heal yourself."

She held the tomahawk out again, shaking it in a way that indicated he had no choice.

Slowly, he reached for it.

But he stopped just shy of gripping the handle.

"Linette," he said, and his eyes filled and overflowed with tears. The tears weren't black this time—they were clear, salty, human tears. Tears of grief. "I killed Herman Melrose."

"And we have forgiven you for it."

Those words hung in the air.

Jonathan took the tomahawk and struck the boards with all his might. This time the blow broke the board into long, large pieces, and Linette reached in and began to pull them out. Jonathan joined her, and between the two of them—and with more help from the hatchet—they cleared away an area of the floor that was four feet by four feet.

Linette closed her eyes for a moment at the sight revealed by the removal of the boards. Relief and joy and wonder all crowded in around her heart.

Deep beneath the floorboards, vines were growing.

New vines, bright green, beautiful. They curled, climbed, and unfurled leaves there in the darkness—sustained by another light, one not visible in this world.

"Come," Linette said. She beckoned to Jonathan even as she led the way, scooting to the edge of the gap and letting her legs down, then jumping the rest of the way. The floor was six feet above the ground, and she found herself standing in a veritable vineyard.

She laughed. And looked up. Jonathan was leaning over the floor, looking wide-eyed at the tangle of life. She beckoned again. "Come!"

As he backed up to begin his descent, she turned and trailed her fingers through the soft leaves. She could hear something ... something running, trickling deeper under the ground.

Water?

"What is this?" Jonathan asked as he lowered himself down. He jumped the last two feet and landed with a soft impact.

It wasn't dark. Light seemed to come from the vines and leaves themselves.

Phosphorescence, Linette thought with amazement.

The light didn't come from the sun after all. It came from something—somewhere—else.

She closed her eyes and breathed in the sweet smell of earth and new growth. Unexpectedly, it was warm here. She felt as though they had fallen into spring in another world.

Wondrous though it all was, Linette shook her head. She needed to come back to reality, enough to figure out what they needed to do next …

But no, she didn't.

This wasn't the time to act.

It was the time to trust and let go.

So she simply turned and smiled at Jonathan, and watched.

The light in the vines grew. As it did, the air grew warmer—but it did not become hot, not threatening. It was warm like the breast of a mother. It was warm like milk on a winter's night. It was warm like blood and like birth, and it surrounded them both.

Jonathan let out a sob and fell to his knees.

His skin, and hers, grew translucent. They saw, both of them, the vines that ran throughout their bodies and the seeds they grew from. They saw black seeds and seeds pulsing with life.

As Jonathan looked down, he saw the massive black seed like a rock near his heart. He sobbed again.

The vines all around them moved as if in a breeze and stretched toward Jonathan, inviting, asking. He opened his hands and let his own vines reach for them … for a moment.

And then withdrew.

Without speaking, Linette walked to his side, knelt down in front of him, and laid her hands on his wrists. Her vines reached out and connected with his. They surrounded his wrists and pulsed with strength. She closed her eyes and let her life, her faith, her assurance flow into him.

He would have to do this himself. But to begin, she could help him. Could stand with him and strengthen him with the life within herself.

You can do this, she silently told him.

You can let go.

You can receive it.

Receive the words you have always known but never believed.

She felt the peace, the calm that came over him as he listened and finally chose to believe what she said. That he was forgiven. That it could be all right. That he could be healed.

She pulled away and watched as the whole vineyard seemed to bow over him and embrace him. To her, the place under the floor grew into something larger, something expansive—the vines not mere vines but whole forests of trees stretching to heaven, soaking up a great and beautiful Light.

Jonathan let his head fall back and his hands open. He swallowed hard.

And the ground beneath him opened.

He fell.

Every word that surged through Jonathan as he opened himself to the forest beneath the floorboards was a word he had heard before.

They were the words of the Creator. He had heard them. Read them himself. Preached them himself. They must have fallen here, to the ground, when they were spoken by the Tremblers in the meeting house.

They were living words, life-changing words.

While you were still a sinner, I died for you.

You love me, because I first loved you.

Though your sins as scarlet be, they shall be white as snow.

He heard them, drank them in. Let them flow into him. Let them fill his vines and fill his heart.

I am your Father, and you, Jonathan Applegate, are my son.

My beloved son.

I am pleased with you.

Tears poured down his face.

And then he heard words he *hadn't* heard before. New words spoken straight to his heart, like the Tremblers said they heard from God.

You have run from me a long time, Jonathan. But I did not make you an orphan; it was the words you chose to believe and the root of bitterness in your heart that drove you from my love. Will you let go of your shame and receive my love and forgiveness instead?

I don't deserve it, he argued.

If you did, it wouldn't be grace, would it?

He couldn't answer that. But he nodded.

It is good that you invite me in through my words. Will you let me wash you in them as well?

He nodded.

That was when the ground fell away.

Jonathan found himself plunged in ice-cold water. He went down, down, down … down until his head, his heart, his feet, his spirit were clean.

CHAPTER
30

Jerusalem Valley Settlement—The New World

"I've told you what happened," Smith told the captain. "He was killed by a wild beast. It's tragic, but he's not the first man lost on the frontier. It's a risk we all take."

"And you expect me to believe this without any witness, when we have it on good authority that the valley has become a hotbed of sedition and intrigue?"

The young captain calling the shots was not the man Serena had told them to expect—someone called Premislav. Instead it was Captain Frederick Almon, the ambitious leader of Fort Collins.

"Forgive me, but I don't know much about your good authority," Smith said. "I'm governor of Jerusalem Valley now, and I'm loyal to kirk and to king alike. You might have orders to take the valley from Herman Melrose, but I don't see how you can have orders to take it from me."

Almon squinted at him. Smith stood intractably on Herman's side of the desk in the old office, with his arms folded over his chest. Almon paced on the other side. Four of his soldiers flanked the office door on the inside, and four more on the outside. Amos Thatcher waited nervously in a corner behind Smith.

"I don't have to explain myself to you, governor though you may be," Almon said. "Melrose had his governorship by order of the king. Whose order do you have it by?"

"We took a vote," Smith said.

Almon barked a laugh. "Much as that doesn't surprise me, the vote of suspected conspirators is not good enough. As of now, you may consider yourselves occupied by the king's army until further notice. Now, if you'll kindly turn over the rogue parson for arrest, the rest of you may remain free for the time being."

"Afraid that's not going to be possible," Smith said.

Almon reared his head back, affronted. He stared Smith down. Amos fidgeted—but Smith didn't move.

"The parson's not been well," Smith said. "He's left us for the time being to find a cure. I don't know where he is, and if I did, I wouldn't turn him over to you. Captain."

"Then I don't suppose there's much use asking you about the where-abouts of two escaped spies, suspected to have come here," Almon said.

"I don't suppose there is."

Almon nodded to his men on either side. "Lieutenant Anderson, put this man in chains," he said. "The Outsiders as well. It doesn't look good on you, *Governor,* that you were consorting with savages when we came upon you."

"That's not right!" Amos burst out. "They're innocent men, free men! They were just visiting here, you can't ..."

"I am acting with the authority of the crown and kirk," Almon snapped. "Though you don't seem to understand the fact, I can do whatever I want. And I am ordering their arrest. Lucky for you, I need a man here to repre-sent the people of this settlement, since your new governor is going to Fort Collins immediately. I hope that gives you better cause to understand your position here."

"Amos, don't fight him," Smith said. He smiled, a thin line across his grizzled face. "Except when you have to."

At another nod from Almon, the soldiers stepped forward and began to snap manacles around Smith's wrists and ankles. Amos choked back a cry of outrage and stood trembling in the corner.

Almon looked at him and laughed. "So that's why they call you Trem-blers. 'Cause you shake with fear."

Amos reddened, but mindful of Smith's orders, said nothing. Lieutenant Anderson and his men shuffled Smith away, and Almon took his place behind the desk. He nodded to his remaining men. "I want soldiers stationed throughout this settlement. Whatever rations you find, they're yours. Commandeer anything else you need."

"Yes, sir," the soldiers said in unison.

"You see any sign of the parson or Premislav's fugitives, bring them in. Man was a fool to play his hand so obviously." He smiled at Smith. "You'll have interesting company in the fort prison, that much is for certain. It seems conspirators are growing like weeds these days. The kirk in the Old World sent a commander to take my position, and what do you think? He turned out to be Sacramenti. Revealed himself by releasing a suspected Imitator in the company of Serena Vaquero."

His eyes narrowed. "One more thing. The elder in New Cranwell wants his daughter returned to him posthaste. Find her, bring her in. Kindly."

Though he still spoke to the soldiers, he fixed his eyes on Smith and then Amos, a slight smile curling his lips. "Be sure to thank her for all her help."

EPILOGUE

Jacques de la Croix sat on a ridge overlooking the valley, gloves in hand.

He watched as the red coats of the soldiers spread through the settlement like players on a chessboard. He was too far to see detail, but he could imagine the heavy hand that was falling on the settlers now. He knew enough about the men directing these pieces to be sure there would be little compassion or humanity shown.

The demon that had driven Jonathan Applegate to unspeakable horrors was gone—vanquished, as they all were vanquished, by the blood.

Not his, of course.

The blood of the Son.

He looked down at his pierced hands. The nail marks were scarred, dark, and ugly. They were his reminder of who he was. Of who he followed.

And of why he was truly here.

Wisps of smoke rose from chimneys. Somewhere down there, Serena was in hiding. He didn't think it would take her long to make her way up here, back to his side. Somewhere down there too, the newly baptized preacher would need to go underground in a different sense than he already had, and the young Trembler woman who had helped him—the daughter of Phinehas Cole himself—would face the greatest challenge of her life.

Jacques saw it all from where he sat.

And he lifted a prayer.

Creator, Father, Spirit, Son.

Maker, Sower, Fire Within.

Be our help and our guide.

We need you.

The End

Rachel would love to hear from you!

You can visit her and interact online.
Web: **www.rachelstarrthomson.com**
Facebook: **www.facebook.com/RachelStarrThomsonWriter**
Twitter: **@writerstarr**

THE SEVENTH WORLD TRILOGY

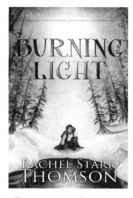

WORLDS UNSEEN   BURNING LIGHT   COMING DAY

For five hundred years the Seventh World has been ruled by a tyrannical empire—and the mysterious Order of the Spider that hides in its shadow. History and truth are deliberately buried, the beauty and treachery of the past remembered only by wandering Gypsies, persecuted scholars, and a few unusual seekers. But the past matters, as Maggie Sheffield soon finds out. It matters because its forces will soon return and claim lordship over her world, for good or evil.

The Seventh World Trilogy is an epic fantasy, beautiful, terrifying, pointing to the realities just beyond the world we see.

"An excellent read, solidly recommended for fantasy readers."
– Midwest Book Review

"A wonderfully realistic fantasy world. Recommended."
– Jill Williamson, Christy-Award-Winning Author
of *By Darkness Hid*

"Epic, beautiful, well-written fantasy
that sings of Christian truth."
– Rael, reader

Available everywhere online or special order from your local bookstore.

THE ONENESS CYCLE

EXILE   HIVE   ATTACK   RENEGADE   RISE

The supernatural entity called the Oneness holds the world together. What happens if it falls apart?

In a world where the Oneness exists, nothing looks the same. Dead men walk. Demons prowl the air. Old friends peel back their mundane masks and prove as supernatural as angels. But after centuries of battling demons and the corrupting powers of the world, the Oneness is under a new threat—its greatest threat. Because this time, the threat comes from within.

Fast-paced contemporary fantasy.

"Plot twists and lots of edge-of-your-seat action,
I had a hard time putting it down!"
—Alexis

"Finally! The kind of fiction I've been waiting for my whole life!"
—Mercy Hope, FaithTalks.com

"I sped through this short, fast-paced novel, pleased by the well-drawn characters and the surprising plot. Thomson has done a great job of portraying difficult emotional journeys . . . Read it!"
—Phyllis Wheeler, The Christian Fantasy Review

Available everywhere online or special order from your local bookstore.

THE PROPHET TRILOGY

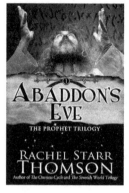

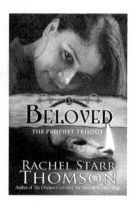

ABADDON'S EVE   COMES THE DRAGON   BELOVED

A prophet and his apprentice.
A runaway and a wealthy widow marked as an outcast.

They alone can see the terrible judgment
marching on their land.

But can they do anything to stop it?

The Prophet Trilogy is a fantasy set in a near-historical world
of deserts, temples, and spiritual forces that vie
for the hearts of men.

Available everywhere online or special order from your local bookstore.

REAP THE WHIRLWIND

Beren is a city in constant unrest: ruled by a ruthless upper class and harried by a band of rebels who want change. Its one certainty is that the two sides do not, and will not, meet.

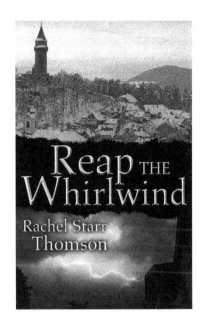

But children know little of sides or politics, and Anna and Kyara—a princess and a peasant girl—let their chance meeting grow into a deep friendship. Until the day Kyara's family is slaughtered by Anna's people, and the friendship comes to an abrupt end.

Years later, Kyara is a rebel—bitter, hard, and violent. Anna's efforts to fight the political system she belongs to avail little. Neither is a child anymore—but neither has ever forgotten the power of their long-ago friendship. When a secret plot brings the rebellion to a fiery head, both young women know it is too late to save the land they love.

But is it too late to save each other?

Available everywhere online.

TAERITH

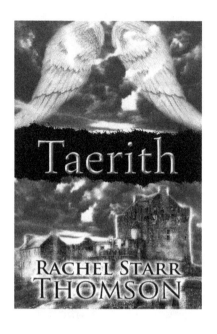

When he rescues a young woman named Lilia from bandits, Taerith Romany is caught in a web of loyalties: Lilia is the future queen of a spoiled king, and though Taerith is not allowed to love her, neither he can bring himself to leave her without a friend. Their lives soon intertwine with the fiercely proud slave girl, Mirian, whose tragic past and wild beauty make her the target of the king's unscrupulous brother.

The king's rule is only a knife's edge from slipping—and when it does, all three will be put to the ultimate test. In a land of fog and fens, unicorns and wild men, Taerith stands at the crossroads of good and evil, where men are vanquished by their own obsessions or saved by faith in higher things.

"Devastatingly beautiful . . . I am amazed at every chapter how deeply you've caused us to care for these characters."
—Gabi

"Deeply satisfying."
—Kapezia

"Rachel Starr Thomson is an artist, and every chapter of Taerith is like a painting . . . beautiful."
—Brittany Simmons

Available everywhere online or special order from your local bookstore.

ANGEL IN THE WOODS

Hawk is a would-be hero in search of a giant to kill or a maiden to save. The trouble is, when he finds them, there are forty-some maidens—and they call their giant "the Angel." Before he knows what's happening, Hawk is swept into the heart of a patchwork family and all of its mysteries, carried away by their camaraderie—and falling quickly in love.

But the outside world cannot be kept at bay forever. Suspecting the Giant of hiding a treasure, the wealthy and influential Widow Brawnlyn sets out to tear the family apart and bring the Giant to destruction any way she can. And her two principle weapons are Hawk—and the truth.

Caught between the terrible truths he discovers about the family's past and the unalterable fact that he has come to love them, Hawk must face his fears and overcome his flaws if he is to rescue the Angel in the woods.

"A beautiful tale of finding oneself, honor and heroism;
a story I will not soon forget."
— Szoch

"The more I think about it, the more truth and beauty
I find in the story."
—H. A. Titus

Available everywhere online or special order from your local bookstore.

LADY MOON

When Celine meets Tomas, they are in a cavern on the moon where she has been languishing for thirty days after being banished by her evil uncle for throwing a scrub brush at his head. Tomas is a charming and eccentric Immortal, hanging out on the moon because he's procrastinating his destiny—meeting, and defeating, Celine's uncle.

A pair of magic rings send them back to earth, where Celine insists on returning home and is promptly thrown into the dungeon. Her uncle, Ignus Umbria, is up to no good, and his latest caper threatens to devour the whole countryside. He doesn't want Celine getting in the way. More than that, he wants to force Tomas into a confrontation—and Tomas, who has fallen in love with Celine, cannot procrastinate any longer.

Lady Moon is a fast-paced, humorous adventure in a world populated by mad magicians, walking rosebushes, thieving scullery maids, and other improbable things. And of course, the most improbable—and magical—thing of all: true love.

> "Celine's sarcastic 'languishing' immediately put me in mind
> of Patricia C. Wrede's Dealing with Dragons series
> —a fairy tale that gently makes fun of the usual fairy tale tropes.
> And once again, Rachel Starr Thomson doesn't disappoint."
> — H. A. Titus

> "Funny and quirky fantasy."

Available everywhere online.

SHORT FICTION
BY RACHEL STARR THOMSON

Butterflies Dancing

Fallen Star

Of Men and Bones

Ogres Is

Journey

Magdalene

The City Came Creeping

Wayfarer's Dream

War With the Muse

Shields of the Earth

And more!

Available as downloads for Kindle, Kobo, Nook, iPad, and more!

CPSIA information can be obtained
at www.ICGtesting.com
Printed in the USA
LVHW102247230522
719565LV00012B/66

9 781927 658468